THE GREAT TRAIN ROBBERY

THE GREAT TRAIN ROBBERY

THE UNTOLD STORY FROM THE CLOSED INVESTIGATION FILES

ANDREW COOK

The History Press

To Alia

First published 2013
Reprinted 2013

This edition published in 2013

The History Press
The Mill, Brimscombe Port
Stroud, Gloucestershire, GL5 2QG
www.thehistorypress.co.uk

British Library Cataloguing in Publication Data.
A catalogue record for this book is available from the British Library.

ISBN 978 0 7509 5454 9

Typesetting and origination by The History Press
Printed in Great Britain

CONTENTS

ACKNOWLEDGEMENTS

I would like to thank all those involved in the research and development of this book, and the following people for their invaluable help:

Jordan Auslander, Bill Adams, David Baldry, Phil Tomaselli, Gavin McGuffie (BPMA), Jamie Ellal (BPMA), Sally Jennings (BPMA), Vicky Parkinson (BPMA), Helen Potter (TNA), Amelia Bayes (TNA), Lizzie Mould (Croydon Local Studies & Archives Service), Bob Askew (Southwark Council, Local History), Martin Robson Riley (National Museum of Wales), Andrew Foster (Railway History Group), Jen Parfitt (Solicitors Regulation Authority), David Capus (Records Management Branch, Metropolitan Police), Philip Barnes-Warden (The Met Historical Collection), Neil Paterson (The Met Historical Collection), Samantha Cardoo (Royal Mail Group Security), Tony Marsh (Group Security Director, Royal Mail Group), Janet Altham (DPP/CPS), John O'Connor (former Head, Flying Squad), Bob Fenton (EMCA), Philip Trendall (BTP), Edward Laxton (formerly of the *Daily Express*), Ray Brown (formerly of Lessor & Co.), Frank Campion (formerly of Lessor & Co.), Harry Lyons (former Assistant Controller, Post Officer IB), Bob Robertson (former Flying Squad), Edward Harris (former Flying Squad), Marlena Wilson (granddaughter of Percy Hoskins), Hazel Collinson (wife of Peter Collinson), Colin Williams (son of Frank Williams), Marian Ikin (daughter of Clifford Osmond), Roger Lemon, James Carpenter and Colin McKenzie.

Furthermore, I would like to thank Bill Locke at Lion Television (Executive Producer of the Channel 4 film *The Great Train Robbery's Missing Mastermind?*), whose support and encouragement enabled me to take this project forward. I am also indebted to all those who were involved in the production of the film, in particular Matthew Whiteman, Luke Martin and Daisy Robertson.

Finally, my thanks to Chris Williamson, Beryl Rook, Alia Cook, Alison Clark, Nabeel Bashir, Simon Hamlet (who commissioned this book) and Lindsey Smith at The History Press.

PREFACE

Just after 3 a.m. on Thursday 8 August 1963, a crime took place that still stands as the heist of the century. A gang of professional thieves made history when they held up the Glasgow to London Travelling Post Office train and seized a record-breaking haul of £2.6 million (just over £50 million in today's money).

Much has been written about it over the past five decades in books, magazines and newspapers. A host of films and television documentaries have also ensured that not one year has passed since 1963 without coverage of the story and the characters involved.

However, despite the wealth and extent of coverage, a host of questions have remained unanswered about the Great Train Robbery: who was behind it, was it an inside job and who got away with the crime of the century? Fifty years of selective falsehood and fantasy, both deliberate and unintentional, has obscured the reality of the story behind the robbery. The fact that a good many files on the investigation and prosecution of those involved, and alleged to have been involved, are closed in many cases until 2045 has only served to muddy the waters still further. To piece together an accurate picture of the crime and those surrounding it, it is necessary to return to square one, starting from scratch in gathering together as many primary sources as possible. The ability to draw upon many formally closed, restricted or hitherto unpublished primary sources have helped in this task immeasurably.

Contemporary, primary source material undoubtedly gives the reader a totally new 'feel' for the case and the social attitudes of the period. The sheer volume of material also brings home just how easy it can be, without the ability to cross-reference other sources and investigations, to overlook certain details and key links. Many theories about the crime were expounded at the time, particularly in the popular press. Some of them were far-fetched; others were rooted in more reliable, off-the-record sources.

Files on the robbery held by the Metropolitan Police, the Home Office, Buckinghamshire Assizes, the British Railways Board and the Director of

Public Prosecutions are vast and impossible to quote in full, as are the files held by Royal Mail, the British Transport Police and the contemporary newspaper reports held by the British Library. Therefore, a degree of selectivity has been applied, but not in such a manner as to compromise the integrity of the source material available. All the main official accounts and reports pertinent to the parallel investigations carried out by the various agencies are included in this book.

The objective of this book is to present as full and factual an account of the Great Train Robbery as is possible, chronologically presented and told by the people who played a role in the story. It is left to the reader to interpret the facts and evidence accordingly. Due to the great extent of abbreviations and initials used in the various documents, the reader is advised to periodically refer to the 'Abbreviations used in Source Notes' at the end of this book.

INTRODUCTION

The term 'The Great Train Robbery' was neither born as a result of the 1963 mail train hold-up, nor indeed the 1855 train robbery immortalised by Michael Crichton in his 1975 novel *The Great Train Robbery* (which was later filmed by MGM in 1978 as *The First Great Train Robbery* starring Sean Connery and Donald Sutherland).

While Crichton's book was a work of fiction, it drew heavily upon real-life events that took place on the night of 15 May 1855 when the London Bridge to Paris mail train was robbed of 200lb of gold bars. Crichton took something of a historical liberty by retrospectively re-christening it the Great Train Robbery. At the time, and for over a century afterwards, it was commonly known as the 'Great Gold Robbery'.

The term 'The Great Train Robbery' has, in fact, no basis at all in any real-life event; it is instead the title of a 1903 American western movie written, produced and directed by Edwin S. Porter. Lasting only twelve minutes, it is still regarded by film historians as a milestone in movie-making. Shot not in Hollywood but in Milltown, New Jersey, its groundbreaking features include cross-cutting, double exposure composite editing and camera movement.

When, within twenty-four hours of the 1963 mail train robbery, the enormity of the heist began to sink in and the British press frantically searched for a suitable iconic headline, Edwin Porter's 60-year-old movie title fitted the bill perfectly. Ironically, Fleet Street went one stage further the following week when, on the discovery of Leatherslade Farm, they dubbed it 'Robbers' Roost'. This secluded location in southern Utah was, in fact, a favourite hideout of the American outlaw and train robber Butch Cassidy and his 'Hole in the Wall Gang' back in the 1890s.

Mail was first carried in Britain by train in November 1830, following an agreement between the General Post Office and the Liverpool & Manchester Railway. Eight years later, Parliament passed the Railways (Conveyance of

Mails) Act, which required railway companies to carry mail as and when demanded by the postmaster general. Trains carrying mail eventually became known as TPOs (Travelling Post Offices). Mail was sorted on a moving train for the first time in January 1838 in a converted horsebox on the Grand Junction Railway. The first special postal train was operated by the Great Western Railway on the Paddington to Bristol route, making its inaugural journey on 1 February 1855.

Because of the wide expanse of territory in the American West and Mid-West, train robbers tended to stop trains by placing obstructions on the track to halt the locomotive, or by boarding the train, jumping into the back of the locomotive and holding up the engineer and fireman.

The location chosen was usually a desolate or isolated stretch of line, miles away from the nearest town, where plenty of time would be available to rob the train and make a getaway well before the alarm was raised. Unlike the 1855 'Great Gold Robbery' in England, there was no need to rob the train while it was in motion. Train robberies carried out by the likes of Jesse James and Butch Cassidy would have been impractical, if not near impossible, in Victorian England due to the short distance between stations and the observant signal box system.

By the time Butch Cassidy and his Wild Bunch hit the Union Pacific train at Tipton on 29 August 1900, the writing was already on the wall for American train robbers. The Board of the Union Pacific Railroad Company had resolved to spend money to save money – by employing the Pinkerton Detective Agency. Their agents, such as the legendary Joe Lefors, were usually well paid, well armed and mandated to take the fight directly to the train robbers. This they did by tracking them, sometimes for months on end, until they were arrested or forced into a gunfight. Unlike US law officers, Pinkertons were not constrained by state boundaries, which escaping robbers had previously exploited by criss-crossing. Pinkertons' strategy, although criticised in many quarters as a shoot-to-kill policy, was to prove particularly effective in combating railroad robberies.

Unlike America, the regional railway companies in Britain (GWR, LMS, LNER and SR) were permitted by Parliament to employ their own railway police constabularies. With the nationalisation of the railways in 1948 and the creation of one sole state-owned company, British Railways, these private-company police forces became one constabulary known as the British Transport Commission Police. In Britain there was no need to employ the likes of Pinkertons to investigate mail crime, as a highly effective official force had operated in the shadows for over 300 years.

The Post Office Investigation Branch (IB) has a just claim to be the world's oldest criminal investigation department, tracing its origins back to 1683, when King Charles II appointed Attorney Richard Swift to the General Post Office (GPO) with specific responsibility for 'the detection and carrying on of all prosecutions against persons for robbing the mails and other fraudulent practices'. On a salary of £200 per year Swift was, according to GPO records, an effective bulwark against post office crime. A Treasury department letter of 1713 affirms that, 'Richard Swift has been Solicitor to the General Post Office for about thirty years in which he has all along acted with great diligence, faithfulness and success.'[1]

During the eighteenth and early nineteenth centuries, reports of the apprehension and sentencing of post office offenders appeared regularly in local and national newspapers. The *Evening Mail* of 8 May 1795, for example, reported in some detail on the case of a letter sorter by the name of Evan Morgan, who had been arrested and charged with 'secreting a letter at the Post Office'. He was hung on 20 May at Newgate Prison. Of particular note was the fact that three of the six men hung that day were postmen.

The sentences for post office crimes were historically harsh, as demonstrated by the records from that era, which show that both capital punishment and transportation to the colonies were common. In 1765, Parliament passed an act that set down the death penalty for 'theft of the mail', 'secretion' and 'embezzlement or destruction of mail'. A further twenty-nine postmen were hung between that date and the passing of the 1837 Post Office Act, which abolished the death penalty for post office offences, replacing it with transportation for terms of seven years to life.

In terms of investigating such offences, responsibility remained with the solicitor to the Post Office until 1816, when much of it was transferred to the Secretary's Office, where the team of investigators were to become known as the Missing Letter Branch. By 1823 the investigators were supplemented and supported by Bow Street Runners. Founded by Henry Fielding in 1750, the Runners (or Robin Redbreasts, on account of their scarlet waistcoats) were London's first band of constables who travelled up and down the country serving writs and pursuing criminals. In 1829, on the founding of the Metropolitan Police by Sir Robert Peel, the Missing Letter Branch used seconded police officers instead.[2]

In 1840 the introduction of the first postage stamp, the penny black, led to a massive increase in the volume of postal traffic. This inevitably meant a consequent rise in the amount of post office-related crime. The Post Office reacted to this by recruiting more investigators who, from 1848, were placed under the supervision of the Post Office inspector general in a separate department. In 1883, the Missing Letter Branch was renamed the Confidential Enquiry Branch and the officer in charge given the title of director. In 1908 the unit once again changed its name to the Investigation Branch, usually shortened to the IB. In 1934 the GPO underwent a radical reorganisation, and in 1935 the Investigation Branch became one of the administrative departments of the new headquarters structure of the GPO. In 1946 the title of the head of the Investigation Branch changed from director to controller. At the time of the 1963 train robbery, Clifford Osmond was controller, having taken over the post in 1957. Formally deputy controller from 1948, Osmond, a native of the West Country, had joined the Post Office at the age of 18 before successfully applying to join the Investigation Branch in March 1934.[3]

In retrospect, the Post Office was most fortunate in having Osmond, a highly motivated, resourceful and effective investigator, at the head of the organisation during a period in which mail crime was to rise significantly and, indeed, culminate in the Great Train Robbery of 1963.

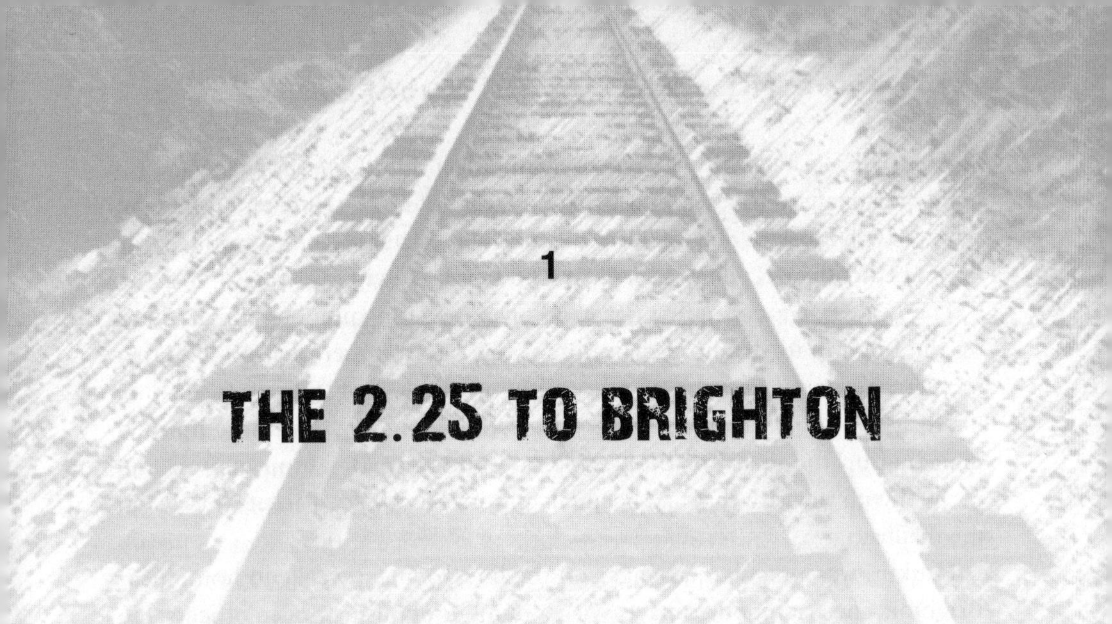

1

THE 2.25 TO BRIGHTON

In the 1950s and early '60s Percy Hoskins was considered by his peers, and indeed many senior police officers up and down the country, to be Britain's foremost crime reporter. As chief crime reporter for Lord Beaverbrook's mass circulation *Daily Express*, he had an almost sixth sense when it came to spotting a unique story angle and a second-to-none ability to get down to its bedrock.

Hoskins was famed for the friendships and acquaintances he cultivated over the years, not only in Britain but also in America, such as Hollywood film director Alfred Hitchcock and FBI Director J. Edgar Hoover. He also had some of the best sources in the criminal fraternity, the Metropolitan Police and the outlying county forces. According to Victor Davis, writing in the *British Journalism Review*, 'Hoskins kept open house for senior police officers at his flat at 55 Park Lane; if you were in trouble with the police you rang Percy before your lawyer.'

According to Davis, Hoskins avoided having a desk at the *Daily Express* HQ at 120 Fleet Street, in the City of London (known unofficially at the time as the 'Black Lubyianka'), so as to avoid Beaverbrook executives keeping a tab on his working hours. During his fifty years working for Beaverbrook newspapers, Hoskins became a personal friend of Lord Beaverbrook and earned a mixture of notoriety and admiration in Fleet Street for the stance he took in his stories. The most noteworthy example being the landmark case of suspected serial killer Dr John Bodkin Adams in 1956, on which Hoskins was the lone voice in Fleet Street not assuming Adams's guilt.

Initially seen by Beaverbrook as an almost suicidal position for the newspaper to be taking, he phoned Hoskins after Adams was found not guilty by an Old Bailey jury and told him, 'Two people were acquitted today' – meaning that

Hoskins would keep his job and his reputation. The *Daily Express* was also highly fortunate to have a second-to-none team of crack crime reporters who worked with Hoskins during the 1950s and '60s, comprised of Edward Laxton, Arnold Latchman, Rodney Hallworth and Frank Howitt.

The *Daily Express* team first got wind of an escalating number of mail thefts on the London to Brighton main line in the late summer of 1960. The first incident occurred in August and resulted in the loss of £7,500 from nine mailbags. The *Daily Express* reported the following day that three hooded men tied up the guard of the 2.25 p.m. London to Brighton express and escaped with the cash that had been taken from High Value Packets (HVPs) in the mailbags.

Hoskins was a regular passenger on the line, having a weekend home near Brighton, and had good contacts with a number of Sussex police officers. He soon picked up on the second incident the following month, 'when a train was halted outside Patcham Tunnel, Preston Park, by a rigged signal'. The *Daily Express* report went on to tell readers that, 'masked bandits over-powered the guard and snatched £9,000 from mailbags'.

By now the Post Office Investigation Branch had become involved and was particularly concerned that the robbers appeared to have a degree of technical know-how in being able to halt trains by manipulating the signals. This is clear from a memo sent by IB controller Clifford Osmond to his Royal Mail security counterparts, Postal Services Department (HMB), on 21 September 1960:

TPO SECURITY

(1) It was reported last night that a passenger train London to Brighton was brought to a halt by thieves who interfered with the railway signals and who stole six bags of mail containing HVPs valued about £9,000 together with a large number of registered letters. It is alleged that the thieves left the train after attacking the guard and escaped by car which was waiting for them at a predetermined spot.

(2) The full facts are not yet available but whether or not they turn out to be as stated I am most anxious that urgent attention should be given to a further review of security precautions that are taken generally on each TPO and sorting carriage particularly when the train is brought to a halt (genuine or otherwise) outside a station. The IB is aware that these are overhauled from time to time.

(3) The IB considers that this exercise could be confined to TPOs and we would be ready to have any discussion on the matter or give any security advice that we might be in a position to offer on TPO routine security measures.[1]

Despite such high-level attention, it seems that nothing much in reality was done to review, let alone improve, TPO security on the Brighton line and, in April 1961, the *Express* told its readers of a further audacious robbery not far from the scene of the Patcham Tunnel hold-up, in which, 'Bandits disguised as railwaymen walked on to the platform at Brighton and got away with a registered bag containing £15,000.'

Bearing in mind that, to the uneducated eye, mailbags containing money in High Value Packets were indistinguishable from regular mailbags, Hoskins became convinced that the men behind these precision raids must have a good deal of knowledge about post office and railway procedures.

A decade before, in May 1952, he had covered the Eastcastle Street robbery with fellow *Express* journalist Tom Clayton, and was sure that it too had resulted from inside information. Someone within the post office must have passed on details to the gang, a view that only hardened when he discovered from a police source that the mail van's alarm bell had been disabled before it had set out to collect its payload. Returning to the City from London's Paddington station, where it had collected High Value Packets from the Great Western Region Travelling Post Office, the van had been ambushed in Eastcastle Street by seven masked men in two stolen cars. At the time, the theft of these eighteen mail sacks, containing £287,000 (£6,150,000 in today's money), was Britain's largest ever robbery.

While the 1952 hold-up remained officially unsolved, Hoskins was led to believe that the police were reasonably sure who was behind it and knew the identity of the seven masked men. To their extreme frustration, a complete lack of tangible evidence that could be presented in court prevented them from making arrests.

Hoskins's sources were proved correct five decades later when the extensive investigation files on the Eastcastle Street robbery were finally opened. In a detailed report dated 20 March 1953, Clifford Osmond, then deputy controller of the IB, noted:

> Within a day or so Supt. Lee (Flying Squad) told me that as the result of information received he considered that the robbery had been planned and executed by the under mentioned team:

Billy Hill (organiser)	Jim Clark	Joe Price
Jock Gwillim	Michael Donovan	Patsy Murphy
George Chatham	George (Billy) Benstead	Teddy Tibbs
Teddy Machin	Sonny Sullivan	

> … of the six or seven men who were seen (by witnesses), the under mentioned criminals of the suspect team would fit the descriptions given: -
>
> Jock Gwillim
> Joe Price
> George Chatham
> Patsy Murphy[2]
> Teddy Machin
> Billy Benstead
> Mike Donovan

While the investigation failed to identify the source of the inside information, Osmond addressed the matter of who he believed acted as the link man between the post office insider and the gang:

> Inquiry and observation finally proved that Billy Howard is (a) a close associate of Billy Hill; (b) lives in the Walworth area where he meets Billy Benstead who also lives there; (c) was, for a time, running a gambling club in partnership with Billy Hill from the rear of canteen premises used by the Meat Porters Union of Smithfield Market and (d) frequents the Red Cow PH, a pub much used by post office staff. It is significant that PHG's sent to the LPR School for training in all branches of registered letter work, sometimes use the meat porters' canteen concerned. Billy Howard was therefore in a position to operate as a 'contact man' and I believe he did so.[3]

In another IB file on the Eastcastle Street robbery, which contains photographs and extracts from the suspects' Criminal Record Office (CRO) files, Billy Howard is shown as residing in East Street, Walworth. Sixteen known associates of his are listed, several of whom will enter our story later in this book.[4]

While the Eastcastle Street robbery was very much seen as a one-off, these new raids on the Brighton main line seemed to fit a pattern and showed no sign of abating. Indeed, each successive incident seemed to be bolder and more lucrative than the last.

After some months, however, it seemed as though the Brighton line raids had petered out. By the late summer of 1961, the *Daily Express* crime team, and indeed the rest of Fleet Street, had become preoccupied by the police manhunt launched on 23 August for the A6 murderer who had shot dead Michael Gregsten and raped and shot his mistress, Valerie Storie. James Hanratty was eventually arrested and charged; his trial opened at Bedford Assizes on Monday 22 January 1962 amid a flurry of media coverage. In the early hours of Friday 26 January, the day the Hanratty case was adjourned for the weekend, an event occurred that caused the *Daily Express* to prematurely use what would, in a year's time, become an iconic headline by presumptuously declaring …

GREAT TRAIN ROBBERY FOILED

A Jesse James-style mail train robbery by moonlight on a lonely stretch of track in Essex failed, it is believed, only because a delayed freight train came along first. The goods train exploded a military-type detonator placed on the line between Colchester and Marks Tey and jolted to an emergency stop. The detonator – the first of 14 found by the driver – was meant for the mail train, police think.

The gang is believed to have been poised to strike, grab mail bags containing thousands of pounds, and escape by car on the A12 London–Ipswich road. Yesterday, police were searching the area of Stanway Woods, alongside the line, for clues. Signalman George Drinkell, on duty at Marks Tey signal box at the time, said: 'Just after 2.30 am Colchester rang to say the goods train had passed through. But it never reached me. Then I heard from Colchester that the driver had phoned to say he had been stopped by detonators. A few minutes later the train arrived at my box. The driver told me he was very frightened when he stopped the train – he thought he would be coshed as he got out'.

'This was no hoax. Whoever put the detonators on the track was obviously after the mail train'.

Minutes after the goods train had gone on, the mail train from Peterborough and Norwich flashed by, unmolested, for London. Three of the ten coaches were travelling sorting offices. British Railways Police and Essex detectives met yesterday to discuss the Great Train Robbery that never was.[5]

Apart from failing in its objective, the Marks Tey incident differed in another significant way from the Brighton line hold-ups: it seemed that the gang responsible did not have the knowledge or ability to stop the train by manipulating the signals. Instead, they employed a rather clumsy and imprecise method of doing so, which had the added disadvantage of attracting unwanted attention. In spite of this, the hold-up location had been well chosen on a lonely stretch of the line, where the railway crossed over a country lane by way of a low bridge. From the lane, the main A12 trunk road was only a minute or two away, giving a fast and direct route of escape from Marks Tey into the heart of East London.

Although the overnight events at Marks Tey were covered in perfunctory fashion by other Fleet Street papers, the *Daily Express* reported in greater detail, making it a major headline story. Uniquely, *Express* reporter Frank Howitt had been sent to Essex to get first-hand accounts from railway officials.

Whilst the glare of the media spotlight was on the small Essex village between Braintree and Colchester, the Post Office Investigation Branch launched their own secret investigation:

SECURITY – TPOS

PSD/HMB

(1) In view of the publicity given in the press on the 27th January 1962 (particularly in the Daily Express) about a suspected attempt to hold up the East Anglia T.P.O, I think we should urgently ensure that TPO security is as good as it should be – particularly when the train is brought to a halt on some pretext.

(2) The question of access by corridor on part passenger part TPO trains and of window/door security on all TPOs are matters which might be reviewed. The IB would send a representative if required.

(3) It may well be that all reasonable steps have already been taken as the result of the IB minute dated 21 September 1960 (copy enclosed) – but risk now is, perhaps, sufficient to warrant this suggested review.

(C G OSMOND)
29 January 1962[6]

Despite this second request to Royal Mail security, it seems that, yet again, no meaningful review of TPO security was undertaken. Four months later, Osmond fired off yet another missive to the PSD/PMB security department, this time as a result of a spate of robberies carried out on mail vans and sub-post offices, which again had all the hallmarks of inside information:

PSD/PMB (Security)
17 May 1962

SECURITY OF THE MAILS, AND OF POST OFFICE PREMISES, CASH AND STOCKS

Postal security arrangements have been under review following on the general intensification of attacks on post offices and on the mails which started just over a year ago. Many additional precautions have been and are being taken which, when fully implemented, should lead to a considerable improvement in our defences against thieves and robbers.

This circular:-

(a) Brings together information and instructions about security which have been issued in various ways but which have not yet been carried into the permanent rule book;

(b) Draws attention to points in the permanent rule books that are of special importance at the present time;

(c) Contains some new instructions, which are sidelined for ease of reference, and

(d) Makes proposals for obtaining, through discussion or local Whitley Committees, the fullest measures of staff co-operation in making local security arrangements effective.

Whilst it is not desired to disturb authorised and long-standing arrangements which are satisfactory and which may have been introduced to avoid irksome attendances, the position in such cases should be reviewed to ensure that the safeguarding arrangements are defensible and that the unavoidable 'waiting period' is as short as possible (POR B3 II 3(a)).

Branch and Sub Offices. Imposters, dressed as postmen, have presented themselves at Branch or Sub Post Offices as the official collector and have been given the registered despatch. Officers making up registered despatches at Branch or Sub Offices should, if the collector is not personally known to them, always insist on the production of one of the means of identification listed in POR B4 XIV 1 and B 4a I 9. They must not release the despatch before the appointed time.

Collections. Where it can be arranged without disproportionate cost, steps should be taken to avoid important collections of registered mail from Branch and Sub Branch Offices or private firms being followed by ordinary collections from firms' or public posting boxes.[7]

As a result of follow-up enquiries, the *Express* men established that there had indeed been a dramatic escalation in post office crime during the past two years, as can be seen from the statistics they obtained:

1955–56	17 offences
1958–59	67 offences
1959–60	76 offences
1961–62	91 offences

It seemed that inside information on when post office vans would leave certain sorting offices, their routes and the amounts of money on board was being supplied to criminals, along with knowledge to assist them in identifying the High Value Packet mailbags from regular ones. In addition to cash, hauls included bulk supplies of postage and National Insurance stamps, which could be sold on in pubs, clubs and indeed to business firms for considerably less than their face value.

A source within the Flying Squad, Chief Inspector Peter Vibart, told the *Express* team, off the record, that the criminals concerned almost certainly had the advantage of floor plans and security details of certain post offices and sorting offices, and knew the location of strongrooms. It was also apparent that keys or copy keys were being used in such raids, as there was never any sign of forced entry. Vibart was an important source, as most Flying Squad detectives (especially Tommy Butler, who would eventually be promoted to lead the squad the following year) had a reputation of remaining tight-lipped.

Vibart had apparently been grateful to the *Express* for not using a story that came their way concerning a highly embarrassing situation he had found himself in not long before. He believed that there were several gangs at work specialising in mail crime, all benefiting to a greater or lesser extent from inside information. Furthermore, he indicated that one James Bryan, who was renowned in the criminal underworld as one of the best 'locksmiths' in the business, was believed to be making and supplying keys for post office jobs to at least one of these gangs, if not more.[8]

Sources on the court circuit also proved useful. Convictions for mail crime were rare, although on 7 July 1962, three men – William Robertson, Michael O'Leary and Arthur Atkins – were remanded at Bow Street Magistrates' Court in connection with receiving £3,740 19*s* 2*d* of stolen National Insurance stamps and £1,540 16*s* of postage stamps. Whether these men were part of a mail crime gang or merely receivers was not apparent at the time. Suspicions remained, however, that at least one of them had a deeper involvement.[9]

At the end of August 1962 the mail crime spree took a more dramatic turn. Even *The Times* began to take more notice, although its coverage was invariably buried deep within the paper:

MAILBAG ROBBERY IN TRAIN FIRE

A mailbag robbery which appeared to have been carried out under cover of a fire in a Victoria to Brighton train on Wednesday evening was being investigated last night by Sussex Police and British Transport Commission officers.

> Two mailbags, one of them containing more than 20 registered packets, were missing from the train.
>
> The fire, in an empty compartment, was noticed when the train reached Preston Park Station, two miles from Brighton. A porter attempted to control it with a fire extinguisher, but was unsuccessful and the fire brigade was called. The robbery is believed to have taken place when the guard left his van to fight the fire. The value of the contents of the bags was not known last night.
>
> In April this year five men in railway type peaked caps made a £15,000 mailbag haul in Brighton as a train was being unloaded just before midnight.[10]

Once more the *Daily Express* crime team were at the forefront of the story. Unlike *The Times* and other press reports that day, theirs was a front page story that was again derived from on-the-spot interviews at the scene:

> **MAIL BANDITS START LONDON TRAIN FIRE**
>
> The mailbag bandits operating on the Victoria to Brighton Line have pulled off a brand new kind of snatch, it was discovered yesterday.
>
> To get at the van carrying the registered mail they set the train on fire. Coshing a lone, unprotected guard is out. It is old hat to dress up as a railwayman to rob the mails. Tampering with the signals to hold up the train – a technique used twice before – is more complicated than luring the guard away from his van by setting a compartment alight with petrol soaked rags. That was what they did on the 10.28 pm train arriving just on midnight at Preston Park on the outskirts of Brighton from Victoria. Old style bandits over the last two years have got away with a total of £32,000.
>
> The post office could not estimate last night the value of the registered mail in two bags now missing. Railway porter George Kay was standing in the booking office at Preston Park when the 10.28 pulled in 18 minutes late. He said last night: 'I saw smoke coming from an empty carriage and ran the length of the platform to warn the motorman. He jumped from the engine and came to help and at the same time the guard came running from his van as the platform roof was getting scorched. I thought the fire was getting worse so I called the fire brigade. I had no idea that while all this was going on somebody was getting at the mail.'
>
> The guard, Mr Thomas Guile, said: 'It seems obvious that one of the gang set a compartment ablaze at Haywards Heath, jumped out and got into another. At Preston Park a porter told me that there was a compartment on fire. I grabbed an extinguisher and ran. There was a small fire in the corner but as soon as I

> pulled the door open it blazed up and out of the compartment. The top of the station canopy started to catch fire and I shouted to my driver, Percy Shepherd, to pull the train out of the station. I would think that the gang then got into my carriage while I was fighting the fire and grabbed the mailbags. I was out of my van for about eight to 10 minutes.'[11]

So far, no clues had been found that might provide any lead whatsoever on any of the mail hold-ups. None of the raiders had ever been seen without masks and no informants had come forward with names or even the merest of possibilities. However, in January 1963 an informant began passing on a series of snippets to Chief Inspector Walker of Scotland Yard's Criminal Intelligence Branch (C11). Early the following month, Walker received information that a big robbery was imminent and a train leaving Weymouth was the target:

> The train was said to travel to London via Woking, that it made four to six stops en-route and at each stop collected surplus monies received at banks. According to the informant each bank carried a certain float and when the bank takings exceeded this float the balance was conveyed on the same train each day. At Woking this surplus money was conveyed from the railway platform onto the train itself by two men who wore yellow around a uniform cap. The precise point of the alleged attack was not known, but it was expected that it would occur en-route and that Woking was the probable point.[12]

Further investigations by C11 concluded that the train in question was the South West TPO Night Up and, as a result, Walker liaised with W.J. Edwards, the assistant controller of the Post Office IB, with a view to strengthening security on the train. Walker also sent out a warning message to all chief constables, who as a result increased the number of police officers present at each of the stations en route.

In Edwards's report he noted that, 'Walker informed me that he learned that about the time of the proposed attack on the train, Robert A. Welch, CRO 61730/58, who was believed to be a member of the gang concerned was attempting to obtain suits of postmen's clothing and hats.'[13]

As February wore on, the attack on the South West TPO failed to materialise. While C11 and the IB were focused on the Weymouth to Waterloo line, a headline-grabbing mail raid on the opposite side of London took everyone by complete surprise:

BATTLE ON MAIL TRAIN

Eight masked bandits battled with dining car attendants along the corridors of the Irish Mail express last night after overpowering a guard and ransacking the mail van. The fight spilled over into first class compartments.

One of the gang pulled the communication cord as the Euston to Holyhead express neared Boxmoor, Hemel Hempstead. After the train jerked to a halt at the station, the raiders jumped to the track, taking with them a bag of stolen packages. The bandits scrambled up a snow-covered banking. An attendant who chased them told police he saw a car waiting in the road. He heard doors banging and a second car move off.

A railway spokesman said early today: 'We do not know yet just what is missing, but I think it must be a fair haul. The raid came at 9.25, 45 minutes after the train left Euston. It picked up speed outside Watford on its 260-mile journey. White-coated attendants prepared to serve the first sitting of dinner. The bandits, who are thought to have split up among other passengers when they boarded the train at Euston, converged on the guard's van.

Six of the gang wore nylon stockings over their faces and carried coshes. They attacked the guard, Mr Owen from Holyhead, and tied him up. They began to rifle the 50 bags of mail. The ticket collector was called into an empty compartment further along the train and coshed. But his cries for help were heard by two dining car attendants. They fought with the bandits in compartments and along the corridor and were joined by two more waiters. But the six bandits barred the way to the guard's van at the rear where two accomplices were steadily going through the mail. Bags were ripped open. A detective said: 'They obviously knew what they were looking for.'

Then the communication cord was pulled at Boxmoor. Night duty porter Peter George, of Ridgeley, Hemel Hempstead, said: 'I had the shock of my life when I saw the Irish Mail train pulling up. There was a terrible hollering and shouting. I ran across the line and the guard, ticket collector and dining car men were tumbling out of the train. A couple of them had blood streaming down their faces and one yelled to the foreman to call the police.'

Five of the train crew had cuts and bruises, but refused to go to hospital for treatment. Police sealed off surrounding roads. Patrol cars throughout the area – West Herts, Beds and Buckinghamshire – were alerted by radio. The mail van was taken off the express at Bletchley. After an hour's delay the Irish Mail continued on to Holyhead – with Guard Owen, the dining car men, and local detectives.[14]

Was this the work of the same gang that had been planning the Woking hold-up? Was the Boxmoor raid carried out because it was obvious to the gang that the police were aware of their plan, or was it a completely different gang and its close proximity to the Woking tip-off a complete coincidence?

C11 and certain Flying Squad officers were also, at this time, beginning to pick up word that a 'big job' was being planned by a specially assembled gang. Other than that, they had little to go on and resolved to keep their respective ears to the ground.

As bold, calculating and successful as this raid was, sceptics at Scotland Yard doubted that this was the 'big job' that was apparently in the offing. While the *Daily Express* crime team were later told by the Flying Squad's Peter Vibart that one of the mail crime gangs might be responsible for the Paul Street bullion job, so far as the paper was concerned it was only a theory and, if true, might suggest that this particular gang were now moving on to bigger things away from mail crime. However, the *Daily Express*, the rest of Fleet Street and, indeed, the general public were – unlike the Post Office IB and Royal Mail security – blissfully unaware of how much money was actually being transported around the country by the Post Office, particularly by train. According to the IB's own official figures, the Post Office was carrying over £4,000 million a year at this point in time.[15]

The Brighton line raids, while being characterised by cunning, boldness and a good degree of technical know-how, seemed somewhat hit-and-miss in terms of sums stolen, which tended to suggest that the inside knowledge they had was not so precise as to be able to target trains carrying the major sums of money. If the Brighton line gang was behind the aborted Woking job, this at least suggested that they were now, by early 1963, better able to identify targets. However, at this stage there seemed to be little awareness by Scotland Yard, the British Transport Police or the IB as to the identities of those who had taken part in any of the hold-ups or attempted hold-ups. Although a number of individuals had been brought in for routine questioning over a three-year period, nothing conclusive was ever discovered.[16] Despite previous IB warnings, and indeed the Woking tip-off, TPO security was still somewhat lacking to say the least. For the likes of C11's Chief Inspector Walker and George Hatherill, head of CID, the question now was whether or not one of the mail crime gangs was planning the 'big job' and, if so, where and when they would strike.

2

THE HOLD-UP

The Glasgow to Euston Travelling Post Office was a night train often referred to as the 'Up' Special or the 'Up' Postal. At the time of the Great Train Robbery it consisted of an English Electric Class 40 diesel locomotive and twelve coaches, none of which carried passengers.[1] The second coach from the locomotive was known as the HVP coach as it carried only High Value Packets. All the packets in this coach originated from banks and were being transported to the East Central District Post Office, in King Edward Street, London EC1, for delivery to the head offices of the various banks concerned. The sorting of these bags and packets into mailbags and sacks was carried out by GPO staff. Altogether there were seventy-seven post office employees on the train sorting mail, under the supervision of a post office inspector who was in the fifth coach.

The Travelling Post Office was comprised of coaches collected on its journey to Euston. The engine and first five coaches left Glasgow at 6.50 p.m. on 7 August 1963, arriving at Carstairs at 7.32 p.m. There it was joined by four more coaches that left Aberdeen at 3.30 p.m. and arrived at Carstairs at 7.15 p.m. These coaches were attached to the rear of the Glasgow train. The engine and nine coaches then left Carstairs at 7.45 p.m., arriving at Carlisle at 8.54 p.m. There, three further coaches were added to the train. These again were attached to the rear. At Carlisle, the original guard on the train was relieved by James Miller, who was with the train until it was attacked.[2]

The train left Carlisle at 9.04 p.m. and stopped at Preston from 10.53 p.m. to 11.03 p.m., Warrington 11.36 p.m. to 11.43 p.m. and Crewe 12.12 a.m. to 12.30 a.m. At Crewe, the original driver and fireman of the train were relieved by Jack Mills and David Whitby respectively. They then drove the train on the remainder of the journey, stopping at Tamworth from 1.23 a.m. to 1.30 a.m., at Rugby from 2.12 a.m. to 2.17 a.m. and, finally, passed Bletchley at 2.53 a.m. The journey continued until, at 3.03 a.m., the train stopped just before the Sears Crossing home signal as it showed red. It was there that the robbery took place.

Thomas Kett was the assistant inspector in charge of the train from Carlisle to Euston. His main duty was to supervise the staff in the second to fourth coaches behind the engine. Frank Dewhurst, a postman higher grade, was in charge of the High Value Packets coach from Carlisle to Euston. Leslie Penn, a postman higher grade, was also employed in the High Value Packets coach from Carlisle to Euston. Joseph Ware, a postman higher grade, joined the train at Tamworth at about 1.30 a.m. on 8 August 1963. Employed throughout the train sorting mail, Ware was in the fifth coach from the engine until just before 3 a.m. when he was instructed to report to the High Value Packets coach. John O'Connor, a postman higher grade, joined the train at Tamworth at about 1.30 a.m. He was employed throughout the train sorting mail. Just a few minutes before the robbery he was instructed to report to the High Value Packets coach for duty.

The stretch of railway line on which the robbery occurred consists of four tracks (two in each direction). The train was travelling on the 'up' fast lane. As the engine approached the dwarf signal that is situated 1,300 yards before the home signal at Sears Crossing, the driver, Mills, saw the light was at 'caution'. He immediately began to apply his brakes. He then noticed that the home signal was red, so he brought the train to a standstill about 5 or 6 yards in front of the signal gantry.[3]

Jack Mills's own statement best captures the events that followed the train stopping at the Sears Crossing signal:

> When I stop in that way it is my duty to tell the fireman to get out and telephone to the signal box. David Whitby was my fireman. He got down on the left hand side. I saw him go to the telephone box. He shouted, 'The wires have been cut'. He then walked back towards the cabin of the train. After David had gone back towards the coaches I saw two men come from the verge on the left hand side. I thought they were railway men. I could not see how they were dressed. It was too dark. I was looking at the controls of the engine and when I looked round I saw a masked man entering the cab on the same side as David Whitby got out; the left side. He had on a blue boiler suit and a balaclava helmet with just his eyes showing. I think the balaclava was green. He was carrying a large staff wrapped in white cloth. It was about 2 feet long. He was holding it ready to strike me, up in the air. I grappled with the man and almost forced him off the foot plate. I was struck from behind. Someone came in from the other cab door. I do not

know how many times I was struck. When I came to I was on my knees. The next I remember the cab was full of men. I was very frightened. One man wiped my forehead with a piece of rag. I could not see who they were; the blood was running in my eyes. They took me into the passage leading to the boiler room. They told me not to look round, not to look on the footplate. They told me to look that way, I would get some more if I did not. David was in the passage with a masked man. He had a balaclava helmet on his head – the masked man. It was dark in the passage but there was some light coming from the cab. There is a light over my seat and a light over David's seat. They were both on. I think someone had tried to move the engine. Someone said, 'Well fetch the driver'. They put me in the driving seat and told me to move the engine. They told me to move the engine and get going and when we shout stop, stop or you will get some more. The cab was full; I would imagine there were eight or nine. I did not notice anything about their hands. They had all got staffs. They told me to keep my head down while I was driving. I did as I was told and moved the engine off. I thought I had got all the train. Nothing happened just then. I had to put the rear ejector on as I thought they had not put the stopper on the back. I had had no similar trouble during the journey. It is the large ejector. I drove the train on until I was told to stop. They just shouted 'stop'. I did not look out of the front of the cab as they told me to keep my head down. I saw no marking flags at the side of the track. When I stopped they pulled me into the engine room again and handcuffed me to the fireman. There was one with David and one pulled me towards him. All the others jumped off the footplate. They took us on to the ground on to the track. They told us to lay face downwards on the grass. I had to walk through the men who were unloading the mailbags. There were only two coaches behind the engine. The men unloading the mailbags were all dressed in boiler suits and balaclava helmets. The men had formed a chain down the bank passing the bags from hand to hand. I should imagine there were about 15 men. One man was standing over us when we were on the grass. He was in a boiler suit and balaclava. He said, 'I'll get your address when this is all over and send you a few quid'. He said, 'Keep your mouth shut. They are right bastards here'. After seven or eight minutes on the grass he told us to climb in the back of the GPO van. I told him I could not climb in so they lifted us both in. In the van I saw four GPO men lying in the corner. I lay on the mailbags. One of the raiders said 'Stay here for half an hour, we shall be back'. Just after he had gone I heard the noise of a motor car engine. It appeared to be one engine. I waited for a few minutes. We stopped in the van until the guard came up. After the guard came another train came up on the slow line and the fireman of this train took my train to Cheddington Station for assistance.[4]

The sequence of events described by Mills is essentially corroborated by fireman David Whitby:

> I had an uneventful journey until the train was held up at Sears Crossing by a red signal. I got down from the left hand side of the cab in order to telephone the Leighton Buzzard signal box. I could not get through to the signal box. I looked under the box and saw that the wires had been cut. I wanted to tell the driver Mr Mills about this. There was a man looking between the second and third coach. I thought he was a postman or somebody out of the train. He had a slop, a cloth jacket on, the same as railway men wear. He had an overall on underneath. The jacket was reasonably light blue. It had been washed a lot. I walked in his direction. I said, 'What's up mate?' He said nothing then. He walked across the line to the down slow. He beckoned me to follow him and said, 'Come here'. The up slow line is on the edge of the embankment. There is a fairly steep embankment at that point. I followed him. I thought he was going to tell me there was something wrong, the train or the signals. He grabbed hold of me just above the elbows, swung me round and pushed me down the embankment. There were two men down the embankment. One of them rolled on to his left hand side and I went underneath him and he came on top of me. He put his hands over my mouth and showed me a cosh. There was white tape bound round the cosh. He said, 'If you shout, I'll kill you'. I was very frightened. He took his hand away from my mouth. I said 'You are all right mate. I am on your side'. I said that to save him hitting me with the cosh. He asked me where I came from. I said Crewe. He said, 'I'll send you some money'. I could not see how this man was dressed. He made me get up and walk towards the engine. I did not see the man who had been looking between the coaches nor anyone else on my way back to the engine. There were five or six men in the cab. They had the same type of overall on as I saw before. They had balaclavas on with just their eyes showing. The one I saw looking between the coaches had a piece of rag round his head. I did not notice any other sort of headgear that they had. I had a view of the man's face who I thought was a railwayman. It was a round face.
>
> They made me get into the cab and turned me towards the engine room and put a handcuff on my left wrist. I was then pushed into the engine room passage. Mr Mills was already there. His head was covered in blood. I could not see anything the men were holding. There was a man behind Mr Mills; the man had a cosh in his hand. It was about 18 inches or two feet long. It had white tape round it. They put me in the engine room and then pulled me out again and pulled Mr Mills out and then pushed me back again. Soon after that the engine started to move. One train went by on the down fast line. One man

stood holding the other end of the handcuffs. I could not see his face or very much because of the light. There was a light. There was a light at the other end of the engine room. It looked like a torch light. I saw no-one but the torch light. The train stopped and I was handcuffed to Mr Mills. I could not see if the men had gloves on. Mr Mills and I were made to get down from the engine. I was taken down towards the other coaches. There were then two coaches on the train. I did not see anyone at the back of the coach; I was looking at the ground. We had been told by the man that was guarding us to keep our eyes shut. We were made to lie on the grass. I had a cigarette and tried to light one for Mr Mills. One of the raiders said, 'I'll have one if you have one to spare'. I gave him one. I have a cigarette lighter which I got out of my pocket. I lit my cigarette. A hand came down for my cigarette lighter. The hand had a glove on it. When he gave me the lighter back the glove looked extra large and as if it had something else underneath it. It was a leather kid glove with stitches round it. While I was on the grass I saw no vehicles but as I was walking I looked down by the side of the bridge. There was a lorry down there. I only saw the side of it. It was flat sided. The back was flat and there were beams on it for a canvas top. My view was from the top of the embankment downwards. I nearly stumbled as I walked along. It was a mailbag which caused me to do that. I could not see how the mailbags were being unloaded. Mr Mills and I were put into the Post Office coach. Mr Mills had to be assisted but I was not.[5]

In Detective Superintendent (DS) Gerald McArthur's report,[6] he relates the statement of Assistant Inspector Thomas Kett who recalled that:

The train stopped between Leighton Buzzard and Cheddington and he estimates the time at 3.15 am. This time is incorrect as will be seen later. A few minutes later the train began to move and he heard steam escaping from the rear of his coach and he formed the opinion that coupling between his coach and the next had broken. Someone pulled the communication cord and others shouted through the windows to attract the attention of the driver. No further action could be taken by them to draw the driver's attention to the position because there was no corridor communication between the High Valued Packets Coach and the parcels van which separates the former from the diesel engine.

Kett said that in accordance with instructions all doors and windows of the High Valued Packets coach were closed and fastened. (This was untrue because the corridor door of the HVP coach was only capable of being locked by a spigot key and there was no indication that this key was turned. A hook and ring higher on the door was not capable of being fastened.) The train travelled for what he estimated to be half a mile and then stopped again. A window of the coach was broken. He shouted to the others that it was a raid and they all began piling mailbags against the sliding doors as a barricade and the other doors were bolted. Someone outside shouted 'They are barricading the doors. Get the guns'. Another window was broken and two men climbed through it into the coach waving coshes. Other men entered through the rear gangway door and one of them was waving an axe. Within seconds Kett says six to eight unauthorized men were in the coach and he could hear others shouting outside. One of the men hit Kett on the arm with a cosh and then all the GPO men were herded into the front of the coach and made to lie down. The man who hit Kett with a cosh stood guard over them making them keep their heads down and eyes closed.

Kett heard the sound of mailbags being unloaded. Afterwards they were told not to leave the coach for half an hour. He saw the driver and fireman come into the back of the coach. He noticed the driver was injured. As soon as things appeared quiet he and Penn left the attacked coach and walked back along the tracks to the remainder of the train. On the way he says he met the guard and told him what had happened. The other Post Office men on the coach, broadly speaking, support the evidence given by Kett. There are, however, differences of opinion as to the exact sequence of events and what part each played in trying to protect themselves or the coach. No doubt their differences are the result of fear which was put into them when mention of guns was made by one of the raiders. None of these Post Office men could identify any of their attackers.[7]

Frank Dewhurst, the post office official in charge of the HVP coach tells a similar story:

Just after 3 o'clock the train stopped. I was in the High Value Package coach then. It started in a matter of minutes. I heard something after it stopped again. Only our part of the train started again. I heard the steam pipe break and made me realise we had parted company. I called out to Mr Kett that the train had broken adrift. He went to the back and shut the door. The train stopped a short time after that. After we stopped the second time one of the offside windows smashed as if something had come in. There was nothing on the floor. At the same time another train went by. Mr Kett called out 'It's a raid'. I tried to stack bags against the glass doors. Mr Kett and Mr Ware were at the gangway door trying I think to put the lock on. I heard someone shout 'Some bastard's putting the bolt on. Get the guns'. I continued to stack bags. The next I knew I turned to my right and I saw a thick set person with an axe raised above his head. I put my

> hands up thinking the person with the axe was going to hit me and as I turned I was hit several times from behind and I fell to the floor. I saw the person who hit me from waist high and I assumed he was a tall person. I do not think he hit me with his hands. It was something hard but not iron. I went face downwards on to the floor. I was not hit while I was on the floor. I was hit about 4 or 5 times before I went on the floor. Someone put their boot into my ribs and asked if I was all right. I did not reply at first but when they repeated it I said 'Yes'.[8]

> In the third coach of the train, that is the coach immediately behind the High Valued coach, were four other Post Office employees. Two of them were Stanley Edward Hall, a High Grade Postman, and Dennis Ronald Jeffries, a Higher Grade Postman. Hall joined the train at Carlisle and was present in his coach when the train stopped at Sears Crossing. After it had been stationary for a few minutes, out of curiosity, Hall opened the nearside door of his coach and saw a man standing between his coach and the High Valued Packets coach. After a few seconds Hall saw another man come from under and beneath the joining bellows of the two coaches. One of them spoke to the other and they then both walked away towards the diesel engine. Hall thought no more of this because he believed the two men to be railwaymen who had affected a repair. Hall closed the door and walked through his coach towards the bellows of the High Valued Packets coach and as he did so he saw it move away and suddenly the steam pipe burst and his vision was impaired due to escaping steam. When the steam cleared he saw that the High Valued Packets coach was drawing further away and one of the GPO employees inside it was closing the corridor door. Hall still did not realise anything was seriously wrong, but he was puzzled because he noticed the signal at red.[9]

Stanley Hall's curiosity actually led to him seeing one of the robbers, who at this stage was not wearing a balaclava:

> After we had been standing for a few minutes, out of curiosity I opened the near side leading door – in other words the left hand door looking towards the train. I was alone at this time and I saw some person standing between my coach and the High Value coach.
>
> As I opened the door the man standing on the permanent way looked at me. He did not have a mask on and he had a roundish face and was wearing glasses. I can't give any idea of age at all, except to say that he was neither very young nor very old. He was bending down most of the time but by the height of the running board I would say he was on the shorter side of about 5' 6". He was

rather thick set. I have got the impression he was wearing a Railwayman's cap but not a shiny topped one as there was no reflection from the light. He was wearing blue material type clothing similar to that worn by railwaymen. When he looked out of the door the man would be about 12 feet away from me. He did not speak to me; he only glanced in my direction. After a few seconds another man came from under and beneath the two coaches.

When the train pulled away there was four of us in our coach, Mr Connell, Mr Jeffreys, myself and someone else I can't remember who it was. I have decided in my own mind that a railwayman must have been involved in this as the uncoupling was done so quickly and it would take an experienced man to do that. He also didn't touch the steam pipe as he must have known he would have been scalded and also it would make a noise.

I have never been approached by anyone to give any information about Post Office trains nor have I heard of anyone else who has. When the two men came out from the train one of them had a torch. I didn't see the actual torch just the light from it. I don't think I would know either of the men again.[10]

Thomas Miller was the guard on the train and he was in his compartment at the rear of the train when it stopped at Sears Crossing. He recorded the time as 3.03 am. Two minutes later he heard the brakes go on and saw the vacuum gauge in his compartment drop to zero. He walked through to the ninth coach and then got down on to the nearside track. He looked towards where the diesel engine should have been but could not see it. Neither did he see anyone. He walked towards the front of the train expecting to meet the fireman. He continued the length of the train and found the engine and first two coaches missing. He could not hear the diesel engine or see any sign of it. He returned to the ninth coach and asked the GPO staff in it to apply the handbrake. He then returned to his compartment, collected detonators on the track at a quarter of a mile, half a mile and one mile from the train. He then returned to Sears Crossing Signals where he found the signal box telephone wires had been cut. He continued along the line believing something serious had happened but not realising that the train had been robbed. He placed detonators at 100 yards from the train and then decided to walk to Cheddington. He came across the remainder of the train at Bridego Bridge.[11]

Miller noticed the nearside door of the High Valued Packets Coach open and also the corridor door. Inside the coach he saw Mills the driver and Whitby the fireman sitting on some bags handcuffed together. He noticed the injuries to Mills. He also saw three of the GPO staff inside the coach. They told him of the robbery and Miller then set off towards Cheddington Station to seek assistance. He stopped a train which was coming toward him, told the guard of the robbery and asked him to stop at the abandoned diesel engine and attended to it. Miller then continued to walk towards Cheddington and en route was picked up by a passing train. At Cheddington Signal Box he arranged for assistance. He recorded his time of arrival there at 4.15 am.[12]

Thomas Wyn-De-Bank was the signalman on duty at Leighton Buzzard No 1 Signal Box, during the night of 7/8 August 1963. At 2.58 am he saw the Travelling Post Office pass his signal box. At 3.00 am he received an indication on a buzzer in his box that the signal lights at the Distant Signal at Sears Crossing were out. He assumed it was a signal failure and took no action but waited for a telephone call from the fireman on the Travelling Post Office. He did not receive such a call and at 3.10 am the signalman from Cheddington Signal Box telephoned him to enquire where the train was. Mr Wyn-De-Bank told him that the train had entered his section and of the signal failure. At 3.15 am Wyn-De-Bank noticed on his indicator that the train had passed the signals at Sears Crossing. At the same time his indicator showed the approach line to Sears Crossing as being still engaged. He assumed that a vehicle or part of the train had been left behind or that there was a track failure. He arranged for a linesman to be called out to check the line and advised the Control Office, Euston, and the signalman at Cheddington Box of the circumstances and his intention to ask the driver of the next 'Up' train to examine the line and report the position of the Travelling Post Office at Cheddington. He later spoke to the driver of the next 'Up' train, a Mr Cooper, and as a result of this action, Cooper discovered the Travelling Post Office and was informed of the robbery. Cooper instructed his fireman, W G Green, to take the front portion of the Travelling Post Office to Cheddington. On the way to Cheddington, Driver Cooper spoke to Euston Control and asked them to arrange for the police and ambulance to attend.[13]

As the official enquiry into the robbery was later to note:

By cutting nearby telephone wires, the gang was able to delay information of the robbery coming to the notice of the police. From the time the train was first brought to a halt at Sears Crossing at 3.03 am and the gang leaving Bridego Bridge at about 3.30 am, it was not until 4.25 am that a telephone call from Cheddington Signal box reached Aylesbury, via Euston and New Scotland Yard.[14]

As a result of the telephone call made to Euston station from Cheddington signal box shortly after Thomas Miller's arrival, the British Transport Commission Police logged an immediate crime report:

BRITISH TRANSPORT COMMISSION POLICE CRIME REPORT

British Railways Board, London Midland Region
PC Blake 7 'M' by Train Control, Euston
Euston 4.30am 8 August, 1963
Sears Crossing, between Leighton Buzzard and Cheddington, Buckinghamshire, 3.05am 8.8.63. Train Crew. Am No4
GPO Mail, High Value Treasury Notes
6.50pm ex Glasgow to London Euston
Driver: Jack Mills – Crewe Loco
Co Driver: David Whitby – Crewe Loco
Guard: Thomas James Miller – Euston

Train stopped at unauthorised signal, signal faked with aid of glove to cover green light and four six volt Ever-Ready Dry Cell batteries to keep 'Red' showing. Driver and Co-Driver attacked and Diesel Engine and two front coaches un-coupled. Driver forced to take it about one mile to a point at Sears Crossing, where raiders attacked GPO Staff in Royal Mail Coach K30204M and 120 Mail bags stolen.

Believed Army type vehicle – 3-Ton with Large Wheels. High Floor. (2) Land Rover Type. Grey or Light blue. (3) Unknown.[15]

By the time the first police car containing two officers arrived at Cheddington at 4.36 a.m., the gang and the money were long gone. As dawn broke, the train was extensively photographed before being moved to Cheddington station to be fingerprinted. The sabotaged signals, the cut telephone lines and abandoned pick-axe handles used to smash into the carriage were caught on film, but no prints were found. It seemed there was very little for the police to go on and the gang was in with a chance of getting clean away.

3

THE 30-MINUTE CLUE

At 8.30 a.m., Detective Constable (DC) Keith Milner from Bucks CID in Aylesbury arrived at Bridego Bridge:

> Just off the south west side of the bridge I saw two rods with white material attached. On the track by the bridge itself I found a railway man's cap and a long crowbar. I took possession of these articles. I then went to the home signals at Sears Crossing, where I took possession of 4 x 6 volt batteries which had been connected to the red signal light, and a glove which covered the green signal light. Inside the glove was a piece of black paper.[1]

At around the same time as Milner arrived at the trackside, Clifford Osmond, controller of the Post Office Investigation Branch, based at St Martin-le-Grand in the City of London, telephoned Brigadier John Cheney, chief constable of Buckinghamshire, and it was agreed that a meeting should be held of all interested parties at GPO Headquarters, London, at 3 p.m. that afternoon.

At 10.30 a.m. a message was sent to New Scotland Yard and to the chief constables of Bedfordshire, Berkshire, Hertfordshire, Oxfordshire and Northamptonshire as follows:

> At approximately 02.45 hours today a mail train robbery occurred between Leighton Buzzard and Cheddington, Bucks. 120 mail bags containing a very considerable sum of money are missing. It is thought that the persons responsible may have hidden up and attempted to get away by mingling with normal morning traffic. Observation and frequent spot checks of traffic vehicles is requested.[2]

Shortly afterwards, Brigadier Cheney telephoned Commander George Hatherill, head of CID at Scotland Yard, asking that the Yard be represented at the GPO conference scheduled for that afternoon. The conference was held at the head office of the GPO in London and some thirty attended, the most prominent being:

> Brigadier J.N. Cheney, chief constable of Buckinghamshire Constabulary, and representatives of his staff including DS M. Fewtrell; Commander G.H. Hatherill, OBE of the Criminal Investigation Department, New Scotland Yard, and representatives of his staff including DS G. McArthur; Brigadier K.S. Holmes, CBE, director of the Postal Services Department, General Post Office, and representatives of his staff; Mr C.G. Osmond, OBE, controller of the Investigation Branch, General Post Office, and representatives of his staff; Mr W.O. Gaye, chief of police, (CID) British Transport Police, and representatives of his staff.[3]

Brigadier Cheney and DS Fewtrell told the gathering about the information in their possession regarding the robbery and the enquiries being conducted. The IB's controller, Clifford Osmond, said that he believed the theft would be in the region of £2.5 million, which was greeted with shock and incredulity.[4]

At the conclusion of the meeting, Hatherill told Cheney that DS Gerald McArthur would be sent to Aylesbury to assist in the enquiries. McArthur and Detective Sergeant (DSgt) Jack Pritchard later left for Aylesbury where they arrived at 10.20 p.m. that evening. On arrival they immediately set about arranging for road checks to be made the following morning for a period of two hours, commencing at one hour before the time of the robbery to one hour after the time of the robbery. It was hoped by this means to trace regular travellers in the area who might have seen something that could assist enquiries. They also conferred with several local farmers and with the aid of an Ordnance Survey map examined the area surrounding the scene of the robbery. Deserted farms and outbuildings, ex-RAF and army camps likely to be used by the thieves as a hideout were also pointed out to them.

Early the following morning, McArthur and Fewtrell discussed the statements made by train driver Mills, fireman Whitby and the GPO staff, who had all mentioned one of the robbers saying that someone would be watching the train for thirty minutes and concluded that this was possibly the time that the thieves had allowed themselves to get clear away from the scene of the robbery to their hideout. They further calculated that if this was so, then the maximum distance they could have travelled would be in the region of 15 to 30 miles.[5]

The possibility was discussed of being able, even with maximum help, to search such a vast area in an attempt to locate the robbers before they vacated their hideout and destroyed any evidence it may have contained. They believed it to be an impossible task but decided to announce to press and radio reporters their belief that the hideout was within 30 miles, knowing that the ensuing publicity might well concern the robbers enough to make them abandon their hideout before they were ready. The announcement to the press was made at the first press conference on 9 August 1963.[6]

DSgt Pritchard remained at Police Headquarters in Aylesbury while DS McArthur and DS Fewtrell left for Cheddington station where the train was now under guard. DS Ray of the fingerprint department, who was to carry out a forensic search of the locomotive, met them at Cheddington only to find the engine missing, which was now apparently in Crewe. After an angry phone call to British Railways officials, McArthur was promised the engine's return the following morning, Saturday 10 August.

On Friday afternoon, a series of conferences were held at Police Headquarters in Aylesbury with officers of the British Transport Police and the Post Office Investigation Branch. It was agreed that the IB would take statements from the GPO employees who had been on the train, other than those in the HVP coach, who had already given statements to the Railway Police. It was also decided to release information to the press, radio and television concerning the 10-ton army lorry seen by David Whitby.

The IB, being a post office department, came under the overall responsibility of a government minister, the postmaster general. Reginald Bevins, the Conservative MP for Liverpool Toxteth, broke off his family holiday as soon as news of the robbery reached him and flew to London. After a one-hour briefing by ministry officials and IB officers Frank Cook and Harry Lyons, Bevins spoke to press and TV journalists: 'I want to find out why the precautions taken were not adequate. Clearly our security arrangements have not been satisfactory … one cannot rule out an inside job.'[7]

On Bevins's instructions, one of the key lines of the IB investigation was to focus on establishing whether or not it was an inside job and, if so, who was responsible for assisting the gang.

When the Post Office held their own post-mortem on TPO security the following afternoon, the issue of possible inside collusion very quickly surfaced:

IN STRICTEST CONFIDENCE

Minutes of a meeting held on the 9 August 1963
To discuss the security of TPOs

1. The Chairman referred to the attack on the Up Special TPO on the 8 August when very heavy losses were incurred. He thought that all the time the Post Office was committed to carrying HVPs our policy should continue to concentrate the traffic on TPOs. The recent attack had demonstrated however that the security of TPOs was not adequate and it was necessary to make them as safe as possible with the minimum of delay. The present meeting had been called to discuss additional security measures that the Post Office thought to be necessary.

2. Repairs to HVP coaches The Chairman explained that there were three special HVP carriages which had been equipped with bars over the windows, additional bolts and catches on doors, lockers and bandit alarms. The up and down special TPOs each included one of these carriages and the other was held in reserve. On the 8 August these three carriages had been withdrawn from service for repairs and an old HVP vehicle had been included in the up special which did not include the special security measures. The LPR confirmed that one of the special carriages had been returned and would be in use tonight. Mr Fiennes confirmed that unless there is something especially wrong with the other two coaches they would be returned to service by the beginning of next week. He would also find out why it took so long to affect the repairs.

3. Reserve HVP coaches The Chairman then suggested that some action was required to avoid a repetition of the situation. It was agreed that an additional reserve carriage should be specially fitted out as quickly as possible. The LPR agreed to make arrangements to let Mr Fiennes have the numbers of the carriages to be so fitted together with a list of the scale of protection required.

4. Security installations LPR confirmed that bolts and throw over catches had been fitted on all the coaches on the up and down specials except on one gangway door. The LPR agreed to arrange for this to be done immediately. Mr. Mitchell confirmed that the bolts and catches were adequate provided they are fitted correctly. The LPR agreed to arrange for all new fitments to be inspected.

> Finally, Mr W O Gaye, Chief of Police (Crime) BR explained that experiments were being made by the railways in conjunction with the Bank of England and the Home Office radio departments with a view to establishing radio communication between the train and the constabularies through which they have passed. He agreed to take the first opportunity of mentioning the post office interests in these experiments with a view to possible participation.[8]

The fact that all three of the special HVP security coaches equipped with barred windows, reinforced doors and bandit alarms had, for the very first time ever, been out of service at the same time due to various defects, raised once more the spectre of possible inside collusion. Earlier that morning, Bevins had again been pressed on the matter by BBC TV News, and had responded:

> BEVINS: These trains have made thousands and thousands of journeys without the slightest mishap, without the slightest loss of money over the past 120 years; this is the first time it's happened.
> INTERVIEWER: Are you blaming British Railways?
> BEVINS: No, I'm not saying that at the moment.
> INTERVIEWER: Are you now more convinced than you were yesterday that this may be an inside job?
> BEVINS: Well, when I was asked the question yesterday, I said I did not rule out the possibility of it being an inside job, I don't rule it out now.[9]

Bevins clearly had the bit between his teeth on this issue, as after the television interview he wrote a memo to his private secretary making his suspicions crystal clear:

> **Private Secretary**
>
> On the mail robbery and the coincidence that all 3 high value vans were off the road on 7 August for the first time ever, do you know whether any of the authorities
>
> (a) Have investigated this detail, since it is very doubtful if the robbery would have been attempted or been successful had one of the 3 vans been in commission;
> (b) Know who, among rail and PO workers, was aware that on that particular night and indeed on earlier nights a van without a bandit alarm would be in use on the down run, ie who knew that 2 or 3 were out of use?

My information about these 3 vans is –

Off road	Repaired	Defect
22 June	Willesden (?)	Hot Box
4 July	?	Hot Box
1 Aug	Willesden	Flat tyre

The more I think about this the more strongly I feel that gang must have known the situation. The question is who could have co-operated with them and also informed them. If the authorities could get an answer to this the rest would not be difficult.

PMG[10]

While keeping a civil servant's sense of perspective, Bevins's private secretary was clearly concerned:

Postmaster General

On the point which you raise in the attached note, your information about the three vans is correct as regards the dates of withdrawal from services and the nature of the defects. In each case however repairs were carried out at Swindon.

Your suspicions about the three vans being out of commission on the night of the 7/8 August are shared by all of us and the Railway Police have been enquiring diligently into this aspect of the case. Mr Osmond is satisfied from what he knows of their investigations that the technical grounds on which the vans were withdrawn from service were in each case unchallengeable and there is confirmation for this in the fact that the vans were taken out of service by responsible people working in three different places, ie Carlisle, Wigan and Euston. It remains a question whether the defects in the vans were brought on deliberately, or their return to service delayed so that the vehicles should be out of commission on the day of the robbery but the Railway Police have so far found no evidence to support this but intensive enquires are continuing.

The possibility of collusion between railway or Post Office staff and the criminals has all along been very much in the minds of both the Railway Police and the Investigation Branch. A considerable number of railway and Post Office people could have been aware of the withdrawal of the vehicles, including the TPO staff and railway staffs at terminal and intermediate stations on the Euston–Glasgow run as well as at the sidings where the TPO vehicles are parked. Enquiries have so far failed to produce any evidence that the gang obtained

> information about the HVP coaches from Post Office and/or railway staff but this aspect is also the subject of intensive enquiry by the Railway Police and the IB.[11]

The issue of possible sabotage was to become a key part of both the IB and the British Transport Police investigations over the following two months and again put British Railways procedures under critical gaze. Having already blotted their copybook for removing the locomotive before further forensic work could be carried out in the cab, it finally arrived back at Cheddington on the morning of Saturday 10 August. DC Keith Milner was again on hand to accompany Scotland Yard's Dr Holden in examining the interior. It is noteworthy that Milner made the following comments in his report:

> On 10 August, 1963, I was present at Cheddington Station when Dr Holden removed blood samples from the engine cab window and from a ledge in the engine. I took possession of these samples, but on 17 August I handed them to Dr Holden.[12]

While the removing of such a vital piece of evidence as the engine and transporting it to Crewe was nothing less than a major blunder on the part of the railway authorities in disturbing a crime scene, it would appear that the crucial blood traces were not unduly harmed or erased. In fact, Milner's remark that blood was found on a ledge in the cab gives some credence to the view that while Mills was indeed struck from behind, he could well have hit his head on the instrumental panel when he fell to the floor, which may or may not have been responsible for accentuating his injuries.[13]

On that same Saturday morning, the first solid information about those thought to have taken part in the robbery reached DS Cummings and Detective Chief Inspector (DCI) Walker of Scotland Yard's C11 Department. They immediately drove over to Aylesbury to discuss the breakthrough with DS McArthur and told him that:

> Bobby Welch (identical with Robert Alfred Welch, CRO No 61730/58), was one of the gang responsible for the robbery. They said that Welch was missing from home and that his wife had received a message that he would be home in two or three days' time. In addition, their information was that the thieves anticipated having twenty minutes in which to leave the scene of the robbery and get safely to their hideout before the alarm was raised. The hideout was believed to be a farm and was somewhere on the outskirts of Aylesbury.

McArthur, Cummings and Walker decided that observation should be placed on Welch's home at 30a Benyon Road, Islington, London N1, and on the addresses of two of his associates.[14]

This was not the only key piece of information that came in by way of an informant on that Saturday morning. Bernard Makowski,[15] who described himself as a London antiques dealer, related a detailed and intriguing story to Chief Inspector Peattie of the Post Office Investigation Branch, which Controller Clifford Osmond wrote up himself in the following memo:

NOTES OF A MEETING WITH AN INFORMANT WHICH TOOK PLACE AT 11 AM ON SATURDAY, 10 AUGUST 1963

The informant is typical of his kind. He often talks in riddles; he leaves much unsaid and he either forgets or does not know the full names of the persons he mentions so that he is forced to refer to them by nickname. The sum total of the information which he gave is described in the paragraphs below.

He said that in January 1963, he was asked to become a member of a team whose job it was to scout a train job which offered a prize, if successful, of about £7m. He described the train as one which was due to run between Scotland and Kings Cross; that the attack was first planned to take place at York and that his part was to watch the unloading of the valuables at Kings Cross and to note the procedure. He said that, in fact, he had watched the unloading arrangements at Kings Cross and that he had counted the boxes as they came off. When asked about the size of the boxes he demonstrated with his hands that they were about 2 feet long and perhaps 1½ feet deep. He said that he thought the boxes were due to be taken to the Bank of England. He pinpointed the particular time of the day and a particular date on which his observation took place – i.e. the 17 April 1963, early afternoon, just after lunch. It was pointed out to him that this could not have been a plan to attack the mails but he said that he was under the impression it was a mail job as the boxes were being unloaded from a train which was standing at the platform which he described as a mail train. On further questioning, however he said that it was not a passenger train but a goods type of coach. He agreed that he did not know what a mail train looked like and he finally said that, although the attack which he had been talking about was due to take place at York on or about the 17 April, the arrangements went wrong – tip-off or something like that occurred – and so the plan was shelved and thereafter he himself was eased out of the team because he was a suspected informer.

The informant went on to say that, although he could not prove it, he felt sure that the same team concerned in what he now found to have been a plan for a bullion attack had carried out the big mail train robbery which occurred on the 8 August. In those circumstances I asked him to name and to describe all the men who might form the team concerned with that bullion plan.

He said that he himself had been invited to become a member of the team by a man whom he knew as Benny Stewart (or Stuart) whose address he does not know but whom he met in the Pubs and Clubs of Soho. He described Stewart as about 40 years of age, a Scot, and a gentlemanly type of crook. He was particularly explicit about his gentlemanly attitude and made it clear that he was not a rough bandit type of man. When questioned, the informant said that Stewart had, he understood, flown to Germany recently and that he has not been seen in London since the attack on the train on the 8 August. He explained that he knew Benny Stewart extremely well and that they had both done some work together at Kings Cross Station in the proposed bullion case. He said that Benny Stewart had, in fact, worked for Billy Hill at one time but that, in his view, Billy Hill was not behind this current mail train robbery. The informant mentioned that on one occasion an 'important' man visited Benny Stewart and himself at Kings Cross Station. He was driving a cream Ford consul and his name sounded something like Falcon, Falcon Faloor. The informant said that he was known to him also as 'Pat', and he has a brother who is also a crook. It was put to the informant that the name might be 'Falco', a criminal who is known to be interested in Post Office crime and who at one time lived in the Angel, Islington, area.

A photograph of Tommy Falco, CRO No 19772/38 was then shown to the informant who alleged, however, that this was not the man he was talking about. He described the man as having a broken nose, slim build, dark hair. On the question of his importance, the informant said that in the bullion case he was what could be called 'an organiser' – i.e. the man who was responsible for establishing train times and Station organisation. The informant maintained that he did not know where Pat Falcon lived but he suggested that he could be found in Hatton Garden as he often worked with (or worked over the shop of) Mansfield of Hatton Garden and that he dealt specially in smuggled watches there. The informant did say, however, that Pat Falcon had a blemish on his cheek and it would appear that Tommy Falcon also has a blemish on his cheek.

Patsy: The informant said that another member of a Kings Cross team was someone he knew as 'Patsy' who was also from the Angel, a man who received a sum of about £6,000 out of the Brighton mail bag theft which occurred from a train. The informant said that he knew Patsy extremely well but he could not give his address although he knew he was another Scot and a school chum of Benny Stewart. The informant described this Patsy as dark, slim and about 38 years of age. Concerning his whereabouts, the informant professed that he would be able to find him very shortly and would eventually give us Patsy's telephone number.

Freddie, the Fox: The informant was particularly anxious to mention Freddie the Fox as a member of the Kings Cross team who were concerned with the proposed bullion case. He said that he knew very little about him but that he would recognise him if ever he were shown a photo of him; that he frequented Clubs in Soho and that he also frequented a pub in the Elephant & Castle area.

O'Leary: The informant said that in the Kings Cross case Mike O'Leary keeps a stall in Leather Lane and has his own vehicle or vehicles and that, in those circumstances, he would suggest that O'Leary would have driven the money away from Cheddington.

Albert Millbank: The informant regarded Albert Millbank as an important man behind the scenes and suggested that he might be organising this particular mail bag offence. In particular, he lived with a woman who is also very important whom he referred to as the 'Julian woman' but it is understood that her real name is De Guillio [sic] who is said to be a Scottish dancer, who lives at Brighton and has a gambling house or club in the Gerrard Street area.

In summing up this information it is clear that the informant regards the people mentioned as some of those who perpetrated the mail bag offence. He stated that, in fact, in his view, there were three separate teams recruited, specially picked for the job – one from the Angel, one from the Elephant & Castle and the third from Soho and that, in his view, O'Leary would have driven the van containing the money to the Leather Lane area. I suggested to the informant that the money might have been held much nearer the scene of the crime but he said that it would have been brought to London definitely, although he could not, or would not, enlarge on that. As an afterthought, the informant said that a Railway employee had given information about the Kings Cross bullion job and that it came particularly from a negro Railway guard whose name he did not know. He was questioned closely about any informant who might be inside the Post Office but he said that, so far as he knew, no inside information had come from that source, although he understood that the fireman on the attacked engine had been involved with the criminals.[16]

The fact that Osmond wrote up the interview and personally passed on the report to Scotland Yard the following day indicates that it was indeed taken seriously. Whether or not Osmond believed that the gang mentioned by Makowski was responsible for the 8 August train robbery, he knew the names mentioned by reputation. He also knew that at least one of them was a known quantity to the IB in terms of mail offences.

Over in Aylesbury, McArthur, Fewtrell and DSgts Pritchard and Fairweather were studying maps and deciding which particular farms and smallholdings should be visited and searched. This was not a particularly easy task as Buckinghamshire has literally hundreds of farms and smallholdings.

At 9 a.m. on Sunday 11 August, about eighty uniformed and CID personnel drawn from Buckinghamshire and Hertfordshire constabularies reported at Bucks Headquarters in Aylesbury where they were briefed. A total of thirteen likely premises had been selected as possible hideouts for the thieves. By midday the searches had been completed with no success reported.[17]

The next day, Monday 12 August, a sergeant from Aylesbury Division and ten men searched a strip of land and buildings between Ordnance Survey grid lines 17 and 22. The search was in a westerly direction from Cheddington. The searchers gathered and set off at about 11 a.m. and had instructions to search buildings in groups of five. On returning to divisional headquarters at Aylesbury at 8 p.m. that evening, the sergeant reported he had reached the village of Quainton and that if the search was to be completed quickly, more search teams were required. As a result, two further teams from the neighbouring division were formed.

It was at this point that Commander George Hatherill's frustration at the state of police organisation on the ground in Buckinghamshire came to the surface. Together with Detective Chief Superintendent (DCS) Ernie Millen, the head of the Flying Squad, he set out for Aylesbury on 13 August and spent two hours discussing the situation with McArthur and Fewtrell. Hatherill insisted that Scotland Yard take over the administration and organisation of the train robbery incident room in Aylesbury, as he considered it was not functioning as smoothly as it should have been.[18]

It was at this time too that DS McArthur was formally made responsible for the progressing of reports and paperwork, and DCS Tommy Butler of the Met's No 1 District (shortly afterwards to replace Millen at the helm of the Flying Squad), assisted by DCI Peter Vibart, was placed in overall charge of the train robbery investigation.[19]

To the media, there was now a very public face leading the enquiry; Tommy Butler, the 'Grey Fox' was the cop who always got his man. He was by nature a very quiet man; a totally dedicated detective who was more than likely aided by his home life – a bachelor living with his mother in West London – Butler was able to dedicate his whole time to pursuing cases and gathering intelligence.

Butler's first move was to set up another incident room, run and staffed by the Flying Squad at Scotland Yard. In the weeks that followed the robbery, at least eighteen Flying Squad officers and often as many as thirty worked exclusively on the case.

At Butler's behest, DCS Ernie Millen directed that no matter what enquiries officers or teams had in hand they were at all times to give priority to the train robbery enquiries. Liaison officers were also set up with the Yard's Criminal Intelligence Department C11.[20]

On 13 August 1963, DS McArthur supplied a number of nicknames to C11 and asked if they could be identified. From the records examined a number of names were put forward which included: John T. Daly, CRO 33321/48; Douglas G. Goody, CRO 4290/46; Roy J. James, CRO 17638/56; Bruce R. Reynolds, CRO 41212/48; Charles Frederick Wilson, CRO 5010/54.[21]

By now, press speculation about the robbery and who was behind it was moving into high gear. The consensus among journalists and editors was that the robbery had been masterminded, although by whom was another question entirely. Every newspaper had its own pet theory.

The *Daily Express* reported that:

> … detectives trying to pick up a whisper about the latest raid in the clubs of London's underworld last night met with silence. For someone has learned to eliminate the gangster's major giveaway – his ability to keep his mouth shut. It is almost certain that one man plotted the raid. This is probably how his raids are planned. First, he gets a tip-off about a train. Usually it comes from an 'ideas' man. He never actually meets the leader, only his contacts. Then a small team of 'officers' are told to hand-pick the raiders. They are given a substantial cash down payment and an assurance that if they are caught their wives and families will be looked after. Contacts have to be made and bought in Glasgow, London and at the scene of the crime. Afterwards raiders go their own ways, knowing the haul will not be touched and distributed for several weeks.[22]

The *Sunday People* was the first newspaper to see a link between the train robbery and the London Airport raid of the previous November.[23] In their opinion, the £62,000 prize from the Heathrow raid was merely a 'curtain-raiser' to meet the expense of the mailbag 'grand slam.'[24] Another theory being probed by Scotland Yard was that the mailbag robbery was the work of the Irish Republican Army. Scotland Yard was, according to *The People*, looking for three Irishmen thought to have been in the gang, who had disappeared from Dublin. The Irish police suspected them of robbing three Dublin banks in the past two years.

The *Daily Mail* claimed that a baronet was being shadowed by the police, 'The check was ordered when it was found that he was associated with men suspected of having taken part in the £2½-million mail robbery,' wrote *Daily Mail* columnist Owen Summers. 'A chapter in the dossier being drawn up by the police is devoted to the activities of the baronet.'[25]

Peter Gladstone-Smith of the *Daily Telegraph* expounded the view that:

> Detectives investigating the Great Train Robbery yesterday know the identity of the criminal who masterminded the £2,631,784 raid. He is a miser and lives alone in one room at Brighton. His home has been searched and he is being watched. There is not enough evidence yet to arrest him. This man has a flair for the most ingenious type of crime. He works with infinite care and patience to prepare a plan which is perfect in every detail. He is known to the underworld by a nickname, travels widely, and meets other criminals in the clubs which they frequent. He has a criminal record but no convictions for more than twenty years.[26]
>
> This man's frugal existence and austere surroundings have defied all efforts to prove his guilt in the past. Detectives believe it has been his ambition to amass a huge sum of money; he is now expected to retire from crime. 'He never takes part in an operation himself. When his plan is complete he takes it to a master criminal, well known in the Harrow Road area of London, who carries it out with confederates.'[27]

Within a few short days the media were to have the breakthrough they had been waiting for when the robber's hideout was finally discovered at a farm near Brill. DS Malcolm Fewtrell later confessed that he had made a tactical blunder that had perhaps delayed the discovery for several days:

> The farm was in fact on the very edge of our 30-mile perimeter and our plan was to search outwards from the centre. During the long months since the discovery of the farm I have kicked myself thousands of times for not having ordered the search the other way round.[28]

The first occasion on which the farm was specifically brought to the notice of the police, as being a likely hideout for the thieves, was late on Sunday 11 August 1963, when Detective Inspector (DI) Densham, head of the Oxfordshire County CID, had a conversation with an informant in an Oxfordshire Club. It was mentioned during the conversation that 'Rixon's place' at Oakley was a likely spot as a hideout for the thieves as it was isolated and in a little known situation. It was known to the informant, as he had met

Rixon in connection with their joint interest in motorcycle meetings and socially. He knew the farm was up for sale and, so far as he was aware, had not been sold up to a few days before the robbery. The informant described it as merely a hunch on his part.

The following day DI Densham made some enquiries to verify the information he had been given. On being satisfied that the information given to him was true and that Rixon was in fact living at the sub-post office at Dunaden, Berkshire, he telephoned the following message to Aylesbury at 11.47 p.m. on 12 August 1963:

> Whilst making enquiries at Wheatley, Oxfordshire, re mail robbery, information was received that the premises at Leatherslade Farm, Brill, Bucks, were on the market for some time with no prospective purchaser. These premises were purchased a few weeks ago for a large sum of money. The informant suggested that this may be of interest to the robbery.

This message was received by Police Constable 78 Lewis in the operations room in Aylesbury. At 9 a.m. on 12 August 1963, Police Constable 145 Peter Collins was on duty in the incident room at Police Headquarters, Aylesbury, when he received a telephone call from John Alfred Maris, herdsman of Glencoe House, Little London, Oakley, concerning his suspicions that Leatherslade Farm may have been the 'hideout' of the train robbery gang. He made a note of this information and handed it to DS Fewtrell. There is no trace of this message anywhere and it was not acted on.

Maris was away on holiday from 26 July until 4 August 1963. From 4 August onwards he saw nothing happening at Leatherslade Farm to arouse his suspicions. On Monday 12 August, after reading his morning newspaper, which mentioned that the police were interested in isolated farms in connection with the train robbery, and knowing that Rixon had left Leatherslade Farm, he went to the farm. He noticed that the curtains were drawn and a large lorry was parked in one of the outbuildings. These facts made him suspicious and he telephoned the police.

At 9.05 a.m. on 13 August 1963, Sergeant Blackman of Waddesdon, on whose section Leatherslade Farm was situated, received a message from Buckinghamshire Headquarters incident room, informing him that a telephone message had been received the night before that Leatherslade Farm, Brill, had been sold recently for a high price and would he examine the place. (This information was passed to Waddesdon as a result of the telephone message from DI Densham of Oxfordshire.) Sergeant Blackman had never heard of Leatherslade Farm and contacted Police Constable Woolley of Brill, and another police constable who had worked the Brill beat. Neither knew Leatherslade Farm. Police Constable Woolley was of the opinion it referred to a farm at Oakley, known to him as Rixon's place.

Whilst these discussions were taking place, a further call was received by Sergeant Blackman from Buckinghamshire Headquarters incident room that a Mr Maris had telephoned again regarding Leatherslade Farm.

It was as a result of this call that more information was given as to the whereabouts of the farm. Sergeant Blackman met Police Constable Woolley at 10.30 a.m. on 13 August, and went to Leatherslade Farm where they arrived at 10.50 a.m. What they found was to change the whole direction of the investigation and, indeed, the lives of all those who took part in the robbery. In the words of DS Malcolm Fewtrell, it was 'one big clue'.[29]

4

ROBBERS' ROOST

Bernard Rixon bought Leatherslade Farm in July 1952. In the spring of 1963 he decided to sell and had lodged sale details with two local estate agents. Towards the end of May he received a telephone call from solicitor John Wheater, whose London office was at 3 New Quebec Street, W1. He apparently had a client who wished to buy the property and who would pay immediately in cash.

Rixon's wife Lily recalled that:

> Sometime in March of this year in answer to an advertisement that was placed in local papers, several people visited our farm at Leatherslade, Brill, which was for sale. Towards the middle of June I remember two men arriving at the farm to inspect the building, I know it was on a Thursday because my husband had gone to Brentford Market in the course of his business. It must have been sometime in the afternoon when they arrived. I know they had a car because they drove their car up to the back door. I had expected someone to call because several telephone conversations had been made by my husband and prospective purchasers during the previous few days. The man who did most of the talking was about 30 years of age, 5' 10" in height, slim build, dark hair, I believe a little wavy. He had a slightly tanned complexion and was clean shaven. He spoke fairly well with a London accent. He was wearing a brown suit. I heard afterwards from somewhere that he was a solicitor's clerk, and now I think of it this description would fit him quite well.
>
> The second man was also about 35 years of age, not much taller than myself – I am about 5' so this man would be about 5' 4" or 5' 6", fair hair, pale complexion. Because of his height he appeared to be broader built than the other one. This man's hair I would say was coloured. He had no grease on it. He was clean

shaven. I can remember him speaking. I can't remember what he was dressed in but it struck me he was not particularly well dressed. I would know both these men again. I heard afterwards that the second man was the proposed buyer and I was very surprised to hear this.

The inspection of the house was made very quickly without hardly any comment made at all. I went out into the yard with them and indicated the toilet which is an outside one. The first man said, 'I don't know what we are going to do with that,' and pointed back towards the house. I said, 'Well what do you want it for?' and he said something to the effect that he was going to do some alteration. There was talk of a swimming pool and other things. He said, 'Is the place still for sale,' and I told him another man was interested in buying it and he replied, 'If he drops out will you send the contract to Wheater's straight away, and he will get it signed up immediately.' The two men then left.[1]

Wheater also told Bernard Rixon that the two men who had casually called at the farm a day or two previously were the prospective purchaser and the other his managing clerk. Rixon consulted his solicitors and eventually a price of £5,550 was agreed. He understood that a deposit of £555 (10 per cent) had been paid to the estate agents Midland Mart, and he agreed with his solicitors that the purchaser could have possession of the premises when full settlement was made. He was later given to understand that full settlement could not be made until 13 August 1963, because the purchaser's money would not be available until that date. The purchaser still wished to take possession of the premises by 29 July 1963, and finally it was agreed that he could take over on that date, providing he paid 7 per cent interest on the balance owing to cover the mortgage on the new property that Rixon was buying.[2]

Rixon left the farm on Sunday 7 July but left his parents and the majority of the furniture in the house. They moved out on 29 July 1963. Before leaving the house, Rixon had a telephone call from a 'Mr Field' asking him to leave the key. By arrangement this was left with Mrs Brooks, who lived at The Bungalow, Thame Road, Oakley. To describe the premises as a farm was something of a misnomer. It consisted of a cottage that has been rebuilt and renovated so that two families could separately occupy it. Five acres of land made up the smallholding, which stands on a rise almost directly below Brill, but which itself looks down on the Oxford to Thame Road, the B4011, and commands an excellent view of the surrounding countryside and approach roads. The farm is not easily seen from the main road. There is only one entrance direct from the Thame Road, a rough but hard surface track about 300 yards in length leading directly to the farm and outbuildings. Leatherslade

Farm is not marked on the Ordnance Survey map but is shown as Nuthooke Farm. Locally it is more generally referred to as 'Rixon's place'.[3]

At the time that Sergeant Blackman phoned the Buckinghamshire Headquarters, giving the information that Leatherslade Farm had no doubt been used as a hideout for the thieves, Commander Hatherill and Detective Chief Superintendent Millen were at HQ. They had spent two hours that morning discussing the crime and its investigations made to date with DSs McArthur and Fewtrell. Immediately the information about Leatherslade Farm was received at Buckinghamshire HQ, Brigadier Cheney, Commander Hatherill and their team of senior officers left for Brill, where they arrived at about 1.30 p.m.[4]

Arrangements were made for the farm to be adequately guarded to ensure that it was secured until an examination by experts from the forensic laboratory and fingerprint department of Scotland Yard could be made. DS Maurice Ray headed the forensic search of the property:

> I went there on the 14 August. I and other officers made a very careful examination of the farm. On the 15 August, in the kitchen at Leatherslade Farm I found a palm mark on the sill of the window in the kitchen nearest to the back door. This was photographed in my presence by Senior Photographer Creer. On the 16 August, I took possession of an unopened tin of Johnsons Travelkit and the cellophane wrapping. There was a tin of Saxa Salt, which had been opened. I removed the cellophane wrapping and handed this and the salt drum to Senior photographer Creer. These things I found on the second shelf of the larder at Leatherslade Farm.
>
> On the 15 August, in the kitchen at Leatherslade Farm I took possession of a Pyrex plate which was in a cupboard under the draining board and which bore a thumb mark. Later the same day at Bucks County Police Headquarters, I received from Detective Constable Milner part of the lid of the Monopoly box which bore a finger mark. On the 16 August, in the larder at Leatherslade Farm, I took possession of a part-used bottle of Heinz Tomato Ketchup which was on the second shelf in the larder.
>
> On the 14 August, I examined an Austin Lorry bearing the index number BPA 260 which was in the shed at Leatherslade Farm. On the outside of the tailboard about 5 feet 3 inches from the ground, I pointed out to Senior Photographer Creer, a palm mark which he photographed in my presence.
>
> On the 15 August, in the bathroom at Leatherslade Farm I pointed out to Senior Photographer Creer a palm mark on the metal handrail let into the side of the bath and he photographed this mark in my presence.

> When I was inspecting Leatherslade Farm I noticed and it was visibly apparent that considerable areas in the house and articles had been wiped. On the draining board in the kitchen were two sponges and from the results obtained when applying powder it was obvious to me that these had been used to wipe down these areas. On 17 August, at New Scotland Yard, I received from Detective Constable Milner nine sacks, mail sacks, containing various papers and on 29 August, I handed the majority of these papers to Mr Moriarty of the General Post Office.[5]

The account of DC Keith Milner, who accompanied Ray, gives a more detailed insight into the wealth of clues that awaited the police inside the farmhouse and outside in the yard, gardens and outbuildings:

> On the morning of 14 August, 1963, I went to Leatherslade Farm, Oakley, and there together with forensic science experts I examined the scene of a bonfire which was situated near the large garage. Here I found a partly burned balaclava, part of a burned nylon stocking in a burned jacket pocket and a piece of burned banknote which was sticking to a small bottle.
>
> There was a full water butt situated by the side of the house. We emptied this and found in it a handle, a pump, a torch, a brace, a pair of wire cutters, 3 pairs of insulated wire cutters, a pair of bolt cutters, a hacksaw blade, a wood saw, a screwdriver, and some sweets.
>
> I was present when Detective Superintendent Ray removed a pick axe handle from behind the nearside seat of lorry BPA 260 which was in the large garage at the farm. I then went into the house itself, and from the cellar I took possession of thirty-three full mailbags, and five empty mailbags. I also took a pair of blue trousers, a blue jacket, a towel, a pair of underpants, a Banlon turquoise shirt and a 'St Michael' pullover from the cellar. There was also one full mailbag in room 'Y' and another full mailbag in the kitchen. In room 'Z' was a foam rubber strip and two dark green sleeping bags. I took possession of all these articles and they were taken to Aylesbury police headquarters.
>
> Later the same day, the mailbags were emptied by Detective Chief Inspector McCafferty, Faber, Detective Sergeant Brown and myself, and I listed the contents. In the mailbags I found a total of £541. There was a large quantity of varied articles in these bags, which included some bandaging, a leather glove which appeared to pair with the glove which was found on the signal near Sears Crossing, three balaclavas, a black hood with eye holes and a nylon stocking mask. There was also a leaflet which bore the instructions for the use of handcuffs. Six sleeping bags, eleven air beds, five air cushions, thirteen blankets

and twenty towels were also found in the mailbags. 4 x 6 volt batteries each of which had wire soldered to the terminals, and which appeared similar to the four batteries at the home signal at Sears Crossing, and forty torch batteries were also taken from the mailbags.

There was also a set of chessmen, part of a game called Monopoly and part of a game of 'Snakes and Ladders' and 'Ludo'. There was a large amount of army type clothing and equipment, which included a Lieutenant's jacket bearing a Special Air Service badge, a Corporal's jacket bearing a badge of the Parachute Brigade, a waterproof jacket, two army cold weather jackets, two army snow jackets, a camouflage jacket, and an army survival kit.

There were also six khaki denim jackets, two pairs of khaki denim trousers, four anoraks, a camouflage gas cape, three berets, two Special Air Service badges, three army housewives, and some army webbing equipment. Eleven blue denim overalls, three blue denim jackets, one pair of blue denim trousers, and a blue bib and brace overall were also found in the mailbags.

On 16 August, 1963, I took these articles to New Scotland Yard fingerprint department. The following morning I returned to New Scotland Yard and handed these mailbags to Detective Superintendent Ray. On that same day I handed to Dr Holden among other articles the 4 x 6 volt batteries, the leather glove and piece of black paper which I had taken from the home signal at Sears Crossing. I also handed to him three balaclavas, a pair of khaki denim trousers, four pairs of blue denim overalls, 3 blue denim jackets, the leather glove and the 4 x 6 volt batteries all of which were taken from the mailbags which were found at the farm.

On the 18 August, 1963, I returned to Leatherslade Farm and took the front and rear number plates from the large new land rover. They were paper type plates bearing the number BMG 757. I also removed the number plates from the lorry. These also were paper ones bearing the number BPA 260.

The following day, 19 August, 1963, I took possession of a number of articles from the parcel shelf of the large new land rover. These articles included a lock, some foreign coins, and matches, a pair of sunglasses and a piece of yellow cord. From the kitchen of the farm I took possession of a gas cylinder, a camping gas stove, six empty tins of 7 pint capacity beer cans, and two full ones.

I also took possession of quantities of cooking and eating utensils, and a large amount of tinned food, eggs, bread, and toilet rolls. These articles were taken from the kitchen and larder of the farm house, and were later photographed by Detective Constable Bailey.[6]

In terms of information given to the police by local villagers, one of the most important witnesses was Mrs Emma Nappin of Brill Road, Oakley, who made a statement to the police on 14 August:

> I am not a very good sleeper. I remember hearing about the mail train robbery on the wireless. After I went to bed the night before I heard about the train robbery I went to sleep and then woke up again at about midnight. I got out of bed. My window faces out on the Brill Road. As I was looking out of the window there was rather a bright light. It came down on the Thame Road before it got to my house. They came past my house. I think it was a motorbike that came first[7] and then it looked like a van to me, then a car. I could see the shape of the van quite easily. I could not see anyone in the vehicles. I went back to bed and woke up again later that night round about 3 o'clock or just after. I stayed awake. I heard something coming again between 3 and 3.30 I would say, I wouldn't say for sure. I know it was before 3.30. I saw the same three vehicles come back as I saw go up. They came down the Brill Road from Brill and when they got to the corner they turned left in the same direction as I had seen them coming from earlier in the evening. When they turned left on the Brill Road they could be anything from ½ to a mile from Leatherslade Farm house. On the return journey they were showing very dim lights. I saw no-one in the vehicles.[8]

Apart from Mrs Nappin, other local people were able to provide information about a number of suspicious vehicles seen at various times in the vicinity of Leatherslade Farm. Lionel Hopcroft, a local wood merchant, for example, gave a particularly significant and detailed account:

> Between 4.30–4.45 pm on Tuesday 30 July 1963 I phoned Luxicars, Oxford, to find out if a Jaguar car I had on order was ready for me to collect. I phoned from the kiosk in the square, Brill, and just as I was leaving the kiosk a Mark VII Jaguar containing four men pulled up alongside me and facing Thame Road. The driver then called out to me and asked where Leatherslade Farm, Brill, was. I told him that there was no Leatherslade Farm, Brill but that it laid between Brill and Oakley. He then asked me if I knew the phone number of the farm. I said I didn't and I didn't think it would be on the phone as no one lives there. He then asked me how they could get there. I gave him directions and the man sitting beside him said, 'I told you we'd taken the wrong fucking turn'. Then they drove off down the Thame Road. Whilst I was talking to the driver I was looking through the driving window, which was wound down. The glove compartment on the side of the front passenger seat was open and I could see inside the glove

compartment a packet of 'Manikin' and the butt of what was either a revolver or an air pistol. The man in the front passenger seat saw me looking towards the glove compartment and immediately closed it with his knee.

The car was a Mark VII Jaguar, in good condition, colour blue, 1951–1955 model. Brown upholstery (the same colour as the dash board) and a most unusual feature of this car was a chrome strip between ½ and ¾ wide ran round each wing following the contour of the wheel-arch, and about 4" to 6" from the edge of the wheel arch. I have been the owner of various Jaguar cars during the past twenty years and have never seen one with chrome strips like these before. I have no idea of the index number of the car. I would describe the driver as follows: 40–45 years, mousy coloured hair, combed straight back and quite thick. I can't estimate the height and I should say he was of medium build. The skin of his upper lip was lighter than the rest of this face as though he had recently shaved a moustache off.[9]

There was no other outstanding feature about his face. He was dressed in a darkish suit, with a white shirt and I believe a checked tie. He was quite smart in appearance. The man in the front passenger seat was 50–55, had dark wavy hair, bald at front with a lot of grey in it. He was of a plump build, clean shaven, roundish face, longish nose, darkish complexion, almost Jewish in appearance.[10]

He was dressed in a grey pinstripe suit. He was of a very smart appearance. He had a small cigar in his right hand and once when he leaned forward to flick the ash off his cigar into the ashtray I noticed he had a gold metal wrist watch on his right wrist. This was round and very large. On the dial were two separate gold hands. There were no numbers on the dial but where 3, 6, 9 and 12 should have been were dashes and the rest of the hours were marked by dots. He flicked the ash off his cigar in a very dainty fashion. His little finger was cocked up and he flicked the ash off with his thumb. Both of these men spoke with cockney accents. I would recognise each of them again.

I didn't take much notice of the two men in the back of the car. These two were about 25 years old; one had mousy coloured hair and the other blonde. Both were biggish built and tough looking. The blonde haired man had very large hands. I saw that they were wearing white open neck shirts but no coats. I wouldn't be able to recognise either again.

Over the next week or so I saw this car on three occasions, each time parked in a gateway off the Thame Road, about 400 yards past the entrance to Leatherslade Farm.[11]

A friend of the Rixon family, Mrs Lillian Brooks, was another local resident who volunteered information to the police:

My husband and I have been friends of the Rixons for a long time. I remember the day when the Rixons finally moved out of the farm. I cannot remember the day but it was a Monday. That day Mr Rixon Senior brought some keys to me. I hung the keys safely on a nail. A gentleman called for them at about ½ past 3 the same day.

He arrived by car and was aged about 35 years, 5' 6" – 7", stocky build with brown hair. He parked the car on the other side of the road. He said 'Good afternoon. Are you Mrs Roberts?' I said 'No. I am Mrs Brooks'. Then he said 'I think you have some keys of mine'. As I did not know the gentleman I said 'Where are you from?' and he said 'From Leatherslade Farm'. I gave him the keys. I said 'Mr Rixon said you were calling at lunch time.' He said 'We have been in the house. We got in through the back'. He turned away to go and I said 'I hope you will be very happy as we are neighbours'. He said 'Yes, I think we shall be very happy', and 'I shall be seeing you in the near future'. I did not see very much of him because he would not look me full in the face. He turned his back on me and looked down my garden. He just turned and jingled the keys and gradually worked his way out to the gate. My house is on the Thame Road between Brill and Long Crendon. When he left he went in the direction of Leatherslade Farm. I am not sure if I could recognise the man again. I could only identify him by his stature.[12]

On Wednesday 7 August, the day the robbers arrived at Leatherslade Farm, Roland Wyatt, a neighbouring farmer, noticed that new occupants had moved into the empty farmhouse. He walked over to Leatherslade Farm to introduce himself and struck up a conversation with a man he thought might be the new owner:

Mr Rixon's father and mother stayed at the house for about a fortnight after their son had gone. Mr Rixon's mother and father had been gone only a few days, when I noticed that curtains were up at the window. I didn't pay much attention as Mr Rixon told me before he went away that the farm property had already been sold. He didn't say to whom, but he did say that the new owners were going to keep pigs. I didn't see anyone at the house until Wednesday 7 August, at about 10 am, when I saw two men standing near a shed where Mr Rixon used to keep his lorry. This shed is just across the lane from the house and is about 10 yards from the house. I noticed that in the shed was an object covered by a green sheet, like a tent covering. From the size and shape, I should think it was a large car or a lorry under the green sheet. I went up to the two men and as I did so, one of them walked away. I asked the one still standing if there were any dogs about because I'm not very keen on dogs.[13]

He told me that there weren't any. I said, 'Are you the new owner?' and he said, 'No. I'm just one of the decorators'. I said, 'Well when do you think the new owners are going to come up here? He said 'He won't be up here for quite a long time'. I said, 'Who is the new owner?' He said, 'Mr Fielding of Aylesbury. If you want to get in touch with the firm who sold it to him, get in touch with Midland Marts, the auctioneers of Banbury.' We then had a bit of conversation about the possibility of me renting a field in the future, as we walked up to the house. I didn't go in though. Sitting in a deckchair was a middle aged man.[14] He was sitting outside the door nearest the french window. I also saw two little mattresses, with a book on each, lying on the ground, inflated, a few yards, from the deckchair. The man I was with told me that the inside of the house was in a bad condition. I thought this was strange because only just before Mr Rixon left, I had seen the inside of the house and it appeared to me to be in good condition. We said goodbye to each other and I left, and returned to my fields. Each morning up to and including Sunday, I saw smoke coming from the chimneys, but I don't remember seeing smoke after then. On several days I heard the sounds of metal being hammered. I think I remember there being a fire outside the house but I'm not sure. I would describe the man to whom I spoke as being about 20–30 years of age, 6' 0" tall, medium build, dark hair, very fresh face, wearing glasses. He was wearing white shorts, mauve shirt, red shoes. He spoke rather like a gentleman as opposed to a workman – the man who was with the man I have just described and who walked away as I said, I'm afraid I didn't see him again unless it was he who was sitting in the deckchair when I reached it. Now the man in the deckchair was aged about 50–60 years, very full in the body and face, ruddy complexion, fair grey hair. He was wearing white shorts and mauve shirt.[15]

Wyatt was not the only person who had witnessed the arrival of the 'new owners' and had seen them at close quarters. That same day, Wednesday 7 August, Brian Currington, a tractor driver employed on the farm adjoining Leatherslade Farm, had stood only a few yards away from three members of the gang as their Land Rover vehicle arrived and stopped at the farm gate:

On Wednesday 7 August I first saw a Land Rover at the gate of Leatherslade Farm. The driver squeezed through between my tractor and the gate. I stood nearby when one of the three men in the Land Rover got out to open the gate. I described him as follows: 6' 0", medium build, 25–30 years, no hat, fair to blond hair, tidily cut with parting on left side. I think it was combed back. He had a pale complexion with fairly sharp features. He was wearing a sports jacket

– a green check – with a faint brown background. The trousers were gabardine – nicely creased and matched the jacket but were a plain colour. He had a smooth cultured accent which I think was natural. I had not seen him before. He had well manicured hands which were not accustomed to work. He seemed very polite. I would most certainly recognise him again. I saw this man three times in all. The second time was when I saw him leaving the farm after the robbery in some sort of vehicle, which I cannot describe. I last saw him on Friday, 9 August but I cannot recall what time of day it was. He was at the farm entrance after having got out of a vehicle which went towards Bicester. I then left the farm on the tractor and turned left towards Long Crendon. When near King's Lane, which is a half mile from the farm entrance, I saw this man walking along the main road towards Long Crendon. He was wearing the same clothes I had first seen him in. He did turn and I gained the impression that he was expecting someone to pick him up. We passed the time of day and I have not seen him since.

There were two other men in the Land Rover. I can only give brief details of the driver. He was about 25–30 years of age and about medium build. He had dark hair, brushed back. A tanned complexion or weather beaten. I only had a side view of him and I noticed his ears were small and close to his head. I think he had a dark sports coat on but I cannot be sure. They drove up to the farmhouse and as they went by I noticed the Land Rover was loaded right up to the roof – it was bulging – but it was fully covered and I could not see what was in it. There were 2 suitcases on the back – on the tail board which was down – they were light grey in colour and very large.

From then until Saturday, 10 August 1963, my work kept me in the vicinity of the farm. I have a faint recollection of seeing the Land Rover leave the farm later on the Wednesday 7 August. On Thursday, Friday and Saturday I would have been in the vicinity of the farm from 9 am until 5 pm each day.

I saw nothing on the Thursday but on Friday 9 August I gained the impression that vehicles were leaving although I saw only one van. This van was an enclosed van, of Bedford 50 cwt type; it was not a dormobile. It was a dull grey in colour with windows at the back. I saw this leaving the farm I think in the afternoon as it turned right into the village at Oakley. I cannot say who was in it. After I had seen this van leave it seemed very quiet. I later noticed that the tracks I had made with my tractor were then undisturbed. On Friday, 9 August I was in the vicinity of the gates entrance to Leatherslade Farm every 20 minutes or so and from late in the afternoon of that day things seemed very quiet. I recall that when I first saw the Land Rover on the Wednesday, 7 August, I remember the fair haired man addressing the driver of the Land Rover as 'Barry' or 'Gary'.

This last comment was of particular interest to the police, who already had knowledge of an individual they suspected was the Land Rover driver. According to DCS Butler, very shortly after the robbery, 'several names of men physically involved in the offence were given to another officer and myself. One of these was Henry Thomas Smith, CRO No 1551/1947, who was living at 262 Fieldgate Mansions, Stepney, a poorly furnished flat.'

The police mused that it could well be that Brian Currington was mistaken and that it was 'Harry' not 'Barry or Gary' that he had overheard. It was therefore decided to immediately take out a warrant to search Smith's flat and bring him in for questioning. This was to be undertaken by three officers with support outside the flat.

DS Jack Slipper's statement explains that:

> On the 14 August 1963 at 2.45 pm with Detective Sergeants Moore and Caple, I went to 262 Fieldgate Mansions, Stepney, a first floor flat occupied by Henry Thomas Smith, CRO No 1551/1947, and Margaret Wade, his common-law wife. Margaret Wade, who was alone in the flat, opened the door. I told her we were police officers and that I had a warrant authorising us to search the premises for stolen bank notes. We entered and searched the premises but with negative result. Mrs Wade indicated that Smith was due home at any time. We remained on the premises and at 3.45 pm the telephone rang. Mrs Wade picked up the phone and said, 'Steam Company. No you must have the wrong number'. She then replaced the receiver. It was obvious that the caller did not have the wrong number and no doubt it was Smith himself. At 4.45 pm the telephone again rang. I picked up the receiver and said, 'Bishopsgate 5235'. There was a short pause and the caller said, 'Who's that?' 'I'm a police officer. Are you Harry Smith, the occupier of this flat?' The caller said, 'Yes, why?' I said, 'I would like to see you about a certain matter'. The caller said, 'What's it all about? Is it about my brother's bother?' I said, 'I don't intend to discuss it over the phone. Are you coming home?' The caller said, 'Yes, I'll be there in half an hour'. He then rang off.
>
> At 5 pm the telephone rang again. I picked up the receiver and said, 'Bishopsgate 5235'. The caller said, 'Harry here. Look I know it's nothing to do with my brother – you've had your card marked. You want me for the train job. If you give me your name I'll get a mate of mine to see you'. I said, 'I want to see you'. The caller said, 'You know I can't afford to see you.' I said, 'You've got three young children here, you can't stay away forever'. The caller said, 'I know that but I'm still not coming and I'll take some finding'. The caller then rang off. We then left the premises. Observations were kept on the premises for the following two weeks and Margaret Wade was followed away on two occasions but Smith was not seen.[16]

Having combed the farm property for clues and interviewed the local inhabitants, the police now turned their attention to how the gang came to acquire the farm in the first place. According to DS McArthur, among the first to be interviewed were Bernard Rixon and his agent Douglas Earle:

> Douglas Anthony Earle is the manager of the Branch Office at Market Square, Bicester of Midland Marts Ltd, the agents who acted for Rixon in the sale of his farm to Field. As Wheater contacted Rixon direct Earle had very little to do with the transaction and did not meet the purchaser. On 23 July 1963, he received a letter and the cheque for the deposit, amount £555, which was drawn on the account of James and Wheater. The cheque was paid into his Company's account at Barclays Bank Limited, Bicester. Joyce Winifred McRoberts of 5, Withington Road, Bicester, is a secretary employed by Midland Marts Limited who describes the visit, in the early part of July 1963, of a man giving the name Richards[17] who wanted particulars of a farm for sale at Brill. Her description of this man could fit one of the train robbers but does not fit either of the Fields.[18]

Police attention now turned to the solicitors who represented the buyers, John Wheater and his managing clerk, Brian Field. McArthur set out in some detail the outcome of interviews with the pair and the growing suspicion that they were not all they initially seemed to be:

> Wheater stated that one Leonard Field first came to see him in connection with the sale of Leatherslade Farm on or about 21 June 1963.[19] Leonard Field produced to him particulars of sale which had been obtained from Midland Marts Limited, the agents for Rixon, the vendor. Wheater then described negotiations in an account which tallies with that given by Mr Meirion-Williams, the solicitor acting for Rixon. Wheater handed over his file of papers relating to the transaction and on the surface had followed the procedure of a solicitor looking after his client's interest in the matter of the purchase of property. Bearing in mind that he was dealing with another solicitor this is not surprising. However, it is apparent that everything possible in the circumstances was done by Wheater to screen the identity of his client. He says that Field paid him the deposit money, the sum of £555, in cash which he paid in to his client's account.
>
> Subsequently, when interviewed by Detective Chief Superintendent Butler he was unable to recall whether or not he issued Field with a receipt and so far has not produced a copy of any such receipt. He states that Field gave his address as 150 Earls Court Road and does not think he has seen him again

since the deposit was paid on 23 July 1963. Prior to this he had written to Mr Meirion-Williams asking for possession upon exchange of contracts and before completion in order that extensive redecoration work could be carried out to the premises.

When contracts were exchanged Wheater signed their half of the contract on behalf of his client. Although it apparently does not affect the legality of the contract and was accepted by Mr Meirion-Williams, this is a most unusual occurrence. The self-evident effect of it is that any subsequent investigator is denied a sight of Leonard Field's signature, something which could lead to establishing identity. This point has not yet been put to Wheater but, assuming for the moment that this was a bona fide transaction, one would expect him to be in possession of a signed document from Leonard Field authorising him to sign the contract.

Although he stated that he had not visited the address given by Leonard Field, 150 Earls Court Road, Wheater admits a connection with the address in that he is acting for a company who are purchasing these premises, which he states consist of a club on the ground and basement floors and letting accommodation for ten rooms on the upper floors. Wheater states that there is no connection between Leonard Field and his managing clerk, Brian Field, but says the two have met in connection with the pending trial of Harry Field on charges of horse doping. He professes to be unaware that his managing clerk, or anyone else from his office for that matter, had been with Leonard Field to view Leatherslade Farm. He didn't think that his managing clerk had any dealings with Leonard Field in the purchase of these premises, adding that he has little knowledge of conveyancing.[20]

Wheater had, of course, contradicted himself in this interview, having told Rixon a different story during their telephone conversation back in July (i.e., that Brian Field had indeed visited the farm in the company of Leonard Field and that clearly Brian Field was closely involved with the conveyancing of the farm.

This contradiction had come out during Rixon's police interview and led the police to dig deeper into the affairs of Wheater and Field. When the police began to delve into the address attributed to Leonard Field, 150 Earls Court Road, more inconsistencies and contradictions in Wheater's story began to surface.

The premises at 150 Earls Court Road were originally part of the property empire of the notorious slum landlord Peter Rachman.[21] When Rachman died on 29 November 1962, his widow, Audrey Rachman, took control of the properties and ran them through a company called Michian Ltd, which was registered at 150 Southampton Row, London WC1.

In March 1963, Michian Limited began negotiations to sell 150 Earls Court Road to a partnership consisting of Anthony Deane, Brian Hocking and Donald Williams.[22] Of the three, Deane was put forward as the nominee purchaser. However, Deane withdrew, leaving the remaining two partners to carry on with the transaction. They formed a company for the purpose, called Jiltslaid Investments Ltd and, on 14 August 1963, Hocking signed an amended contract on behalf of this company.

According to Wheater, he was acting for Hocking, whom he had represented in a previous property deal, and was also asked by Hocking to look after the formation of Jiltslaid Investments Ltd. Hocking had, however, told a number of others in confidence, including tenants at the property, that he was merely a front man for the real purchaser, i.e. Wheater himself. When put on the spot during his police interview, Hocking gave the following account:

> I am in the process of buying the premises at 150 Earls Court Road, SW5. The negotiations started in about February 1963, and originally a Mr Deane was also in the partnership but he dropped out at the end of June, 1963. A company is being formed for the purchase, named Jiltslaid Investments Ltd, but to date no return of directors has been made.
>
> James and Wheater Solicitors, of 3 New Quebec Street, W1, are acting for us in the purchase of the property which is being sold with vacant possession, apart from the basement which is used as a club. I paid a £1,000 deposit to Mr Wheater on 2 July, 1963, and I signed a contract on behalf of Jiltslaid Investments Ltd on or about 13 August, 1963. Completion was due within about eight weeks.
>
> I had asked to be given access to the premises upon signing the contract and this permission was given verbally to Mr Wheater by the vendors' solicitors. The vendors were a company named Michian Ltd. I have known Sergiusz Paplinski for some years and I knew that he ran 150 Earls Court Road on behalf of the owners. I was given to understand by Sergiusz that the tenants were being given notice to leave so that the premises would be vacant before completion. Sergiusz himself had a first floor studio at the address and was affected by this. Sergiusz found a new flat at 6 Southwell Gardens, SW7, and I introduced him to Mr Wheater who acted for him in negotiating his lease. When Sergiusz was about to leave I visited him at 150 Earls Court Road, and as far as I could tell only he and one other tenant, a woman, were left there. When Sergiusz

> left he told me the place was empty of tenants. I understood that the owners' agents were removing furniture. I should mention that the rooms had all been let furnished. I told Sergiusz that I was only a nominee for the purchasers of 150 Earls Court Road, but this was not strictly true. My reasons for this were that I did not wish to disclose the identity of my partner. We have not yet completed the purchase, delay having been caused by difficulty in raising a mortgage. However, we hope to complete within a week or two.[23]

When the police interviewed Paplinski, he confirmed what Hocking had originally told him back in the spring of 1963, months before the robbery, and the revised account of his role:

> I lived at 150 Earls Court Road, SW5 until about the end of July or beginning of August, 1963. I rented a studio room there. Until March 1963, apart from living at the address, I looked after the house for the landlord. He then died and his widow decided to sell the house. Her solicitors began to negotiate the sale and on or about 22 March, 1963, I was sent Notices to Quit to be served on all the tenants there. I knew Brian Hocking who was acting for the purchaser of the house. He told me that the real purchaser was a solicitor named Wheater.
>
> When I found a new studio flat at my present address, 6 Southwell Gardens, SW7, Brian Hocking introduced me to Mr Wheater and he negotiated the lease for me. I went with Brian Hocking to see Mr Wheater at his office near Marble Arch. When I moved, all the other tenants at 150 Earls Court Road had already left. Brian Hocking knew this as he was arranging for builders to go in and re-decorate. I never discussed with Mr Wheater the fact that I was the last tenant to leave. Brian Hocking would know for himself as I had given him a key to the premises before I left.[24]

While these enquiries were in progress, a dramatic discovery was made by a couple in woods just outside Dorking. According to DS McArthur:

> On 16 August, 1963, a discovery was made which definitely connects Brian Field with the train robbers. At about 8.35 am that morning, John Ahern, a Clerk, was riding his motor cycle along a road near Coldharbour, Surrey, accompanied by a pillion passenger, Mrs Esa Nina Hargreaves, a Supervisory Clerk. The motor cycle engine began cutting out and Ahern stopped the bike.

In his statement, John Ahern recalls:

> We both left the machine to let it cool off and began walking down the track away from the road. I was talking to Mrs Hargreaves and after going a few yards I saw three cases on the ground among the trees and about 20 yards off the Dorking Road. I could see that it was not rubbish, and both Mrs Hargreaves and I went to check them. They were placed side by side in a straight line. There was nothing around to indicate why the bags were left there. I said to Mrs Hargreaves that someone had had a picnic and left their cases behind and that I would strap them on the bike and run them to the police station. I saw the one with the zip and thought that I had better look inside to see if there was any identification inside. Mrs Hargreaves was with me when I opened the holdall. I saw what appeared to be bundles of £1 Bank of England notes with brown adhesive bands around. Both Mrs Hargreaves and myself were shocked and I re-zipped the bag. I immediately thought of the big train robbery and told Mrs Hargreaves not to touch the other bags. I did not touch them. My thoughts were to get the police as soon as possible, and keeping the bags under observation. Both Mrs Hargreaves and myself went back to the road. We eventually stopped a car with a man, woman and girl in and took them back to the bags, un-zipped the hold-all and showed them the contents and then asked them to contact the police. Mrs Hargreaves and myself went back to the road again because I was uneasy as there may have been someone still about who was connected with the money.[25]

DI Basil West of Surrey Constabulary attended the scene and went to the spot indicated by Ahern and Hargreaves, where he took possession of the bags which he describes as a camel leather briefcase, a brown leather briefcase and a holdall. Upon searching the immediate vicinity he discovered a suitcase about 50 yards away from the original find. The bags, which were all filled with banknotes, were taken to Dorking Police Station. DC Alexander Illing, of Surrey Constabulary, later received the bags from Inspector West to examine them for fingerprints.[26] When Illing examined the bags at Dorking Police Station he discovered not only banknotes totaling £100,900, but also a hotel bill in a pocket inside the leather holdall. The hotel bill was made out to Herr and Frau Field, relating to accommodation at the Sonnenbichl Hotel, Hindelang, southern Germany between 2 and 16 February 1963. The next day DC Illing made a further statement:

> Further to my previous statement, I now add that on Friday 16 August when I took possession of a camel leather briefcase, a brown leather briefcase and a hold-all from Mr Ahern and Mrs Hargreaves, the brown leather hold-all was completely enclosed in two polythene bags, one drawn onto the bag from each end. One polythene bag was plain, the other bore markings showing it had originally contained a candlewick bedspread. I did not remove these bags until I reached Dorking Police Station, where I did so. I then handed them to Detective Constable Illing for fingerprint examination.[27]

The prints DC Illing found were photographed and the resulting negatives passed on to DS Ray at Scotland Yard's fingerprint department. He carefully analysed them and concluded that:

> There were in all 13 photographs which I received of impressions on this case. One of which is a comparison with Brian Field's. Of the remaining 12 photographs, four of them were useless. Three have not yet been identified. The other five disclosed fragmentary finger marks from which I formed an opinion but they were not of a standard necessary to bring before a Court. Of the 13 impressions, three were made by a hand other than Brian Field's. I can say that with certainty. The four were useless because they were not sufficiently defined to make comparison possible.[28]

The mystery surrounding the discovery was now twofold: whose money was it and why had it been abandoned there?

Scotland Yard's Criminal Intelligence Section, C11, had at this time received information that the robbers' original plan was for Leatherslade Farm to be thoroughly cleaned up by a close associate of Bruce Reynolds and John Daly after they had left. His name was William Still and, according to his C11 file, he had been in partnership with James MacDonald since 1959 in an antiques business that now operated from 69 Portobello Road, London W11, which Reynolds and Daly were also associated with. Apparently, Still was to receive a full share of the robbery proceeds for undertaking this task. The plan to clean up the farm had come unstuck when Still was arrested with three associates on 25 June in Euston Square. When the four men were searched, police found in their possession 'explosives, detonators, drills, putty, a pick handle, jemmy and nylon stockings'. While Still's solicitors, Lessor & Co., made a valiant attempt to get him bail, the application was dismissed. It was at this point that Brian Field volunteered to clean up the farm for the same sum as had been promised to Still. Field's reward for handling the purchase of the farm, along with Wheater, had apparently been £40,000, and he no doubt saw Still's arrest as an opportunity to increase his share of the spoils. However, according to C11's source, he had lost his nerve at the last minute and the farm was never cleaned up as intended.[29]

With suspicion now very much pointing to Brian Field's direct involvement in the crime, the police sought a statement from Field himself. DCI Mesher of Scotland Yard's Fraud Squad (Section C6) deals with Field's account of matters concerning Lenny Field in his twenty-two-page report on the purchase of Leatherslade Farm:

> Brian Field saw Leonard Field on a few occasions in connection with Harry Field's defence but does not recall discussing the purchase of the farm. Subsequently Leonard Field came to the office saying that he would like someone to accompany him to the farm. Brian Field is not sure whether Wheater was present or whether he saw Leonard Field on his own. However, for some reason which he cannot recall, Wheater was unable to go and therefore Brian Field agreed to accompany Leonard Field to the farm. They drove down in Field's motor car, a black Zephyr, and saw the owner's wife. Prior to leaving a telephone call was made by someone in the office, first to Rixon's solicitors and then to Mrs Rixon making an appointment for the visit to take place.
>
> They arrived at the farm and were shown round by Mrs Rixon, thus confirming that they were, in fact, the two people seen by this witness. On leaving the farm they met Mr Rixon and introduced themselves to him. Afterwards, Leonard Field drove Brian Field back to the latter's home address since when he has had no more dealings with him regarding the purchase of the farm.
>
> Dealing with his movements during and immediately after the night of the train robbery, Brian Field states that on Friday 9 August, he spent a normal day working at the office and then going home and going to bed. He had no visitors that night. He had no visitors the following night and on Sunday 11 August, went to a neighbour's christening party. The significance of his account of the happenings of these days will be dealt with later.
>
> Field's wife is a German woman and he mentions trips to the Continent with her including a visit to Hindelang, southern Germany, where they stayed at the Sonnen Bichl hotel for two weeks from 2 February 1963.[30]

Field's story about a quiet night in with no visitors on Friday 9 August was quickly to collapse when the father of one of Field's neighbours contacted the police:

A Mr L.E.D. Parker, of 'Abbeydale', Sunnyhill, Derby, has come forward and given the following facts to Derby Police. During the week-end he visited his daughter and son-in-law who live at Bridle Path, Whitchurch Hill, Berkshire, for the purpose of attending the christening of their youngest child.

The daughter and son-in-law are friendly neighbours of Brian Field who is also well known to Parker himself. They understand him to be a solicitor. According to Parker, on the Friday evening, 9 August, 1963, he saw a van parked in the drive to Field's house. It was also noticeable that a fair number of motor cars kept calling at Field's house that evening. The van left at mid-night but still a number of cars visited the house. Parker and his wife found difficulty in getting off to sleep in a strange bed and saw the lights of these vehicles shining on their bedroom window at the front of the house which is apparently opposite Field's residence.

The traffic continued throughout Saturday into the small hours of Sunday morning. Field attended the christening and made reference to the number of visitors he had had during the preceding days. He said something to the effect that 'the Brighton horse racing gang case starts in September' and that he represented them.

Mr Parker declined to make a statement in writing and is loath to become involved because of his family who are unaware that he has approached the police. However, I am quite confident that he can be persuaded to make a statement and will agree to give evidence.[31]

With the net closing around Field and suspicions that Wheater might not be all he seemed, another major breakthrough in the case was about to occur, along with a further recovery of cash.

5

THE POPPY

With little more than the '30-Minute Clue' to go on, the task facing the police investigation seemed a daunting one, but thanks to the fingerprint evidence left at Leatherslade Farm the prospects for early arrests seemed more promising. While it took some ten days to complete the challenge of dusting down the entire farm, outbuildings and vehicles left behind, the first arrests were down to pure luck (or bad luck from the point of view of those arrested).[1]

Roger Cordrey had left Leatherslade Farm on Saturday 10 August, met up with an old friend, Bill Boal, in Oxford, and together with his family and Cordrey's share of the robbery money had gone down to Bournemouth. Cordrey's immediate plan was to hide the money in two second-hand cars they had bought and secure them in two rented garages. Boal apparently saw an advert in a newsagent's window for a rented garage and, along with Cordrey, set off to meet the owner, 67-year-old Emily Clarke, who unbeknown to them was a policeman's widow. She immediately became suspicious when the pair offered to pay the garage rent three months in advance in cash. Mrs Clarke accepted the money, gave them the key and phoned the police the minute they left her house:

> They were both arrested at just after 9 pm on 14 August by Detective Sergeant Stanley Davies and Detective Constable Charles Case of the Bournemouth Police, following on information given to the police by Mrs Emily Clarke of 45 Tweedale Road, Bournemouth. Keys found in the possession of Boal were used to unlock an A35 car UEL 987, in the garage at 45 Tweedale Road, and a suitcase in the car which contained a quantity of banknotes. The amount of money found in the car was £56,047.

> Another car TLX 279 was found in a garage at 59 Ensbury Avenue, Bournemouth. The garage was opened with a key found in Boal's possession. Six suitcases were found in the boot of the car. These contained £78,982.
>
> At 3 am on 15 August 1963, a flat was searched at 935 Wimborne Road, Bournemouth. In a bedroom there was found a briefcase containing banknotes and under a pillow on the bed was £840. The total money recovered from the flat was £5,910, giving a grand total recovered of £141,017. Both Boal and Cordrey admitted that the monies found had come from the train robbery.[2]

On arrest, Cordrey had resourcefully hidden the car key in his rectum. After a few hours in custody, acute discomfort and panic at being unable to remove it had led to an anguished admission to the custody sergeant, who immediately summoned a local GP:

> I am a registered medical practitioner residing at 61 Grove Road, Bournemouth. On the 15 August 1963 at 1.15 pm I removed a Yale type key from the rectum of Roger Cordrey and handed it to a police officer.
>
> M.J. Saunders[3]

The London addresses of Cordrey and Boal were searched by Flying Squad officers, which resulted in the arrest of Mrs Rene Boal (wife of Boal), and Mr Alfred Pilgrim and his wife May Florence Pilgrim, brother-in-law and sister of Cordrey, for receiving part of the stolen money.[4] Cordrey and Boal each made statements under caution to DS Fewtrell and DSgt Pritchard, giving their version as to how the money came to be in their possession and their activities since the day of the train robbery.[5]

On 14 August the *Daily Mirror* reported that names and information from underworld informants was coming in thick and fast. Under the headline 'The Squealer gives Yard 10 Names' it was suggested that a 'snout' had also tipped off the police about Leatherslade Farm. Members of the public were also sending in letters to the police and the GPO in record numbers.

In the early hours of 14 August, Flying Squad officers had raided the home of Robert Welch at 30a Benyon Road, London N1. Welch was not at home, although his wife was, and a search was made of the house. On 16 August Welch was interviewed at Scotland Yard by Inspector Reginald Roberts, to whom he gave a written statement of his whereabouts on 7–8 August. According to Welch, he had met two friends, Jimmy Kensit and Charles Lilley, in the Express Café at the Elephant and Castle at 10.30 a.m. on 7 August. He was there for about an hour and then went to a betting shop in Aldgate, where he claimed the proprietor, Len Rose, had seen him. He left the shop around 5 p.m. and spent the evening with Charles Lilley at Wimbledon greyhound track. The pair left the track at 9 p.m. and Welch states he then went home and spent the night with his wife. The following day, Welch and Lilley met at the Express Café at 9 a.m. and then proceeded to Beckenham golf course.

Following this interview, Inspector Byers sent out officers to bring in Lilley and Kensit, two of Welch's three alibis. Kensit could not be found, but Lilley was brought in and interviewed by DI Roberts. In his statement Lilley confirmed that he was with Welch at the times and locations mentioned in Welch's statement. According to DS McArthur's report to CS Millen:

> Charles Gervaise Lilley, CRO No 27967/42, born 11 January 1921, a printer of 112 Knapmill Road, Bellingham, London SE6, has made a statement in which he supports, in the main, Welch. This is not surprising as Lilley and Welch are, I understand, firm friends. However, he is unable to say what Welch did between 10.00 pm, 7 August and 9.00 am, 8 August 1963.[6]

Two days after the *Daily Mirror* report, Tommy Butler sent the Post Office Investigation Branch a list of the eighteen names on his 'suspects list',[7] which included the ten names referred to by the *Daily Mirror*. This list appears to be somewhat of a 'pick and mix' that drew together information from a number of sources, some reliable and others not. Indeed, as the Flying Squad began working through the list, nine of the 'suspects' were found to have cast-iron alibis – indeed, one had even been dead for nine months:

Mr Butler's Confidential List 16/8/63:

Douglas Goody	Michael Kehoe[9]	Hayden Smith[14]
Charles Wilson	Terry Sansom[10]	Charles Lilley
Bruce Reynolds	George Sansom[11]	Roy James
James White	Frederick Robinson[12]	Billy Ambrose[15]
Robert Welch	Jack Cramer[13]	Kenneth Shakeshaft[16]
Harry Pitts[8]	Henry Smith	John Daly

On Tuesday 13 August 1963, Mary O'Rourke, a sales assistant at Coronel, a lady's dress shop in Church Street, Reigate, Surrey, became suspicious of a woman customer who bought a quantity of clothing and paid in twenty-six dirty £1 notes. When Miss O'Rourke asked the customer for her address, she refused to give it and left the shop.

According to DS McArthur's report:

The conduct of the woman was sufficiently suspicious to cause the shop assistant to follow her and note the number of a small grey sports car the woman got into as REN 22. On returning to the shop she immediately contacted the police. Police Constables 401 Donald Cooper and 183 Gerald Bixley located the car and kept observations on it and subsequently saw a man who gave his name and address as James Edward Patten of 66, The Woodlands, Beulah Hill, Croydon, SE19. He was accompanied by the woman who had been in the dress shop. After some conversation he satisfied the Police Constables and drove away.

Further enquiries were made by Reigate Police and it was learned the couple had been to a number of other shops and purchased goods. At one shop Patten had given his name as Mr Ballard, Clovelly Caravan Site, Bexhill Road, Boxhill, Surrey. This site was visited and it was learned that a man giving the name of Ballard had, on 11 August 1963, bought a caravan there. The caravan was searched and £136 in £1 notes was found in a jacket pocket.

Observations were kept on the caravan by Dorking police officers and on 18 August, Harry John Browne, CRO 32240/45, was stopped entering the caravan. He was interviewed but there was insufficient evidence to arrest him.[17]

During police questioning, Browne gave the following explanation for his presence at the Clovelly caravan site:

I am on sick benefit, but have worked for about 1½ years, on and off, in the Betting Office of M & M Regan, 38, Aldergate Street, EC1 (In their office).[18] I have known Jim Bollard for about 2½ years. I think I got to know him in a pub or club in London. I met him casually in a number of Clubs and Pubs and he and his wife came to my home on a few occasions. He was betting at my shop before he took the café. Seven to eight months ago he took over an empty shop at 37, Aldersgate Street, EC1, and turned it into a café and he's run it as such ever since.

I used the same Clubs, so I have met him on and off in such places over that period. I've met him in The Starlight Club; Stratford Place; Regency Club, Great Newport Street; and others. Last Friday evening, 16 August, 1963, I went to The Starlight Club, with Terrence Durnford, Mr Regan (John), Fred Allen, where we met some girls and had a drink. At about 10.15 pm I met Jim Bollard at the Club. He was with a friend, Bob. I don't know his surname. We were all talking in general about holidays and Jim said that my wife, two kids and I could use his caravan at Boxhill for a week if we would like to. I had heard then that he had a caravan somewhere, but this was the first time he had one at Boxhill.

I said that if it was a nice day on Sunday I'd take the wife and kids down to see if she liked it and if she did we'd spend some time there (I intended going back on Sunday evening for clothes if we were to stay). I asked him for the key and he said that the lady on the site in the lodge had the key, and I could collect it from her. He asked me, that if I went on Sunday, I could save him a journey by collecting a refrigerator from the garage proprietor, Mr Collins at Boxhill.

I intended going into his café tomorrow morning to let him know whether we were staying or not. This morning, when I asked the lady for the key I told her Mr. Bollard had given me permission to use his caravan, and she said she only had the shed key. I said I had got the refrigerator I had collected from Collins, and would leave it in the shed. I've never been to Bollard's home and don't know where he lives except that its somewhere in Mitcham. I've gathered that much in conversation with him.

I describe Jim Bollard as aged 35–36 years, 5' 11"–6'; medium build; dark brown hair, straight with a kink at the front, greased and smart; oval face; fresh complexion; clean shaven; I think grey eyes; no glasses; good teeth. I've noticed no marks, scars or tattoos; London man, London accent. I described Bob 30 years; 5'11"–6'; medium build; dark hair; clean shaven; no glasses; London accent.[19]

In McArthur's report he confirms that:

Subsequent enquiries identified Ballard/Patten as being James Edward White, CRO 26113/55. A search of the paneling of the caravan revealed a large amount in notes which was counted by the manager and a clerk of the Midland Bank, Dorking. The amount was £30,440. Some of the notes were identified as being part of the money stolen by the robbery. It was all handed over to Detective Superintendent Fewtrell on 20 August 1963.

On 19 August 1963, Detective Sergeant Wright of C3 Department went to the caravan and examined it for fingerprints. He took possessions of a number of articles on which he developed finger marks which have since been identified as those of White, and Lily Mercy Price, alias Sheree White. A thorough enquiry was made respecting the address given to the two police constables at Reigate. It was learned that the Pattens took tenancy of 66 Woodlands, Beulah Hill, SE19 on the 25 March 1962, at £295 per annum and paid their rent quarterly in advance. No payment had been made since the last quarterly payment commencing on 24 June 1963. Mrs Patten was last seen at the flat on 27 July 1963. On Monday, 29 July 1963, Mr Patten telephoned the daily woman and said that his wife had gone away on holiday. Nothing has been heard of them since at 66 Woodlands.

> The Austin Healey car REN 22 was purchased by a man giving the name of John Steward, Rock House, Chaunston Road, Taunton, Somerset (false), at 5.30 pm, 9 August 1963, from Allery & Bernard Limited, 372/4, King's Road, SW3, for £900. This was paid in cash in £5 notes. Steward has been identified as White. On Wednesday, 14 August 1963, a man since identified as White left the Austin Healey REN 22 at Zenith Motors Limited, 170 Aldersgate, EC1 for repair. He failed to collect it and on 21 August 1963, Police Constable C Bartlett, C10, New Scotland Yard removed the car to Chalk Farm Police Garage. James Edward White, CRO 26113/55 is still wanted for the robbery.[20]

By complete coincidence, Jimmy White was not the only robber who, on 9 August, decided to spend some of his new-found wealth on an Austin Healey sports car. Car salesman Dennis St John clearly recalled the chain of events:

> I am a car salesman employed at the Chequered Flag Sports Car Specialists, Chiswick.
>
> On Friday the 9 August, my attention was drawn to a man looking at an Austin Healey 3000.[21] He returned later on that day. At a much later stage that day he went and fetched a woman. They both had a conversation with me. When he returned the second time I did not see what car he came in. He came into the showrooms alone the second time. I took him out for a demonstration run in a black Austin Healey 3000 index number NFC or NPC 222. After the demonstration run I had a further conversation with the man. He fetched a lady. I could possibly recognise the lady if I saw her again. The gentleman said they would buy the car. I believe the lady said to the man, 'Have you driven it?' I believe the man said, 'No, but it will be all right'. I took them in to the office. I cannot remember whether either of them said anything to me.
>
> I told them that the car was subject to a three month guarantee, but if, as they mentioned, they were going abroad the following day, we should like to service it before. I said, 'Before you go, if you get time, at any time after 8 o'clock in the morning, bring it back to our workshop'. I cannot remember if I used the word 'Abroad'. He said, 'I will try', when I mentioned bringing it in for service. I said, 'Your name, Sir is?' He said, 'Would you invoice it to the lady'. I asked the lady for her name. She said, 'Mrs Mary Manson'. She gave me the address 209 Mitcham Lane, Streatham, London, SW16. I wrote it down in the invoice book. The lady signed her name across a 6d stamp.
>
> The price of the car was £835; it did not include anything in respect of insurance. The lady paid for the car. She paid for it in £5 notes. She took the notes from her handbag. They were in bundles of 100 with elastic bands round them.

> She handed me nine bundles. I counted them and returned some. I counted off seven £5 notes from the last bundle and then handed them back to her. I gave them the log book of the car and the signed stamped invoice. It is a copy of the invoice which I have produced. I made no arrangement for insurance for the car. The woman did not ask me to do so.[22]

Clearly suspicious, Dennis St John eventually decided to call the police the following week. Once they had had the opportunity to process the enormous number of leads and telephone messages that came in from the public during the days immediately after the robbery, it was decided that this was worth releasing to the media. The story about the black Austin Healey appeared in the press on the morning of 19 August and immediately brought forward several key witnesses. James Morris informed the police that a man answering to Reynold's description had parked the car at the Cranford Hall Garage in Hayes, Middlesex. Leonard Robinson, a company director from Somerset, had spotted the car in Bristol at around 8.40 a.m. on 16 August.[23]

Even more significantly, a travelling salesman by the name of James Bryning, who lived at 12 Walpole Lodge in Culmington Road, Ealing, told the police that:

> Since reading the 'Daily Express' this morning respecting the Black Austin Healey Sports car which was bought from the 'Chequered Flag' Chiswick, I am sure that this car has been parked outside my block of flats during the last week. I know for certain it was there Tuesday, Wednesday and Thursday. I am almost certain the number of the Austin Healey was 222 NFC as stated in the newspaper.
>
> I live in a third floor flat at Walpole Lodge. No 10 is opposite my flat on the same floor. I have seen the man who lives at No 10 Walpole Lodge, driving the car and putting it in his garage at the rear of the block of flats. I don't know his name. He is about 5' 7" tall, stockily built, with fair, short cropped hair and round face. He is well-dressed.
>
> He has been in company with a woman, aged about 23 years, short, slim, dark hair, wearing coloured blouses and skirts. I have seen the man wearing dark glasses. I have not seen the Austin Healey during the week-end 17/18 August, 1963. I have seen the man in a green 'Zodiac' motor car. It looked like a new one.
>
> During the last week I noticed quite a few men visiting the flat in the evenings. Also, another woman has been staying at the flat during last week. She was about 30/35 years of age, well built, light blonde hair. I have seen her in the Austin Healey with the man from No 10.[24]

As a result of Bryning's information, DC Frank Cowling of the local Ealing 'T Division' police, to whom Bryning had initially reported the matter, visited 10 Walpole Lodge:

> On Sunday 18 August 1963, at about 8 pm, I called at No 10, Walpole Lodge, Culmington Road, Ealing W5, and saw Terrence Hogan. I said to him 'I am making enquiries to trace the owner of an Austin Healey motor car, Registration No 222 NFC; this car is believed to have been outside this block of flats recently'. Hogan said, 'I don't know anything about it. I have never had a Healey; my car is outside, the Zephyr.' At that time I had no reason to question Hogan further. Outside the flats in Culmington Road, I saw a Green Ford Zephyr motor car, Registration number 591 FGX, which Hogan had pointed out as being his.[25]

At Scotland Yard, Cowling's investigation report was read by Flying Squad officers who immediately recognised the name of Hogan:

> The occupier of 10 Walpole Lodge is Terry Hogan, a friend of Bruce Reynolds.[26] Hogan was, on 19 August, in possession of a green Zodiac, index number 591 FGX. Reference to Mr Morris's statement will show that when Reynolds parked the Austin Healey at Cranford Hall Garage, Hayes, he walked along the Bath Road and got into a Ford Zodiac or Zephyr of the latest model which was of a dark colour.[27]

Both Manson and Hogan were questioned on 21 August at Scotland Yard. Hogan, when interviewed about the Austin Healey, and indeed his whereabouts on 7–8 August by DI Frank Williams of the Flying Squad, claimed that he had been in Cannes, and returned to England on 9 August. He was released without charge.[28]

Williams also reported that:

> At just before 12 noon on Wednesday, 21 August, 1963, in company with Detective Chief Inspector Baldock, I saw a woman I know as Mrs McDonald and her solicitor, Mr Stanley, at New Scotland Yard.[29]
>
> Chief Inspector Baldock said, 'As you probably know, we wanted to see you in connection with the train robbery at Aylesbury', and following this, he put a number of questions which I recorded in writing, together with the answers she gave. Mrs McDonald signed the document after it had been read over to her in the presence of the solicitor. The solicitor then left.

> At about 2.30 pm the same day, I left New Scotland Yard with Mrs McDonald, accompanied by Detective Sergeant Moore and Woman Detective Constable Willey, and went to Mrs McDonald's address at 4 Wimbledon Close, The Downs, Wimbledon. During the journey in the Police car, Mrs McDonald said to me, 'Do you remember me? I was at Judge in Chambers and saw you there when Billy Still applied for bail. Do you know that he's applied two or three times and it was up again a few days ago? I'm glad he didn't get bail otherwise I knew he would have been in the Aylesbury job with Reynolds. I cautioned her and she said nothing further.
>
> We arrived at the address, and I searched the flat. During the course of the search I was in one of the bedrooms with Mrs McDonald when she said to me, 'I'm scared stiff about this. I saw my solicitor on Monday first thing and he kept me there all day, and then advised me to hide until he'd sorted it all out'. I reminded her of the caution, and said to her, 'What exactly do you mean by that remark?' and Mrs McDonald said, 'Just what I've said, now what is going to happen to me?'
>
> I said to her, 'Your shop and all your other accommodation is going to be searched, and then you will be taken to New Scotland Yard.'[30] The search was completed at the flat and shop, and a warehouse at 18 Thornton Road nearby, and then we returned to New Scotland Yard, where she was detained. Later that evening Mrs McDonald was again seen by Chief Inspector Baldock and I. Mr Baldock said to her, 'You will be detained overnight and tomorrow morning you will be taken to Aylesbury Police Station, where you will be charged with receiving the sum of £833, knowing the same to be stolen'. She was cautioned, and said, 'I've got nothing to say.'[31]

With the results of the fingerprint work of DS Ray now becoming available, a debate began at Scotland Yard as to how to proceed.[32] George Hatherill's view, which was supported by Flying Squad chief Ernie Millen, was to immediately publish photographs of the wanted men and their wives via posters, newspaper releases and television news bulletins. However, other senior Flying Squad officers such as Tommy Butler and Frank Williams were opposed. They felt that such a move would drive the suspects underground, making it harder to track them down. Despite their objections, Hatherill and Millen decided to press ahead. On 22 August photographs of Bruce Reynolds, Charlie Wilson and Jimmy White (along with extracts from their CRO files) were published and the police manhunt began.[33] This was an almost unprecedented move for the police and underlined the unchartered territory the investigation was now entering. There were also concerns at the Director of Public Prosecutions (DPP) that this move might be viewed in some quarters as prejudicing a fair trial.

The Flying Squad's first target was Wilson, who, unlike Reynolds and White, was still going about his normal, everyday business. Wilson's name had been one of the first that came forward from informants during the first forty-eight hours after the robbery. C11 believed that he had connections with a number of criminals in the East End of London, such as Harry Smith, whom he had worked with, as well as West London criminals that included Gordon Goody, Bruce Reynolds and Ronald Edwards. C11 believed that Wilson, Goody and several others had been involved in a robbery at the National Provincial Bank in Clapham on 14 August 1962. No evidence to prove Goody's involvement had ever been obtained and Wilson, although charged, was found not guilty when the case came to court. Also found not guilty was a close associate of Wilson's, Joseph Hartfield. The Flying Squad were therefore keen to interview Hartfield, a steel fixer, of 1 Isabella House, Cottington Street, London SE11 as part of their enquiries.

DS McArthur's report refers to Wilson's arrest:

> On 22 August 1963, Charles Frederick Wilson, CRO 5010/54, aged 31 years, a greengrocer of 45 Crescent Lane, Clapham, London, SW4, was arrested. At 12.55 pm Detective Sergeant Nigel Reid of the Flying Squad, New Scotland Yard, was waiting at Wilson's home, when Wilson entered.[34]
>
> According to Reid's report, Wilson:
>
> … came into the house shortly after we arrived. I told him that we were police officers. I asked him to wait in the sitting room of his house until Inspector Byers returned. At about 20 minutes past one, Inspector Byers came into the room. He said to Wilson, 'Are you Charles Frederick Wilson?' Wilson replied, 'Yes that's right.' The Inspector then said, 'I am Detective Inspector Byers of the Flying Squad and I want to see you in connection with the mail train robbery. You know the one the Press have been writing about which took place at Cheddington.' Wilson replied, 'I know what you mean. I've never been there. I understand about it.' The Inspector then said, 'Although you've never been there, I want to search your house. And I want you to accompany me to Cannon Row Police Station for further enquiries to be made'.
>
> Inspector Byers and the other officer left the room and started to search Wilson's house. Wilson remained with me in the living room at the front of the house. As we were there he switched on the record player and after a while he said to me, 'Can you tell me the strength of this?' I said, 'I can't as we are only carrying out instructions to bring you in for further enquiries to be made.'

He said, 'You are taking me in then? It must be something strong for you to do that.' He said nothing more which was relevant. Soon after that Inspector Byers and the other officers came back after having searched the house. I and the other officers took Wilson to the Police Station. Just as we were coming from the living room to the passage of Wilson's house, he turned and shouted to his wife who was through in the kitchen, 'Ring him won't you' and she answered, 'You bet'. I got into a police car with Inspector Byers and Wilson and some other police officers. As we were on the way Inspector Byers said to Wilson, 'You are going to Scotland Yard and not the local station because this is a big job.' Wilson said, 'What put you on to me? Not as though you would tell me.' Inspector Byers did not reply. A short while afterwards Wilson said, 'I didn't think you would.'[35]

It is significant that this thorough search of Wilson's home was carried out without a search warrant.[36] Neither was Wilson cautioned, either at his home or in the police car taking him to Scotland Yard.[37] The 'other officer' Reid referred to was DS John Vaughan. His statement gives precise details about the nature of the search carried out at 45 Crescent Lane:

In the first floor rear bedroom, from a wardrobe, I took possession of a pair of black crepe soled shoes 'John White' make, a pair of blue jeans, and a pair of Police issue trousers. In the ground floor lounge, from the rear of a cushion where I had seen Wilson sitting, I took possession of a key. I also searched the garden at the rear of the house, and from the remains of a bonfire situated in the centre of the garden about eight feet from the rear of the building, I took possession of pieces of burnt cloth and also samples of the ashes and soil of the bonfire. The same day I handed the shoes, two pairs of trousers, pieces of burnt cloth, and the remains of bonfire to Dr Holden. I also handed the key to Chief Superintendent Butler.[38]

On arrival at Scotland Yard, Wilson was interviewed by DS Tommy Butler:

On the 22 August 1963, at 2.50 pm, in company with Chief Inspector Baldock, I saw Charles Wilson detained in the cells at Cannon Row Police Station. I said, 'I'm Chief Superintendent Butler and this is Chief Inspector Baldock. On my instructions you have been brought here in connection with the mail robbery at Cheddington, Bucks, on the 8 August, 1963. From my enquiries I have reason to believe that you and other persons are responsible for this offence. Do you know Cheddington in Buckinghamshire? Wilson replied, 'No, I have never been there in my life'. I said, 'Do you know Leatherslade Farm, near Oakley,

> Buckinghamshire?' Wilson said, 'No, I have never been there in my life, but I have read about these places in the newspapers'. I said, 'Would you care to tell me where you were on the morning of the 8 August, 1963?' Wilson replied, 'I was in Spitalfields Market. I left home about 5 am'. I said, 'Have you any receipts or proof of business done?' Wilson replied, 'No, they don't give receipts. I saw a few friends there though'. I pointed out the location of Leatherslade Farm and its surroundings. Wilson said, 'Yes, I have seen it all in the papers. I'm telling you, I have never been there in my life. Nobody can say I have'. I said, 'Are you quite certain that what you are saying is correct, because I have reason to think it is not'. Wilson replied, 'You obviously know a lot; I have made a ricket somewhere, but I'll have to take my chances'.
>
> I said, 'You will be detained and taken to Aylesbury Police Station, where you will be charged in being concerned with others in robbing a Travelling Post Office train at Cheddington on the 8 August 1963. Wilson was cautioned, and he said, 'I don't know how you can make it stick without the poppy and you won't find that'. Later, Wilson was charged and formally cautioned at Aylesbury Police Station, and replied, 'Not guilty, that's all'. Just prior to having his fingerprints taken, I said to him, 'I understand that you have an interest in a greengrocery business at High Street, Penge, which is run for you by someone else; what do you sell there?' I cautioned him and he replied, 'Fruit and vegetables, of course'. I said, 'Do you sell any tinned goods?' He replied, 'No, I don't think so'. I said, 'Don't you know what you are selling at the shop?' and he replied, 'I think we sell a bit of tinned fruit, that's about all'. I said, 'Do you sell groceries of any type?' He replied, 'No nothing like that. Why are you asking me? You can go there and see for yourself.'[39]

Wilson flatly denied making the now famous quote about not knowing 'how you can make it stick without the poppy'. This quasi-admission was certainly totally out of character for Wilson.[40] So-called 'verballing' (i.e. fabricating quotes used in police statements) by police officers was relatively common at this time.[41]

This was not the first occasion on which a suspect's home had been searched without a warrant. Although no fingerprint evidence had been found at the farm to incriminate Gordon Goody, and although his details were not included in the 22 August police media appeal, he remained on the suspects list due to his known association with some of the other suspects. The week before officers searched Charlie Wilson's home without a warrant, they had searched the home of Goody's mother, again without a warrant. Goody took this as a sign that the police were determined to nail him and dropped out of circulation.

He moved into an old bolt-hole above the Windmill Public House in Blackfriars. On the day of Wilson's arrest, Goody borrowed the landlord's car and set off for Leicester, by way of the M1, to meet a girlfriend. Before leaving he wrote a letter addressed to a police officer who had been involved in the London Airport robbery the previous year:[42]

22/8/63

Dear Sir

No doubt you will be surprised to hear from me after my double trial at the Old Bailey for the London Airport Robbery.

At the time of writing I am not living at my home address because it seems that I am a suspect in the recent train robbery. Two Flying Squad officers recently visited my home address whilst I was out, and made a search of the premises and honestly Mr Osborne, I am now very worried that they connect me with this crime. The reason I write to you now is because you always treated me in a straight forward manner during the Airport Case. I will never forget how fair and just yourself and Mr Field were towards me.

That case took nearly eight months to finish and every penny I had, and to become a suspect in the last big robbery is more than I can stand.

So my intentions are to keep out of harm's way until the people concerned in the train robbery are found.

To some people this letter would seem like a sign of guilt, but all I am interested in is keeping my freedom.

Hoping these few lines find you and Mr Field in the best of health.

Yours faithfully
D G Goody[43]

The car broke down in Cranfield, near Bedford, but Goody eventually got to Leicester in a hire car. While staying at the Grand Hotel, he was ironically mistaken for Bruce Reynolds (whose photograph had been in the papers that morning) and the Leicester police were called. Goody was taken to Leicester police headquarters to await the arrival of Chief Inspector Peter Vibart of the Flying Squad, who reported:

At 3.15 pm on Friday, 23 August 1963, in company with Detective Sergeant Read, I went to Leicester City Police Headquarters where I saw Douglas Gordon Goody. I said to him, 'I am assisting in enquiries regarding the mail robbery which occurred at Cheddington, Buckinghamshire, on 8 August 1963. Where were you at about 3.00 am on that night?' He replied, 'I was about'. I said to him, 'Have you ever been to Leatherslade Farm at Brill in Buckinghamshire', and he replied, 'That's a funny old question, is he (pointing to D/Sergeant Read) all right, have you been to the Windmill and seen Alexander because it was his car I had when I was having it away. I have been staying there since they turned the "Old Lady" over'. I then said to him, 'I know you were using his motor car when it broke down in Bedford and that you later travelled to Leicester by hired car to meet a Miss Perkins but why were you using the name of Alexander and his vehicle? You have two motor cars, a Jaguar and a Ford Zodiac of your own'. He replied, 'Did you see the smudges in the paper? I wouldn't have got a hundred yards in mine. I thought if I was with the bird it would take the dairy off'. I said, 'Are you telling me you were implicated in the mail robbery because known associates of yours are now wanted for interview?' He replied, 'Look. I was away out of it over the water on the Green Isle so you can't fit me in'. I said, 'Do you mean you were in Ireland on the 8 August 1963?' He replied, 'I am not trying to be awkward but I am not saying where I was as alibis are alibis, Mr Vibart.' I then said, 'Would it not be a simple matter to tell me where you were on the 8 August as you are aware a great deal of publicity has been given to the mail train robbery'. He replied, 'I had to get away for a month or two as the smokes empty. They've all had it away so what could I do? – stand around and mow the lawn till you came and laid bands on me, so I borrowed the car and phoned the bird; I borrowed a "flim" from her. I am skint, what do you think I buried it?' The interview was then concluded.

At 6.00 pm the same day I again saw Goody and said to him, 'I have seen Miss Margaret Perkins and although you have not seen her since last July you had arranged to send her some postcards from Ireland to an address of a friend nearby. These have now been destroyed but according to Miss Perkins the last card was received on Thursday, the day of the robbery'. He replied, 'That puts me there doesn't it'. I then said to Goody, 'I am not satisfied with your explanation and you will now be taken back to Aylesbury Police Station pending further enquires'. He replied, 'My brief will be there, I have arranged if I don't turn up for the necessary to be done'. I then returned with him to Aylesbury Police Station where he was detained.

At about 12 midnight on the 23 August 1963 with D/Chief Superintendent Butler, I again saw Goody at Aylesbury Police Station. Superintendent Butler said to him, 'I understand you were detained at Leicester having travelled as far as Bedford in a motor car belonging to someone else and you were using the name of Alexander. Would you care to explain these facts?' He replied, 'I was going to keep out of the way until things died down. Them blokes who are all in the paper are friends of mine and that puts me in it and all according to you'. Mr Butler then asked, 'What do you mean by that?' He said, 'Because of the aggravations over the Airport job and I had to sweat for eight months.' Mr Butler then said, 'That matter is over and done with. I would like you to tell us what your movements were on the 7/8 August, as that is the reason for your being brought here, as you well know'. Goody was silent for a few moments and then said, 'Look, I want to think about that; I am tired because I didn't have much sleep last night what with these aggravations and all.' He was then informed by the Superintendent that he would be detained and he replied, 'So I'll be detained, see you later'.

At about 1.00 pm on the 24 August I was present when Goody was seen by Superintendent Butler at Aylesbury Police Station, Mr Butler said to him, 'You have had ample time to think about the matter we discussed last night. Would you now tell us of your movements and your location on the 7/8 August?' He replied;,'I was touring Ireland doing a bit of fishing and shooting'. He was then asked, 'Where did you stay whilst you were there?' He replied, 'I can't tell you that; if I am charged it will be part of my defence'. Mr Butler then said, 'If you were in Ireland as you say then it follows you were not at Leatherslade Farm that night doesn't it?' He replied (indicating myself), 'He mentioned that yesterday; I don't know the place. What would I be doing on a farm?' The Superintendent then said, 'You could be there preparing for the commission of this very serious offence or taking part in the division of the proceeds of it'. He replied, 'You don't expect me to admit that do you?'

Superintendent Butler then said to him, 'I suspect you were at Leatherslade Farm at the time already mentioned'. He replied, 'Nobody saw me there; I'll stand on any ID parade you like to put up.' Mr Butler then said to him, 'It may come to that. In the meantime enquiries are still in progress and we will see you later in the day.' The interview was then concluded.

At 11.45 pm on Saturday 24 August 1963 with D/Chief Superintendent Butler I again saw Goody and Mr Butler said to him, 'It has been said by you that on the 8 August 1963, the date of the mail robbery, you were in Ireland. I have now ascertained that you travelled by air to Belfast on the 2 August 1963 with your mother and a man named Knowles and stayed with a relative, but you returned alone on Tuesday 6 August 1963 leaving Knowles and your mother there. These two persons returned home on Wednesday 7 August 1963 and both travelling in the name of Goody' – Goody interrupted and said, 'Look, I am saying nothing more; I'll have to see my mouthpiece; he will fit me up with something else'.

> At 12.15 am on 25 August, 1963, Goody was released on the undertaking that he again returned to Aylesbury Police Station on Saturday 7 September 1963. He was taken to his home by police transport.[44]

With apparently no fingerprint evidence against him, Goody was optimistic that his luck would hold. However, the police were convinced that he was not only involved but had played a major role in the commission of the crime. A key police informant had come forward and mentioned Goody by name, and had also given groundbreaking new information which was to open up a whole new angle for the investigation.

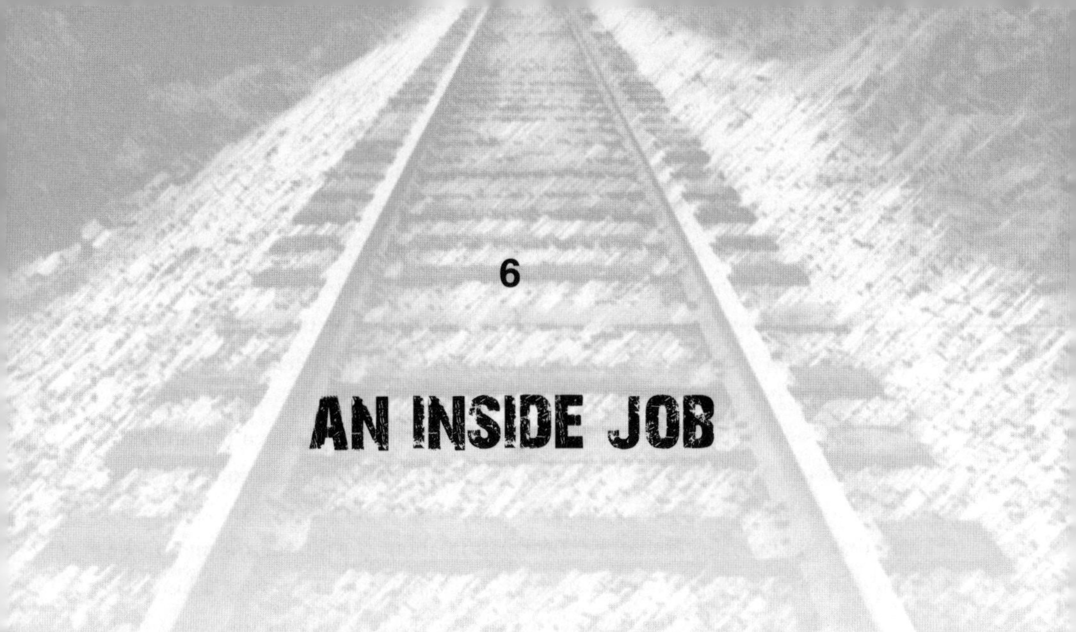

6

AN INSIDE JOB

For nearly fifty years, one question has remained unanswered: did someone tip off the robbers about the millions on board the train – was there an inside man at the Post Office who provided the intelligence and helped the robbers plan the crime? A team of highly specialised Post Office investigators were tasked by the postmaster general with determining whether or not the robbery had been, as he strongly suspected, an inside job. The Post Office case files on the robbery have remained closed for the best part of fifty years, but are now, in the majority of cases, open for the first time.

From the outset, the police agreed to share information gleaned from their network of underworld informers with the Post Office Investigation Branch. One of the first informer reports held tantalising clues for the Post Office investigators – the report of a mysterious phone call made to one of the train robbers, Gordon Goody. The background to this major development is given in an internal report by IB Deputy Controller R.F. Yates:

> On the 29 August, 1963, Mr Osmond and I attended a special detective conference held at New Scotland Yard. Commander Hatherill was in the chair and Chief Superintendent Millen (Flying Squad) and Chief Inspector Bradbury were also present. Mr Hatherill said that on the previous Tuesday he had seen an informant who had given him a list of 14 names of the bandits who had formed the robbery team; that he (Hatherill) was satisfied that those 14 criminals were the 'certain' offenders and that the money had already been divided into 18 lots – i.e. one each for the 14 offenders quoted; one each for 2 Post Office insiders; one for the organiser and one for the man who had bought the farm (i.e. about £145,000 apiece).

Mr Hatherill said that, according to the informant, the story of the case was, briefly, that Brian Field had made the first contact with the Post Office insider from whom he had obtained information about HVP mails carried on the Up Special TPO; that this enabled Brian Field to plan the robbery; that Field first put the plan to another London gang who rejected it; that he then put it to Bruce Reynolds who accepted it and carried it out with a team specially recruited for the job; that this team met at Leatherslade Farm at 11.30 pm on the 7 August, 1963; that only one man – Goody – arrived late (said to have been half an hour, which would make it about 11.30 pm) and that Goody's explanation of his late arrival was that he had been waiting for 'the message'. The informant apparently said that 'the message' contained information about the number of men to be found in the HVP coach at the time of attack and that there were 'a hundred bags on the train'. Mr Osmond and I put it to Mr Hatherill that the times quoted would be important and he agreed that the alleged information given in 'the message' must have been available to Goody by about 11.30 pm on the 7 August and certainly not later than midnight. Mr Hatherill explained that the informant had also said that the information came from a Post Office man 'on the train' who, in turn, had passed it to his brother and that it was this brother, an Irishman, who had passed on 'the message'. Discussion did not further clarify the informant's story – i.e. whether 'the brother' was also a Post Office employee in view of the two shares of money; whether the message was passed direct to Goody or to Brian Field; whether, if 'the brother' was an Irishman, the man on the train was also Irish or a step brother. It was suggested to Mr Hatherill that 'the brother' might have been a railwayman who had assisted with the possible sabotage of the HVP van and Mr Millen – who was, apparently, also present when the informant was seen – said that although there was no information about a railwayman, he would not entirely discount such a possibility. It was generally assumed by Police that the information from the 'man on the train' had been passed on by telephone but I explained at once that on the 9 August I had taken steps to trace and check every ticketed call made to the London area from stations and towns at which the Up Special TPO had stopped and that the only suspicious call traced was one from Rugby to Wicken, Bucks (pub to pub). There is, however, an STD service from some places on the route. Mr Millen asked us to get out the personnel papers of all 70 odd TPO staff who were on the train that night and then to discuss the problem of concentrating inquiries on any Irishman or officers with Irish names. Mr Millen further said that another clue was the identity of the 'man on the train' was that he would be known to Brian Field – i.e. he might have been represented in Court by Messrs Wheater or Field might have been concerned in a house purchase for the Post Office man.

The build up of HVP sacks did not reach the total of 100 until the Up Special TPO reached Tamworth at 1.23 am and that if any information about loads were given out by a member of the train crew in time to reach Goody by 11.30 pm it must have been at Preston where the TPO stopped at 10.50 pm – or, if given some time latitude – at the next stop, i.e. Warrington 11.36 pm. Even at Warrington, however, there were only 46 HVP bags on board. The train reached Crewe well after midnight and by this time Goody had, apparently, reached the farm. There were only 91 mail bags on board at Crewe. It was clear, therefore, that there was something radically wrong with this information, and it became a question for consideration, as in all 'informant' cases, whether when some information can be disproved, other parts of the story could be relied on. One further part of the story did not ring true – i.e. that which deals with the number of officers to be found in the HVP coach by the time the train reached Cheddington. It is, of course, impossible for any man on the TPO to say hours ahead how many officers could be found in the HVP coach. The Inspector on the train has full authority to switch staff to that point and indeed on this very night he sent two additional officers to assist with the heavy load. Mr Osmond and I felt somewhat sceptical about the accuracy of this information but I pushed ahead with IB inquiries on the basis that some latitude might, perhaps, have to be allowed. There were 16 officers on the train that night who could be regarded as Irishmen, particulars of whom have been supplied to New Scotland Yard. Of those, only 10 have one or more brothers, and of the 10 only two would have had normal and free access to the HVP coach – i.e. Mr M R Lyttle, PHG London, who travelled from Carlisle to London and Mr T McCarthy, PHG Glasgow, who travelled from Glasgow to Crewe. IB and Police inquiries have so far failed to direct suspicion to either man but observation is being maintained on their movements from time to time for signs of any lavish spending.[1]

Having had the Friday and the weekend to work on the 'matters arising' from the conference, Osmond and Yates returned to Scotland Yard on Monday 2 September where they put to Hatherill the results of their own interim investigation. In particular they expressed their scepticism about the reliability of certain aspects of his informant's information about the 'Goody message'. Significantly Hatherill responded by telling them that, 'Some of the information concerned had reached him second-hand and it could well have lost some of its accuracy on the way.[2]

Commander Hatherill's list of fourteen suspects was a particularly significant development, as it provided a list of names, the majority of which were already linked by previous offences and relationships. Unlike DCS Butler's 16 August suspect list, which was very much a patchwork of names flagged up by a variety of informants whose information varied in terms of quality and past reliability, Hatherill's list came from one source regarded as knowledgeable and reliable. It is therefore unsurprising, as previously noted, that a good many of the names on Butler's earlier list were eliminated from the enquiry within days of its compilation.

Hatherill's list comprised the following names:[3]

Douglas Goody	CRO 4290/46
Charles Wilson	CRO 5010/54
Bruce Reynolds	CRO 41212/48
James White	CRO 26113/55
Henry Smith	CRO 1551/47
Roy James	CRO 17638/56
John Daly	CRO 33521/48
Ronald Edwards	CRO 33535/61
Thomas Wisbey	CRO 26362/47
Danny Pembroke	CRO 27206/56
James Hussey	CRO 40455/49
Brian Field	
Roger Cordrey	CRO 3716/42
Robert Welch	CRO 61730/58
Two Post Office men	(Irishmen?)[4]

The tip about the two post office insiders and the specific information they allegedly gave Goody was, as conceded by Hatherill, second-hand and possibly distorted to some extent by the passage of its journey. Despite the IB's reservations concerning the specific nature of the information given by the alleged insiders, they certainly seem to have been convinced by the proposition that there were at least one or more insiders, as R.F. Yates's report makes clear:

Inside Information

General: One of the important aspects of this case has been the possible leakage of information to the bandits from a member of the staff concerning HVP traffic. This possibility was envisaged from the outset and the result of the detailed inquiries made about 35 officers,[5] but no evidence has come to light that any detailed inside information, or any general knowledge of the movement of HVP money has been passed on.

Scope: Information regarding the general treatment of HVPs and their transit on the Up Special Travelling Post Office is known to a wide section of Post Office staff and to some professional criminals. It is also widely known in the Post Office that, after a Bank Holiday, a large sum of money would be in transit and therefore, the number of HVPs would be greater than normal. Whilst such general information would be sufficient to stimulate interest amongst criminals to plan a robbery, it would be totally inadequate for a gang to be able to launch a successful attack of the nature of that under review. I hold the view that meticulous planning would be undertaken by criminals of this calibre, that the arrangements would be precise and that, consequently, detailed information would be essential before embarking on such a venture. Furthermore, I think that provision would be made for any changes in procedure to be notified to the gang. Post Office employees in general would not, of course, be in a position to keep abreast of daily changes in TPO working, and the only officers apart from some of high rank or those employed in special security postal work who would be able to furnish impeccable information, are those actually employed on the Up and Down Special TPOs; those attached to the HQ of the TPO Section itself or those employed at railway stations in the loading and unloading of HVP mails from the Up Special TPO.

Administrative Staff: Discreet but general inquiries have been made without success concerning the supervising and administrative staff at GPO HQ and in LPR but this was cut short when the information mentioned in the below paragraph came to hand, although all the known facts have been passed to police.

TPO Staff: At the start of this inquiry the IB arranged for all officers who were on the attacked TPO to be questioned and finger printed and for a CRO check to be carried out. Some TPO officers were questioned again by police but no evidence of collusion came to light. It was found, however, that three officers who travelled on the Up Special on the night of the 7/8 August have criminal records, but the Police discovered no evidence to connect them with the known members of the gang.[6]

Significantly, Deputy Controller Yates identifies four groups of post office employees from whom the leak or leaks might have emanated:

GPO officers of 'high rank' at GPO HQ;
GPO officers employed in special security postal work;
postal workers on board the TPO;
GPO officers attached to the HQ of the TPO section.

The thirty-five officers on whom detailed enquiries were to be made are listed in an IB investigation file:[7]

Davison, James	PHG	M&T Section (PTO)
Delaney, Edward	"	"
Frost, Derrick Joseph	"	"
Maguire, Michael Joseph	"	"
McNamara, William John	"	"
McNeil, Davis	"	"
Morrison, William	Postman	"
O'Connell, Joseph	PHG	"
O'Connor, Joseph William	"	"
O'Regan, Patrick Joseph	"	"
Reilly, James Patrick	"	"
Rogers, Alan	"	"
Rooney, Michael Patrick	"	"
Spencer, Raymond Frederick	"	"
Walters, John Edward	"	"
Barrs, Robert Edward	"	SWDO
Bates, James	"	"
Denby, John Terence	"	M&T Section (TPO)
Kett, Thomas Walter	A/I	"
Millbank, Alfred	P&TO	SEDO
Moss, Ernest Frederick	A/I	M&T Section (TPO)
Penn, Leslie Oliver	PHG	"
Roberts, Frank Ernest	Techn I	Ravensbourne Tel Ex
Ward, W.R.	Asst Cont'	M&T Section
Wilkinson, Joan	TP Teleph'	Balham Red Ex
Lyttle, Michael Raymond	PHG	M&T (TPO)
McCarthy, Thomas	"	"
Howard, William	EO	"
Wicks, Frank Alvin	PHG	"
Bish, Albert William	PHG	"
Flood, Bernard Alfred	Inspector	IS
Foley, Thomas John	PHG	IS

If the tip about the two informers being Irish was correct, then the two men on the list who were both Irish and had brothers were Michael Lyttle and Thomas McCarthy. Both men were, therefore, thoroughly investigated, as a memo written by IB controller Clifford Osmond makes clear:

ROBBERY – UP SPECIAL TPO MEMORANDUM

It will be remembered that on the 29 August 1963 information came to hand at New Scotland Yard suggesting that information concerning the number of HVP bags carried on the Up Special TPO or likely to be carried, had been given to the bandits by a member of the Post Office staff who travelled on the train that night and the only clue given by the informant was that the man on the train had passed the information to his brother who was an Irishman.

Of the 16 Irishmen who travelled on the Up Special TPO that night, only 3 would in normal course have had access to the HVP coach and 2 of those were:-

(a) Michael Raymond Lyttle, PHG who travelled from Carlisle to London, and who lives at 79 Watcombe Road, London SE25, and
(b) Thomas McCarthy, PHG Glasgow, who travelled from Glasgow to Crewe and who lives at 16 Egilsay Crescent, Glasgow.

It is important that observation is urgently maintained upon the movements of both these officers in order to establish whether or not either is spending money more freely now than he did before the robbery took place. I should like to have IB Assistants allocated to this work without delay and reports submitted to me via Mr Edwards, as soon as possible.

Lyttle, Michael Raymond
Joined train at Carlisle. Employed in No 5 coach (No 3 Division). Would have been due officially to visit HVP coach.
General Information:
Speaks with cockney accent. Lives with his wife (believed to be Irish) and two children (two girls – 4 years and 2 years respectively) at the home of his wife's mother (Mrs Phyliss I Letts). Lyttle's father – Patrick Joseph, has married again and resides at 45 Watcombe Road, SE25.

Michael Raymond Lyttle is a heavy spender and drinks heavily, mostly at The Gladstone, Portland Road, SE25, and attends a working man's club at 12 Enmore Road, Norbury. He appears to borrow money at the beginning of each week. He owns an old Alvis car, index No KPO264.

No further information has been forthcoming on his brother Kevin Edward Lyttle, but Vincent Lyttle is believed to live at 210 Durnley Drive, New Addington. No CRO but thought to mix with 'wide boys' in the West End.

McCarthy, Thomas

Joined train at Glasgow, left at Crewe. Employed mainly in No 4 coach (Division 4). During the journey however he assisted in HVP at Carlisle Station owing to heavy transfer of mails.

General Information:

No obvious Irish accent. Lives with his wife and two children (10 and 12 years respectively) in a terraced house which he rents from Glasgow Corporation. He is not regarded too highly locally as he is known to drink and gamble frequently. Apart from this, there is no evidence of excessive spending.[8]

Could one of these two men be the 'insider'? Lyttle lived in South London, an area associated with a number of the train robbery suspects, and his brother was possibly mixing with members of the criminal fraternity in London's West End clubs. McCarthy, on the other hand, lived in Glasgow, which, according to an IB report, was also closely tied to ongoing enquiries:

> ... there is evidence that Reynolds and Daly flew together to Glasgow in May 1963. If that trip had anything to do with the planning of this offence it might mean that a Post Office or Railway accomplice lives in Glasgow.[9]

While Lyttle and McCarthy's links to the train robbers were purely speculative, IB enquiries turned next to a man whom C11 at Scotland Yard believed had concrete links to one of the robbers:

> Detective Chief Inspector Walker also reported to me that he had ascertained that Welch or his associates had gained information regarding transit of mails from a man in the Post Office at Mount Pleasant. Furthermore, that this man had formerly been the Secretary of the local union and had been in trouble with the Police for attacking a woman with a knife.
>
> In pursuing this aspect I established that Thomas John Foley, CRO 36217/50 formerly a PHG at the London Parcel Section had in fact been previously employed at the Inland Section and had held the office of Secretary of the IS Branch of the UPW. Foley was suspended from duty following Police action on 10 November 1962. The CRO File on Foley shows that he was born in Southern Ireland on 26 April 1925. His associates in crime have been:-

Denis Foley (brother)	CRO 40988/56
James Sydney Moore	CRO 19060/60
John Galvin	CRO 57427/62

The CRO Files of the above mentioned have been examined and it has been established that Denis Foley was represented by Messrs Wontner and Son, Solicitors, West Central 2, and there is no evidence that James, Wheater & Co or Brian Field have been concerned in defending either of the Foley brothers.

The possibility that Foley was the source from which the robbery gang attacked the Up Special TPO has been discussed at various times with Detective Chief Superintendent Butler. He is quite sceptical about the information given by the informants of both Detective Superintendent Walker and Commander Hatherill,[10] but he agreed with me that further enquiry to alleviate any suspicion was in fact warranted. I promised to acquaint him with the result of the enquiries in due course. Some further enquiry is, it is thought, called for and this File is now being passed to Mr Edwards.

I have discussed this case with DI Huntley of C11. Foley obtained for Welch two postmen's hats which were taken to his address. There is no information connecting Foley with the Great Train Robbery. On 8 August 1963 he had been in prison for 4 months serving a sentence of 3 years imposed by the CCC on 29/3/63.[11]

With Thomas Foley now effectively eliminated from the enquiry by virtue of his current tenure at Wandsworth Prison, IB controller Clifford Osmond returned to the conundrum of Hatherill's tip about the Goody phone call:

In order for this information to be accurate, the man on the train would be required to pass his information to his brother either at Preston or Warrington and, in that event, it would be necessary for the TPO man to assess that a total of 100 bags would be available at Cheddington. This would not be a difficult assessment to make for any skilled TPO officer.

Inquiries so far made by both Police and the Investigation Branch have failed to find any TPO officer who fits the bill but some special inquiry should now be made about Leslie Oliver Penn, PHG who lives at 147 Lucas Avenue, Chelmsford, who was in the HVP coach at the time of the attack. Copies of the statements already made by Mr Penn are enclosed in this separate file in order to facilitate these further inquiries. The important features of Mr Penn's statements can be summed up by the fact that he has two brothers with criminal records – ie, William Arthur James Penn of 13 Sheffton Road, London N1, and Cyril Edward Penn, who is said to be living at Peabody Buildings, London.

The other fact calling for some inquiry is that Mr Penn has a brother who lives at Warrington – ie, John Owen Penn who is said to be 39 years of age but whose address not been quoted, although he is described as a lorry driver. As the

Up Special TPO stopped at Warrington at 11.36 that night, it is important that some inquiry should be made in the town concerning the background and movements of John Owen Penn and some special trace should be set in motion in an effort to prove whether or not any telephone call was made from Warrington between 11 pm and midnight on the 7 August to a London subscriber or to a Pangbourne subscriber, or perhaps to Arthur James Penn, another brother who lives at 86 Windsor Avenue, Hillingdon, Middlesex, and who at one time was a member of the Post Office staff.

It will be seen, therefore, that in some ways the information to hand could fit Mr Leslie Oliver Penn, PHG but so far there is no information to suggest that any of the Penns are Irish themselves or have Irish connexions. This is a matter which should receive attention during the forthcoming inquiry into this aspect of the mail train robbery.[12]

Within a week, IB officer Dennis Geall, who had been despatched to Warrington, reported back to Osmond:

Enquiries at Warrington made in connection with Leslie Oliver Penn's brother have identified him as John Owen Penn of 4 Prestbury Drive, Thelwall, Warrington. Penn's date of birth is 24 April, 1923 and he is employed as a long distant lorry driver by G L Baker, Ltd (Transport), Thelwall Lane, Warrington. John Owen Penn has a CRO No 16711/41 and the address quoted on that form, ie, 26E, Peabody Buildings, Roscoe Street, London, EC1, was given by Penn in his application for a mortgage to the Halifax Building Society.

Penn was on holiday during the week ended 10 August, and at present it has been established that he was away from his home on 5 and 6 August, and returned on 7 August, but his whereabouts during his absence have not been ascertained. During my enquiries, I received active co-operation from the Warrington police and Cheshire County, Stockton Heath Sub Division, Police who, should they obtain any further information in respect of Penn, will convey it to this Branch via G C Molsom, Esq, the Head Postmaster of Warrington.

I should perhaps mention that the Manager of Messrs Baker's Depot in Thelwall Lane is not well regarded by the Warrington police and, in the event of further enquiries having to be made by this Branch, of his employers, it is suggested that local police be approached in the first instance.[13]

Osmond finally closed the file on the Penn brothers when he received further reports that seemed to put them in the clear:

It has been ascertained that no outgoing telephone calls whatsoever are recorded as having been made from the Warrington area between 11.00 pm and midnight on the 7 August 1963, to either a Pangbourne or Hillingdon (Uxbridge) telephone number. In so far as calls to London exchanges are concerned such calls would normally be made by means of the STD systems but nevertheless it has been confirmed that no ticketed calls are recorded against that area during the relative period.

Enquiries have also been made in an attempt to establish whether or not the firm of James & Wheater Solicitors represented any one of the Penn brothers in the course of the criminal proceedings instituted against them in the past, the most recent of which took place on the 2 March 1961. In this connexion it has been ascertained that prior to the 1 May 1961 when Mr J D Wheater entered his present firm and undertook criminal practice for the first time since he became a solicitor on the 1 March 1949, he was engaged solely on civil actions and in the circumstances it would appear probable that he was not in a position to have been concerned in any of the prosecutions against the Penn brothers.[14]

Having hit another dead end, Clifford Osmond resolved to return to square one and search for the origin of the Goody phone call:

While I feel that this information in some respect or other cannot be completely accurate, we must do our best to test it out step by step. Hence, all telephone calls made from stations on the route of the mail train have been checked and one leg of the inquiry dealt with in these papers concerns a telephone call recorded as having been made at about 10 pm on the 7 August from a public call box situated in the Prince of Wales Hotel, Drury Lane, Rugby, to another public house in the village of Wicken, which is only a few miles from Cheddington where the attack took place.

An examination has, therefore, been made of all ticketed calls made, before and after the attack, from the Prince of Wales Hotel, Rugby, and in the course of those investigations it was found that calls are frequently made to J C S Boyd, 18 Redcar Street, Belfast 6 (Tel: Belfast 56398). This was an interesting feature, to say the least, because information reaching the Police suggests that an Irishman is in some way concerned with this leakage of information. In those circumstances, we have now examined the ticketed calls made in turn from Boyd's Belfast telephone and a copy is enclosed together with a copy of the ticketed calls made from the Prince of Wales Hotel, Rugby.

It is important to establish what Mr Boyd does for a living and as much information as possible about his background, remembering that this might very well be an innocent aspect of the case. At the same time it will be seen from the attached lists of telephone calls that calls have been made from both the Belfast and Rugby numbers to Harthill 390 – subscriber G S Bowie, 16 Westbenhar Road, Harthill, Lanark. In those circumstances, it is essential also to find out what Mr Bowie does for a living and as much information about his background. During these investigations, which must be made with great discretion, it is essential that a report should be submitted urgently if Mr Boyd or Mr Bowie turns out to be a member of the Post Office staff or a railway employee or to have connexions with the Post Office or railway.[15]

This seemed to be an intriguing possibility and one that made a great deal of circumstantial sense so far as Hatherill's tip-off was concerned. As a result of further extensive investigations, Osmond committed the results to paper:

Post Office Insider – Bowie

In the course of following up inquiries into the possibility of inside information having, been passed to a member of the mail train gang to a spot not far from Cheddington, all telephone calls made from places at which the train stopped on its journey from Glasgow to London were checked as it was found that a call was recorded as having been made at 10.06 pm on the evening of the 7 August from a renter's call box situated in the Prince of Wales public house, Drury Lane, Rugby to another public house – ie, The Fox and Hounds, Denes Hanger, Wolverton, which is not very far from the scene of the crime. It is, of course, true that the Up Special TPO had not reached Rugby by 10.06 pm. that night. Nevertheless, some inquiry should be made to see whether or not the barman at the Fox and Hounds can identify any of the published photographs or describe strangers who might be in such a small village that night. The second leg of such an inquiry should be directed to establishing the identity of G S Bowie, who lives at 15 Westbenhar Rd, Hartill, Lankshire (Tel: 390). The reason for such inquiry is that there has been information from time to time that the leakage took place by an Irishman and it is found that frequent calls are made from the Prince of Wales public house, Drury Lane, Rugby, to Mr J G S Boyd, 18 Redcar Street, Belfast, to Bowie frequent calls are also made by Mr Boyd in Belfast to Mr Bowie in Scotland and to the public house in Rugby. It would be sufficient I think, if it were established beyond any doubt what Mr Bowie does for a living and in particular that he is not a member of the Post Office staff or a Railway employee.[16]

To take the enquiries forward, Osmond deputed DCI Peattie and Sergeant Meller to undertake undercover enquires into Bowie's background. They reported back within a week:

Mr G S Bowie

As a result of discreet enquiries it has been established that Mr G S Bowie is an electrician employed at the Reddich Hill Colliery. He has resided at 15 Westbenhar Road, Harthill, Lanarkshire, for about eighteen years. It has been confirmed that he has at no time in the past had any connection whatsoever with the Post Office or British Railways, and indeed is regarded locally as respectable.

The Fox and Hounds

I have pursued this enquiry at the Fox and Hounds, Denes Hanger, Wolverton, where I interviewed both the Licensee and his wife, Mr and Mrs G B Brazier, who serve at the bar at the public house and know all their regular customers. Neither could recall any strangers having been on the premises during the relevant period, and explained that their daughter, Susan Kay Brazier, was responsible for making the telephone calls from the Prince of Wales public house, Drury Lane, Rugby. Both Mr and Mrs Brazier have been previously interviewed about these telephone calls by PC Underwood, Denes Hanger, and I have ascertained that they are well respected in the neighbourhood and their good faith and integrity is beyond reproach.

Chief Inspector Peattie
Sergeant J H Meller[17]

Again, another lead that in many ways looked too good to be true had seemingly come to a dead end, with an innocent explanation found. However, as one lead went cold, the telephone record checks turned up another intriguing possibility that set Osmond's mind racing, as his report reveals:

Memorandum

It is known that John Daly, CRO 33521/48, the brother-in-law of Bruce Reynolds and one of the main suspects in the Mail Train robbery, has been in touch by telephone in the past with The Victoria Wine Company, 18 Akeman Street, Tring, Herts. This is extremely close to Cheddington where the train robbery took place and the contacts between Daly and someone at this Wine Company are being investigated by the Bucks Constabulary.

However, there is another aspect of this subsidiary inquiry which interests me. On the 17 April 1963, a ticketed telephone call is recorded as having been made from The Victoria Wine Co, Tring, to Gipsy Hill 5462. This telephone line stands in the name of F E Roberts, 1 Eden Hill, West Norwood, London, SE27. Further inquiry has disclosed that Mr Roberts is a member of the Post Office staff employed as a Technician Class I on external work in the Ravensbourne Telephone Exchange area, LTR/SE Area. Unless this has already been done, I should like to have some early inquiry made designed to give some background information concerning Mr Roberts.[18]

Again, the wheels of undercover investigation moved into motion providing a full report of Roberts's personal and professional background:

As a result of discreet enquiries designed to give some background information concerning Mr Frank Ernest Roberts, Technician I, Ravensbourne TE, it has been ascertained that he is married and resides with his wife and son, age about 16 years, in an old type one storey end terrace house which he is believed to be purchasing at 1 Eden Road, West Norwood, SE27.

A form P141X is attached from which it will be seen that he first entered the Engineering Branch of the Post Office in the London South East Area on 5 October 1936 and apart from the period 8 October 1939 to 19 October 1945 when he served in the Royal Navy, he has been employed continuously in that area of the Post Office to date.

On 7 August 1963 Mr Roberts was employed on external work in the area from 7.45 am to 5.15 pm and similarly on the following date from 7.45 am to 6.30 pm. During the course of his duties of each of those dates he was in possession of an official vehicle (Mini Minor YXF 409). A schedule outlining his hours of duty during the w/c 5 August 1963 and giving details of ticketed telephone calls from his private telephone number viz, GIP 5462 is associated. Whilst the possibility that Mr Roberts assisted the raiders on the night in question cannot at present be refuted, it may be considered that having regard to the fact that he is known to have commenced duty at Ravensbourne Telephone Exchange at 7.45 am on 8 August 1963 makes this somewhat unlikely.

In so far as the telephone calls to the Victoria Wine Company, 18 Akeman Street, Tring, are concerned, despite the frequency of these calls during the periods February to May 1963 when nine such calls are recorded, it has not been found possible to establish the reason for them.[19]

Despite the Roberts connection turning out to be a tenuous one, to say the least, Daly's calls to the wine merchant suggested the shop was or had been used as some kind of 'dead letter box'.

DCI Peattie had not only been on the trail of the Rugby telephone caller, Messrs Boyd, Bowie and Roberts, he had also been tasked with investigating the information given by his informant Bernard Makowski on 10 August, which, in spite of initial scepticism, was about to provide a vital lead.

7

THROUGH THE LOOKING GLASS

Bernard Makowski's information concerning the gang headed by Benny Stewart was thoroughly investigated by DCI Peattie. He passed on his conclusions to IB controller Clifford Osmond along with CRO photographs and information concerning all those referred to in the statement about the proposed 'King's Cross' line robbery. Osmond, in turn, forwarded a copy to IB investigator Frank Cook on 19 August:

CONFIDENTIAL

> Mr Cook
>
> The attached report from Chief Inspector Peattie relating to the latest information from his informant will no doubt be passed to Chief Supt Butler for his information. As regards Lucraft, the previous reference was not, of course, to 'Mickie the Fox' or 'Mickie the Fly' but to 'Freddie the Fox' who I understand from Mr Butler is a criminal known as 'Titch Lucy'.
>
> Mr Peattie has today told me that he considers that Benny Stewart has been, or is still, in Germany and that a German criminal who has been deported to Germany recently is one of Stewart's associates. Mr Peattie is at present following up this inquiry with the Aliens Office in an effort to identify the German criminal and to search the CRO for any trace there. It is a question for consideration whether or not this further inquiry relating to Benny Stewart or any other member of the team quoted by the informant should continue and perhaps you would be good enough to let me know confidentially what Mr Butler thinks about this.[1]

Within three days, Peattie had identified Stewart's German associate:

> The German associate of Stewart has been identified by the informant as:- Hans Wilhelm Schaefer CRO 21154/62, who was deported from this country on the 21 June, 1962, and is believed to be a native of Kefenrod, Germany. Schaefer has convictions in Australia and was deported from that country on 9-11-59.
>
> Correspondence reveals that Schaefer sailed from Dover to Ostend on SS Prince Baudouin en route to Aachen, Germany. Whilst the records show Schaefer as being penniless, information has been received that this man perpetrated crime on a large scale in this country and successfully smuggled the money so obtained to Germany. Schaefer is believed to have had military training and the informant is confident that he, Schaefer, has been in the West End of London since being deported. He is described as the type of criminal Stewart would recruit as a member of the 'Gang'.
>
> If there is reason to suspect that Stewart is involved in the Mail Train Robbery, the informant is prepared to accompany me to Germany, provided that his expenses are paid, with a view to tracing Stewart, if subsequent enquiries reveal that there is a possibility he may have linked up with Schaefer.[2]

With new and reliable information from Commander Hatherill regarding the identities of the mail train gang, it seems clear that Clifford Osmond was about to close the file on Makowski's information. None of the names Makowski had mentioned had been corroborated in any way by other Yard informants, and while the story in itself was certainly of interest in terms of previous attempted mail train robberies, it seemed an unlikely current lead. However, at 9.30 p.m. that same evening, C11 received significant new information about Bruce Reynolds, which was copied to DCS Butler and Clifford Osmond.

According to Osmond:

> A series of events has led to some important developments in the mail train robbery which came to a head on the 27 August 1963. The information relates to three different addresses:-
>
> (a) Edith M Simon
> 85 Hermitage Court
> Woodford Road
> Wanstead, E18
> Telephone: Wanstead 5078

(b) Mrs Doris May Golding
42 Winchester Road
Fulham
London, SW6
Telephone: Renown 3592

(c) Mr L Heller
69 Belsize Park Gardens
Hampstead
London, NW3
Telephone: Primrose 02183

Apparently, these addresses were thought to be linked to Bruce Reynolds's support network. Although official permission for telephone taps to be placed on these three lines had not yet been sought, let alone approved, it seems likely that some unofficial tapping had already occurred in order for these suspicions to be formalised.[4] Clifford Osmond's memo confirms this:

> At the request of Chief Supt Butler, observation was arranged on the 27 August, and was kept on each of these three addresses by Mr Balm, Mr Hood and Mr Gray, IB Assistants. At about lunch time Mr Gray reported that whilst outside 69 Belsize Park Gardens, Hampstead, he saw a man who resembled Albert Millbank leave the house in company with a blonde woman who was carrying a poodle. They drove away in a car bearing a registration number which was recorded and a quick search through the records revealed that, in fact, this car was registered in the name of Albert Millbank who was using his mother's address in the registration particulars.[5]

Millbank, of course, was named by Makowski in his statement about the proposed King's Cross mail train job as being 'an important man behind the scenes and suggested he might be organising this particular mail bag offence.'[6] Subsequent enquiries into Millbank through the Criminal Record Office revealed an offence in 1939 and a cross reference to the Garda Criminal Records Office in the Irish Republic. This indicated that Millbank and one Charles McGuinness had been arrested by the Irish police at Kingsbridge railway station in Dublin on 12 September 1955. A warrant was already out on McGuinness, who was wanted in connection with a £44,000 mail van robbery in Glasgow on 19 July 1955. There was no warrant out on Millbank, although Glasgow police did want to interview him about the robbery. Both

Millbank and McGuinness were charged by Dublin police with 'loitering at Kingsbridge Station between 7.00 pm and 8.00 pm for the purpose of committing a felony' and also with 'having £232/4*s*-9*d* unlawfully in their possession'.[7]

Osmond concluded his memo by asserting that:

> There is some reason for thinking that Bruce Reynolds might be hiding at the Belsize Park Gardens address in view of the fact that information now to hand suggests that a message might have reached him from his girl friend on the night of the 22 August.[8] This was the day on which Mary Manson was arrested and it is known that she is the girl friend of Bruce Reynolds and that she was attempting to get a message through to him urgently on that day. This information has been passed to Chief Supt Butler who has requested that telephone observation should be set up on all three addresses without delay. I suggested to Mr Yates that the Post Office, as yet, has insufficient information to justify a request to the Home Office for such authority but that we would be prepared to do the work if Scotland Yard would obtain the Home Office warrant. However, I said to Mr Yates that as Bruce Reynolds is the organiser of this team, I would be prepared to persuade the DDG to put a letter to Sir Charles Cunningham if there is any difficulty foreseen by Scotland Yard.[9]

Further C11 information was to quickly lead to Home Office permission to tap the line:

> Memo.
> As a result of information received from DI Pickles, C11, I arranged for the Supervisor, Wanstead Exchange, to trace calls incoming to Wanstead 5078. The subscriber on Wanstead 5078 is Edith B Simons, 85 Hermitage Court, Woodford Road, Wanstead, E18.
>
> At 10.05 pm I was informed that a call was in progress and that an attempt was being made to trace the origin. The trace was lost at Toll B Exchange. The callers were heard to say:
>
> Male voice: 'Things are a bit fresh. Would you take it over the road and put it in the fridge in case it goes off.'
>
> At 10.55 pm there was a further call with a message from Barney's girl friend:
>
> Male voice: 'Thanks for getting the message through, will try and get another message later.'
>
> Female voice: 'Thanks, it's a pleasure'.

> Again the trace was lost although engineers at the Toll B were on duty. These engineers traced a call on the Wanstead No1 Junction in which a female voice said, 'Get clothes ready will arrive in the morning'.
>
> At 10.58 am 23 August the subscriber of Wanstead 5078 called Renown 3592 (Mrs Doris May Golding), 42 Winchester Road, Fulham, SW6) and spoke to Mr Brand re picking up a coat. Called subscriber (Mr Brand) said; 'Coat will be ready today, make arrangements to pick it up tomorrow.' Mention made of Mr Heller and phone No Primrose 0218 and address 69 Belsize Park Gardens. Arrangements made for meeting 8 pm – 9.30 pm tomorrow (Saturday). Information passed to C11.[10]

While none of this new intelligence led to the arrest of Reynolds, it did open the door on a new line of enquiry. As a result of the telephone taps, teams of IB 'tailers' were assigned to all the new persons of interest and C11 began looking in earnest at these individuals and their movements. As a result of further enquiries, police concluded that George Stanley, the managing clerk at the solicitors Lessor & Co., was the common denominator linking these new suspects.

Stanley, real name George Albert Sturley, was the brother of Arthur Leonard Sturley, a man with a criminal record and known to the police in connection with a number of fraud offences in and around London. George Stanley had apparently bought his way into Maurice Lessor's business after the war, possibly with his brother's money, and although not qualified, now held a pivotal position within the company as managing clerk. His cousin Charles Sturley had been a suspect in the 1952 Eastcastle Street TPO robbery.

According to an IB summary report written by R.F. Yates, entitled 'Stanley, Simons, Isaacs, The Millbanks and Heller' C11's information and the IB's observations had led to the following interim conclusions:

> (i) This group of suspects have been kept under observation from time to time by IB officers and this has produced proof of association. Police believe that stolen money is being held or controlled by this group of suspects. Detailed reports are given in File 10, but the brief facts are as given in (ii) below.
>
> (ii) Mr George Stanley is the Managing Clerk for Messrs Lessor & Co, Solicitors, London, E15 and came to notice very early in the inquiries. Stanley is a shrewd man and the Police know him as an able advocate for the criminal classes. The actual part he was called upon to play is not known but there is reason to think he may be controlling some part, at least, of the stolen monies. Observations on Stanley by Assistants of this Branch established

> that he made regular visits to 85 Hermitage Court, Wanstead, a flat owned by Miss Edith Simons in a luxury block. Other persons who have also visited the flat (sometimes when Stanley was present) were Harry Isaacs (CRO 19314/41) and Albert Millbank (CRO 2019/39). Isaacs was traced by the IB to 10 Saddleton Road, Whitstable, Kent. Millbank was traced to 69 Belsize Park Gardens, NW3, also occupied by a German Mrs Heller who is believed to be in touch with Reynolds. Both Isaacs and Millbank are known receivers, or minders, of stolen property and both are associates of James Edward White who is wanted for questioning. Isaacs is somewhat of a mystery man. For some considerable time Albert Millbank has been suspected by Chief Inspector Peattie of receiving property stolen as a result of Post Office break-ins. His brother, George Milbank [sic] has, in fact, been convicted for Post Office break-ins. Another relative is Amy Millbank who has been seen in White's café at 36 Aldersgate Street, London EC1. Further inquiries need to be made about this group of suspects.[11]

While George Stanley lived at Tinkers End, Red Oakes, Theydon Bois, Essex with his wife Marjorie, C11 soon came to the conclusion that Edith Simons was Stanley's mistress and that she was acting as the conduit between him, Isaacs, Millbank and Heller. A man matching Harry Isaacs's description had been identified as having visited Leatherslade Farm with Jimmy White before the robbery, although the identification by Lionel Hopcraft was not considered sufficiently strong to take matters further.[12] Isaacs's tailers also observed him visiting Bruce Reynolds's associate Mary Manson at her address in Wimbledon on several occasions during the weeks and months after the robbery.[13]

With George Stanley able to operate behind the shield and legal privilege of Lessor & Co., it seems that the IB focused most of their tailing efforts on Albert Millbank in the hope of furthering the investigation and indeed recovering more of the stolen money:

> **Observation Maintained by Officers of the PD/IB**
>
> At 1.45 pm on 27 August, 1963, Mr Gray observed a man later identified as Albert Millbank to leave the address, 69 Belsize Park Gardens, Hampstead, NW3. Mr Millbank drove away in a Ford Zephyr Saloon AMH 536 which is registered in his own name. Mr Millbank was seen to frequent the Belsize Park Gardens address on a number of occasions between 27 August and 1 September, 1963, in the company of a blonde woman who appeared to have a close connection with a perfumery shop at 14 Sicilian Avenue, London, WC2.[14] The motor vehicle 996 ELW was frequently to be seen at the Belsize Park Gardens address.

> The registered owner of this vehicle is Stanley Alfred Gooch, 19 Parliament Hill Mansions, London, NW5. Observation maintained on this address however, proved negative.[15]

The 'blonde' referred to in the observation reports was one Catherine Mary de Guilio. She was also mentioned by informant Bernard Makowski (who refers to her as the 'Julian woman') in the account he related on 10 August 1963 to Inspector Peattie.[16] According to IB controller Clifford Osmond she apparently lived in Brighton and had a club in Soho's Gerrard Street.[17] The IB, with police assistance, therefore turned their attention to the Brighton area, the results of which are outlined in a report written by Inspector Forsyth to Clifford Osmond:

> On the 28 August, 1963, I commenced observations on the residential premises situated at numbers 5 and 27 Goreham Way, Telscombe Cliffs, near Newhaven, Sussex. Those observations were continued until the 6 September 1963, but were broken for intermittent periods as a result of relative enquiries being made in the surrounding district the result of some of these being subsequently reported herein.
>
> Number 5 Goreham Way is a detached bungalow at present occupied by a Mrs Mary Catherine De Guilio widow of Anthony Paul De Guilio CRO No 14406/61, who died on the 25 September, 1962. They previously resided at No 3 Goreham Way, a semi detached bungalow next door to No 5 and Mrs De Guilio is at present endeavouring to sell No 3 at approximately £5,000. Apparently, as a result of discreet enquiries, she would also appear to be the owner of No 7 Goreham Court, a self contained flat in a block of flats opposite Nos 3 and 5 Goreham Way. No 7 Goreham Court is at present occupied by a Heather and Leslie Gale (not known to local Police).
>
> 27 Goreham Way is a detached chalet bungalow and is occupied by Dominic and Josephine De Guilio. The former is the registered owner of a blue Vauxhall motor car index No 443 AUF. It was hoped that these observations might well reveal a link between the occupants of these premises and Albert Millbank, CRO 2019/39. However, those hopes have not been fulfilled to date as at no time during the observation has Albert Millbank been seen visiting any premises in Goreham Way.
>
> Before leaving London, Mr Yates, Assistant Controller, discovered that Albert Millbank was the registered owner of a blue Zephyr motor car index AMH 536A, which I ascertained was bought new by Millbank on the 22 March, 1963.

However, when registering this vehicle Millbank used his usual 'covering up' address, namely, 127 Arlington Road, London, NW1, which is his mother's. It is well known that any Police enquiries thereat concerning Millbank meet with negative results.

During my observations and enquiries I have had the utmost co-operation from the local Police and in particular Superintendent Taylor of the East Sussex Constabulary. At my request he circulated the description of Millbank's motor car in an endeavour to 'house' or discover what places Millbank visited.[18]

With no sign of Millbank in the Brighton area, the search returned to London the following day:

OBSERVATION REPORT

Date 29 August 1963
Officer(s) Reporting Fowler and Rees
Address on which observation kept – 69 Belsize Park Gardens, NW3
Time commenced 10.45 am

Blue Zephyr Reg Number AMH 536A arrived at above address at 1.30 pm driver of car (Millbank) entered house. At 2.50 pm, Blue Fiat 600, Reg Number 996 ELW arrived. Driver a man about 6' six tall, fair hair and a full beard alighted from this car, carrying a briefcase, and entered the house (Reg owner of 996 ELW is Stanley Alfred Gooch, 19 Parliament Hill Mansions, Lissenden Gardens, London, NW5). At 2.10 pm Millbank and a woman, aged about 40 years, height about 5'6"/7", silvery blonde hair and carrying a white poodle, left the house. We followed and temporarily lost them in traffic. Zephyr was again picked up at Bloomsbury Square. Woman left the car carrying white poodle and went into 14 Sicilian Avenue, off Southampton Row. 14 Sicilian Avenue is a shop, Perfumery and Cosmetics. Apparently the woman works in or owns this shop. The Zephyr was then lost. At 6.30 pm Millbank arrived at Sicilian Avenue. At 6.50 pm Millbank and the woman left in the Zephyr and went to 69 Belsize Park Gardens, NW1. Observation was maintained on this address but they were not seen again.

Time observation ceased 10 pm.[19]

Having lost Millbank's Zephyr in traffic, and not having located him elsewhere, Fowler and Rees returned to Belsize Park Gardens the following day, patiently waiting for him to reappear:

OBSERVATION REPORT

Date 30 August 1963
Officer(s) Reporting Fowler and Rees
Address on which observation kept – 69 Belsize Park Gardens
Time commenced 10.45 am

Driver of car 996 ELW arrived at 4.45 pm left car and entered house. At 4.56 pm Blue Zephyr with Millbank and silvery blonde woman carrying white poodle, left car and entered house. Millbank was carrying a few parcels. At 5.40 pm Millbank left in blue Zephyr on his own. We followed but lost him at Regents Park. We then went to 14 Sicilian Avenue but could not find him. We then went back to Belsize Park Gardens. 996 ELW had left. Millbank was not seen to return.[20]

Having lost Millbank in traffic for a second time in two days, the IB was no doubt relieved to receive a brief report from the East Sussex Constabulary two days later:

As a result of Millbank's photograph being circulated by East Sussex Police, a sighting was made on 1 September: 9.45 am – believed car (AMH 356A) seen travelling from Newhaven to Seaford. Driver only occupant.[21]

Millbank's driving skills were in evidence the next day when he made a quick exit from the house, catching Fowler and Gray off-guard:

OBSERVATION REPORT

Date 2 September 1963
Officer(s) Reporting LV Fowler and BA Gray
Address on which observation kept: 69 Belsize Park Gardens, NW3
Time commenced 11.30 am

At 1.25 pm Ford Cortina 154 FLN arrives. Male and female enters above address i.e. Garden Flat. At 2.08 pm blonde woman carrying white poodle dog leaves address and enters taxi No PUV 148; we follow. She pays off taxi at Selfridges, Oxford Street; then we lost sight of her in Oxford Street. Later return to the above address. Blue Zephyr No AMH 536A parked outside. At 4.45 pm Millbank enters car and drove off at speed, unable to follow. 5.10 pm blonde woman seen at door. At 6.30 pm Austin Cambridge 940 FYX parks outside. Man enters house: Age 30–35 yrs. Height 5'.8"–9". Dark hair, ruddy complexion, dark suit. At 7.05 pm taxi 138 EEU arrives at address. Woman enters house. Description: – Age 25–30 years, height 5'3", dark hair, carrying suit case. Car not seen any more.

Time observation ceased 9 pm.[22]

Back in East Sussex, Millbank was again spotted by the local police:

On 3 September – at noon AMH 356A seen travelling south in Cooden Sea Road, Bexhill. Driver only occupant, boxes in back of car. When driver saw police constable he turned round and travelled off in opposite direction. Unfortunately, in both of these cases the PCs were unable to follow the car and the wireless cars upon receiving the relative messages were unable to make contact with AMH 356A. Photographs of Millbank have been circulated to the local CID officers and any developments as a result of these steps will be passed to this branch immediately.[23]

On the same day that Millbank had once again eluded his tailers on the streets of Bexhill, a new witness, Reginald Billington, came forward. He had spent the best part of three weeks mulling over whether or not he should do so. Being a post office employee he eventually spoke to his supervisor, who called in the IB. Clifford Osmond decided to interview Billington personally:

Memorandum

On the 3 September 1963, Mr R N Billington, Inspector of Wireless Telegraphy, Wireless Telegraphy Section, RSD came to see me in order to appraise me of some happenings which occurred on the 8 August 1963, at a house next door to him – ie, 99 Pollards Hill South, Norbury, London, SW, occupied by a Mrs Willard who is supposed to be a physiotherapist.[24] Mr Billington said that at 9.10 pm on the 8 August an open Mini-bus drew up outside 99, Pollards Hill South, Norbury. He was unable to see the registration number but he thought that it was a blue Volkswagen. He saw that it contained about 30 pillow cases (stripped ticking) and each of them was filled with something or other and each had its neck tied with string or rope. He said that two men were in the Mini-bus and that his wife saw the men take the pillow cases, together with some sacks or bags, into the house. He wondered whether this had any significance in view of the fact that he knows Mrs Willard to be a prostitute and that some 18 months ago he was instrumental in assisting the police to arrest a criminal who had frequented that house and who eventually was prosecuted to conviction for violence. Mr Billington explained that this background story was necessary in order to show that his next door neighbour is no ordinary neighbour. At about the same time a Mini-van, green in colour, stopped on the other side of the road with two men in it. He could not say whether or not those two men had any connexion with 99 Pollards Hill South. There is apparently a son of Mrs Willard about 16 years of age and there are two friends who call frequently at the house – a blonde woman and a balding man, middle aged.[25] Mr Billington says that he thought there might be something extraordinary going on because he had seen a black Anglia car some distance from the house with a man in it who seemed to be keeping observation on his next door neighbour's house. He emphasised that this information was given for what it is worth and that in no circumstances should his name or his wife's be made known to the police without his consent. I promised that his wishes should be met and that we would look into the possibility that the pillow cases might have contained some of the proceeds of the mail train robbery, although I did point out to Mr Billington that the information so far received suggests that the money was taken in bulk to Leatherslade Farm and kept there until Friday the 9 August.

C Osmond[26]

The police were particularly intrigued with this report, having recently interviewed a number of Brian Field's neighbours. Kenneth Barnes, who lived close to Brian Field in Whitchurch Hill, mentioned in his statement that he saw a dark blue dormobile at Field's house at 7 p.m. on 9 August 1963. The police report concludes that: 'the point of interest is that Field was insistent that the van should be put in the garage whilst the Jaguar car was left outside in the open. Mr Barnes saw inside the back of the van. It was empty.'[27]

Another Whitchurch Hill resident, Peter Rance, also mentions seeing 'a Dormobile type of vehicle driven into Brian Field's garage before 11 August 1963'.[28] Field's next door neighbour, Miss Patricia Higley, also saw the Dormobile van being driven into the Field's driveway at '8.30 pm on 9 August'.[29] While noting that Higley and Barnes gave different times for the arrival of the Dormobile, the police concluded that the accounts given by all three witnesses were essentially consistent. Miss Higley was clear that the driver of the Dormobile was not Brian Field, and described him as being 'aged 30 years and dark haired'. She also saw the Dormobile depart from Field's house on 11 August at 10.30 a.m. Again it was driven by the man she saw driving it on 9 August; this time, however, he was accompanied by a young blonde woman.[30]

Although, as Clifford Osmond states, information received thus far was that the money remained at the farm until 9 August, the police did not rule out that some of it might have been moved beforehand, and belatedly conducted a search of 99 Pollards Hill South. However, unsurprisingly, given the three-week impasse, nothing was found at the address.

This development and Millbank's association with previous mail offences further reinforced the postmaster general's suspicion that the train robbery was indeed an 'inside job'. Conscious of the grilling he would no doubt receive when the House of Commons resumed after the summer recess, and in particular MP's questions on the possibility of an inside job, Bevins and his post office officials set about trying to tie up loose ends.

On 30 September, after several weeks of memos circulating around the Post Office, British Railways were, for the first time, formally pressed to respond to the sabotage issue:

> Dear Mr Ibbotson
> As you know, a good deal of play was in the press about the fact that on the night of the attack on the Up Special TPO all three of the specially fitted HVP coaches were out of service.
>
> We have not previously asked the Board in correspondence to give reasons for this, but as the Postmaster General will possibly be questioned on these matters when the House resumes, I should be grateful if you would be good enough to let me have an explanation for all the coaches being out for the delay in having them repaired. It would be most helpful to us if you could let me have this soon.
>
> Yours sincerely
> D Wesil[31]

British Railways were quick to respond, and did so the following day:

> Dear Mr Wesil
> It is the case that the three vehicles in question were out of traffic as a result of defects for varying periods prior to the incident on the morning of 8 August, viz:-
>
> 39. Stopped at Carlisle on 4 July due to hot axle box. Repaired and sent south but again stopped at Wigan for the same cause. Repaired and returned to Willesden. In service 9 August.

81. Stopped at Euston on 1 August with flat tyres. After examination was ordered to Swindon Works on 9 August and despatched on the 10 August.

1177. Stopped at Wigan on 23 June with hot axle box. Necessary materials ordered but later vehicle found to have bogie defects and required at Swindon. Some delay in arranging this, and vehicle stopped three times en route due to hot axle box.

As was pointed out in discussion at Willesden when the Postmaster General was present, the vehicles which had been taken out due to defects were replaced by others as agreed with Post Office representatives and our staff had no knowledge that they were specially fitted from a security point of view. The total number of vehicles available was never less than that required to cater for requirements, and there was no indication that any special urgency attached to the reinstatement of these particular coaches. The first intimation of this was a letter received on 6 August, but even this made no mention of security.

Yours Sincerely
Ibbotson[32]

British Railways were clearly on the back foot as they and the Post Office sought to shift the blame for this unfortunate chain of events. It is clear from IB records that while they were never able to establish anything more than a highly circumstantial case for sabotage, the belief remained that this was indeed the reason why on the night of the hold-up, an inferior HVP coach, lacking the updated security features, was used on the train. The police, too, seem to have taken a similar line. Commander Hatherill expressed this view in his contemporary reports and later stated publicly that:

> Shortly before the robbery was due to take place, a preliminary operation was performed. Although it was later suspected that there might have been tampering with three vans specially built for carrying HVP, we could find no proof at the time.[33]

After the re-arrest of Charlie Wilson in 1968, his wife Patricia was questioned by police, and later published her story in a newspaper serialisation. According to Hatherill, Mrs Wilson had 'confirmed that our suspicions were correct' with regards to sabotage; 'the vans were put out of action so as to ensure that an older and less secure type of van without corridor access to the following coach would be in use for the Glasgow–Euston run on the night on 7–8 August'.[34]

While the IB and the police had a growing stack of files containing unproven or uncorroborated suspicions, phone-tap transcripts and informants reports, they now had a dossier of forensic evidence that would enable them to arrest more of the names on Hatherill's list of suspects during the months of September and October.

8

BLIND MAN'S BLUFF

Before fingerprint evidence was available, Metropolitan and Surrey police officers conducted a huge trawl in August of all known associates of the men on Commander Hatherill's suspect list. Builder Ronald Biggs, whose name was not actually on the Hatherill list, was initially visited at his home on the basis that he was a former known associate of Bruce Reynolds. They had initially thought that Biggs might be handling some of the stolen money, but soon dismissed this suspicion, as DI Basil Morris of Surrey CID explains in his statement:

> At 6.45 pm on Saturday, 24 August 1963, in company with Detective Sergeant Church, I saw Ronald Biggs at his home at 37 Alpine Road, Redhill. His wife was present at the time. I told him that we were police officers from Reigate and that we had heard that his wife had recently been spending quite a lot of money. He said, 'Yes, I expect she has. I won £510 at the races and we decided to spend that and use the money I get from the business towards the houses'.
>
> I told him that I understood that the bookmaker concerned was a man named Inkpen and he said, 'Yes'. I told him that Inkpen had already been seen and that we had verified that he had, in fact, won £510, and that I understood that the winnings had been collected by a man named Stripp. He said, 'Yes, he is my partner'. I then asked him why he had not collected the money himself, and he said, 'I had to go down to Brighton that day so he collected it for me.' I asked him if he knew any of the men who were wanted in connection with the train robbery in Buckinghamshire, and he said, 'I knew Reynolds some years ago. I met him when we were doing time together in Wandsworth. Then he used to come down to Mrs Atkins place at Malmstone Avenue when I used to go there,

> and I met him there once or twice afterwards, but I haven't seen him now for about three years'.[1]
>
> I then asked him if any cases or boxes had been brought to his house recently, and he said, 'No. We had a party last night and we brought a crate of beer in, but that's all that's been brought in here'.[2]

Once the fingerprint evidence garnered by DS Ray and his C3 fingerprint section at Leatherslade Farm was available, it was realised that Biggs was more than an associate and a warrant for his arrest was immediately issued. DI Frank Williams of the Flying Squad and a team of officers arrived at Biggs's home at 37 Alpine Road, Redhill at around 2.45 p.m. on 4 September, just as Charmian Biggs was about to leave with her two children for a doctor's appointment. Mrs Biggs was allowed to proceed to the doctors but was accompanied by three police officers. Williams and the other officers remained at the house. On her return from the doctors she found the police carrying out a full forensic search of the house.

DI Williams's statement gives his version of what took place when Biggs arrived home from work that evening:

> At about 6.20 pm, Ronald Arthur Biggs arrived there and I said to him, 'We are Police officers. We are here in connection with the train robbery in Buckinghamshire recently, and I am in the process of searching your house'. He said, 'What again? The local law turned me over some time ago about that. You haven't found anything, have you?' I said, 'No, nothing has been found'. He said, 'That's all right then.'
>
> The search was continued in his presence, and when this had been more or less completed, I said to Biggs, 'It is proposed to take you to New Scotland Yard in order that further enquiry may be made'. He replied, 'That don't sound too good. What are my chances of creeping out of this?' I left the address with him, and on the way to New Scotland Yard he said, 'I don't know how you've tied me in with that lot in the papers'. I said, 'Do you know any of them?' He said, 'Well, I've read all about it, but I don't know any of them'. I said, 'Are you sure?' and he said, 'I know what you are getting at. Yes, I know Reynolds. He'll want some catching'.
>
> At 7.30 pm the same day I introduced Biggs to Chief Superintendent Butler at New Scotland Yard. I was present when Biggs was asked a number of questions which were taken from a prepared questionnaire, and I saw the replies written down by Chief Superintendent Butler as Biggs uttered them. He refused to sign the document when he was asked to do so.

> Chief Superintendent Butler then said to Biggs, 'I am satisfied that you have been consistently lying. You will be taken to Aylesbury Police Station and charged with being concerned with others in committing robbery'. Biggs was cautioned and he said, 'Get on with it. You will have to prove it all the way. I'm admitting nothing to you people.' He was taken to Aylesbury Police Station, accompanied by Chief Superintendent Butler, Detective Sergeant Moore and myself. During the journey Detective Sergeant Moore was instructed to take Biggs' antecedent history. He did so, and when this officer asked Biggs to account for his employment during the last two months, he said, 'I've been working on four different jobs with my partner, who is named Stripp'. Sergeant Moore asked him to specify each job, and he then gave the name and address of one firm. He then refused any further details. Chief Superintendent Butler pointed out to him that it was in his own interests to explain where he was working on or about the 7 and 8 August 1963, whereupon Biggs said, 'I'm not saying. I'll keep that up my sleeve'. I later formally charged and cautioned Biggs at Aylesbury Police Station, and he replied, 'No'.[3]

Once Biggs's fingerprints had been discovered and confirmed, the police undertook an in-depth investigation into him and his known associates, which would ultimately lead to a new line of enquiry. For some weeks it had been erroneously thought by the police and the IB that forcing Jack Mills to drive the train for the half-mile journey from Sears Crossing to Bridego Bridge had been part of the robbers' original plan. Mills, too, believed this and in an interview with the *Daily Mirror*'s Tom Tullett had said: 'I think they might have killed me, but I was too important to their plans … I'm certain they didn't know how to drive the diesel and that's what saved me.'[4]

However, as the IB's R.F. Yates relates in his report, it was during the first week of September that:

> Information came to hand that Biggs had recruited an ex Railway Engine Driver known as 'Old Alf'[5] to drive the TPO after Driver Mills had been knocked out but that 'Old Alf' had failed to get the train to move because of the broken vacuum and that Driver Mills had to be brought back to the foot plate. 'Alf' has not so far been identified.[6]

As a result of further information received by DCI Frank Williams, a warrant was obtained on the morning of 6 September to search the home of Daniel Pembroke, CRO No 27206/56. Flying Squad officers, led by Williams and DS Slipper, searched 22 Hood House, Elmington Estate, Camberwell SE5, but nothing incriminating was found. Pembroke, who was in the flat at the time, was then taken to Scotland Yard where he was interviewed by DCS Butler in the presence of DCI Williams.

In Butler's report to Commander Hatherill, he states that Pembroke was 'closely interrogated and denied complicity in the case. His palm prints were taken and compared with several palm prints left at Leatherslade Farm by the robbers, but no identification was made.'

Likewise, when a forensic search was undertaken at Leatherslade Farm, pubic hair had been found in a number of the sleeping bags left behind. Pembroke was therefore asked to give samples in order that Dr Ian Holden could undertake a comparison. These also proved to be negative, and Pembroke was allowed to leave.[7]

The following day, 7 September, a warrant was issued to search the home of painter and decorator James Hussey. Hussey had been under observation for a while, although nothing suspicious had been noted. He was not spending any more money than normal and was doing nothing that might support the information the police had that he was one of the robbers. It was decided, however, that the flat should be searched and Hussey brought in for questioning. DSgts Nevill and Slipper were sent over to the flat where Hussey lived with his parents. In DS Nevill's statement he says that:

> I went to 8 Eridge House, Dog Kennel Hill, London, SE22 in the company of another officer, Detective Sergeant Slipper. I saw a man, James Hussey. I said to him, 'We are police officers and have a warrant to search this address in connection with the mail train robbery at Cheddington on the 8 August 1963'. Hussey said, 'Help yourself, there is nothing here.' We searched the premises with a negative result. I said to Hussey, 'You will be taken to New Scotland Yard where enquiries into this matter are to be continued'. He said, 'OK, I have no objections'.[8]

In the car to Scotland Yard, Hussey allegedly asked Slipper, 'Guv'nor, what's this really all about?' When Slipper replied again that it was in connection with the train robbery, Hussey said, 'Guv'nor, you keep saying that, but what do you really want?' After Slipper repeated yet again that it was about the train robbery, Hussey said, 'I feel much better now as I had nothing to do with that.'

According to Nevill, 'We arrived at New Scotland Yard at 10.45 am. Hussey was introduced by me to DCS Butler.' Tommy Butler later wrote an account of the interview:

> On the 7 September 1963, at 11 am, Hussey was introduced to me by Detective Sergeant Nevill. I said to him, 'I am making enquiries in connection with the Mail Train robbery and I have reason to believe that you were one of the men concerned.' Hussey said, 'I had nothing at all to do with it. I don't know Buckinghamshire at all.' I said, 'Do you know Leatherslade Farm?' Hussey replied, 'No I don't.' I said 'Do you know of villages named Brill and Oakley?' Hussey said, 'No, never been there as far as I know.' I said, 'Do you know any of the persons already charged with this matter?' Hussey replied, 'No, I don't know any of them.' I then said, 'Do you know any of the four men whose names and photographs have appeared in the press in connection with this case?' Hussey replied, 'No, they're all strangers to me.' I said, 'Have you any objections to your palm prints being taken?' Hussey replied, 'No. I've no worries.' Hussey's palm prints were then taken by Detective Sgt Nevill and when concluded I said to Hussey, 'Would you care to make a written statement concerning what you have told me?' Hussey said, 'Yes, that's fair.' Detective Sgt Nevill then took a written statement, under caution, which at its completion Sergeant Nevill read to Hussey and he signed it as being true.[9]

At this point DS Ray had a number of palm prints found at Leatherslade Farm that had not yet been identified and set about trying to find out if Hussey's matched any of these. Eventually, over an hour later, he found a match. Butler further records in his statement that:

> I had left the office and returned at 1 pm. I reminded Hussey of the caution and said, 'I want to ask you about a lorry and a Land Rover which were used in the commission of this offence.' Hussey said, 'Ask what you like about them, they're nothing to do with me.' I said, 'Did you take part in the purchase of a Land Rover from Humphries at Winchmore Hill in July, or an Austin lorry from Mullards by a man Blake of Kenton, Middlesex, in the same month?' Hussey replied, 'I don't know anything about those people or the motors.' I then said, 'Do you wish to make a further written statement concerning this?' Hussey said, 'Yes, I don't mind.' Detective Sgt Nevill then took a further written statement under caution, which at its completion Hussey read and signed as being true.

Hussey was then told that he was going to be taken to Aylesbury Police Station where he would be charged with involvement in the robbery.

While still unable to find any fingerprint evidence on Gordon Goody at Leatherslade Farm, the police had asked the IB to shadow him and record the comings and goings at Courtneys, the ladies' hairdressing salon he owned in

Lower Richmond Road, SW15. While a great deal of time was clearly invested in the Goody observation exercise, the operational files make clear that very little of value was achieved by it. Typical is a report from IB officers E.H. Hood and F. Underwood on 10 September, three days after Hussey's arrest:

> 12 Noon: Two men, aged about 30 years, 5' 10", smartly dressed arrived at Courtneys in a car – Maroon Consul 722 CFY (first registered in 1961 to James Pemberton, flat 89, Kings Court, London W6). In the shop about 2 minutes and drove in direction of Putney Bridge. Unable to follow.
> 3.15 pm: Saw a man, recognized as Goody, arrive at 6 Commondale in a black and White MG car 894 AMW.
> 4.45 pm: Mr Goody left the house and drove in the direction of Putney Bridge, where he was lost from view. Not seen again.[10]

IB and Flying Squad officers were also keeping the home of turf accountant Thomas Wisbey under observation. He had initially been questioned shortly after the robbery, not as a suspect but on account of the fact that he and his wife Rene were close friends of Ronald and June Edwards. When Wisbey's fingerprint had been found at Leatherslade Farm it had been decided that rather than publicising his name, the Flying Squad would wait for him to surface. Initial enquiries had established that he had not been seen around his usual South London haunts for the past week. In light of this, DI Frank Williams thought that Wisbey might be hiding out at home, and therefore raided his third-floor flat at 27 Ayton House, Elmington Estate, Camberwell at 7 a.m. on 7 September. Wisbey lived close to Daniel Pembroke on the Elmington Estate and they were known to be close friends. According to Williams's report, Rene Wisbey made tea while the flat was being searched. However, neither Wisbey nor anything else of assistance was found at the flat. Wisbey's tearful wife told Williams that he had left her for another woman and that the pair were now in Spain on holiday. A disbelieving Williams thanked her for the tea and returned to Scotland Yard.

In spite of the raid, Wisbey was clearly confident that the police had no evidence against him, so much so that four days later he telephoned Frank Williams at Scotland Yard and offered to meet him. Williams knew Wisbey well, although this is not apparent from his somewhat formal and measured report:

> On 11 September 1963, at about 11 am at New Scotland Yard I received a telephone call from a man who said, 'I am Wisbey, I understand you want to

> see me.' I said, 'That's right, where can I see you?' He said, 'I will be in my shop in half an hour.' At 11.30 am I saw Thomas Wisbey in a betting shop at 1 Red Cross Way, SE1, I was with Detective Sergeant Moore.[11] I said to Wisbey, 'I would like you to come with me to New Scotland Yard where you will be questioned in connection with the train robbery in Buckinghamshire.' He replied, 'I thought so, that's why I rang you up. I'll come now.' He was taken to New Scotland Yard where Detective Sergeant Moore took his palm impressions. Following this at about 12.15 pm he was interviewed by Chief Superintendent Butler in my presence and that of DSgt Moore.[12]

Butler asked Wisbey the same set of standard questions he had asked the others, which were designed to compromise them in light of the fingerprint evidence from Leatherslade Farm, which thus far he had not disclosed to them:

> I said to him, 'I am making enquiries into the robbery of a train at Cheddington, Buckinghamshire, on the 8 August of this year and I have reason to believe that you can assist us in this case'. Wisbey replied, 'I don't know anything about it'. I said to him, 'Do you know villages called Brill or Oakley in Buckinghamshire'. He replied, 'No, I've never been there as far as I know'. I said, 'Do you know Leatherslade Farm?' He said, 'No, not at all, except what I've read in the newspapers'. I said, 'Can you tell us in greater detail than we have at present what your movements and location were on the 7 and 8 August 1963?' Wisbey said, 'I have already told the other officers that. It was all written down'. I showed Wisbey a typed copy of the statement he had made earlier. He read it and said, 'That's it, that's the absolute truth. You can ask those people I have mentioned. They will tell you so as well'. I said, 'Do you know any of the persons charged in connection with this case?' Wisbey said, 'I only know Jimmy Hussey, I've known him a few years. I don't know the others'. I said, 'Do you know the persons whose names and addresses were in the papers recently?' He replied, 'I saw their photos, I don't know any of them'. I asked him if he would be prepared to make a written statement fully covering his movements at the material time and he said, 'Sure I will'. A written statement was taken under caution from him by Inspector Williams in my presence and Wisbey signed it as correct after it had been read to him. I left the office and returned later after about five minutes. I said to Wisbey, 'I have reason to believe that you were in fact one of a number of men directly concerned in this crime. You will therefore be taken to Aylesbury Police Station and charged with robbery'. He was cautioned and said, 'All right, I know it will be done on its merits'.[13]

The contents of Wisbey's statements were referred to by Superintendent Gerald McArthur in the fifth of his series of reports about the ongoing train robbery investigation:

> I refer to my fourth report which dealt with the arrest of and evidence against Wisbey. In all he made two statements offering an explanation of his movements on 7/8 August 1963. He said that his parents, two sisters and a brother could vouch for the fact that he was at home in bed on the night of 7 August 1963, and that a licensee of a public house could verify that he was in the public house between 9 pm and 11 pm on 7 August 1963. The following witnesses have been seen and statements taken from them (1) the father Thomas William Wisbey born 23 October 1907, a wholesale bottle merchant, (2) a brother Ronald Charles Wisbey born 23 November 1937, a painter, both of 37 Simpson House, St Oswald place, London, SE11 and (3) another brother George Frederick Wisbey born 1 January 1934, a bottle merchant of 14 Voltaire Sceaux Gardens, London, SE5. The first two say that the prisoner has lived with them, following a row with his wife, for about six weeks including 7/8 August 1963, and the second witness further says that they slept together on the night of 7 August 1963. George Wisbey merely confirms the statement of his father and brother that the prisoner had been living at home for about two months.
>
> William Edward Coupland born 5 April 1914, the licensee of the Newington Arms Public House, King and Queen Street, Walworth, SE17, originally refused to make a statement but a few days later agreed to make one. Very briefly the statement refutes the suggestion by Wisbey that Coupland could confirm he was in the public house on 7 August 1963 between 9 pm and 11 pm. Coupland says he was out with his wife that evening and that Wisbey's claim could not be true.[14]

On 14 September, Leonard Field, a 31-year-old merchant seaman of 262 Green Lanes, Harringay N4, was arrested in connection with the robbery and the farm purchase. DS Ray had examined the bank authority that Brian Field had identified as bearing the signature of Leonard Field, and found a fingerprint on the document, which he identified as belonging to Leonard Field. The fingerprint, together with the signature, in the view of the police established Leonard Field as the prospective purchaser of Leatherslade Farm. When under arrest at Scotland Yard, Field had demanded his solicitor, John Wheater, be called in. This was exactly what DCS Butler had wanted – an engineered confrontation between Wheater and Field:

> Wheater was sent for and arrived at New Scotland Yard at about 11.55 am. He was seen by Mr Butler, Mr Bradbery and Detective Inspector Williams. Mr Butler then told him that Leonard Field was in the building and had asked him to act on his behalf. Chief Inspector Bradbery and Detective Inspector Williams left the office, returning about five minutes later with Leonard Field. As Field entered the office he said, 'Hullo Mr Wheater'. Mr Butler said to Wheater, 'This is Leonard Dennis Field who has asked you to act for him. We believe he is the man who paid you a deposit for the purchase of Leatherslade Farm which as you know, was used as a base and hideout by the criminals who robbed the train.' Wheater said, 'this puts me in a very awkward position. Under the circumstances do you think I should act for him?' He was told that it was a matter for his decision and said, 'very well'. Field then interjected, 'I never purchased any farm, did I Mr Wheater? You know I didn't Mr Wheater.'[15]

Wheater was now flustered and caught in an impasse:

> Wheater stood up, loosened his collar, turned quite pale, looked hard at Field for about twenty seconds and then said, 'I'm confused. I'm confused. I am not sure now. I thought he was the man at first but now I'm not certain.'[16]

Wheater and Field were then taken out to separate offices where they made further written statements, each sticking to their own version of events. Unlike Field, Wheater, for the time being, was permitted to leave. With a rising tide of evidence now implicating him, Brian Field was arrested the following day by DCS Butler and DS Luis Van Dyck and taken to Scotland Yard. Amongst property found in his possession when arrested was a £5 bank note, serial number A15 901750, which was within 200 of a stolen note, A15 901857. On 16 September 1963, both Brian and Leonard Field were taken to Aylesbury Police Station, where Brian Field was confronted with Leonard Field and denied that he was the man who had acquired the farm. They were later both charged with conspiracy to rob and obstructing the course of justice.

The Fraud Squad's DCI Mesher, who had received the latest statements by John Wheater and Leonard Field, and the material on Brian Field's arrest, concluded his report on Leatherslade by summarising his view of the legal position:

> Anyone who acquired Leatherslade Farm and remained in possession and control during the relevant period, in default of a water tight explanation, must be an accessory to the robbery. Anyone else assisting with guilty knowledge

> must be party to a conspiracy to rob. Brian Field, on his own admission, shortly before the robbery, examined this farm with a Leonard Field whom he knew to be the relation of a convicted criminal. There is ample corroboration of this admission. Upon reading about the connection of the farm with the robbery, he made no effort to contact police with his knowledge.
>
> An abandoned brief case, full of bank notes from the robbery is shown to belong to Brian Field by the overlooked hotel bill which he admits is his. I would say that it is a clear inference, that as police enquiries were closing in, he discarded his share of the loot, paid for helping to provide the robbers with a base for operations. Upon arrest, he was in possession of a bank note, the serial number of which falls within the sequence of numbers relating to stolen ones. Mr Parker can say that Brian Field's house was used as a traffic centre for two days after the robbery, when Field himself says he had no visitors.
>
> There is a lack of substantive evidence against Wheater, although much which could corroborate that he was a partner in this enterprise. He accepted a substantial cash deposit from a man he knew to be the brother of a convicted criminal without apparently issuing a receipt. He signed the contract for sale himself, thus suppressing Leonard Field's distinctive signature. We have yet to discover his authority to do this, likewise the position about insurance of the farm. A point I have not previously mentioned is that the address, 150 Earls Court Road, London, SW5, appears to have been added to the contract in manuscript by Wheater as an after-thought.
>
> The demeanour of Wheater, when confronted with Leonard Field underlines the obvious falsity of his contention that he couldn't recognise him as the prospective purchaser. His contradictory statements also imply guilty knowledge.[17]

Mesher and his Fraud Squad colleagues had been brought in by Commander Hatherill to untangle the complex web of lies and deception that had surrounded the acquisition of the farm. Having worked his way through this initial quagmire, he eventually established that Field and Wheater were involved in a much wider network of fraud and money laundering.

Unlike Wheater who, on paper at least, had a distinguished and unblemished background, Brian Field's was a more checkered one. Born on 15 December 1934, he was immediately adopted by a South London couple, Reginald and Ivy Field. On leaving school in 1951 he obtained a position as a junior clerk at a South London solicitors, which he held until he was called up for National Service as a private in the Royal Army Service Corp in April 1953. According to his army record, the solicitors gave him a reference stating that he was 'conscientious and of excellent character'. Following basic training he briefly saw action in the Korean War prior to the armistice that ended the conflict on 27 July 1953. On discharge in April 1955, the Royal Army Service Corp described his character as 'good'.[18]

After leaving the army, Field spent the next year or so drifting from one menial job to another. In May 1955, for example, he became an accounting machine clerk, but 'left of his own accord' four months later. After two months of unemployment he became a linotype operator but left after three months, being described by his employer as 'unsuitable for this type of work'.[19] He then seems to have found his forte as a clerk at Dyne Engineers Co. Ltd, where he eventually worked his way up to become company secretary. In fact, he also became company secretary of another linked company, Richard Baines Ltd, before both went into liquidation in May 1958. Shortly after liquidation, a police investigation followed, which resulted in Douglas Carroll, Brian Field and John Cosworth-May being charged with 'conspiring with Albert Grossman and other persons unknown to cheat and defraud the creditors of Dyne Engineers Co Ltd'.[20] Grossman, who ran a whole web of companies, disappeared but was arrested in Paris the following year. The case against Grossman, described as one of the most complex frauds of its time, dragged on for the best part of three years. Eventually, Grossman was found unfit to plead and was released in 1961.[21] Carroll, Field and Cosworth-May eventually had their cases dropped due to insufficient evidence.

Following his first scrape with the law, Field again became a solicitors' clerk in April 1959, leaving in May 1960 to take up employment with John Wheater as managing clerk at his recently opened firm of TW James & Wheater.[22] There, Field (a natural networker) was able to develop the laundering skills he had learned under Albert Grossman and build up the firm's criminal law business through a host of underworld contacts.

During their investigation into the conveyance of Leatherslade Farm, the Fraud Squad had discovered that the address given by Wheater on the sale contract for Leonard Field was 150 Earls Court Road, London, which turned out to be an empty property owned by the widow of slum landlord Peter Rachman. The property was currently in the process of being sold to a company called Jiltslade Investments Ltd, and police encountered a host of contradictory accounts by Wheater and others associated with the purchase as to who was actually the real purchaser. Wheater maintained that it was one Brian Hocking,[23] a director of Jiltslade Investments Ltd, while Hocking maintained that he was simply a front for the real purchaser, Wheater himself.[24] While no firm conclusion was ever reached on this matter, the Fraud Squad suspected that if Wheater was the real purchaser, he was probably obtaining the property as an investment for one of his firm's criminal clients. Investigations also discovered that Jiltslade was just the tip of the iceberg in terms of linked companies that Field and Wheater had an involvement with. These included: Brusteric Investments Ltd, Fusigrand Investments Ltd, Stramquish Investments Ltd and Trizweeks Investments Ltd.[25]

Indeed, when Wheater sought to procure a mortgage for Jiltslade Investments Ltd, it was he (rather than Hocking) that filled in and signed the application form. Furthermore, when fraud officers later read the application form during their investigations, they wrote in green ink 'downright lying' next to Wheater's claim that he owned the property in which he lived at 60 Otterways Lane, Ashtead, Surrey.[26]

Field and Wheater were also found to be fronting a number of other companies and enterprises and had close links to the newly legalised betting industry, which was a heaven-sent opportunity for laundering large sums of money. On 6 September 1962, for example, TW James & Wheater had registered at Companies House a new company called Bookmakers Guardian Co. Ltd (registered office 4th Floor, 93–97 Regent Street, London W1). With a nominal capital of £1,000, the shares were held by Field and Wheater, with Derek Ruddell (of 2 Sherard Mansions, Well Hall Road, Eltham SE9) as director and Field as company secretary.[27]

DCI Mesher's knowledge of the fledgling bookmaking industry in London was also to be of great assistance to DCS Butler's investigation of Harry Smith, as Butler makes clear in a report to Commander Hatherill:

> It is well known that Danny Regan is a close friend of Smith and that their degree of friendship goes back to at least 1946. Regan is one of several brothers who, between them, operate several betting shops in the metropolis under the name 'M & M Regan' and 'Michael Regan.' One of the shops owned by the brothers is situated at No 38 Aldersgate Street, City, EC, next door to a cafe owned by James Edward White, CRO No 26113/1955, who is another associate of Smith and Regan. Information has been received by another officer that one of the men who took part in the actual robbery was named Danny. He was thought to be identical with Daniel Pembroke, CRO No 27206/56. This man who lives at No 22 Hood House, Elmington Estate, Camberwell, SE5, was brought to this office on 6 September 1963. Pembroke is a close associate of several of the men already dealt with for this crime, so he cannot be completely eliminated from suspicion. When the even closer association between Regan and White and Smith and probably others became known to us, it was thought highly probable

> that this was the man Danny. On 27 September 1963, Regan was brought to this office and closely interrogated concerning the offence. He staunchly denied all knowledge of it. His palm prints were taken and compared with those left at the farm, but no identification was made. Regan admitted knowing White and Smith and several of the other persons who at the time had been arrested for complicity in the offence, but said he had not seen any of them for many weeks. He was allowed to leave. Regan is one of those close-mouthed individuals who counteract interrogatory subtleties by monosyllabic replies and refusal to elaborate. He will admit nothing that cannot be proved to the hilt and is quick to demand the attendance of a legal representative.[28]

As a result of Mesher's ongoing enquiries into the Leatherslade conveyance and the activities of the firm TW James & Wheater, the decision was eventually made by Commander Hatherill to give DCS Butler an arrest warrant for Wheater. Butler was also to document the arrest:

> At 7.40 am on Thursday the 17 October 1963, with Chief Inspector Mesher and Detective Sergeant Pritchard, I went to 60 Ottways Lane, Ashtead, Surrey and there saw Wheater. I said to him, 'You already know Detective Sergeant Pritchard and myself. This is Chief Inspector Mesher. May we come in?' We accompanied Wheater into the lounge, where I said to him, 'We hold a warrant for your arrest for conspiracy to stop a mail train with intent to rob it at Cheddington on the 8 August 1963, and also for being an accessory after the fact. Shall I read the warrant?' He said, 'May I read it myself?' The warrant was handed to him and he read it.
>
> Whilst reading it, he said, 'I don't know any of these or at least only half of them'. I cautioned him and said, 'Briefly, it is alleged that you have concealed the identity of the purchaser of Leatherslade Farm, signed the Contract yourself, and gave a false address of Leonard Field in that you said he lived at 150 Earls Court Road. Do you remember that?' He replied, 'Yes'.
>
> He was told that it was proposed to search the address, and he said, 'Yes, I'll explain to my wife later'. We commenced to search the lounge. Wheater stood quite near me and said, 'This is a mistake, you know. This will ruin me'. He walked to the window and then said, 'Don't think I am being rude, but I would like to search you people first. I don't want anything put on me.' I said to him, 'Surely you don't mean that. You must have been listening to too many fairy tales from your clients.' He said, 'Yes, probably I have, I'm sorry, I should not have said it.'
>
> The search continued. Wheater was in no way obstructive. We took possession of certain documentary exhibits, including a Telephone Directory dated

> February 1963, which was on a shelf in the dining room near the telephone. Written on the back of the Directory were some telephone numbers. They were STA 7857 (Stamford Hill), CAN 3593 (Canonbury) and BAY 3921 (Bayswater). Later, the four of us went to Wheater's office at 3 New Quebec Street W1, and searched it in his presence and that of his staff. He was requested to indicate files of recent cases in which he was concerned and these were put aside. We took possession of only documentary exhibits. Included was a sheet of paper from a file of two men Wheater defended in May 1963, which bore handwritten notes, including the telephone number STA 7857 (Stamford Hill). There is also a notebook in which is written this telephone number and the name was 'Lenny'.
>
> Stamford Hill 7857 is the telephone number allocated to 262 Green Lanes N4, which Field gave as his address, and at which he was seen on two occasions by Detective Inspector Tappin. Canonbury 3593 is the telephone number allocated to 2 Liverpool Road, Islington, N1, a florists shop owned by the Field family. Bayswater 3921 is the telephone number allocated to 26 Colville Road, Notting Hill W11; the subscriber being Alexander Henry Field, who is the brother of Leonard Dennis Field.
>
> Wheater was taken to Aylesbury Police Station, where he was charged and formally cautioned and said, 'I am absolutely innocent of both charges'. A list was prepared by Detective Sergeant Pritchard of all the items taken possession of, both at Wheater's house and at his office. Wheater inspected the List and signed it as correct.[29]

While the investigation so far had made reasonable progress in terms of identifying those who had robbed the train on 8 August, very little of the stolen money had thus far been recovered. In a renewed effort to recover cash, the Flying Squad began searching the homes of certain known associates of those thought to have been involved.

Two weeks before Wheater's arrest, 28-year-old driver Martin Harvey was arrested by Flying Squad officers and charged with receiving money from the mail train robbery. Harvey was the brother of Bob Welch's associate Ronald Harvey. The arrest team was led by DS Louis Van Dyck:

> On the 1 October, with Detective Constable Thorburn, I went to 17 Michaelson House, Bowen Drive, London SE21. It is a flat. Mrs Harvey admitted us to the flat. In the dining room I saw Martin Harvey. I told him we were police officers and that we had a warrant to search his flat. 'We are looking for bank notes stolen in the mail train robbery in Buckinghamshire.' He said, 'You're joking, we haven't got any of that here.' I said, 'Have you any money at all here?' He said,

> 'No nothing except that up there.' He indicated a small wad of notes on the mantel shelf and said, 'There is no more'. I took the notes from the mantel shelf and found 18 £1 notes. 'That's my wages. No, I mean my holiday pay. This is my last week of the holiday.' I then searched the room. Detective Constable Thorburn found a brown paper bag in a corner recess of the room and the bag contained a wad of £1 notes. There was £500 in £1 notes. Detective Constable Thorburn said to Harvey, 'What about this. Where did this come from?' He replied, 'What can I say. I'm bang to rights.' DC Thorburn said, 'I believe this money is from the mail train robbery or have you some other explanation?' He said, 'No, how can I? You are dead right. It's from the job. Someone brought it here for me to look after. There is a monkey there. I'm getting £200 to mind it.' I said, 'What about this?' and showed him the £18. He said, 'Yes that as well. It is a bit of spending money for now'. I said to him, 'Who brought it here and what were you told about the money?' He replied, 'I can't tell you that. How can I? I'll have to swallow it because I haven't got any choice. I guessed where it came from and I'll have the receiving but I wasn't in on the job and that's Gospel.' I told him that he would be arrested for receiving. I cautioned him and told him he would be taken to New Scotland Yard and later to Aylesbury Police Station. He said, 'I'm not arguing. It's fair enough.' He later asked to examine the search warrant [which] was [dated] 27 September. He pointed to the date and said, '27 September. I wish you had come then. I never had it then. I've only had it two days.' He was taken to New Scotland Yard. He there made a statement under caution. Taken down in writing by DC Thorburn and signed by the accused Harvey. He was later taken to Cannon Row Police Station and detained there.[30]

On the morning of Thursday 10 October, as a result of further information received, Flying Squad officers led by DS Nevill and DS Slipper went to 14 Linel House, Murray Grove, Shoreditch, N1. During the search of the flat, which was occupied by bookmaker's marker Walter Albert Smith and his wife Patricia, DS Slipper became suspicious of Mrs Smith's stocky appearance, which he was not convinced was the result of her weight. When he challenged her on this, she became abusive and he informed her that he would have to summon a WPC to search her.

At this point Mrs Smith pulled up her skirt to reveal that her knickers were stuffed with money. When the WPC arrived it was discovered that the money concealed in her knickers totalled £470 in rolled-up £1 notes. When Mrs Smith was asked why the pound notes had been individually rolled up it was revealed that the couple had received a sack of £2,000 in £1 notes and had hidden it on the roof. However, it had rained and the money had been soaked.

One of the earlier London–Brighton mail train robberies in August 1962 reported in the *Daily Express*. (Author's collection)

Mail bandits start London train fire

Express Staff Reporter

THE mailbag bandits operating on the Victoria to Brighton line have pulled off a brand new kind of snatch, it was discovered yesterday.

To get at the van carrying the registered mail they set the train on fire.

Coshing a lone, unprotected guard is out. It is old hat to dress up as a railwayman to rob the mails.

Tampering with the signals to hold up a train— a technique used twice before—is more complicated than luring a guard away from his van by setting a compartment alight with petrol-soaked rags.

That is what they did on the 10.28 p.m. train arriving just on midnight at Preston Park on the outskirts of Brighton from Victoria.

Old-style bandits over the last two years have got away with a total of £32,000.

Two missing

The Post Office could not estimate last night the value of the registered mail in two bags now missing.

Railway porter George Kay was standing in the booking office at Preston Park when the 10.28 pulled in 18 minutes late.

He said last night: "I saw smoke coming from an empty carriage and ran the length of the platform to warn the motorman.

"He jumped from the engine and came to help and at the same time the guard came running from his van as the platform roof was getting scorched.

"I thought the fire was getting worse, so I called the brigade. I had no idea that while all this was going on somebody was getting at the mail."

The guard, Mr. Thomas Gulle, said: "It seems

BATTLE ON MAIL TRAIN

By EDWARD LAXTON

EIGHT masked bandits battled with dining car attendants along the corridors of the Irish Mail express last night after overpowering a guard and ransacking the mail van. The fight spilled into first class compartments.

TOO LATE

Brown comes back and misses meeting

By IAN AITKEN

GEORGE BROWN

The haul

Two deaths riddle

Britain's Ersatz Army

Soldier flees with girl over the Wall

MARRIED COUPLE BANNED FROM SECRETS

By JOHN GRANT

SWITCHED

Police fly to riot town

Guns seized

February 1963. The boldest train robbery yet failed to go to plan but succeeded in making the front pages. (*Express* newspapers)

Bridego Bridge, half a mile down the line from where the train was ambushed. It was here the robbers unloaded the HVP coach and passed the mailbags down the embankment by human chain. (Thames Valley Police)

Discovered five days after the robbery, Leatherslade Farm was dubbed 'Robbers' Roost' by BBC TV News reporters. The police referred to it as 'one big clue'. (Thames Valley Police)

On 15 August, four bags containing £100,900 were found in woods near Dorking. Recently opened files at last reveal who the money belonged to and why they dumped it in the middle of the night. (Thames Valley Police)

Mekay QUALITY SHIRTS

Evening Standard

THURSDAY, AUGUST 22, 1963

3d.

FINAL NIGHT EXTRA

KEEP YOUR SEAT AND SAVE YOUR LIFE FIT Britax SAFETY BELTS

These names are issued: Bruce Richard Reynolds, Charles Frederick Wilson, James E. White

3 MEN THE YARD WANT TO SEE

Cherie, the baby and the poodle called Gigi

Evening Standard Reporter

Scotland Yard today named three men they would like to see in connection with the Great Train Robbery gang investigation.

This statement was issued this afternoon:

Shortly after 2 a.m. on Thursday, August 8, 1963, at Sears Crossing, Cheddington, Bucks, a number of men stopped an express travelling Post Office and stole from it approximately £2,500,000.

The police are anxious to trace the following three men who may be able to assist them in their inquires. They are:

BRUCE RICHARD REYNOLDS, 41, motor dealer and antique dealer.

He is 6ft. 1in., built proportionately; has a slightly suntanned complexion; light brown hair with grey eyes and speaks with a Cockney accent.

'A CLEFT CHIN'

He has a slight cleft in his chin and wears horn or rimless spectacles.

The second man is CHARLES FREDERICK WILSON, 31, turf accountant. He is 6ft., slimly built and fresh complexioned with dark brown, well-greased hair.

He has blue eyes and a scar on the knuckle of the first finger of his left hand. He also speaks with a Cockney accent.

The third man is JAMES E. WHITE, 43, cafe proprietor, 5ft 10in., slimly built. He has a sallow complexion with brown staring eyes and brown hair in a slight quiff and receding at the temples. He is reasonably well spoken and on his right forearm is tattooed a Royal Artillery crest.

'WOMAN, BABY, POODLE'

White is said to have recently removed a small moustache which he had had for some time. He may be accompanied by a woman and a six-month-old baby and a white miniature poodle called Gigi.

The woman's name is probably Cherie.

If you have seen these men or have heard of them recently seeking accommodation in hotels, boarding house or lodgings or think that have any information that may help the police would you please get in touch with the nearest police station or to headquarers of the Bucks Constabulary, Aylesbury 5818.

The three descriptions were flashed to every police force in the country today. Air and sea ports were also alerted.

WOMAN TO BE CHARGED

At noon today a woman who had spent the night

◆ Back Page, Col. Three

BRUCE RICHARD REYNOLDS

CHARLES FREDERICK WILSON

JAMES E. WHITE

These pictures were issued by Scotland Yard today.

WEATHER—Dull.—See Page THIRTEEN

ENGLAND LOSE TWO WICKETS

HALL WARNED ABOUT BUMPERS

Bumpers slung down by West Indies Wes Hall drew comment from the umpire to captain Frank Worrell in the final Test at the Oval today.

Soon after the warning England lost two quick wickets. Bolus and Ea... were both caught behind, off Sobers. They had put on 58.

England had chosen to bat after winning the toss. Titmus was 12th man, and with Kanhai fit Nurse became 12th man for the West Indies.

John Clarke—Page 23.
Scoreboard—Back Page.

School-leuvers cause jump in unemployment

School-leavers caused a slight rise in Britain's mid-August unemployment figures.

The total unemployed on August 12, according to Ministry of Labour figures issued today was 501,213—2.2 per cent of the estimated number of employees. This compares with two per cent in July and 2.1 per cent in August 1962.—PAGE THREE.

£1600 ingots vanish

A lorry loaded with seven tons of copper ingots worth £1600 was stolen today in Woolwich New Road, Woolwich.

Judge puts ban on Ward papers

Mr. Justice Faulks today ordered *Dr. Stephen Ward's* literary agent, Mr. Pelham Pound, not to disclose the contents of documents in his possession.

It was said that 25,000 words had been prepared for sale.

There was a further plea to stop an exhibition of paintings. But this failed.

Dr. Ward's estate was revealed today as £14,820 gross (£4420 net).

The full story is on PAGE TWELVE.

Amusements Guide
PAGE TEN

The police announce the names of the first three suspects. (*Evening Standard*)

Concealed behind a timber panel in Jimmy White's Reigate caravan, police discovered £30,440 in stolen banknotes. (Surrey Police)

As the result of a mystery phone call, police found two sacks of stolen money in a Camberwell telephone box. New information suggests a deal had been done between the police and one of the gang. (Author's collection)

Commander George Hatherill, head of CID at Scotland Yard, had been given a list of those who had taken part in the robbery by an informant. (Author's collection)

Daily Mirror

3d. Wednesday, August 14, 1963 • • • No. 18,553

At the end of a long country lane—the train gang's hideout

'THE SQUEALER' GIVES YARD 10 NAMES

By TOM TULLETT and HOWARD JOHNSON

AS the underworld yesterday started to "squeal" on the £2,554,000 train robbers, Scotland Yard men knew they had achieved a breakthrough in their massive hunt for the bandit gang.

It was an informer—"snout" in criminal slang—who gave the police their first big tip-off when he told them the gang had used a remote Buckinghamshire farm as a hideout.

And the same man gave the police an even more vital lead—the names of ten men who took part in the Travelling Post Office ambush at Sears Crossing, Bucks, at 3.15 a.m. last Thursday.

The *Daily Mirror* dubbed Commander Hatherill's informant 'The Squealer'. (*Mirror* group)

Detective Superintendent Gerald McArthur and Detective Superintendent Malcolm Fewtrell co-ordinated the Buckinghamshire side of the investigation from Aylesbury Police Station. (Author's collection)

The Flying Squad's Train Robbery team: (*left to right*) DS Van Dyke, DS Moore, DS Neville, DI William, DS Slipper and DCI Bradbury. (Author's collection)

Antique dealers Bruce Reynolds and John Daly with their wives. (Author's collection)

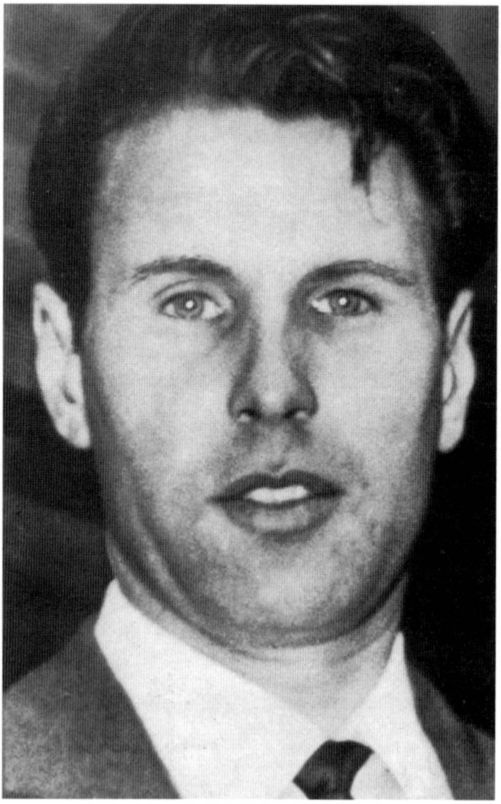

Charles Wilson, a Clapham bookmaker. He was one of the first to be arrested on 22 August as a result of fingerprint evidence. (Author's collection)

Above: Ronald 'Buster' Edwards. This 1962 photograph was found when police searched his flat shortly after the robbery and was used on the 12 September 1963 Metropolitan Police 'Wanted' poster. (Author's collection)

Gordon Goody – one of the gang's leadings lights. Despite his guilt it remains highly probable that the evidence against him was fabricated by police. (Author's collection)

Ronald Biggs. Despite being the best known of the robbers today, in reality he played a relatively minor role in the robbery itself. (Author's collection)

Above: Roger Cordrey, the railway expert. Despite leaving no prints at Leatherslade Farm, he was arrested when he tried to rent a garage in Bournemouth which turned out to belong to a policeman's widow. (Author's collection)

Roy James. An accomplished cat-burglar and a talented motor racing driver, he had beaten future world champion Jackie Stewart four times in the previous year. (Author's collection)

Robert Welch, a South London club owner who already had a successful track record of train robberies on the London to Brighton line. (Author's collection)

Above: Bookmaker Thomas Wisbey. Convinced that he had left no prints at the farm, he voluntarily telephoned Scotland Yard and told them of his whereabouts. (Author's collection)

Brian Field, the wily solicitor's managing clerk. Originally sentenced to twenty-five years' imprisonment, he served just over three years as a result of his 1964 appeal. (Author's collection)

Solicitor John Wheater, seen at the time as being manipulated by his shrewd managing clerk Brian Field; it now seems that he was more centrally involved than was thought in 1963. (Author's collection)

Above: Lenny Field, no relation to Brian Field, was used as a front man in the purchase of Leatherslade Farm. (Author's collection)

Jim Hussey; put under observation shortly after the robbery and eventually arrested at the flat he shared with his parents on 7 September 1963. (Author's collection)

Bill Boal – the forgotten victim of the Great Train Robbery. He had no involvement whatsoever in the robbery but was found guilty and sent to prison, where he died in 1970. (Author's collection)

John Daly's arrest at a flat in Eaton Square on 3 December 1963 was, like a number of other robbers' arrests, only made possible by a tip-off from an associate who was minding his money. (Author's collection)

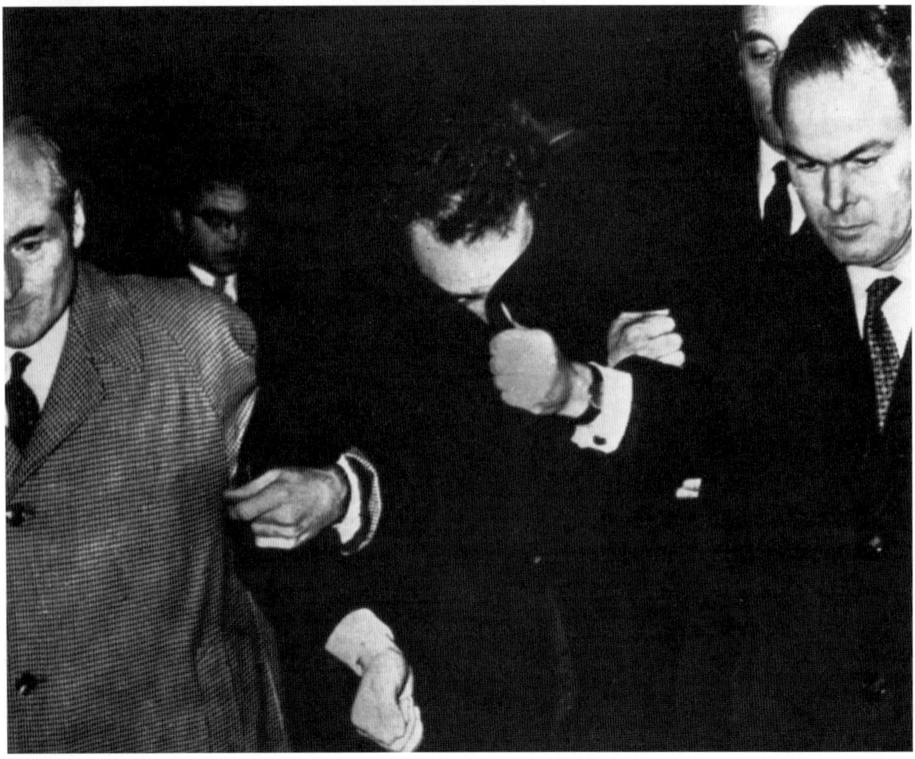

When Ronald Edwards left the country for Mexico in 1965 he had plastic surgery and a new identity. This photograph was taken for his new passport. (Author's collection)

Ronald Biggs, alias Terrance Furminger – the passport Biggs used to travel to Australia in December 1965. (Author's collection)

The 'Grey Fox', Detective Chief Superintendent Tommy Butler and Harry Lyons of the Post Office Investigation Branch leaving court in Aylesbury. (Author's collection)

John Daly is released from custody after his shock 'not guilty' verdict on 14 February 1964. (Author's collection)

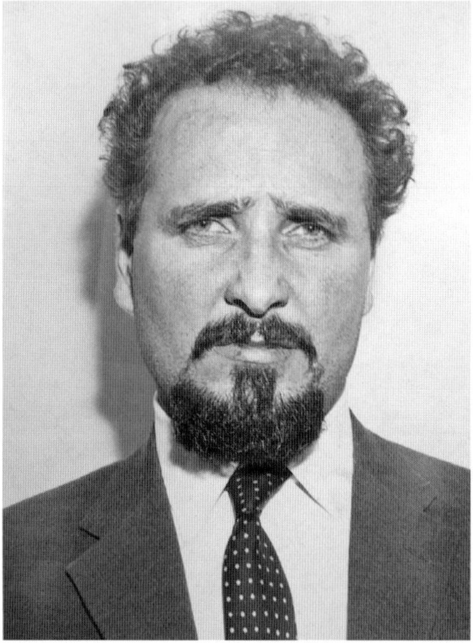

When John Daly was finally arrested, Flying Squad officers barely recognised him as he had lost several stone in weight and now sported a beard. (Author's collection)

John Daly's appearance before he went into hiding shortly after the robbery. (Author's collection)

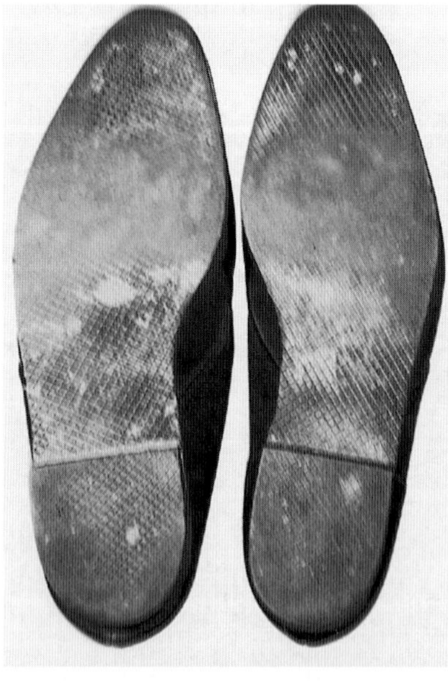

The shoes that convicted Gordon Goody – how and when did the yellow paint get onto the soles? (Metropolitan Police)

Evening Standard

'The game is not worth even the most alluring candle'

ROY JAMES · DOUGLAS GOODY · CHARLES WILSON · THOMAS WISBEY · RONALD BIGGS · ROBERT WELCH · JAMES HUSSEY

SEVEN GET 30 YEARS EACH

the GREAT TRAIN ROBBERY

Sentences total 307 years

Evening Standard Reporter: Aylesbury, Thursday

It was the crime of the century . . . the £2,517,975 raid on a mail train in the 3 a.m. darkness of Buckinghamshire. And today came the reckoning: 307 years in jail for 12 of the men involved.

Sentences on all counts totalled 573 years but because they were concurrent the period of imprisonment was cut by 266 years.

It took Mr. Justice Edmund Davies 32 minutes to pass the sentences at Buckinghamshire Assizes, Aylesbury, after trials lasting 57 days.

A WINK . . . A 'THANK YOU'

Seven of the men found guilty of taking part in the raid and conspiracy were each jailed for 30 years. They were ... Goody, Charles Frederick Wilson, Thomas William Wisbey, Robert Welch, James Hussey and Roy John James.

The other sentences ranged from 25 to three years.

The 12 men heard their sentences calmly.

Biggs, a slight smile on his face, winked at his wife as he left the dock. Wisbey drummed his fingers on the dock rail but gave no sign of emotion. Wilson paled . . . and said nothing.

Welch worked his mouth as if he was chewing gum. Then he bowed low.

From Hussey came an almost inaudible "Thank you, your Honour." James held his hands clasped behind his back.

Goody, grim-faced, gave a toss of his head and clenched his fists as he was led away.

'OH, MY POOR BOY'

The only outburst came when Leonard Field, 31, was sentenced to 25 years for conspiracy.

His 75-year-old mother, a grey-haired tiny figure in a black velvet coat with fur collar screamed: "Oh, my poor boy . . ."

As she was led out Field called out: "Never mind,

Back Page, Col. Five

"This conduct constitutes a menace to society . . . It is nothing less than a sordid crime of violence inspired by vast greed . . .

The consequence of this outrageous crime is that the vast booty of £2,500,000 remains almost entirely unrecovered.

It would be an affront if you were to be at liberty in the near future to enjoy these ill-gotten gains. I propose to secure that such an opportunity will be denied to you for an extremely long time."

MR. JUSTICE EDMUND DAVIES, THE JUDGE AT THE MAIL ROBBERY TRIAL TODAY.

'FERRANTI COMPANY BEAT WHITEHALL'

The MPs' "watchdog" committee on public accounts reported today on the Ferranti contract. The committee find that THE COMPANY was able to beat Whitehall's technical cost estimate by "an enormous margin"; and THE MINISTRY—"one of the most disturbing facts"—had not been able to establish how it happened.

The MPs consider that the firm made an "excessive profit." This was contested by Mr. Sebastian de Ferranti, the chairman and managing director.

Fuller report—Page FIVE

LEONARD FIELD · BRIAN FIELD · ROGER CORDREY · WILLIAM BOAL · JOHN WHEATER—Three years

The 'wild ones' get priority in big crime probe

Royal wedding in September

THERE IS NO QUESTION—the AUSTIN A60 IS THE CAR FOR QUALITY and COMFORT see it!—try it!—at Car Mart Ltd

THE KENNING & Car Mart MOTOR GROUP Britain's Largest Motoring Service

WEATHER—Cloudy—See Page 17.

The sentences handed down by Judge Edmund Davies totalled 307 years. (*Evening Standard*)

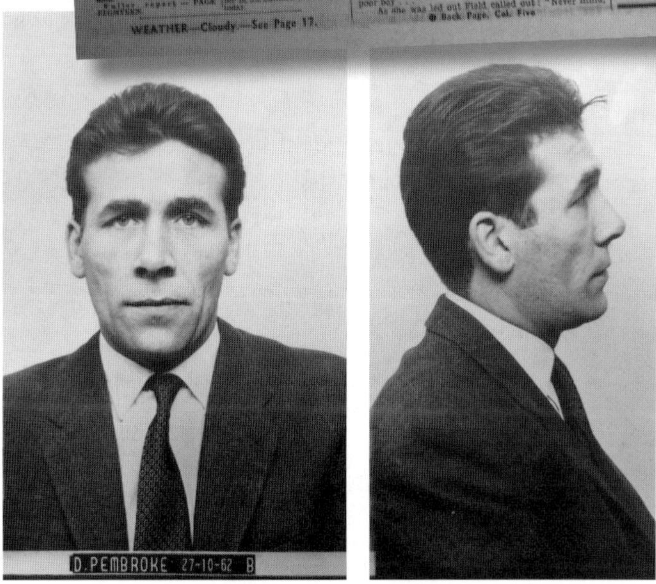

Danny Pembroke. Taken in for questioning in September 1963, the DPP concluded that there was no tangible evidence to prove his involvement in the robbery. (Metropolitan Police)

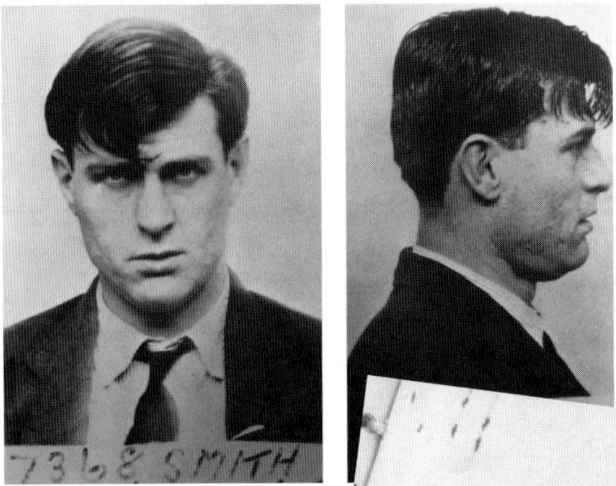

Harry Smith. After a nine-month manhunt, he was finally arrested by Flying Squad officers in South London in May 1964 and taken into custody at Aylesbury. The DPP eventually decided not to press charges. (Metropolitan Police)

Criminal Intelligence Section,
New Scotland Yard.
WHI 1212 Ext. 886/887.

NAME William Frederick John STILL

ALIASES 'Billy' 'Shooting-brake Billy'

DESCRIPTION Born 30.5.21. Mitcham, London. Height 5' 7". Broad build; dark brown hair (receding); brown eyes; thick dark eyebrows. Is cleanshaven at present but at times had a beard. Scar on left forearm. Scar on right calf.

DRESS Recently seen wearing a light fawn three-quarter length leather coat, with white sheepskin collar. No hat.

ADDRESS Living at 4 Wimbledon Close-a luxury block of flats at The Downs, Wimbledon, S.W.20. (Telephone No: WIM 6393) together with James Stuart McDONALD and his common-law wife, Mary McDONALD alias MANSON.

C.R.O. No: 11815/38.

Xd 1398
STILL W.F.J.

PHOTOGRAPH Is still a good likeness, although 10 years old.

CONVICTIONS Has convictions for 'breaking, suspected person, taking and driving away m/vehicles, and gaming. Last conviction; (9) On 16.11.54. at Leeds Assises was sentenced to 4 years imprisonment for warehousebreaking.

CARS USED In December, 1963, a new blue Ford Cortina, Index No:4438 P.H. registered in Mary McDONALD'S name, and in January 1964, a dark green Ford Zephyr, 7222 P.L. registered in James McDONALD'S name.

Billy Still. Police suspected that it was his job to clean and burn down the farm – he was, however, arrested in Euston Square in connection with another offence before the train robbery took place. (Metropolitan Police)

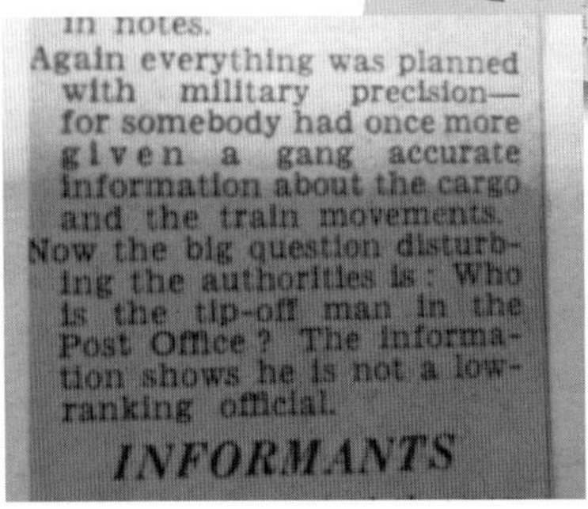

in notes.
Again everything was planned with military precision—for somebody had once more given a gang accurate information about the cargo and the train movements.
Now the big question disturbing the authorities is: Who is the tip-off man in the Post Office? The information shows he is not a low-ranking official.

INFORMANTS

April 1964. Percy Hoskins of the *Daily Express* highlighting the view that the Post Office insider must be a relatively high-ranking official. (*Express* newspapers)

A very rare photo of Jimmy White taken while he was in hiding. (Author's collection)

Mrs Smith had subsequently been rolling up the notes (to try and get rid of the crinkles caused by the rain) and drying them in her airing cupboard. In the airing cupboard a further £363 was found. Elsewhere in the flat, £325 was found in £5 postal orders. They were both arrested and charged with receiving £2,000 in stolen money.

According to an IB report:

> The two Smiths had, in fact, embarked on a plan of exchanging the stolen money by purchasing £5 postal orders and then en-cashing them. As a result of this, and at the request of Detective Chief Superintendent Butler, a special notice was issued on 17 October 1963 to all counter officers in the LPR area drawing attention to persons purchasing or en-cashing an abnormal number of £5 postal orders. There was a good response to this circular but although some apparent irregular practices on the part of bookmakers were brought to light it did not result in any further person being apprehended in this mail case. The circular has been withdrawn.[31]

While there was no certain evidence, the police suspected that the Smiths had received the money from Patricia Smith's brother, Daniel Regan, and had been gradually laundering it by the purchase and cashing of postal orders. It was equally believed that Regan was minding some or all of Harry Smith's share of the robbery money.

While making enquiries to trace Smith, DS Slipper learnt that his father Henry had recently left the East End and moved to 41 Rochford Way, Croydon, a house owned by his sister-in-law. On 18 October, a warrant was obtained to search the property and this was carried out by DS Nevill, DS Van Dyck and DS Slipper. While the search proved negative, they spoke to Henry Smith Snr who made a statement to Slipper:

> I am a married man and live with my wife. I have six sons Henry Thomas, Patrick Joseph, Leonard James, Heydon Francis, Charles Gordon and Kevin Barry who is the only one who lives at home. I also have two daughters Beryl Florence who is married to Walter Probyn and Rosemary who is married to Richard Aldridge. Henry Thomas who is my eldest son married Shirley Young about 1950 and they had two daughters. When Henry who is nicknamed 'Harry Boy' got into trouble last time his wife who had threatened to leave him in fact did so taking the two children with her.
>
> Harry then went to live with a woman named Margaret Wade. She already had two children of her own. This was about four years ago. Since then she has

> given birth to a son Harry being the father. Up until 12 August 1963 I lived at 263 Chatham Avenue N1. I only left that address as a sister-in-law offered me better accommodation in Croydon. On 18 May this year Harry bought a school of driving business from Mr John Muskett of 1 Chatham Avenue N1 and Mr Charles Poulton. Harry paid them £400 for the business and agreed to take over the Hire Purchase outstanding on the cars. Harry asked me if I would run the business for him and I agreed to do so.
>
> I remember going round to his home on the Sunday previously to the big train robbery in Buckinghamshire. Why I am so certain of this is because I saw Margaret Wade and told her I wanted to see Harry. She said, 'He's gone away for a few days. He's on a big job that's coming off'. I then left. This was not unusual for her to tell me when Harry was going out to do a job in fact she tells everybody and seems to want to brag about it. When I read in the newspaper a few days later about the big train robbery I realised that's what she was talking about. Since then I've heard conversations in Shoreditch and Hoxten [sic] that both Harry and his mate were involved in the train robbery. I haven't seen Harry or Margaret since the job or heard from them. I have heard that Harry has changed his address three times since the robbery and nobody seems to know where he is. Harry has always brought his children to see me on a Sunday but since the train job I haven't even seen them. What I have said is perfectly true and although my son is involved I am willing if need be to give this evidence in Court.[32]

Of those believed by the police to have taken part in the robbery, Roger Cordrey, Bill Boal,[33] Charlie Wilson, Ronald Biggs, Thomas Wisbey, James Hussey, Brian Field and Lenny Field were now in custody. John Wheater was also under arrest as an accessory. Six more – Bruce Reynolds, Buster Edwards, Jimmy White, John Daly, Bob Welch and Roy James – were either on the run or in hiding. Daniel Pembroke and Daniel Regan had been taken in for questioning but had been released without charge, and Harry Smith was still being sought for questioning.

In the absence of fingerprint evidence, Gordon Goody also remained at liberty while the police thought out their next move in marshalling a case against him. Commander Hatherill and other senior officers were also more than aware from their informants that three, possibly four others who had been at Bridego Bridge on 8 August, were unaccounted for, but in the absence of hard evidence there was little if anything that they could do at this point.

Not only were half the gang still at large, so too was most of the money. Somehow, £2,300,000 or thereabouts, weighing around one and a half tons, had disappeared without trace. How could it have been got rid of without attracting attention? Britons travelling to the Continent during the autumn and winter of 1963 brought back stories of delays at banks and currency exchanges while English £5 notes they handed over were checked by tellers against lists of serial numbers. *The Guardian* declared in an editorial that the numbers of more than half of the stolen banknotes were known to the police, who had circulated lists throughout Britain, Europe and the United States. The story, more than likely sourced from someone at Scotland Yard, was totally inaccurate, as the banks had the serial numbers for only 15,000 £5 notes. The *Daily Mirror*, the *Daily Mail*, the *Daily Herald* and the *Daily Sketch* all ran stories that the police were confident the money was still hidden in London and were concentrating their search in the capital. But what had really happened to the money and how did those still at large plan to make good their new-found fortunes?

9

AND THEN THERE WERE SIX

Following the release of Gordon Goody on 25 August, the police stepped up their efforts to find something that might stick, something that would enable them to charge him. Two days earlier, on 23 August, a search had been conducted by DS John Vaughan at The Windmill public house in Blackfriars:

> On the 23 August 1963, I went to the Windmill Public House, 17 Upper Ground, SE1, in company with Dr Holden. There I saw the licensee, Mr Alexander, who after brief conversation took me to the second floor front bedroom. There he said, 'This is my daughter's bedroom but she is away at the moment and Mr Goody is using it'. I said, 'How long has he been using it?' Mr Alexander said, 'He is an old friend of mine and has been here some weeks.'
>
> I said, 'Whose property is this?' Mr Alexander said, 'All the male clothing is his'. He then opened the wardrobe and said, 'Everything in here is his except my daughter's clothes'. He pointed to a pair of shoes under the wardrobe saying, 'Those are his'. He then indicated a pair of boots under the bed and a pair of slippers saying, 'Those are his as well'. Then, pointing round the room he said, 'All the rest of the male clothing, and the books and bag are Mr. Goody's'. He then left the room. Dr Holden and I then commenced to search the room. I took possession of the pair of brown suede shoes, 'True Form' make size 10, which were under the wardrobe.[1]

Interestingly, it would be nearly a month before any significance was attached to these shoes. On 28 August DC Keith Milner took custody of a partially squashed tin of yellow paint at Leatherslade Farm. While in his later statement he recalled seeing 'this tin of paint on my first visit to the farm on 14 August and subsequent visits there', he gave no explanation as to why he finally decided, on 28 August, to take the tin and hand it over to Dr Holden the following day.[2] A further three weeks passed before Dr Holden, in Milner's presence, removed some yellow paint from the clutch and break pedal of a Land Rover at Leatherslade Farm, along with a sample of khaki paint on 19 September.[3]

Scotland Yard also appear to have got it into their heads that Bill Boal was also one of the robbers. Unable to find any trace of his fingerprints at Leatherslade Farm, they set about securing alternative evidence of his guilt. As a result of an in-depth search of his Fulham home, three items were passed on to Dr Holden on 26 August by DS Price; a pair of knuckledusters, a blue jacket and a peaked cap.[4]

DS McArthur was later to report that:

> A jacket which was found at Boal's house was also examined and a knurled knob of yellow paint was found in the right jacket pocket. This paint was the same colour and chemical composition as that found on Goody's shoes. Dr Holden was quite satisfied that the shoes must have been at Leatherslade Farm.[5]

As a result of Dr Holden's conclusions, DCS Butler was now confident he could charge Goody:

> At 2.50 pm on Thursday 3 October 1963, at Putney Police Station, with Chief Inspector Vibart, I saw Goody in the presence of Mr Brown of Lesser and Co solicitors. I said to Goody, 'You know us both. Enquiries have now been completed in connection with yourself in relation to the mail robbery which occurred at Cheddington, Bucks, on the 8 August, 1963'. I showed him a pair of size 10 brown suede shoes by True Form, and said, 'Would you examine these, as they were found in a room at the Windmill Public House, Blackfriars, where you were staying when you left for Leicester on the 22 of August this year. Are these your shoes?' Goody examined them and said, 'Yes, Mr. Butler, they are mine'. I said, 'Have you ever loaned them to anybody?' He replied, 'Of course not'. I said, 'You will recall being questioned regarding your visit to Ireland between the 2 and the 6 August, 1963. Would you now care to tell me how and on what date you travelled back?' Goody replied, 'My going to Ireland and coming back had nothing to do with what you're enquiring about. It was all personal and certainly not incriminating'. I said, 'Would you care to say what it was?' He said, 'Can I speak to my Solicitor alone?' I told him that he would be arrested and charged at Aylesbury Police Station with being concerned with others in

robbing a mail train at Cheddington, Bucks, on the 8 August, 1963. He was cautioned, and he said, 'Yes, I see'.[6]

With Goody in custody, there were now six suspects – Bruce Reynolds, Buster Edwards, Jimmy White, Roy James, John Daly and Bob Welch – who were effectively in hiding or on the run. While there were other suspects in the frame, police believed that they had enough tangible evidence to charge the six and DCS Butler now focused his manhunt on arresting them as quickly as possible.

Reynolds had gone to ground almost immediately, hiding out in London flats and safe houses. After he had been publicly named as 'wanted' on 22 August he had to move yet again. In December, Reynolds was almost arrested when a police patrol car spotted a ladder up against the first-floor window of the flat he and his wife were sharing above a dry-cleaning shop in Handcroft Road, Thornton Heath. Unbeknown to them, they had just been burgled. When the police rang the doorbell and asked to look over the flat they found a naked man in the bedroom. The woman who opened the door to the police officer explained that her husband was away and that the man in the bedroom was her lover. They had, she explained, been in bed when he rang the doorbell. The naked Reynolds gave a false address in Battersea and the two officers left. Only when they got back to the police station did they recognise him from a poster. By the time they raised the alarm and informed Scotland Yard, Reynolds and his wife were gone. After the flat had been raided and subjected to a fingerprint search, prints belonging to Roy James were found in the kitchen.[7] Reynolds had been lucky in more ways than one; the Thornton Heath area had been staked out for some weeks by Flying Squad officers who had information he was living in the neighbourhood. Had it not been for his unplanned departure they might well have eventually located him.[8]

From Thornton Heath, the Reynolds moved to a house in Albert Mews in South Kensington where they stayed for six months until a new identity in the name of Keith Miller had been secured for him. He eventually flew out of the country from Elstree Aerodrome in June 1964 heading for Mexico via Brussels.

Reynolds had taken great care to arrange that the bulk of his share of the money was transferred to Switzerland and paid into a Zurich bank account. His brother-in-law John Daly was not so circumspect; according to DCS Butler: 'Reliable information has been received here to the effect that Daly had split up his share of the proceeds of the robbery into three equal parts. One part held by (William) Goodwin, one by (Michael) Black and the third by a jeweler in the Folkestone district.'[9] Daly would later discover (to his cost) that, contrary to the old saying, there was in fact no honour among thieves.

Shortly after the robbery, a man giving his name as Grant (an alias Daly used while on the run) approached a number of boat yards in Cowes, Isle of Wight. Arthur Scardifield, a director of the Medina Yacht Company Limited, later recalled that:

> About 6.00 pm on Friday the 9 August 1963, I know it was the Friday of Cowes Week, I was in my firm's yard at Birmingham Road, Cowes, when I was informed I was wanted in the office. In the office I saw a man, aged about 50 years, 5' 11", average build, fairish hair – greying, clean shaven. He was wearing a darkish grey suit and carrying a camera. The suit jacket may have been lighter or darker than the trousers.
>
> He told me that he had just come into the sum of £25,000 and that his friend, who was a Superintendent in the railway in South Africa, was retiring in January 1964, and together they wanted to purchase a boat – about a 9 tonner, and they were not worried about the price.
>
> I then showed the man different types of brochures and we went into the various boats in detail. I then took him into the boat yard and showed him a number of boats, but unfortunately at that time I did not have any readymade ones for sale. I told him this and he said he was interested in getting one built. He took photographs whilst in the yard of the inside of boats.
>
> The man later gave me his name as Grant of 83 Sloane Square, London, and told me he would telephone his friend and get in touch with me as soon as possible. I was with him for about an hour, and I gave him some brochures and my card.[10]

On the same day, Grant visited FS Dinnis Ltd, Marine Engineers, in High Street, Cowes. The manager, Colonel Richard Stoney, told an identical story to Richard Scardifield. When he was shown photographs of the train robbers, he told the police: 'As I remember him, his likeness would be to that of the man Ronald Edwards or John Daly, with a preference for Daly. I believe I would be able to identify Grant if I saw him in person.'[11]

Daly had then headed for Margate in Kent. Information passed to DI Frank Williams indicated that Daly and his wife were staying at a boarding house in the town. Williams felt that door-to-door hotel enquiries would alert Daly and so adopted a more low-key presence in the town. Daly and his wife had in fact checked in to the Endcliffe Hotel, First Avenue, Cliftonville, where they stayed from 14 August to 26 August. According to the hotel manager,

Roger Parr, they had with them an excessive amount of luggage and were in possession of a green Jaguar car.[12]

According to DS McArthur's investigation report:

> … during their stay at the hotel they were joined for the nights 16 to 19 August by a woman who signed the register M Manson and gave her address as 301 Wheatland House, SE and on the nights 24 to 25 August 1963 by a man who signed the register J Bloor and gave his address as 12 Gribble Place, London E17.[13]

On 26 August 1963: 'Daly unexpectedly asked for his bill saying that his wife was experiencing pregnancy pains and that they should be getting home.'[14] 'I was to learn much later' said DI Frank Williams, 'that the publication of Daly's photograph scared him and he fled from the hotel we had traced before we could get there.'

Daly now shrewdly decided to return to London where he could go to ground with the help of William Goodwin. He also resolved to radically change his appearance by growing a beard and shedding several stone in weight through a punishing diet of fish and slimming pills. Once he had lost weight his appearance was indeed transformed. On 8 November he left London with Goodwin and journeyed to the small Cornish village of St Juliot, near Boscastle, where Goodwin's mother and niece lived in a house called 'Endelstowe'. There, they buried a sum of approximately £100,000 under the vegetable garden at the back of the house. Goodwin told his niece, Audrey Sleep, that only three people were to touch the money: himself, Daly and Michael Black. Before burying the money, Daly gave Sleep £100 for looking after his newly born baby and took some money for himself to pay rent for where he was staying in London. Two days later, on 10 November, Goodwin and Daly were involved in a car accident at Cold Northcott on the A395. Their Ford Zephyr had been involved in a collision with some cattle. The car was badly damaged and a police patrol car was soon at the scene. Goodwin, the driver, identified himself with his driving licence, as did his passenger 'Michael Blake'.[15] Daly's new appearance totally fooled PCs Richards and Hancock. Later shown a photograph of Daly in the *Police Gazette*, both swore blind that 'Michael Blake' was definitely not Daly.

Daly then drove back to London with Goodwin in a hire car, where his wife Barbara was waiting. While DI Frank Williams heard talk that Daly was back in town, he had no indication at all as to where he might be or who might be sheltering him.

In contrast, Williams was beginning to make progress in his search for Bob Welch, who had gone missing from his home some weeks earlier:

> Welch had disappeared from his usual haunts. Through snippets of information we later uncovered his movements. He stayed at the Harbour Lights Hotel in Mevagissey from 30 August to 8 September when he left for the Headland Hotel in Newquay. The reservation had been made by Charles Lilley who had booked in on 2 September with his wife and daughter. Welch stayed in Newquay until 13 September.[16]

The IB's R.F. Yates describes the events that followed:

> During early October I was told that some of the suspects in this case were staying at an isolated farm near Beaford, Devon and that over £200,000 of the stolen money was being held there or at a bank in the area.[17] In discussions with Chief Superintendent Butler, I undertook the task of trying to establish directly who were at Beaford, the vehicles used and habits of the suspects and I sent an IB team to Devon, together with IB radio sets. The villages were small and the risk of being spotted was, therefore, great. However, the IB officers took a Sub-Postmaster, his wife and a postman into their confidence who quickly established some basic information as regards descriptions of strangers and car registration numbers. Patient and continual observation from remote points, coupled with efficient radio communication, then enabled these suspects to be followed to important spots including Exeter and Barnstaple and they were identified as:-

Charles Lilley	CRO	27967/42
John Sturm	"	19274/54
Ronald Harvey	"	1196/51
Bobby Welch	"	61730/58
Danny Pembroke	"	27206/56[18]

By examining records at the local telephone exchange, the IB fixed the group's arrival at Beaford House as being approximately 17 September. From that date, regular calls were made by the suspects from telephone number Beaford 305 and a tap was placed on the line.

According to the IB's log of calls, the majority were made to their home addresses back in London and to South London bookmakers, where bets were placed. However, looking at the list of calls, three in particular stand out. The day after their presumed arrival, 18 September at 9.06 a.m., a call was placed to Lincoln & Lincoln solicitors in Armitage Road, London NW1.[19] The call apparently lasted for three minutes and seven seconds. Later in the afternoon, at 4.38 p.m., a call was placed to Whitehall 1212, lasting for two minutes and one second. Just over an hour later, at 5.58 p.m., a further call was made to the same number that lasted for six minutes and two seconds. Unlike the other calls logged in the report, no destination name or address appears opposite Whitehall 1212. The number is, in fact, the telephone number for Scotland Yard. Why would one of the five men make two calls to the Yard shortly after arrival? According to Welch, he had fled to Devon as the result of a tip-off from a police officer that the net was closing in. Was the call placed to this officer at the Yard or is there an alternative explanation?[20]

On 7 October Yates reported further details about the farm:

> Beaford House is a country house standing in its own ground of approximately five acres 1½ miles from the village of Beaford. The property lies back from the approach lane well concealed by trees. The owner occupier of the property, Mr LW Wickett, purports to be a farmer, but in addition he and his wife run Beaford House as a residential country guest house and it is thought that they derive the greater part of their income from this source. There are numerous outbuildings associated with the property but it has nevertheless been established from observations that the guests park their vehicles on the forecourt in front of the house. Prior to taking over Beaford House two years ago, Mr Wickett was a farmer at Holsworthy, Devon, and he does in fact still bank with the Holsworthy Branch of Lloyds Bank Ltd. Mr Wickett is the owner of a green Ford Consul motor-car Index No 897 ADV.
>
> The suspected offenders in this case were using a white Ford Consul motor-car Registration 587 AYE which is believed to be registered in the name of Lilley. During the course of the observations four of the suspected offenders were seen in the Exeter and East Devon Districts. Mr Sturm was not seen at any time.
>
> The four suspects were frequent visitors of the Globe Hotel in Beaford where Messrs Boniface and Petrie are the joint landlords. It has been learnt that the suspects drank lavishly at the Globe and that the landlords were frequently embarrassed by having to change £5 Bank of England Notes.[21] The suspects were exceedingly generous in the village and the local vicar has been heard to comment that he had never known such a remunerative harvest festival. The landlords at the Globe are known to bank with Messrs Lloyds Bank at Torrington. A brother of Mr Boniface was a former Police Officer in the Brighton Constabulary where he was believed to have been an Inspector.

> Whilst at Beaford House Lilley and Welch enjoyed the local country amenities to the full, eg fishing and hunting etc. They were however accepted by the local population with some reserve and casual remarks had been passed that they could have been concerned in the Mail Train Robbery. From observation it was noted that of the five suspected persons, one always remained at Beaford House during the periods when the party went shooting in the woods.
>
> It was later speculated in a Flying Squad report that, 'The house commands an extensive view of the woods. This may be one of the main reasons for one man always remaining in the house. With a pair of binoculars he could, from an upstairs window, see strange persons in the vicinity of the woods and warm his confederates. One is forced to the conclusion that the men have a cache of stolen money somewhere in the woods.'[22]

IB officers in Devon sent regular reports to IB controller Clifford Osmond, who liaised directly with DCS Butler:

> At 8.00 am on Friday 11 October 1963, I left Exeter, equipped with short range wireless, bound for the Winnleicth area via the A377 and B3220 roads. I reached the area shortly after 9.00 am.
>
> At 1.05 pm from my concealed vantage point, I saw an off-white Ford Consul index number 587 AYE moving very fast along the B3220 on the direction of the A377. I followed at a discreet distance until I reached a telephone kiosk at the junction of the B3220 and A377 where I stopped to telephone and inform Mr Bond, the time then was 1.20 pm.
>
> I then continued to Exeter where I established radio communication and was instructed to continue observation on foot. At 2.50 pm I was outside Lyons café in company with other officers when I saw four men leave, three of the men I believe to be R A Welch, CRO 61730/57, Daniel Pembroke, 27206/56 and R C Harvey, 1196/51, description of the fourth man 5' 7" in height, thick set build, broad shoulders, greying hair and full faced, aged about 40 years, wearing a light blue sweater.[23]

It was during this observation that large rolls of £5 notes were first observed on the suspects:

> I kept the four men under observation until they reached the entrance of the car park at Central Station. The time then was 2.55 pm. I next saw the men leave the station car park in 587 AYE and I followed them to St David's Station, which was reached at 3.00 pm. A few minutes later I was in the telephone kiosk which

> is situated in the booking hall and was about to telephone Mr Bond when the four men entered the booking hall. I saw Harvey purchase a ticket and obtain three platform tickets from the appropriate machine. He re-joined the group who were near the kiosk and I could see the man wearing the blue sweater had a roll of £5 notes in his hand. There appeared to be some friendly banter about the notes and I saw the man jokingly offer them to Welch, who jokingly pretended to accept them. The notes, however, did not exchange hands and I heard Welch exclaim amid chuckles, 'They are only worth three pence a-piece now'. I saw the men go on to the station but made no attempt to follow them.[24]

DCI Frank Williams believed that the earlier tip-offs he had received from informants about large sums of stolen money being with the five suspects was verified by IB reports such as these:

> I believed the time had now come to raid the farm. I felt certain that none of the other members of the train gang was going to use it and at least we could catch Welch and recover some of the money. It was reasonable to assume, through the free spending, that a substantial part, if not all, of Welch's £150,000 share was there.[25]

Apparently, Williams was overruled by DCS Butler, and no raid was authorised by Scotland Yard. However, Williams's belief that at least some of the money had been banked in Exeter seems to be confirmed by an IB observation report from 11 October:

> At 2.25 pm the man in the blue sweater detached himself from the rest of the group and went into the Midland Bank, Queen Street. He remained in the Bank until 2.35 pm when he left and proceeded to Lyons Café in High Street where he rejoined the group. At 2.55 pm the four men returned to the parked vehicle and drove to St David's Station. They reached there at 3.00 pm and remained in the car for some minutes conversing.[26]

An IB report from L.V. Fowler to Clifford Osmond on 17 October describes one of a number of shopping expeditions undertaken by the party while in Devon:

> On entering Exeter some 15 minutes later Mr Bowerman and myself observed 587 AYE to be parked in Goldsmith Street. I left Mr Bowerman to park his car and proceeded on foot to the Exeter shopping centre. At 5.30 pm I observed

> Mr D Pembroke to leave the outfitters shop at 'Lillywhites' in the High Street and cross the road into 'Horne Bros' on the opposite corner. As I looked into this shop I saw Mr C Lilley descending the stairway leading from the first to the ground floor of these premises. I am unable to say what purchases these two men made in Exeter.[27]

The following day IB Officer E.J. Hattersley observed the return to London of two of the five men and reported back to Clifford Osmond:

> At about 5.40 pm the white Consul drove past me in Paul Street where it was held up in traffic. I observed the four occupants to be Mr Harvey (driving) who was wearing dark clothes, Mr Welch sitting next to him, with Mr Lilley and Mr Pembroke in the rear passenger seat. The car then turned left into Queens Street in the direction of St David's Station, to where I proceeded on foot ... I then obtained a platform ticket to Platform 5, where the 6.00 pm Exeter to London train was waiting. I then saw Mr Lilley and Mr Welch standing on Platform 5 talking to someone in the train. Observing the two men to be standing directly outside a Gentlemen's Toilet, I proceeded to the toilet where I could see the two men in the train to be Mr Harvey and Mr Pembroke. I then left the Station and entered the observation van (43CLY) which was parked opposite the white Consul (587 AYE). At about 6.07 pm I saw Mr Lilley and Mr Welch leave the Station and approach their car.[28]

Frank Williams continued to pick up information about Welch's movements:

> We heard from another informant that Welch was to travel to London one evening to meet his brother.[29] This meeting was to be at London Bridge Railway Station. I briefed my team and we set ourselves up, out of sight, near the station. I saw Welch come from the station, meet his brother, and they both walked towards our waiting car. We had a team of five men in the area, two waiting in nondescript cars and others strolling casually in the street. As Welch opened the door of the car we pounced. He stood absolutely still with a look of blank astonishment on his face. He was dumbfounded and had difficulty in speaking when I told him who I was.[30]

> At about 8.50 pm on Friday 25 October 1963, I was with Detective Sergeant Van Dyck in Railway Approach, London Bridge, SE1, when I saw Robert Welch. I said to him, 'We are Police Officers, what is your name?' He replied, 'Robert Welch, what's the trouble?' I said, 'I intend to take you to New Scotland Yard in

connection with enquiries into the robbery at Cheddington, Buckinghamshire, in August of this year'.

He replied, 'Do you mean the train job, I don't know anything about that, I don't even know Cheddington'. He was put into a police car and on the way to New Scotland Yard, I said to Welch, 'Where are you living now?' He said, 'The same place as when I was pulled in about this last time. He was taken to New Scotland Yard where I introduced Detective Chief Superintendent Butler who said, 'Enquiries are being made into the train robbery at Cheddington, Bucks on the 8 August of this year, and I have reason to believe that you were concerned'. He replied, 'I don't know anything about it, I've never been to Cheddington'.

Mr Butler said, 'Do you know a farm called Leatherslade Farm which is near a village called Oakley in Buckinghamshire?' He replied, 'No, I've never been there'. Mr Butler said, 'Have you ever been in the locality of Leatherslade Farm which includes Brill, Bicester or Thame or Waddesdon?' He replied, 'No, I don't know that part of the country at all and never been there'. Mr Butler then said, 'I am going to mention some names to you and I want you to tell me if you know the persons, Bruce Reynolds, John Daly, Roy James, Ronald Edwards and James White'. He replied, 'No, I don't know any of them people'. Mr Butler said, 'A number of persons have been charged with this case, do you know any of them?' He replied, 'I've been following the case in the papers, the only two I know out of that lot are Wisbey and Hussey.' Mr Butler said, 'How do you know them?' He replied, 'Through spieling'. Mr Butler said, 'How do you get a living?' He said, 'I've just told you, for the last three years I've been spieling, before that I was in the club game'. Mr Butler said, 'An appointment was made by me to see you with a legal representative on the 25 September last, but you failed to keep it. Enquiries made by other officers and myself show that you were not living at home, can you explain that?' He replied, 'I didn't think it was urgent. I was about though'. Mr Butler said, 'Where?' He said, 'No, I'm not saying where, look I've already made a statement about this'. Mr Butler said, 'We know that, but I believe the contents are untrue. You will be detained pending the result of further enquiries. He was cautioned and said, 'If you say so'. Mr Butler said, 'Do you want your solicitor informed?' He replied, 'No; the morning will do'.

His finger and palm prints were taken by Detective Sergeant Van Dyck at Cannon Row Police Station. He was searched and a car key was found in his possession. He was asked if he had a car and he said, 'Yes, a red Cortina, it is parked in the road where you stopped me'. Mr Butler said, 'Is it yours?' He said, 'A friend of mine hired it for me in his name'. Mr Butler said, 'Who is this friend and why didn't you hire the car yourself?' He replied 'I don't want to say'.

> At 3 pm the following day, Mr Butler and I saw Welch at Cannon Row Police Station. Mr Butler said, 'As a result of the complete information we now have, you will be taken to Aylesbury Police Station and charged with being concerned with others in robbing a mail train at Cheddington on the 8 August 1963'. He was cautioned and said, 'All right'.
>
> He was taken to Aylesbury Police Station where he was formally charged with two offences. The charges were read over to him and he was cautioned and replied, 'I have nothing to say'.[31]

When questioned at Cannon Row, Welch had been asked about the police search of his home on 14 August. A paid hotel bill for £19 7*s* 0*d* made out to a Mr Richards by the proprietors of the Flying Horse Hotel, Poultry, Nottingham had been found in a sideboard. When the bill was examined for fingerprints by Dr Holden, a print identified as that of James Hussey was found on it. According to the hotel records, five men who gave false London addresses had stayed there on the night of 22 May 1963. Although the hotel receptionist picked out only one man (James Hussey) in an identification parade held at Aylesbury Police Station on 20 November 1963, the IB believed that Reynolds and Welch were among the other four men. The IB speculated that the journey may have been connected with meeting a post office or railway informant. A male caller (thought to be Reynolds) had again contacted Midland Marts Ltd in Bicester (the agents for Leatherslade Farm) on 24 June using the name Mr Richards.[32]

In Welch's statement he explained the matter directly:

> I want to state straight away that on 22 May 1963 I was one of five men at the Flying Horse at Nottingham, although I have not been identified and there is nothing sinister about this visit nor was it in any way connected with this case. We gave false names it is true because we were attempting to get black market Cup Final Tickets, and had already got some from Manchester the day before.[33]

DCS Butler was somewhat sceptical of Welch's story, particularly on the matter of the black market FA Cup Final tickets for the Manchester United v Leicester City game.[34]

When Welch had been interviewed back in August he had given a detailed statement of his movements on the 7–8 August, and named Charles Lilley[35] and Jimmy Kensit[36] as being with him on those two days. While Lilley had confirmed this in a separate statement made after he had been taken to Scotland Yard for questioning, police had not been able to locate Kensit.

However, two weeks after Welch's arrest, DI Frank Williams finally succeeded in making contact with Kensit:

> At 12.05 pm on the 7 November 1963 I received a telephone call at New Scotland Yard from James Kensit. I know Kensit and recognized his voice. He said to me, 'I understand you wish to see me because Robert Welch has said he was with me about the time of the train robbery.' I replied, 'Yes, I do'. He then said, 'This is not true, he is taking a liberty, but you must see my point that I cannot make a statement about it and I am not willing to see you. I have been in touch with Lincoln and Lincoln and told them what I have told you. They are upset because I will not support Welch.' I tried to persuade Kensit to see me about this matter but he absolutely refused to meet me. I then recorded my conversation with him as a message.[37]

For much of the previous week, Flying Squad officers had been carrying out observations on a property where they were assured they would find Harry Smith. DS Slipper recorded that:

> Enquiries led me to 496 Barking Road, Plaistow. Numerous observations were kept on the house, even to the extent of borrowing a GPO hut and van which were placed opposite the premises for two days, but Smith was not seen, although Mrs Wade and the children were seen on many occasions. It was then considered that Smith might be on the premises and afraid to go out. As a result, a search warrant was applied for and executed on 4 November 1963 but again proved fruitless.
>
> Mrs Wade, who was at home, was very abusive and stated that she had no money and Smith was living rough, but in her purse was found ninety-three £1 Bank of England notes. When questioned about this money she claimed to have won it at a local Bingo Hall, which she refused to name. This money was taken possession of and the numbers checked against the stolen notes, but none was found to be identical. In a pram was found the Deeds of the house. These showed that on 7 October 1963 it was sold to Daniel Patrick Regan, CRO No 217/47, an associate of Smith.[38]

Throughout this period, Frank Williams was also liaising on a regular basis with contacts of Buster Edwards, who he thought might be persuaded to give himself up.

Edwards had not returned to his home at 214 St Margarets Road, East Twickenham, where after the robbery he and his wife June lived under the aliases of William and June Green. Edwards instead went to a Richmond hotel; his wife stayed on at the St Margarets Road flat for a few days while she sought out a new home. On Monday 12 August, Edwards telephoned Philip Tookey, the estate agent for the property. Tookey recalled that Edwards:

> Said that he wanted to give a month's notice and wanted an inventory checked out at 11.00 am on Thursday 15 August 1963. I told him that it was by far too short notice and that I could not let him have the key as he wished after the inventory had been taken. I asked him what the panic was over and at first he said that he was going on holiday and then that he was leaving the country and going to Persia.[39]

When Tookey visited the flat on 19 August he found that the family had 'moved out with all their possessions, leaving the flat fittings and furnishings in good and clean order'.[40]

The couple and their daughter Nicolette (Nikki) had by now moved to Old Forge Crescent, Shepperton, where they rented a house from a geologist for twelve guineas a week. Not long after they had moved in, a neighbour's babysitter locked herself out of the house, along with the 3-year-old child she was looking after, and went to the Green's home for help. Edwards used a stepladder to try to open the neighbour's first-floor window, but the ladder was too short. The neighbour later knocked on their door and asked Mrs Green if she could personally thank Mr Green. She was told, however that Mr Green was out.

On 12 September, a police poster showing a photograph of Buster and June Edwards was published. Within twenty-four hours the police had received a phone call from a neighbour in Old Forge Crescent who gave them the address of Mr and Mrs Green, who so much resembled Mr and Mrs Edwards.

The police immediately raided the house, only to find that 'the Greens' had hurriedly moved out only hours before the publication of the photographs. They had apparently left in a red Morris 1100 that was found abandoned by the police in Ealing the following day. It seems highly likely that a police officer had tipped off Edwards, thus allowing him to escape.[41]

So far as the police and IB were concerned, the trail now went cold. As they would discover over two years later, the 'Greens' had in fact moved a comparatively short distance to 'Sunnymede', a house in Wraysbury, Buckinghamshire, which they rented for £20 per week and which backed on to the River Thames.[42]

Within two months of the move to Wraysbury, an incident occurred that police later believed had been a blind to convince the authorities that Edwards had already successfully managed to flee the country. Since the date of the robbery, the police and the coastguard had been observing sea ports for any suspicious activity or vessels. During December, their attention was directed towards a 5-ton motor yacht named *Christine*, which was owned by a 30-year-old South London garage proprietor, Edward Anderson, who was thought to be an associate of Buster Edwards. When the yacht was reported missing at sea on 3 January 1964 after sailing from Ramsgate, there was immediate concern that its disappearance had something to do with the train robbery money.[43]

According to police observation reports, Anderson had taken the yacht down the Thames on 18 December to Margate, where he discovered it was taking on water. He therefore sought out John Halmes, a marine engineer, who took it to his yard in Ramsgate for temporary repairs. When Anderson said he intended taking the yacht back to London for permanent repair, Halmes strongly advised him not to and loaned him a large barge motor pump in case he got into any further difficulties prior to seeking a permanent repair.[44]

Immediately the yacht was reported missing, helicopters, planes and lifeboats searched relentlessly off the south-east coast but the only trace of the vessel found was an empty rubber dinghy tied to a buoy 7 miles north-east of Broadstairs. Edward Anderson, like *Christine*, had also disappeared.

Percy Hoskins of the *Daily Express* had picked up the story from Scotland Yard sources at the outset and immediately went about investigating the lead and the fate of Anderson. Three weeks later, on 24 January, Anderson was found by *Daily Express* reporters in Dublin. Somewhat tight-lipped, he said that he had not sailed with the yacht but that his friend Dennis Bassett had gone to sea in her with two other men. He also implied that the disappearance of the boat, and indeed his flight to Dublin, was in some way connected with the train robbery.[45] Three days later, Bassett's body was washed up off the Belgian coast. It was identified and brought back to England, where notice of an inquest was immediately given. Despite being tracked down by the *Daily Express*, Anderson gave an exclusive interview to *The People* newspaper shortly after.

On Sunday 1 March, Ken Gardener of *The People* printed a full statement given to him by Anderson. The newspaper apparently considered the story so important that it took the front page, taking precedence over the previous day's Innsbruck air disaster in which eighty-three Britons were killed.

According to Anderson's statement, the yacht was carrying two of the train robbers and £1 million in banknotes. He had only broken his silence because he was in fear of his life. 'I am dead scared that my fate will be the same as Danny Bassett's,' he said,'I know too much.' Anderson claimed that a few days after Christmas a friend phoned and asked to see him urgently. When they met he asked Anderson if he would like to earn £5,000 by taking a few parcels over to France. The yacht was to cross the Channel and rendezvous off the coast with another boat that would take the parcels.

He was later told that he would take two passengers who would bring the parcels and transfer with them to the other boat 8 miles off Dunkirk. After various delays for repairs to *Christine*, he fixed the sailing day for 2 January. Shortly after 11 p.m. that night, a man came aboard carrying two large suitcases. A second man, carrying a large canvas holdall, arrived shortly thereafter.

Anderson at once recognised them from police posters. One of them said to him, 'I suppose you know all about it, Eddie. I'll be glad when all this is over and done with.' He said that his wife was 'on the other side' and indicated that a car would be waiting to take him to her when he landed in France at dawn. Anderson asked if he had the money. The man replied by bending down and snapping open the fasteners on one of the suitcases. The lid flew back to reveal a case tightly packed with £5 notes. Anderson asked if the other bags were also packed with notes. He had responded: 'What do you think?'

Ken Gardener reported that Anderson then apparently made a sudden decision to back out. 'Well, I'm not coming with you,' he said to Bassett. Then he grabbed his holdall of personal belongings and jumped from the yacht on to the quay. Bassett and the others shouted after him but nobody attempted to follow. 'That was the last I saw of my yacht the *Christine*,' said Anderson.[46]

The police were by no means convinced that his story held together. How, for example, could two men have carried £1 million worth of notes aboard in two suitcases and a canvas holdall? Such an amount of money would have weighed between 400lbs and 500lbs. When the inquest on Bassett began at Dover, Anderson gave a more detailed account. He claimed that the passenger he recognised as being one of the men wanted in connection with the train robbery was Buster Edwards. 'I recognised him straight away,' he told the coroner. 'I have met him in the past. He was wearing dark glasses as a disguise and he had lost a lot of weight. He went below and Bassett poured him a drink.' Edwards told me, 'You know what it's all about Eddie. We are the package.' Anderson described how Edwards opened one of the suitcases and produced a large wad of notes, mostly in £5 notes. But when the coroner asked him if

Edwards had told him some of the money was for him, he refused to answer on the grounds that he might incriminate himself. While the story seemed plausible on the surface, the coroner was sceptical. The police eventually took the view that it was a well-planned decoy.[47]

On 3 December, as a result of information received, Flying Squad officers raided flat 65a Eaton Square, where they found and arrested John Daly. Frank Williams had been aware for a few weeks that Daly was holed-up in a flat somewhere in Belgravia. He hardly left the address, apparently, and on the rare occasions he did, he was disguised as a City gent. When the definitive information as to Daly's address was received, DCS Tommy Butler and DI Frank Williams were deputed to carry out the arrest. Other officers were brought in for support and to cut off possible lines of escape in the back garden and surrounding streets.

At 4.15 p.m. Butler and Williams, supported by DS Steve Moore, DS Bernard Price and DC John Estensen, descended the steps to the basement flat. They knew that there was a special doorbell signal (two short rings followed by a longer one) that had to be given in order for the front door to be opened. The two men stood either side of the peephole in the door and Butler gave the special ring. When Mrs Daly duly answered the door:

> We burst in. Daly stood up from a settee, which was behind a table on which were the remains of a fish meal. Daly was wearing a red dressing gown, pajamas, sporting a black beard and claimed to be Paul Grant. I said, 'Now come on, you remember me.' He looked at me and said, 'Hello Mr Williams. I'm caught.'[48]

Butler, Williams, Moore and Price drove Daly to Scotland Yard for questioning while the other officers searched the flat. Among the possessions taken from the flat were a host of documents belonging to Michael Black, including a driving licence, gun licence, two items of personal correspondence and a receipt from a Harley Street consultant.[49]

According to DCS Butler's report to Commander Hatherill:

> After Daly had been removed from the premises, officers were left there to detain any person visiting the flat. Into the trap walked William Goodwin, CRO No 18605/29, laden with groceries. It became very obvious that Goodwin was assisting Daly to evade arrest, and doubtless was receiving heavy payment for his labours.
>
> When Daly was asked to explain his possession of these items belonging to Michael Black he replied; 'I'm not answering any more questions'.[50]

According to DS McArthur's report, when interviewed by DCS Butler at Scotland Yard, Daly:

> … denied that he had ever been to Leatherslade Farm. He was told that he was going to be arrested and charged with robbery of the train and after caution said, 'I expected it sooner or later but you are not taking her (indicating to his wife) are you?' When he was eventually charged at Aylesbury, he replied after caution, 'Nothing more to say'.[51]

Police soon established that the flat was owned by a Mrs Margery Beaumont Grover and that her daughter Gillian Stovell acted on her behalf. In a statement, Gillian Stovell explained how Daly (known to her as Mr Grant) came to be living at the address:

> I reside with my mother who is the owner of the lease of a garden flat at 65A Eaton Square, London SW1. The flat at 65A Eaton Square was put in the hands of the Estate Agents Douglas, Lyons & Lyons of 33 Kinnerton Street, SW1 with a view to letting it. Sometime at the beginning of October 1963 I received a telephone call from Mr Douglas at the Estate Agents who informed me that he was sending a Mr Selway along to see the flat. An appointment was made for me to see Mr Selway at 11.30 am that same day at 65A Eaton Square in order that I might show him the flat on behalf of my mother. I kept the appointment and a man who announced himself as Mr Selway duly arrived. I showed him the flat and he asked that he might be given first refusal until 3.30 pm that same afternoon, so that he had a little time to make up his mind.
>
> Mr Selway said that he was a Financial Adviser connected in some way with the film industry. He said that he wished to take the flat on behalf of a friend of his, Mr Bryant. Mr Selway was aged about 38–40, 5'11", well built; well dressed; well-spoken and quite a pleasant sort of man. I would know him again. He telephoned my house at 3 pm the same day and said that he wished to take the flat. I did not see him until two or three days later when I went to the flat and handed the keys (two sets) to him. An inventory of the flat was taken by a Mr O'Neil on my behalf and this was checked by Mr Selway. About a week afterwards, or about a week after the new agents moved in, I received a telephone call from the porter who asked me if I was in possession of the main street door key. I said I was and shortly afterwards I telephoned the flat at 65A Eaton Square (BEL 1319) and spoke to a woman. I told her that I would bring a key round. I went to the address at about 8.30 pm and was met in the entrance hall of the flat by a woman who was accompanied by a bald-headed man. I introduced myself and in turn the woman introduced herself as Mrs Grant and

said she was waiting there to collect the key. I did not know if Mrs Grant was the occupant of the flat; as far as I was concerned she might have been a friend of Mr Bryant. Mrs Grant introduced the man who was with her as Colonel someone or other, I cannot remember his surname. I had no conversation with him apart from introductions and handing over the key. As soon as I had done this I left.[52]

Michael Selway, a property dealer, was then sought and questioned. DI Frank Williams was somewhat suspicious of Selway and went so far as to caution him before Selway made the following statement:

To the best of my recollection I met a man named Grant in a bar at the Mayfair Hotel, I think it was in the Beach Comber Bar. It was either at the end of September or early October. I think I was alone at the time and I think he was also alone. I got into conversation with him but I cannot remember who started the conversation. He was well dressed and quite well turned out, he was about my height and had a beard and was between 30 and 40 years of age.

During the course of general conversation I said that I was a property dealer and also he said that he was looking for a flat. I said that I would try to get him one. He implied that he wanted the flat for a girl friend of his and that he would be living with her. He only wanted to lease a flat for a short period. I gave Grant my telephone number. He did not give me a telephone number or address but implied that he lived somewhere outside London. I am not sure where or how our subsequent meetings took place but during the course of conversation with Estate Agents and people connected with property I did bear in mind that he requested a flat.

I have been cautioned by Detective Inspector Williams that I am not obliged to say anything unless I wish to do so but that whatever I do say will be taken down in writing and may be given in evidence should this matter be taken to court.[53]

While suspicions lingered that Selway knew full well who he was dealing with, this was not sufficient to press charges of aiding and abetting. When forwarding the investigation files on Daly to the DPP, DS McArthur noted that:

When the search of Leatherslade Farm was made, in one of the mailbags was found a piece of green slotted cardboard and in another a number of tokens used in the game of 'Monopoly'. All these items were examined by Detective

> Superintendent Ray of the Fingerprint Department, New Scotland Yard. On the green card he identified the finger impressions of Daly, Bruce Reynolds and Biggs. Altogether there were eleven marks, eight for Daly, two for Reynolds and one for Biggs.
>
> In 1961 Daly took out a mortgage on property at 73 Burleigh Road, Sutton, Surrey with the General Building Society who advanced him £2,850 repayable over a term of 20 years at monthly repayments of £22 8.11*d*. The mortgage was completed on 5 January 1962. He gave as his employer J S McDonald of Mac's Antiques of 69 Portobello Road, London, W11.
>
> Daly was well known to officers at New Scotland Yard. He had been seen frequently prior to 21 June 1963. He was clean shaven and weighed between sixteen and seventeen stone. On the 14 of May 1963, Daly bought under a hire purchase agreement a Jaguar motor car, index number 2162 PK. On the 28 August 1963, Jaguar motor car 2162 PK was left in a garage in London, by a man described as 40, 5' 9" tall and very well built. He asked to garage the car for about a week. On the 7 October 1963, the car was still at the garage when it was taken into police custody by C10 Branch, New Scotland Yard.[54]

Of the six wanted men originally on the run in early October, Daly's arrest took the number down to four. Within a week that number would fall again to three.

On 7 December a female informant called Scotland Yard to say that Roy James was in hiding at 14 Ryder's Terrace, St John's Wood NW8, just off Abbey Road. He had been on the run for over three months following police announcements that he was wanted.

On 16 August at Leatherslade Farm, DS Ray of Scotland Yard's fingerprint department had examined a blue-glass Pyrex plate and a Johnson's travellers kit: on the plate and on the cellophane wrapping of the traveller's kit he developed some finger impressions that he identified as those of Roy James. On a loose page in an American magazine called *Movie Screen*, he also developed finger impressions that were identified as those of James. The police therefore issued appeals on 23 and 27 August to representatives of the press, radio and television to help trace James.

The informant had also cautioned police that James had apparently boasted to her that he had an escape route out of the flat if his whereabouts there were ever discovered. According to DCS Butler:

> She was also able to give a detailed outline of James' physical appearance, the manner in which it differed from the published one (he has grown a beard), the

> location of the address in which he was living and the description of a Jaguar 'E' type motor car. She has impressed upon me the necessity for absolute secrecy regarding the part she played in this matter, assuring me that disclosure would have grievous results for her. I share her concern on this point. For this reason she does not wish to give her address (which is known to me), but has expressed her willingness to meet anyone connected with the General Post Office, if it is considered that her valuable endeavours to assist warrant a monetary reward.[55]

DS Slipper and DSgt Nevill were therefore deputed to investigate escape routes before a raid on the flat was sanctioned. Plans of the building and the surrounding area were obtained from the St Marylebone borough engineer and plans of underground sewers and tunnels were also studied. During a search of the area, a piece of waste ground behind a 12ft brick wall at the end of the mews was also thoroughly examined. While the area behind the wall was strewn with rubbish, old bottles, bicycle wheels and weeds, an area some 20ft in circumference had been cleared and looked freshly dug. On further investigation, it also appeared to have been dug several feet in depth. DCS Butler took the view that this was quite possibly a 'soft landing' point for a jump off the roof. Apart from being an expert driver, James was also known for his reputation as a cat-burglar. The freshly dug patch was directly below a flat roof that overlooked the adjacent Blenheim Terrace, and Butler reasoned that if James had rehearsed an escape he would know the exact spot on the roof to jump from, even in the dark.

Extra officers were therefore drafted in to cut off all possible lines of escape from Ryders Terrace; five in particular were to surround the freshly dug patch of ground.

According to DS McArthur's report:

> Detective Chief Superintendent Butler, Detective Sergeants Moore, Nevill, Matthews and Price of the Flying Squad and Police Constables 99 Lewis and 586 O'Loughlin of 'D' Division, Metropolitan Police and other officers went to the vicinity of Ryders Terrace, St John's Wood, London, NW8. After WPC Willy had met with no success, Detective Chief Superintendent Butler repeatedly knocked at the door of No 14 but no one answered although there were obvious signs that someone was on the premises. Detective Chief Superintendent Butler gave certain instructions and acting on these Detective Sergeants Moore and Nevill climbed onto a balcony outside a first floor window. Detective Sergeant Moore smashed a large window and climbed through a hole into a bedroom. He was followed by Detective Sergeant Nevill. Moore went into an adjoining bedroom

> and saw James disappearing through a fanlight window. Moore climbed after him on to the roof and shouted to his colleagues, 'He's going over the roof'. He noticed that James was carrying a bag or holdall. Moore chased James across the roof and over further roofs of adjoining houses. James then jumped from the roof and was detained by Detective Sergeant Matthews and Police Constables Lewis and O'Loughlin. He denied knowledge of the holdall he had been carrying.[56]

James was then taken to Scotland Yard where he was seen by DCS Butler and admitted his identity:

> He was asked why he had run away instead of opening the door and he replied, 'Open the door? I should think so. Just to get myself nicked?' He was then asked to explain where he was on the night of 7/8 August of this year when the mail train was robbed at Cheddington. He replied, 'Nobody can remember that far back. One thing for sure, I wasn't at the farm I've read so much about.' Detectives Chief Superintendent Butler asked him if he meant Leatherslade Farm and James said, 'Yes that's it. I haven't been there'. He was then told that he was going to be arrested and charged with being concerned in the robbery of the mail train and conspiring with others to rob it. He was cautioned and he replied, 'Well that's it. I suppose I'm lucky I didn't break my neck'. Detective Chief Superintendent Butler showed James the holdall which contained packets of money and asked him if he would like to explain his possession of it. He was cautioned and replied, 'You don't want me to tell you blokes anything about that, surely'.[57]

James was the third robber in two months to be arrested as the result of an informer's phone call. When searched he had £131 10*s* on him and £12,041 in the holdall. The numbers of two £5 notes found in his possession, J69 5007 47 and J94 284281, were both among those reported stolen. A scrap of paper in the holdall showed amounts totaling £109,500, which police suspected might have been his share of the robbery.[58]

The police were more than pleased to be able to add the sum of £12,172 10*s* to the meagre total they had so far recovered over the past four months. The circumstances surrounding this recovery, however, were clear and transparently documented – as compared to a mysterious incident that had occurred only hours before James's arrest.

10

OPERATION PRIMROSE

Great mystery still surrounds the events that took place on the evening of Tuesday 10 December 1963 on a busy South London street, less than half a mile from the Elephant and Castle. The official version is succinctly outlined in a recently opened DPP file:

> On 10 December 1963 at about 6.35 pm, as a result of information, Detective Chief Superintendent Butler and Detective Inspector Williams went to a telephone kiosk at Great Dover Street SE1, at the junction of Blackhorse Court. They found two sacks containing bundles of money. It was at first examined by Dr Holden and Detective Superintendent Ray. The former took away the sacks and debris for forensic examination whilst Detective Superintendent Ray removed two top and two bottom notes of each bundle for fingerprint examination. Superintendent Ray took away with him notes to the value of £401. The remainder of the money was counted and examined by Mr Charles of the National Provincial Bank Ltd. He counted £46,844 which added to that taken by Detective Superintendent Ray makes the total amount found in the sacks as £47,245.[1]

The officer who received the telephone tip-off was, according to the police report on the find, DCI Sidney Bradbury. Apparently the caller had with him 'a person who has got £50,000 of train robbery money with him in sacks'. The sacks would be left at the Great Dover Street kiosk. The caller then hung up after telling Bradbury to 'be there in five minutes'. Bradbury then immediately passed on the message to Williams.[2]

However, there is reason to believe that Williams had prior awareness of the drop and had in fact been expecting it. Furthermore, he may well have participated in an earlier aborted attempt to pass over the £50,000 at Nunhead station in Peckham, South London, a few weeks beforehand that was never disclosed in his reports.[3]

The two potato sacks found in the kiosk were taken back to Scotland Yard by Williams and Butler, where they were opened. Inside were bundles of Irish, English and Scottish banknotes apparently in 100 lots of £500. DCS Butler then instructed DCI Bradbury to sleep in his office overnight with the two sacks, prior to their collection and dispatch to Aylesbury Police Station the following morning.[4]

The Buckinghamshire CID was equally puzzled by this turn of events. DS Malcolm Fewtrell first heard the news about the £50,000 from a reporter. His immediate reaction was to privately wonder how the Flying Squad knew that there was £50,000 in the two sacks when no one, so far as he knew, had yet counted the money. His bewilderment heightened the next day when the money was delivered to him at Aylesbury Police Station. On examination, the money was found to be still damp and musty, suggesting that it had recently been dug up from its hiding place; many of the notes were, as a consequence, stuck together. Tellers from the National Provincial Bank, who were called in by Fewtrell, took two days to peel the notes apart and count them. Their final tally was £46,844. When this was added to the £401 taken by DS Ray, the total came to £47,245, £2,755 short of £50,000.[5]

While Hatherill was given only the briefest information by Butler about the find (and indeed no reason for its presence in the telephone box), his view was that the money was left there by one of the robbers who had been questioned at length but not charged. Hatherill's theory was that the money was getting too hot for him.[6] However, it seems clear that Hatherill was not privy to the activities of Frank Williams and that in spite of assurances to the contrary given to Williams by Butler, both Hatherill and Millen were clearly out of the loop so far as Williams's overtures to those still on the run were concerned.[7]

From Williams's reports it is clear that he was dealing with several intermediaries in order to pass on messages to those robbers still at large and used code letters to protect their identities. He was trying to do deals with several of those on the run to turn themselves in with reasonably large sums of money – in exchange for playing down their role in the robbery.[8] There is equally a suggestion that the Great Dover Street episode was part of a deal to hand over money in exchange for the police not pursuing those on whom there was little or no evidence to connect them to the train robbery.[9]

Ten days after the Great Dover Street drop, Williams was to hear from Scotland Yard's C11 Section, that they had received information that another train robbery was possibly being planned, this time on the Weymouth–Waterloo line. Most intriguing was the suggestion that some members of this gang 'were connected with the gang concerned in the Up Special TPO Robbery (on 8 August)'.[10]

It was on the same day that the IB's R.F. Yates also heard about C11's information:

> Whilst at Scotland Yard on the evening of 20 December 1963 I saw Commander Hatherill. He mentioned that he had received information from three sources indicating that an attack on the TPO running from Weymouth to Waterloo was being planned. The attack, he said, was expected to take place early in the New Year and he asked that I furnish him with brief factual details of: -
>
> (i) the TPO concerned, with running times;
> (ii) the make-up of the train;
> (iii) the approximate number of HVP bags carried;
> (iv) the number of Post Office personnel on the train.
>
> On Monday 23 December, I handed to Commander Hatherill a copy of the schedules and pointed out that immediately following Christmas large amounts of monies would be remitted by the banks, in HVPs, to their Head Offices in London. Commander Hatherill said that he intended to call a Conference at an early date to which he proposed to invite Chief Constables of the area of the route of the TPO, the Post Office, and Railway Police. He said that at that Conference he would disclose the full facts of his information and attempt to arrange for security and detective measures to be stepped up. So far as I could gather the venue of the suggested attack is not, as yet, known.[11]

This information confirmed the somewhat vague earlier intelligence that came to the attention of C11 back in September, to the effect that a raid on the Weymouth–Waterloo line was being planned. Senior IB investigator William Thomas wrote a memo that day following receipt of the information:

IN STRICTEST CONFIDENCE

Threatened attack on SW TPO

1 Information has reached New Scotland Yard (C11) which suggests that the threat of attack on high value mails carried on the SW TPO Up (Weymouth–Waterloo) has been renewed.[12] The information, which is

somewhat nebulous, is to the effect that a raid is again being planned with mention of Weybridge as the possible target. This information was passed to PD/IB (Mr Yates) by C11 officers late on Thursday 5 September 1963.

2. PSD/PMB(S) and D/LPR (TPO Section) were advised of the above development early on Friday 6 September. At the same time I confirmed by direct enquiry of BTC Police (Supt Ward) that the SW TPO Down and Up are included in the special precautions currently being taken by BTC Police for the protection of certain TPOs – ie that 2 BTC Police officers travel as escorts on both down and up journeys of the SW TPO from Monday to Friday nights inclusive.
3. Follow up action has been taken by PSD/PMB(S) to alert LPR, HCR and SWR as to the renewed threat so that security arrangement connected with the TPO, station and feeder services security may be checked and local Police forces advised of the possibility of attack.
4. At the request of PD/IB (Thomas-Supt, Ward), BTC Police have undertaken to provide two additional Police officer escorts who will travel on the TPO Up from Southampton to Waterloo on Tuesday and Thursday nights commencing Tuesday night 10/11 September, 1963. This arrangement will continue until further notice subject to review after four weeks.

W Thomas
6 September 1963[13]

As Thomas's memo stressed, the information at hand in September was somewhat non-specific. With new and more detailed information now coming forward, security was to be significantly ramped up in the new year. Commander Hatherill took the initiative in calling a round-table conference at Scotland Yard immediately after the Christmas/New Year holiday on 8 January 1964, to put the wheels in motion. The same day that invitations to the conference were sent out by Scotland Yard, IB assistant controller R.F. Yates summarised the progress of the investigation, so far as the hunt for those who were still at large was concerned:

On 4 December, 1963, it became known that Bruce Reynolds and his wife had been residing in West Croydon but had left hurriedly on the night of 3 December. He has not been seen since but finger prints found at the West Croydon house established that both Daly and James had visited there.

To summarise the situation up to that stage, offenders who have so far been arrested:

12 were charged with robbery
8 were charged with receiving stolen money
1 (Mr Wheater) was charged with conspiracy

The total sum recovered amounted to a little less than £350,000 which is about 14% of the total stolen. It is important to note that these recoveries were effected despite the fact the identifiable notes recorded by the Banks amounted to about .05% of the notes despatched.

Detective inquiries continue concerning three groups of criminals:-

Group A: Reynolds, White and Edwards – Definite evidence exists against these men.
Group B: H T Smith CRO 1551/47 and Daniel Pembroke CRO 27206/56 – Both these criminals are strongly suspected of being members of the criminal team led by Reynolds. Pembroke has already been questioned, with negative result.
Group C: Terry Hogan CRO 38593/45 and Ronald Harvey CRO 1196/51 – Suspected.[14]

Commander Hatherill's sources seem to be the same ones that provided much of his inside knowledge about the planning of the robbery and those who had taken part in it.[15]

As a memorandum on this highly secretive meeting shows, Hatherill's informants were clear that those behind this second potential train robbery included some of those connected with the Great Train Robbery the previous August:

MEMORANDUM

1. A meeting took place this morning at Scotland Yard of Metropolitan Police and the Chief Constable on the route of the SWTPO. Mr Morgan Philips, Chief of Police in the British Railways Police, was present and from the Post Office Messrs Wesil, Osmond, Yates (IB) and Shires (LPR) were present. The meeting was called by Commander Hatherill but in fact it was chaired by Mr Bacon Assistant Commissioner of the Metropolitan Police.
2. The object of the meeting was to discuss a threatened attack on the SWTPO. Commander Hatherill explained that information had been received which suggests very strongly that an attack on this TPO was being planned by criminals some of whom were connected with the gang

concerned in the Up Special TPO robbery. The timing of the attack was not known but was likely to be in the early part of the year extending into spring and early summer.

3. For the Post Office we explained what the arrangements were on this train, what amounts were carried and when the peak periods of values carried were likely to be and we stressed that in the present season the greatest amount carried was likely to be tonight. We said that although we had taken certain measures to improve the protection of the sorting coaches on this train, it was impracticable for us to make it impregnable and that in any event some of the measures which we wanted to take could inevitably be carried out only in the longer term. We were bound to rely on the Railway Police and the Police Force through whose territory the train passed for proper protection and on this I stressed the supreme importance of everyone concerned of avoiding another successful attack.

9 January 1964[16]

It was only after the Scotland Yard conference had taken place that Postmaster General Reginald Bevins was told about the new information and how Hatherill intended to combat the threat:

Postmaster General

You will wish to know that the Police have received information which suggests that an attack may take place on the South Western TPO which runs from Weymouth to London. The information is not precise about the date when the attack can be expected, but the early part of 1964 has been mentioned and the threat may hang over us until the spring or even early summer. The attack would be carried out by a large gang at least on the scale of the one that carried out the Up Special robbery on the 8 August.

Yesterday a meeting took place at Scotland Yard of Chief Constables of the police forces along the route of the TPO and adjacent forces. It was chaired by an assistant Commissioner of the Metropolitan Police and was attended by the Head of the Crime Department of the British Railway Police. We were represented by members of the administration, the Investigation Branch and the London Postal Region.

The meeting decided to form a working Party of the police forces directly concerned, under the chairmanship of the Chief Constable of Hampshire, to deal with the threat. The first meeting of the Working Party is taking place today at Winchester. We are attending and will, of course, give the Police every assistance.

At the same time we have done what we could to strengthen the physical defences of the train, which is not wholly a Post Office train but carries passengers. For the time being Railway Police and Investigation Branch Officers are travelling on the train each night.

We will keep you informed of developments.

9 January 1964[17]

The whole exercise now took on a distinctly melodramatic air by naming it 'Operation Primrose'. The day after the Scotland Yard conference, another meeting was held in Winchester, the first of the 'Primrose' taskforce meetings,[18] which pulled in representatives from a wide range of organisations in the areas seen as possible locations for the hold-up.

SECRET

'PRIMROSE'

Meeting of Planning Group held on Thursday 9 January 1964 at West Hill, Winchester

Purpose of Group:

Reliable information of intended robbery of travelling post office Weymouth/Waterloo, one night during the coming 3–4 months.

Agreed:

Object of the exercise would be to ensure that if such an attempt is made those responsible would be apprehended. It follows that all arrangements should be secret and no disclosure to the press of plans in hand. Post Office and Railway Police would take steps to ensure maximum physical security of train and persons travelling thereon. Railway Police travelling on the train might well be employed in plain clothes.

Survey of Railway Line:

In view of the considerable mileage involved, it was pointed out that it was essential to eliminate unlikely areas of attack as far as possible. Mr Duck (Assistant to Traffic Superintendent, SW Line) agreed to supply aerial photographs of route on basis of one master copy of whole route to the Chief Constable, Hampshire, with additional copies to Chief Constables Dorset and Surrey, covering their own areas.

Agreed:

Survey of railway line in each Force area should be carried out forthwith by Police in conjunction with Railway Police and Railway Authorities. In addition to unlikely areas of attack, particularly vulnerable points should be noted. The Chief Constable Hampshire, agreed to set up a special Control Room equipped with communications which would operate each night throughout the period of the running of the train. Other County Forces would, of course, have to make local arrangements for receiving signals and acknowledging but Dorset and Surrey frequencies would be monitored from the Central Control Room. The Chief Constable, Hampshire, would also provide two officers to act as intelligence officers. One of these would be the officer on duty at the appropriate time in the Central Control Room. These officers would also co-ordinate and disseminate all intelligence received regarding the exercise. They would work in close co-operation with Mr Walker, C11. GPO intelligence at London end would be passed through Mr Walker.

Detective Chief Superintendent Jones would produce a circular for distribution to officers directly concerned showing particulars of two principal suspects, this circular to be distributed to detective officers on vicinity of the railway line. Officers receiving this circular would be strictly instructed as to secrecy.

If suspects seen, not to be interrogated but information passed with code word 'PRIMROSE' to Central Operations Room, Hampshire Constabulary. (Note: The two officers appointed are Inspector Childs and Sergeant Head, with direct telephone line at Winchester 61627 in operation from noon on Friday, 10 January. Alternatively, intelligence to be passed to Detective Chief Superintendent Jones or Detective Chief Inspector Stuchfield at Winchester 3333. Preference to be given to the first telephone number.)

ENQUIRIES TO BE SET IN TRAIN

(a) Run-In: The probability was that the criminals would seek to find a run-in within 20 miles of the railway line. Accordingly checks should be made forthwith of all vacant and suitable premises in this area and where agents-reliable arrangements made for the Police to be notified of enquiries regarding purchase or tenancy of such premises.

(b) Attention to be given to the possibility of use of caravans for this purpose, particularly in New Forest area. Caravans not permitted in New Forest area until after the 1 April, so particular attention to be paid to any such vehicles in the meantime.

(c) Possible that no run-in would be acquired and attempt made to transfer proceeds to other vehicles such as agricultural vehicles, oil tankers, etc. Added importance of check points.

(d) Manning of check points in the light of commitment revealed by survey of check points. Arrangements for manning will be discussed at next meeting. It must be accepted that this operation will entail a considerable drain on manpower in the coming months but first priority must be given to provision of adequate men and vehicles to deal with the emergency for the whole length of line. Emphasised that check points should be capable of providing physical barrier to traffic.

DATE OF NEXT MEETING

Thursday, 16 January 1964, at 11.00 am at West Hill Winchester

If this attack took place and succeeded through lack of the physical security referred to I need hardly say what trouble we should be in.

10 January 1964

Brigadier K S Holmes, CB, CBE[19]

The new security measures to be taken were quickly set out in a memo:

IN STRICTEST CONFIDENCE

Measures adopted or accelerated to meet the threat against SWTPO:-

1. Windows on all coaches barred
2. Steel mesh covers to windows of HVP coach
3. HVP cupboards strengthened
4. Mechanical bell alarms installed in all coaches
5. Loud hailers temporarily installed in HVP coach

6 VHP radio temporarily installed

7. 2 IB escorts on up train.
8. 7 BT police escorts on up train.
9. Train included in signalman reporting procedure
10. TPO staff augmented
11. Police supervision at stations during loading
12. Telephone communication between stations and police
13. Mechanical bell alarm at stations
14. High standard of security between stations and offices

15. Loading of HVPs into ordinary coaches at TPO stopping points (to avoid opening of HVP coach)

9/1/64[20]

Four days later, the chief constable of the Hampshire & Isle of Wight Constabulary introduced a degree of dissention into the equation by questioning the length of time the new security measures could be kept up for:

HAMPSHIRE & ISLE OF WIGHT CONSTABULARY

13 April 1964

SECRET

Dear Sir

Exercise 'PRIMROSE'

The question must now arise as to the length of time over which the arrangements for this exercise should be kept in being. I know that all concerned have been prepared to keep the arrangements in hand as long as there seemed to be any likelihood of an attack being made. In the considerable time since the information was first received, however, no intelligence of any significance whatsoever has been collected which would tend to confirm the original information, and it is difficult to believe that if an attack was intended some further indication would not have been forthcoming.

I should like, therefore, for the Working Party which considered these arrangements to meet again at West Hill, Winchester, at 3.00 pm on Wednesday 22 April, 1964, in order that we can make a single decision amongst ourselves as to how long this operation should continue, and, if it is discontinued, what other steps might be desirable. It will, of course, be borne in mind that, having made all these arrangements, it should not be difficult to remote the exercise at short notice if considered advisable.

I should be glad therefore if you would attend this meeting or send a representative who is competent to speak on your behalf, so that early decisions can be made.

Yours faithfully,
Chief Constable
Hampshire and the Isle of Wight[21]

The other issue concerning the bottling up of such an explosive story was just how long could it be kept from the media with so many various officials involved in the taskforce. The answer was soon apparent, when ten days after the Scotland Yard conference the story was broken by the crime editor of the *Daily Express*:

> **YARD MEN FOIL NEW RAIL RAID PLAN**
>
> By Percy Hoskins
>
> Plans of another Great Train Robbery have fallen into the hands of Scotland Yard. The target this time: a West Country express carrying £5 million to £6 million in notes. Again, everything was planned with military precision – for somebody had once more given a gang accurate information about the cargo and the train movements. Now the big question disturbing the authorities is: Who is the tip-off man in the Post Office? The information shows he is not a low-ranking official.
>
> The Yard learned of the new plot from underworld informants three weeks ago and elaborate precautions were taken by Commander George Hatherill. The Chief Constables of every county the train passes through were called to a secret conference at the Yard. A defence scheme involving road blocks and the abandonment of county 'frontiers' for pursuit purposes was drawn up. Ever since, on the nights the train has carried valuable loads there has been a general standby at selected 'danger spots.' Although no raid has been attempted, Commander Hatherill does not believe the scheme has been abandoned, but that the thieves noting the precautions have changed the target.[22]

Hoskins put his finger right away on the issue of inside information. It seems clear, as he concludes, that whoever the mysterious inside man was at the Post Office, he had to be a particularly high-ranking official.

The day after the *Daily Express* broke the story, post office security officials got together to discuss strategy now that the story was public. From the official account of the 'Primrose' meeting they attended on 22 April, it seems clear that they and their colleagues were much more interested in trying to discover who leaked the 'Primrose' story to the press than who leaked the inside information about the South West TPO train to a criminal gang bent on robbing it:

1. Messrs McMorran and Link (PSD/PMB/S), Osmond and Edwards (PD/IB) and Shires (LPR) met on the 21 April 1964 to discuss Post Office tactics at the meeting of 22 April in connection with 'Primrose'.
2. It was agreed that the question of whether the threat to SW TPO was still alive and the extent to which the special security arrangements would be relaxed were matters for the police to decide. Subject to the concurrence of the police we would be prepared to:-
   (a) withdraw the 2 IB men travelling on the train;
   (b) withdraw the TPO Inspector travelling on the nights when HVPs were heaviest;
   (c) agree to a reduction in the number of escorting BT police.

The other security arrangements which had been made by the Post Office would remain as permanent features.

3. It was agreed that in discussing the extent to which the police could relax their efforts, we should express the hope that they would continue their supervision at TPO stopping points.
4. During the scare the civil police forces had maintained close radio contact with the Up TPOs throughout their respective territories. They might want to curtail this procedure to checking in and out of each constabulary. We would prefer calls from the train to the police every 10 minutes (the time interval Chief Constables had been asked nationally to agree to) but it was agreed that the frequency of calls must ultimately be left to the Chief Constables.
5. Mr Osmond explained that he was committed to attending the meeting and would take Mr Edwards with him. It was agreed that they should speak on behalf of all Post Office interests and Messrs. McMorran and Shires need not attend. Mr McMorran would advise the Chief Constable, Hampshire accordingly. Mr McMorran also agreed to let Mr Osmond have a list of the security arrangements on the SWTPO made by the PO and a list of TPO stopping points which had telecommunication with the Police.
6. Mr McMorran mentioned DDG's enquiry as to who gave the information about 'Primrose' to the press. Mr Osmond confirmed that so far as he was aware it was not given by a member of the Post Office staff. He did not know whether the press release had been inspired by the police but agreed to let PSD/PMB/S know if he got any information from the meeting at Winchester.

7. Mr Osmond asked about progress with development of an odometer. Mr McMorran said ED/W had now reached the point where a practical test was imminent: there had been a lot of design snags to overcome.

Note: Mr Hyatt ED/W, has since stated that development work has been slow because the novelty of the device had thrown up serious design problems which had never before been tackled eg the need to take account of wheel wear, and wheel slip, to ensure accurate mileage recording. It would probably be a month or two yet before design could be finalised.

(G McMORRAN)
22 April 1964[23]

By the end of April, Commander Hatherill had decided that the threat level had reduced sufficiently to stand-down many of the security measures on the SW TPO route. However, he and his Flying Squad subordinates seemed little interested in pursuing the question of who had sparked off the whole episode by furnishing the inside information necessary to rob the Weymouth–Waterloo express.

11

FISH ON A HOOK

The English court system under which the train robbers were tried in 1964 had hardly changed since the Middle Ages. Until 1967, committal proceedings were heard in order to determine whether criminal offences should be dealt with by the Quarter Sessions or referred to the Court of Assize.

The Courts of Quarter Sessions were local courts that were held at four set times a year.[1] They did not have jurisdiction to hear the most serious crimes and were usually held in the seat of each county or county borough. They were named after the four meetings held at Epiphany, Easter, Midsummer and Michaelmas each year from 1388 onwards. The Courts of Assize heard the most serious criminal cases that were committed to it by the Quarter Sessions.[2] Both Quarter Sessions and Courts of Assize were abolished in England and Wales by the Courts Act of 1971, which replaced them with a single Crown Court.

At the committal proceedings it was generally only the prosecution that would give evidence, with the defence reserving its case. Until 1967 these proceedings were often reported in the press, so that it was virtually impossible to find an unbiased jury for the Assize trial. This indeed was one of the key reasons for the 1971 reforms.

Despite the 1,700 exhibits that were to be produced in court, along with 2,350 witness statements and 209 witnesses,[3] the Crown was unable to bring before the court one single witness or piece of forensic evidence to identify any of those in the dock as being present at the scene of the crime in the early hours of 8 August 1963.

Was the political establishment out to make examples of the robbers whose actions it perceived to be a direct attack on the very fabric of the state?

Were the police encouraged to get convictions at any price, and did the judge allow flagrant abuses of the judicial process in order to facilitate this? Immediately after the trial, the Conservative Attorney-General Sir John Hobson MP,[4] wrote personally to Judge Edmund Davies:

> You must be thankful that the trial is over as it must have been an appalling burden on you. Nobody can congratulate or thank a Judge for administering justice in the way it is expected to be administered, but I think it would not be improper for me to say that no single word of criticism from any quarter (whether connected with the law or not) has been heard over the conduct of this trial, and all those concerned with the administration of the law must indeed be grateful for that achievement.[5]

However, it is clear from the correspondence that Edmund Davies received after the trial and sentencing that Hobson's claim that 'no single word of criticism from any quarter' had been heard was untrue. In addition to the large volume of letters from members of the public agreeing or disagreeing with the sentences handed down, there are detailed memorandums from a number of noted legal authorities who expressed degrees of reservation concerning his conduct of the trial.[6]

The committal proceedings against the train robbers so far charged commenced at Aylesbury on 26 September 1963. Between then and 2 December, the court sat for nineteen days. As a sign of things to come, the ten prisoners were taken to and from court by twenty constables. On 2 December, all those charged appeared before the Linslade Magistrates sitting at Aylesbury. It was at this point that Mr Sabin, a junior counsel for the prosecution, told the chairman of the bench that the prosecution had decided to withdraw the charge against Mary Manson for receiving, and would not in fact be proffering any other charge against her. He then outlined the case against her and spoke of her connection with Reynolds.

He told the bench that:

> It would be quite unfair for the prosecution to ask the bench to regard Reynolds as any other than the person with whom she went to the Chequered Flag Car Showrooms. No evidence had been produced to connect Reynolds in any way with the crime.[7] Reynolds was simply a man with whom she went to the garage and no more, and the prosecution could not prove that any of the money that came from her bag came from the train robbery.[8]

Mr Sabin concluded his address by asking for all the other accused to be committed for trial on the charges that had been placed before the court. Mary Manson was then dismissed and the chairman of the bench said that costs would be allowed from public funds.

Lewis Hawser QC then submitted that Brian Field had no case to answer on the charge of robbery, on the basis that the evidence to support the charge of conspiracy was extremely thin and that Field should only be tried for receiving.

The court adjourned and on its return the chairman of the bench announced that they rejected all the submissions. Submissions were then made by all the defence counsel for the case to be committed to the Central Criminal Court (the Old Bailey). The reason given by the defence was that such a relocation would be more convenient for all concerned: defendants, counsel, witnesses etc. The chairman rejected the submissions and committed the prisoners to stand trial at the Buckingham Winter Session of Assize at Aylesbury, which was scheduled to begin the following month.[9] Applications for bail were made on behalf of Brian Field by his counsel Ivor Richards and for Gordon Goody by Wilfred Fordham. The magistrates' bench, however, refused both applications.

Finally, solicitor Ellis Lincoln asked that the prisoners be sent to await trial at Brixton Prison, claiming that it would be more suitable for the prisoners and more convenient for the counsel. This application was also refused, probably on security grounds, the authorities preferring a location well away from London.

Following on the arrests of John Daly on 3 December and Roy James on 10 December 1963, both appeared before the magistrates at Linslade Magistrates' Court. They were then remanded in custody until 27 December, when they were further remanded until 31 December 1963. It was on New Year's Eve that the committal proceedings were held at a special sitting of the Linslade Magistrates at Leighton Buzzard. Part of the prosecution evidence was given and both prisoners were then remanded in custody for trial before the Buckinghamshire Assize Court.[10]

By the time of the 1964 Assize case, nine of the sixteen men believed to have taken part in the mail train robbery were in custody awaiting trial. A further three had already been publicly identified by the police and were on the run: Buster Edwards, Bruce Reynolds and Jimmy White. Four more remained publicly unidentified and still at large.

Looking back from today's perspective in terms of court procedure and the rules of evidence, the case presented by the Crown was an exceptionally thin and circumstantial one. Their argument was essentially that if it could be proven that an individual had been at Leatherslade Farm then they were, by implication, at Sears Crossing and Bridego Bridge too and hence guilty of conspiracy and robbery. Even on this flimsy hypothesis, the Crown was on thin ice, as the fingerprints of Ronald Biggs, John Daly, Jimmy Hussey, Roy James and Bob Welch were all on movable objects that could plausibly have been made before they were taken to the farm. Other evidence presented by the prosecution was even more dubious. While the judge raised the eyebrows of many trial observers by ruling as admissible a number of clear breaches of Judges' Rules of evidence, other breaches were so blatant that he had no option but to overrule them.

When the case opened on the cloudy, rainswept morning of 20 January 1964, all the prisoners appeared in the specially constructed spike-topped wooden dock at the Buckingham Winter Assizes, which was held in the Rural District Council Chambers, Aylesbury. The usual court building was far too small for such a major case, so it was decided to convert the Council Chamber instead. Each prisoner in turn was asked to enter a plea to the court in the respect to each charge against him. The following charges were laid against the following individuals:

1 For that they:
Roger John Cordrey
William Gerald Boal
Charles Frederick Wilson
Ronald Arthur Biggs
Roy John James
John Thomas Daly
Thomas William Wisbey
James Hussey
Leonard Dennis Field
Brian Arthur Field
Douglas Gordon Goody
John Denby Wheater
Robert Alfred Welch

On divers day unknown between the first day of May 1963 and the ninth day of August 1963 in the County of Buckinghamshire conspired together and with other persons unknown to stop a mail with intent to rob the said mail.
Against the peace of our Sovereign Lady the Queen, Her Crown and Dignity

2 For that they:
Roger John Cordrey
William Gerald Boal
Ronald Arthur Biggs
Roy John James
John Thomas Daly
Charles Frederick Wilson
Thomas William Wisbey
James Hussey
Leonard Dennis Field
Brian Arthur Field
Douglas Gordon Goody
Robert Alfred Welch

On the eighth day of August 1963, in the County of Buckinghamshire, being armed with offensive weapons or being together with other persons robbed Frank Dewhurst of 120 mailbags.
Contrary to Section 23(I) (a) of the Larceny Act 1916

3 For that he: William Gerald Boal

On a day unknown between the seventh and fifteenth days of August 1963 received £56,037 in money the property of the Postmaster-General knowing the same to have been stolen from and out of a mailbag and to have been sent by post.
Contrary to Section 54 of the Post Office Act 1953

4 And or that he:
On a day unknown between the seventh and fifteenth days of August, 1963, received £79,120 in money the property of the Postmaster-General knowing the same to be stolen from and out of a mailbag and to have been sent by post.

5 And for that he:
On a day unknown between the seventh and fifteenth days of August 1963 received £5,060 in money the property of the Postmaster-General knowing the same to be stolen from and out of a mailbag and to have been sent by post.
Contrary to Section 54 of the Post Office Act 1953

6 For that he: Roger John Cordrey

On a day unknown between the seventh and fifteenth days of August 1963 received £56,037 in money the property of the Postmaster-General knowing the same to have been stolen from and out of a mailbag and to have been sent by post.
Contrary to Section 54 of the Post Office Act 1953

7 And for that he:

On a day unknown between the seventh and fifteenth days of August, 1963, received £79,120 in money the property of the Postmaster-General knowing the same to be stolen from and out of a mailbag and to have been sent by post.
Contrary to Section 54 of the Post Office Act 1953

8 And for that he:

On a day unknown between the seventh and fifteenth days of August 1963 received £5,060 in money the property of the Postmaster-General knowing the same to be stolen from and out of a mailbag and to have been sent by post.
Contrary to Section 54 of the Post Office Act 1953

9 For that he: Brian Arthur Field

On a day unknown between the seventh and seventeenth days of August, 1963, received £100,900 in money the property of the Postmaster-General knowing the same to have been stolen from and out of a mailbag and to have been sent by post.
Contrary to Section 54 of the Post Office Act 1953

10 For that he: John Denby Wheater

Between the seventh day of August 1963 and the tenth day of September 1963 in the County of London well knowing that one Leonard Dennis Field had robbed Frank Dewhurst of 120 mailbags did comfort, harbour, assist and maintain the said Leonard Dennis Field.
Against the Peace of our Sovereign Lady the Queen, Her Crown and Dignity[11]

The public gallery (with seats for sixty people) was full, with disappointed queues filing down the street outside the council building. The press benches were equally full to capacity with correspondents from all over the world sitting alongside some of Fleet Street's most prominent reporters. An equally prestigious army of nearly forty counsel, including twelve QCs, and their juniors were positioned in the centre of the improvised court room. A full list of counsel can be found in Appendix 3.

At 10.27 a.m. on the dot, the accused rose to answer the charges made against them. With the exception of Roger Cordrey all pleaded not guilty. Cordrey pleaded guilty to count one, in which he was charged with conspiracy to stop the mail, and counts three, four and five in which he was charged with receiving various large sums of money. He pleaded not guilty to count two in which he was charged with robbery with aggravation. The pleas by Cordrey were accepted by the prosecution and he was put back in custody to await sentence.[12]

Arthur James QC, leading the prosecution team, opened the case for the Crown, which took just over ten hours, beginning with a description of the hold-up and proceeding to the alleged role of each of the accused in the plot.

On day three James produced the first of the prosecution's parade of 206 witnesses who would appear over the next thirteen days. Jack Mills, the engine driver, looking tired and strained, was allowed to give his evidence from a chair. Unable to identify any of the robbers from among the men sitting in the dock, his evidence was perfunctory and at times almost inaudible.

One of the most contentious parts of the prosecution case was that against Gordon Goody:

> On 28 January 1964 Detective Chief Inspector Peter Vibart was giving evidence regarding the questioning of Gordon Goody at Leicester when his Counsel, Mr Sebag Shaw QC told the Judge he had a submission to make which should be made in the absence of the jury. Justice Edmund Davies agreed and the jury retired. The submission was that at the time Detective Chief Inspector Vibart saw Goody at Leicester he was in custody and should have been cautioned under Rule 3 of Judges' Rules before being questioned and that any statements attributed to him after that time were contrary to the rules and inadmissible in evidence. After arguments Justice Edmund Davies decided not to admit the evidence. This meant that the whole of the statements attributed to Goody from the time he was first seen by Detective Chief Inspector Vibart at Leicester on 23 August 1963 until he was allowed to leave Aylesbury Police Station on 25 August 1963 were ruled inadmissible.[13]

The judge was also forced to issue a stiff reprimand to another police officer giving evidence against Goody. DSgt John Swain of the Flying Squad had related an account of a search he made at the home of Goody's mother when she was the only person in. Mr Sebag Shaw vigorously pressed Swain on what he suspected was a clear abuse of the law of search: 'You were told to search the house without a warrant?' Swain replied evasively and without conviction that, 'If Mrs Goody had said, "you can't come in" we would have got a search warrant.'

Sebag Shaw now had Swain on the ropes, as he knew full well that Swain had told Mrs Goody that he had in fact got a warrant on him. Forced to admit that he had said this, Swain attempted to mitigate himself by responding that, 'It was a mistake not a lie. I had other warrants to search other houses on me and I was told to go to Mrs Goody's home.'

Judge Edmund Davies immediately rebuked Swain – 'See that it never happens again.'

While this was a very small victory for Goody, both he and his counsel knew that the biggest challenge to the evidence against him was yet to come in relation to the claim by the prosecution that shoes belonging to him had paint on them that matched paint found at Leatherslade Farm. The Crown was additionally claiming that a little knob, found in a jacket belonging to Bill Boal, contained in the grooves traces of yellow paint, which according to Scotland Yard's Dr Ian Holden was more than likely the same paint as that on Goody's shoes.

However, before this could be contested, there were other submissions to be made concerning other alleged breaches of Judges' Rules of evidence:

> On the 31 January 1964, Detective Inspector Harry Tappin was giving evidence when Michael Argyle QC, Counsel for Leonard Field, asked to make a submission in the absence of the jury. Justice Edmund Davies agreed and the jury retired. The objection raised, was that evidence which was about to be given by Tappin of the questioning of Leonard Field by Detective Chief Superintendent Butler, was not in conformity with Judges' Rules because his client had been in custody and had not been cautioned. Justice Edmund Davies ruled that the oral evidence, up to the time Field was put into the detention room at Cannon Row Police Station, would be admitted in evidence. Justice Edmund Davies also ruled that the written statement taken from Field after he had been in the detention room should not at this stage be admitted.[14]

While this was the second submission that the judge agreed to, he was to inexplicably change course following the third submission:

> Lewis Hawser QC, Counsel for Brian Field then raised an objection to evidence which Detective Inspector Tappin would later be giving against Field. Hawser's objection was that an oral statement made by Field just before he was charged in which he denied the identity of Leonard Field as the potential buyer of Leatherslade Farm was inadmissible in evidence. After certain arguments had been made, Justice Edmund Davies decided to exercise his discretion and admit the evidence. The jury then returned and the trial continued.[15]

Perhaps the biggest error in terms of police evidence was to come on 6 February when DI Basil Morris, of the Surrey Constabulary, gave evidence regarding an interview he had with Ronald Biggs, when he asked whether or not Biggs knew any of the train robbery suspects. He gave Biggs's reply to one question as being:

> 'I knew Reynolds some years ago. I met him when we did time together.' At the conclusion of Morris's evidence he was cross examined by Wilfred Fordham who afterwards, in the absence of the jury, made an application to Justice Edmund Davies to discharge Biggs without a verdict from the jury. Justice Edmund Davies granted the application and on the return of the jury he told them that they would be relieved from considering the case of Biggs. Biggs then left the dock and the trial against the other accused continued.[16]

This was clearly an improper and prejudicial statement by Morris before the jury: that Biggs had served a prison sentence in the past. Judge Edmund Davies immediately realised that this would mean a re-trial for Biggs, which would, from his point of view, waste a large sum of public money.

Whether it was chagrin at Morris's error or the resultant burden upon the public purse that prompted Judge Edmund Davies to publicly castigate Morris can only be speculated on. However, he certainly did not mince his words:

> That the inspector, who, of necessity, must be a man of great experience in his duties, should have so far forgotten his duties as to bring in a phrase of that kind gratuitously is grossly improper and cannot be too strongly condemned.[17]

A further controversy occurred on 10 February 1964 when Lewis Hawser QC submitted to the judge that the questioning of Brian Field at New Scotland

Yard about the case, and the hotel bill found following his arrest at his home in Oxfordshire, was plainly a breach of Judges' Rules. Justice Edmund Davies then ruled that although he agreed that Judges' Rules No 3 had been broken, he was, nevertheless, going to exercise his discretion and allow the evidence to be heard by the jury.

John Mathew, counsel for Charles Wilson, also submitted that he objected to the questioning of Wilson by DCS Butler, without caution, on the grounds that Wilson was already in custody. Judge Edmund Davies then ruled that the whole of DCS Butler's evidence regarding Wilson until the moment he was formally charged and cautioned at Aylesbury Police Station was not to be put to the jury. The jury then returned to the court and the trial continued.

John Mathew then drew to the judge's attention the implication of his ruling and asked him, as a consequence, to rule that Wilson had no case to answer on either counts 1 or 2, the only ones concerning him in the indictment. He argued that the only evidence against Wilson was that three 'prints' of his were found at the farm. The evidence against him of his denial of ever visiting the farm had been ruled as inadmissible and therefore the Crown was put in the unenviable position of having to rely solely upon the evidence of the 'prints' at the farm with no explanation as to how or when they got there. He also submitted there could be four possibilities in terms of how the prints had got there, i.e. before the robbery (either innocently or in a guilty manner) or after the robbery (either innocently or in a guilty manner). He submitted that the evidence against Wilson was three to one against him being guilty on either count, and that it was the duty of the prosecution to prove which explanation was true – and they had failed to do so.

On 12 February Joseph Grieves QC submitted that Wisbey had no case to answer as there was no evidence to show the dates that the prints had been left at the farm and, as both the conspiracy and the robbery was complete by the morning of 8 August, if they had been left there after that date, even in a guilty manner, then Wisbey could not be guilty. He also asserted that Wisbey's denial of having visited the farm might have been an innocent mistake.

Mr Ashe Lincoln QC followed a similar argument on behalf of Robert Welch, but with the additional assertion that 'there was not one tittle of evidence' against his client on the second count of robbery.

Ronald Brown QC for James Hussey asked the judge to rule that there was insufficient evidence on either of the counts upon which Hussey was charged. He echoed the submissions already made by other counsel and particularly those put forward by Joseph Grieves QC. He reiterated some of the previous counsel arguments and added that Hussey's 'prints' were found on the lorry at the farm, which had not been proved to have been used in the robbery.

Walter Raeburn QC, counsel for John Daly, also asked Justice Edmund Davies to rule that there was no evidence that amounted to proof on either of the counts upon which Daly was charged. This contention was, according to Raeburn, 'disarmingly simple' in that the evidence against Daly fell into two categories: 'the finding of his fingerprints on a set of Monopoly and the other is that he went underground when the hue and cry had been raised'. Raeburn dismissed the first, asserting:

> … there is only a tenuous connection in that the fingerprints are found not on anything remotely connected with the crime, but upon a toy which was introduced into the farm; nobody knows by whom, nobody knows to whom it belonged and it is not at all a matter of inference that the fingerprints came upon the particular parts of that toy at any time subsequent to its having come to the farm. The rest of the evidence is at the highest, mere suspicion. It is consistent with a man who realises that people with whom he has associated are being sort [sic] by the police and while no doubt, being wise after the event, one can see that it would have been very much better in such circumstances for him to have voluntarily assisted the police in their enquiries, that is a very long way from saying that it amounts to any sort of proof that he was a party to a conspiracy.[18]

Roy James's counsel, William Howard, also echoed the same argument, to which he added that the Crown had not proved that the money found in James's possession was stolen or produced evidence to show that it was the result of the conversion of stolen money. The Crown was in a slight predicament on this point, as only two £5 notes out of the £12,130 found on James at the time of his arrest were among the small minority of notes of which the serial numbers had been recorded by the respective banks. To admit in court that most of the money was untraceable would not only have been somewhat embarrassing but would have potentially made life easier for those still on the run by revealing there was little need to launder their money.[19]

Mr Sebag Shaw QC, for Gordon Goody, asserted that there was no case for Goody to answer on counts 1 and 2, the only ones concerning him. He argued that so far as the khaki paint found on Goody's shoes was concerned it did not connect him physically with Leatherslade Farm, but only with a Land Rover found there after the robbery. The yellow paint did not therefore necessarily connect Goody physically with the farm. He then drew the judge's attention to the evidence of Charles Alexander, who asserted that Goody's shoes had been at his public house from the end of July 1963 until 9 August 1963 and that Goody had no access to them during that time. Alexander also said that he had moved them from one room to another during that period and he had seen that they were free from any paint marks of any kind. In those circumstances, he added, the worst that could be said against Goody was that sometime after the robbery his shoes had become contaminated with two types of paints. On this argument alone he submitted that there was no evidence against Goody.[20]

Lewis Hawser QC, Brian Field's counsel, sought to argue that there was not sufficient evidence on which the jury could safely convict on the charge of receiving because the Crown had not established sufficiently that Field was in possession of £100,900, or indeed any of the money found in the bags in the Dorking Woods. The fact that two of Field's bags were found in Dorking Woods eight days after the robbery was itself, in Hawser's view, insufficient evidence of Field having been in possession of the bags at the time the money was in them – and when they were dumped there by somebody.

On 14 February 1964 Justice Edmund Davies was to give his judgements on all the submissions. The submissions were made on sound legal grounds and, on past precedent, no one in court that day expected anything other than an across the board rejection by the judge. As Edmund Davies dismissed each submission in turn, there was audible shock throughout the court when he arrived at the one made in respect to John Daly:

> I propose to uphold the submission in relation to Mr Daly in respect to both counts, and when the jury returns they will be directed to acquit him.[21]

No one in court appeared more startled or shocked than Daly himself, who immediately left the dock with a one man police escort. Outside the court he told waiting journalists:

> I was innocent from the start … now that I have been acquitted I hope they will take down all those 'Wanted' posters with my photograph on them. I don't want to get arrested again.[22]

Why was John Daly's the only submission accepted? In many ways, his circumstances were little different from those of Welch, Hussey, James and Biggs. Indeed, Hussey's palm print on the tailboard of the truck was arguably a more persuasive submission. Was it the eloquence of Walter Raeburn that convinced the judge or was Daly just plain lucky?

12

CASE FOR THE DEFENCE

John Daly's acquittal was apparently 'a great blow to the Police and to everyone connected with the prosecution – especially to those who were aware of the true position'.[1]

The report, written by IB assistant controller R.F. Yates, goes on to say that:

> It was felt that Daly's case should have been allowed to go forward to the jury for consideration of a verdict. It is of interest to note that after his acquittal, a celebration party was arranged for Daly by Mrs Mary Manson and that criminal associates of both Daly and Manson were present.

Immediately on news of Daly's acquittal, Bill Goodwin and Michael Black went to Endelstowe, the house in Cornwall:

> They dug up the cash containers, took them into the house and split the cash content two ways. Half was put into a suitcase and carried off by Black. The remaining cash was counted and amounted to just on £50,000. This was placed into a large briefcase and hidden in the aperture of an old boiler in the kitchen, and the hole cemented in and painted to cover traces of new work.[2]

Following the party, Daly and his friend Billy Still drove down to Cornwall at top speed to retrieve the £100,000 that had been buried in the back garden of Bill Goodwin's house near Boscastle. One can imagine how the elation of Daly's acquittal immediately turned to shock and disbelief when on arrival he was told by Goodwin's niece, Kathleen Sleep, that shortly after his arrest in December, Michael Black had double-crossed him, dug up the money and disappeared.

Black apparently went abroad but returned due to ill health and died in London of a heart attack.

According to police reports: 'Daly apparently accepted Miss Sleep's story that Michael Black had collected all of it [the money] following his arrest. The local police knew that Daly and Still were in the area because their car was stopped for a traffic infringement but they were allowed to proceed.' The IB was told by Scotland Yard that: 'Chief Superintendent Butler is of the opinion that Daly is not aware of Black's death and is still looking for him.'[3]

Back in Aylesbury, the proceedings were now in their twentieth day and the case for the defence was about to begin. The defendants were cautiously optimistic, as were their counsel. Each of them had a well thought out, logical explanation as to why their fingerprints were found at Leatherslade Farm. Had their cases been held separately and in London, some of these defences may well have been viewed as plausible and resulted in not-guilty verdicts. However, put together, they seemed less believable. In the same way that the sum of the prosecution case was greater than its constituent parts, the defence case was the opposite and, in retrospect, suffered for this disadvantage.

In the witness box Bill Boal told the court that he had been beaten up on arrest and denied a number of statements that police alleged he had made, such as, 'fair enough, it [the money found in his possession] came from the train job'. He also made clear that he didn't know Leatherslade Farm and had never been there. Neither had he been '... anywhere near the train spot. And if you were to offer me my freedom now, I wouldn't be able to find my way there.' He claimed he was a dupe of Cordrey who owed him money and that remaining with Cordrey was the best way of ensuring that he got his money back. His story, while uniquely true, lacked corroboration. There appears to have been some consideration given by his counsel to calling Cordrey as a witness to back up Boal's account. However, it was considered in retrospect that this might do more harm than good; they clearly feared that Arthur James QC would respond by asking Cordrey, who then was guilty, why Boal was not. Cordrey could only respond to this by refusing to answer, which would inevitably lose him the credit he had built up by pleading guilty. Boal was therefore caught between a rock and a hard place.

Welch, Hussey and Wisbey had banded together to concoct a joint defence. According to Hussey's statement on 10 August, a friend known as 'Dark Ronnie' wanted help in delivering some groceries. When 'Dark Ronnie' arrived at Hussey's flat, Wisbey and Welch arrived about the same time to see if Hussey wanted to go for a drink:

> Hussey said a friend of his, a Mr Dark, had to take a lorry to somewhere in Oxford and whilst they were discussing as to how he would get back, Hussey, innocently put his hand on the tailboard. At that time, which was lunch time on Saturday 10 August 1963, Welch, who was in his own car and accompanied by Wisbey arrived on the scene. Hussey asked Welch if he would follow Dark in the lorry to where he had to deliver it, and then bring him back. Welch agreed and Wisbey went along for the ride. Hussey himself remained at home in London.
>
> Welch accompanied by Wisbey, then followed Dark into Oxfordshire where they met a Land Rover and the three vehicles continued on to a house in the country which both Welch and Wisbey later identified as Leatherslade Farm. Upon arrival they unloaded the lorry which contained vegetables etc., and the driver of the Land Rover took them into the house where Wisbey washed his hands and innocently left his palm impression on the bath rail. Welch was offered a drink from 'Pipkin' can of beer but he refused. He did, however, take hold of the can out of curiosity and examined it and thus his palm impressions, quite innocently, remained upon it. Dark attended Court the following day and gave evidence for Welch, Wisbey and Hussey.[4]

While Dark fully corroborated this story in the witness box, he did not perform well under cross-examination and was not the type of witness to impress a jury.

On 19 February 1964, the defence of Roy James commenced. One of the witnesses called was Derek Brown, who swore under oath that at 10.30 p.m. on 7 August he had picked up James from his flat at Nell Gwyn House in Chelsea and taken him to the Bagatelle Club. He also claimed to have picked up James from the club at 2.30 a.m. and taken him back to his flat where the two stayed up talking and drinking tea until 4 a.m. He went on to say that he visited James on seven occasions at Aylesbury Prison but that he had not discussed the case with him because of the presence of two warders at each visit. Like Ronnie Dark, Brown did not go down well in the witness box when cross-examined by Niall MacDermot QC for the prosecution. Brown admitted that he was a cab driver employed by the same company as a man who was an associate of James. He also admitted that he paid not seven visits to James in prison but seventeen. James, however, offered no explanation for how his fingerprints came to be on a cat dish, a first aid kit and a tin of salt.[5]

While it was not disclosed at the time, the DPP had a witness statement from one Arthur Eeles, who had previously made a statement about seeing the lorry used in the robbery on 8 August. According to Eeles, at around 2 p.m.

he was driving between Ashendon and Brill when he saw a Vauxhall motor car and a green six-wheel lorry facing each other in the middle of the road. He saw two men and a woman standing by the vehicle. One of the men got into the lorry and the woman got into the car. The second man walked across the field towards Dorton. On 11 September, after photographs of the wanted men had been published in the press, he approached the police and gave the following statement:

> I would like to say that I have seen several photographs in the daily newspapers of Roy John James. There is definitely no doubt in my mind that he was one of the two men I saw with the lorry in Westcott Brill Road, on 8 August 1963; in fact he was the man [who] walked away across the fields. I am prepared to give evidence if necessary.[6]

The DPP, being satisfied that James's fingerprints constituted a sufficiently strong case on their own to establish his guilt, decided not to use Eeles's statement as evidence.

On 20 February Mr Sebag Shaw QC presented the defence case for Gordon Goody. His contention that Goody was in Ireland smuggling watches was very much a compromise defence following the downfall of Goody's Irish alibi. It also involved admitting to dishonesty, which in turn allowed the prosecution to imply that Goody had been fortunate to avoid prosecution for the London Airport robbery the previous year. The following day Goody, who was immaculately dressed and wearing a Royal Artillery tie, was recalled to the witness box. He was cross-examined about the shoes that had been taken by police from The Windmill public house and the evidence given by landlord Charles Alexander. Justice Edmund Davies interjected during the cross-examination:

> One of the ugliest issues in this case is the assertion by Mr Alexander that on 23 August 1963, when Dr Holden came, there were no marks on the shoes. Therefore, the suggestion is implicit that after the shoes were collected somebody had applied khaki paint and somebody had applied yellow paint to those shoes after they got into the hands of the police. There is no bucking that issue. The defence are not as I gather withdrawing any suggestion which the jury might like to draw from that evidence of Mr Alexander.[7]

Mr Sebag Shaw QC, defending Goody, agreed that the judge had represented the position accurately. After the prosecution's cross-examination, he re-examined Goody at some length, and one of the questions he asked was if he had any idea of how the paint came to be on the shoes. Goody replied that he had no idea. Sebag Shaw then called Raymond Brown, of Lessor & Co., Goody's solicitor, to the witness box. Brown confirmed that on Goody's arrest DCS Butler had refused to allow Goody to try on the suede shoes and that he had not disclosed that there was any paint on them. Sebag Shaw then gave notice that expert evidence regarding the paint would be presented to the court on a later date.

On 6 March 1964, the expert evidence on behalf of Goody was presented to the court. Cecil Robbins BSc FRIC, a director of Hehner & Cox Ltd, took the stand to confirm that his company was an established firm of analytical chemists. He summarised his evidence by saying that the paint on the Land Rover and the paint on the shoes were two different paints. The defence then called Douglas Nicholas of the Fulmer Research Institute. He also took the view that there were differences in the compositions of the paint on the shoes and that taken from the Land Rover.

Arthur James QC for the prosecution then asked for permission to call Dr Holden to give evidence of rebuttal. Holden reiterated his previous conclusions made in his statement of 24 October 1963, in which he asserted that the khaki paints came from the same source and that the yellow paints could also have come from the same source. These expert testimonies can be seen in Appendix 4.

On 24 February the defence for Brian Field commenced:

> Field's QC, Lewis Hawser, agreed that two of the four bags found at Dorking Woods, containing £100,900 of stolen money were his but that he did not put the bags there and had indeed lost them sometime before. He admitted that he had lied to Detective Chief Superintendent Butler when he said it was not Leonard Field who went to the farm with him. Another witness, Brenda Field,[8] a secretary at TW James and Wheater, gave evidence to show that he had left the two bags in the office at 3 New Quebec Street, W1 and that he discovered them to be missing from that office before the robbery. The remainder of the evidence was an attempt to prove an alibi.[9]

On 28 February the defence for Leonard Field began, led by Michael Argyle QC. Unlike previous defences, Argyle chose not to make an opening address but immediately called Field into the witness box, where he remained for most of the day:

> He immediately told the Court that in certain matters he had lied and that in fact he learnt from Brian Field on 9 August 1963 that Leatherslade Farm had been used by the robbers. He said that on that date Brian Field told him that the farm had been bought in his [Leonard Field's] name, that it had been used by the robbers and that he [Leonard Field] would get a considerable sum of money if he would just stay away from the office. Brian Field added that Wheater and he would take care of everything and see that he [Leonard Field] was not involved. When he heard Wheater and Brian Field deny his identity he was satisfied that they were keeping to their agreement not to disclose he was the person who bought the farm. He continued by saying that he had not bought the farm, knew nothing of the conspiracy or the robbery and that his only error was in refusing to disclose to police the true position, and that he had entered an agreement with Wheater and Field not to disclose the information.[10]

According to Leonard Field, Brian Field had told him that he would get £5,000 if he kept his mouth shut about his involvement in the Leatherslade purchase, but as it turned out he was never in fact paid a penny:

> I knew I wasn't doing this for nothing, and that something would be involved. I asked him [Brian Field] there and then what would happen if anything came about the police. I was assured that I couldn't be implicated. I was told to stay away from the office and that Mr Wheater would take care of everything.[11]

Brian Field, brought back to the witness box by his QC, denied every word of Field's new story.

On 3 March 1964 the defence of John Wheater commenced. Mr G.R. Swanwick QC did not address the court himself but called witnesses to testify to Wheater's good character. These included Paul Bryan MC, vice-chairman of the Conservative Party and MP for Howden. Bryan had been Wheater's commanding officer in Italy during the Second World War. Wheater was, Bryan told the court, 'certainly brave, certainly loyal, and liked by the men. His honour and integrity could not be questioned.' Brigadier Geoffrey Barratt, another of Wheater's wartime superiors, told the court that he was 'a real fighting soldier'.[12]

When it became time for Wheater to again go into battle, this time to fight for his innocence, he was the picture of composure and confidence. He told the court that the first time he had heard about the Leatherslade Farm purchase was when Brian Field had brought Lenny Field into his office:

> Brian Field said Leonard Field wished to purchase the property and asked if I would deal with it. Leonard Field produced particulars of the sale. He merely said he was interested in buying the property and that he wanted to try to get it for less than the advertised price. He said he wanted it as quickly as possible.[13]

Wheater's case to the court was succinctly cued up by his QC, who asked him, 'Do you feel that you are a person who is by nature particularly cut out to be a solicitor or not?' Wheater replied, 'I decided some time ago that I was not, and I feel that a lot of our clients have suffered through my carelessness.' By the time Wheater finished his evidence on 6 March, his stance of integrity, naivety and an inability to realise what was going on under his nose had been very succinctly put across to the jury.[14]

Probably the most damning piece of evidence presented to counter the defence of Wisbey, Welch and Hussey was that of the farmer John Maris, who was called back to the witness box by Arthur James QC:

> He was milking in the cow sheds at the bottom of the lane leading to Leatherslade Farm from 3.15 pm to 5 pm on Saturday 10 August 1963 and that if a convoy of vehicles as suggested by the accused Wisbey and Welch, and the defence witness Darke, had entered the lane he would have heard them and been so interested as to have looked through the window of the cowshed and seen them. He did not hear or see such a convoy.[15]

Three days later on 9 March, the evidence of both the prosecution and the defence came to an end on what was the thirty-sixth day of the trial. Arthur James QC then outlined the points he would put to the jury and announced that the Crown would now drop the charge against Brian Field of aggravated robbery.

With all the closing addresses to the jury having been completed, the court was adjourned until 17 March 1964, when Justice Edmund Davies delivered his summing up. This lasted until Monday 23 March and was over a quarter of a million words long. The jury then retired. On the third day of their deliberations, after sixty-six hours of confinement – the longest in British legal history – they finally reached verdicts on all the charges and returned to court at 10.30 a.m. on Thursday 26 March.

'Are you agreed on your verdicts?' asked Judge Edmund Davies.

'We are,' replied the foreman of the jury. The foreman then proceeded to tell the clerk to the court that the jury found all the remaining defendants guilty as charged, apart from Brian Field who, although found guilty of conspiracy to rob and obstructing the course of justice, was found not guilty of aggravated robbery or of receiving £100,900. John Wheater was found not guilty of conspiracy to rob.

Judge Edmund Davies told the court that the sentencing would be held over until the remaining trial of Ronald Biggs had been held.[16]

On Wednesday 8 April 1964 the retrial of Ronald Biggs commenced at the Buckinghamshire Assizes, held this time at the Crown Court at Aylesbury, and not at the RDC building. Before Judge Edmund Davies sat a new jury of twelve, alongside the two legal teams from the previous case (see Appendix 3).

On 9 April 1964 DCI Frank Williams, New Scotland Yard, commenced his evidence. Michael Argyle QC immediately asked Justice Edmund Davies for the jury to be withdrawn to enable him to make a submission. This was granted and Argyle made his submission that:

> ... once Biggs had been taken from his home by Detective Inspector Williams he was in custody and he should have been cautioned. Anything he said after that to a police officer in reply to questions was inadmissible in evidence being contrary to Judges' Rules.[17]

Argyle then asserted that certain police statements put before the court were either 'mistaken or false'.[18] DCI Williams and DCS Butler were then called to the witness box and were cross-examined by Argyle, who put this charge to them directly. Both officers denied this. The prosecution then called DS Moore (who had been present when Williams arrested Biggs and at the interview conducted by Butler) to the witness box. Moore supported the answers and statements given by Williams and Butler. Michael Argyle QC then called upon Biggs to give his account.

Despite rulings to the contrary in the cases of Charles Wilson and Gordon Goody, Judge Edmund Davies declared that whilst he ruled that part of the evidence given by police was contrary to Judges' Rules, he would, in fact, use his discretion to admit it. This was not only a setback to Biggs's case but flew in the face of established judicial protocol.

The prosecution relied to a very large extent on the answers Biggs allegedly gave when interviewed by DCS Butler at Scotland Yard, and on the comments he supposedly made to DCI Frank Williams when arrested. Williams's statement dated 6 September 1963 claims that when he arrested Biggs at his home on 4 September and told him he would be taken to Scotland Yard for further questioning 'in connection with the train robbery in Buckinghamshire recently', Biggs had replied, 'that don't sound too good. What are my chances of creeping out of this?'[19]

According to the interview statement signed by Butler on the same day (6 September), he had asked Biggs on the evening of his arrest if he knew Leatherslade Farm, to which Biggs had allegedly replied, 'No, never heard of it. I've got no interest in fucking farms.' According to Biggs, he had in fact replied, 'I think everybody in the country must know it. It's been on television, on the radio and in all the newspapers for weeks.' When the statement was written up Biggs had refused to sign it on the grounds of these inaccuracies.[20]

Before the opening of the original trial in January 1964, Butler had deleted the word 'fucking' from the statement, but the rest of the account he had written up of his interview with Biggs on 4 September stood. This evidence was clearly highly prejudicial to Biggs's case when put to the jury by the prosecution, who finally completed their case at 4 p.m. on 10 April.

Michael Argyle QC then made an opening speech for the defence and declared that Biggs's evidence would be that he went to Leatherslade Farm with a man named Norman Bickers, to caretake the premises in connection with an unlawful purpose that was unknown to them both. They arrived there at about 1.30 p.m. on 6 August 1963 and stayed until 8 a.m. on 7 August 1963. During this time, they prepared and ate meals from foodstuffs stored at the farm, thus accounting for the fingerprints of Biggs on the Heinz tomato ketchup bottle and a Pyrex plate. He also said that Biggs had handled the Monopoly set, which would account for his fingerprints on that.

With regard to the fingerprint evidence, the prosecution had contended throughout the main trial – of all seven defendants on whom fingerprint evidence had been put before the court – that when the Rixon family had moved out of Leatherslade Farm, they had entirely removed all of their possessions. Therefore, the objects on which fingerprints were found were either immovable (such as the window sill or bathroom rail) or had been brought to the farm by the defendants themselves. This meant that none of them could argue that they had been at the farm prior to the robbery and had inadvertently handled or touched an object that had been left at the farm by the Rixons. Indeed, a police statement had been secured from Hilda Rixon who stated:

> This summer we all moved from Leatherslade Farm to where we are living now. My son moved a month before me and my husband. We moved on Monday 28 July or 29 July. When my son moved he moved just a few things

> that he really needed. When the final move took place my son came up to help. The furniture was moved. We took the curtains down. Everything was cleared out because I looked everywhere.[21]

DS Ray had taken fingerprint samples from all members of the Rixon family for elimination purposes. Not long after he and his team had begun work they discovered a Kilner jar with Pauline Rixon's fingerprints on. Because of this, all members of the Rixon family were asked to report back to Aylesbury Police Station, where they were all closely questioned again about the possibility that they had, after all, left some objects behind at the farm when they moved out.

As a result of this, Hilda Rixon recanted and made the following statement: 'I had a Pyrex plate with a blue border which I used to feed the cat. I think I left it behind because when I got to Dunsden,[22] and unpacked I found I was one short with a blue border.'[23]

Furthermore, it soon became apparent that the ketchup bottle was probably not brought to the farm by the robbers either. In a report from DS McArthur to DCS Butler on 11 September 1963, he stated that:

> ... impressions found by Detective Superintendent Ray on a blue edged pyrex plate and a bottle of ketchup at the farmhouse can be identified as those of Biggs. The pyrex plate is undoubtedly one left behind at the farm by Hilda Hannah Rixon. The bottle of ketchup may be one left behind by Lily Elise Rixon.[24]

McArthur continued:

> Detective Superintendent Ray is forwarding details of the evidence he has in his possession by hand to the Director of Public Prosecutions, and for that reason, at present, his statement and that of his colleague from the Photography Section are not attached to these papers.[25]

This report about the fact that the Rixons had, after all, left a number of items at the farm (including two on which Biggs's fingerprints were found) does not appear to have been disclosed to Biggs's defence. Had such a disclosure been made, it would no doubt have been a key part of Michael Argyle's defence, and may well have been relevant to other defendants whose prints were also found on these two objects.

Michael Argyle then continued with his defence, submitting that both Bickers and Biggs examined the contents of the farm and Biggs saw a large amount of army uniforms stored in one room. Biggs had commented to

Bickers that if the unlawful purpose was to be a raid on an army depot he could 'count him out'. Bickers agreed but said that he had to meet someone in Oxford when he could find out more details. At 8.30 a.m. on 7 August 1963 they left the farm and went to Oxford. Bickers left Biggs to keep the 'meet' and afterwards rejoined him. He then told Biggs that he had 'counted both of them out' because the farm was to be used to stop a mail train. Biggs agreed that it was madness and said he was going home. Bickers insisted that Biggs stayed with him to prevent Biggs from communicating with anyone, adding that if anything went wrong on the raid the robbers would put the responsibility for it at their feet. Argyle concluded his speech by saying that whilst Biggs went to Leatherslade Farm originally with the idea of committing an unlawful act, when he found out it was to be robbery of a mail train he immediately withdrew from it and was not guilty of either the conspiracy or the robbery with aggravation. At 10.30 a.m. on Monday 13 April 1964 Biggs was called into the witness box and cross-examined by Arthur James QC. Biggs admitted he had lied to his wife, to a witness called for the prosecution and to the police. He agreed that he lied if he considered it expedient.[26]

On 14 April Judge Edmund Davies commenced his summing up, which lasted for the remainder of the day and part of the following morning, after which the jury then retired. It took them but ninety minutes to reach a guilty verdict on both the charges against Biggs.

At 10.30 a.m. on 16 April 1964 the court was reconvened and Judge Edmund Davies passed sentence on all prisoners one by one:

> ROGER CORDREY
>
> Roger John Cordrey, you are the first to be sentenced out of certainly eleven greedy men whom hope of gain allured. You and your co-accused have been convicted of complicity, in one way or another, of a crime which in its impudence and enormity is the first of its kind in this country. I propose to do all within my power to ensure it will also be the last of its kind; outrageous conduct constitutes an intolerable menace to the wellbeing of society.
>
> Let us clear out of the way any romantic notions of dare-devilry. This is nothing less than a sordid crime of violence inspired by vast greed. The motive of greed is obvious. As to violence, anybody who has seen that nerve-shattered engine driver can have no doubt of the terrifying effect on law-abiding citizens of a concerted assault by masked and armed robbers in lonely darkness. To deal with this case leniently would be a positively evil thing. When grave crime is committed it calls for grave punishment, not for the purpose of mere retribution but so that others similarly tempted shall be brought to the sharp realisation that

crime does not pay and that the crime is most certainly not worth even the most alluring candle. As the higher the price the greater the temptation, potential criminals who may be dazzled by the enormity of the price must be taught that the punishment they risk will be proportionately greater.

I therefore find myself faced with the unenviable duty of pronouncing grave sentences. You, Cordrey, and the other accused vary widely in intelligence, strength of personality, in antecedent history, in age and in many other ways. Some convicted on this indictment have absolutely clean characters up to the present. Some have previous convictions of a comparatively minor character and others have previous convictions of gravity which could now lead to sentences of corrective training or even of preventive detention.

To some the degradation to which you have all now sunk will bring consequences vastly more cruel than to the other. I have anxiously sought to bear in mind everything that has been urged on behalf of all the accused by your learned Counsel, to whom I am so greatly indebted, but whatever the past of a particular accused and whatever his position, all else pales into insignificance in the light of his present offences. Furthermore, the evidence, or rather the lack of it, renders it impossible to determine exactly what part was played by each of the eleven accused convicted of the larger conspiracy or the eight convicted of the actual robbery. I therefore propose, after mature deliberation, to treat you all in the same manner with but two exceptions.

You, Cordrey, are the first of the exceptions. On your own confession you stand convicted on the first count of conspiracy to rob the mail and on counts 3, 4 and 5 of receiving in all nearly £141,000 of the stolen money, but when arrested you immediately gave information to the police which enabled them to put their hands on nearly £80,000 and the remainder was eventually recovered. Furthermore, at the outset of this trial you confessed your guilt and I feel I should give recognition to that fact in determining your sentence. I do this because it is greatly in the public interest that the guilty should confess their guilt. This massive trial is the best demonstration of the truth of that proposition. In respect of the four counts you must go to prison for concurrent terms of 20 years.

WILLIAM BOAL

William Gerald Boal, you, who are substantially the oldest of the accused, have been convicted of conspiracy to rob the mail and of armed robbery itself. You have expressed no repentance for your wrong-doing, indeed, you continue to assert your innocence but you beg for mercy. I propose to extend to you some measure of mercy and I do it on two grounds. Firstly, on account of your age, you being a man of 50 and, secondly, because, having seen and heard you, I cannot believe that you were one of the originators of the conspiracy or that you played a very dynamic part in it or in the robbery itself. Detective Superintendent Fewtrell has confirmed me in that view of you which I had already formed, but your participation in any degree nevertheless remains a matter of extreme gravity. In the light of these considerations the concurrent sentences you will serve are, upon the first count, 21 years and upon the second count 24 years.

CHARLES WILSON

Charles Frederick Wilson, you have been convicted of conspiracy to rob the mail and of armed robbery. No one has said less than you throughout this long trial. Indeed, I doubt if you have spoken half a dozen words. Certainly no word of repentance has been expressed by you. I bear in mind those matters which your learned Counsel has urged upon your behalf, but my duty, as I conceive it, is clear. If you or any of the order accused still to be dealt with had assisted justice that would have told strongly in your favour, but you have not. The consequences of this outrageous crime is that the vast booty of something like £2½ million still remains almost entirely unrecovered. It would be an affront to the public weal that any of you should be at liberty in anything like the near future to enjoy any of those ill-gotten gains.

Accordingly, it is no spirit of mere retribution that I propose to secure that such an opportunity will be denied all of you for an extremely long time. Nevertheless, the plea of Mr Wilfred Fordham for a gleam of light at the end of the long dark tunnel to be left for his client, is a plea I intend to heed in respect of all of you. On the first count you will go to prison for 25 years and on the second count you will be sentenced to a concurrent term of 30 years.

RONALD BIGGS

Ronald Arthur Biggs, yesterday you were convicted of both the first and second counts of this indictment. Your learned Counsel has urged that you had no special talent and you were plainly not an originator of the conspiracy. Those and all other submissions I bear in mind, but the truth is that I do not know when you entered the conspiracy or what part you played. What I do know is that you are a specious and facile liar and you have this week, in this court, perjured yourself time and again, but I add not a day to your sentence on that account. Your previous record qualifies you to be sentenced to preventive detention; that I shall not do. Instead, the sentence of the court upon you in respect of the first count is one of 25 years' imprisonment and in respect of the second count, 30 years' imprisonment. Those sentences to be served concurrently.

THOMAS WISBEY

Thomas William Wisbey, you stand convicted on the first and second counts. Your previous record qualifies you for corrective training but any such sentence is plainly out of the question in the present circumstances. In your case again I have no evidence upon which I can measure the degree or quality of your participation in the vast criminal enterprise which has given rise to this trial. Your learned Counsel has urged that you are plainly not a dominant character and that the part you played was subsidiary and was perhaps connected with transport matters. You yourself have thrown no light upon that or upon any other topic and you have not sought to mollify the court by any admission of repentance. The sentences upon you are concurrent sentences. In respect of the first count, 25 years' imprisonment and in respect of the second count, 30 years' imprisonment.

ROBERT WELCH

Robert Alfred Welch, you have been convicted on the first and second counts of this indictment. Your Counsel has urged upon me that there is no evidence of any sudden flowing of money into your pockets or as to when you joined the conspiracy or what you actually did. These and all matters urged in mitigation and your antecedents, I have sought faithfully to bear in mind. The sentence of the court upon you is that on the first count you go to prison for 25 years and upon the second count you go to prison for 30 years. Those sentences will be concurrent.

JAMES HUSSEY

James Hussey, you have been convicted on the first and second counts of this indictment. You have previous convictions of gravity, including two involving substantial violence. On the other hand, I accept that as a son you are warm-hearted and it is obvious you have qualities of personality and intelligence which you might have put to very good stead. I balance these and all other matters to the best of my ability and having done so the concurrent sentences that you will serve are, on the first count, 25 years' imprisonment and on the second count, 30 years.

ROY JAMES

Roy John James, you have been convicted on both the first and second counts. You are the only one out of the accused in respect of whom it has been proved that you actually received a substantial part of the stolen moneys. On your arrest you still had in your possession over £12,000 which I have no doubt was the result of exchange out of the original stolen moneys received by you. I entertain no doubt that the original sum you received substantially exceeded that figure. Your record in the past is a bad one and corrective training seems to have done you little or no good. Yet you have ability of a kind which would have assured you an honest livelihood of substantial proportion; for in a very short space of time you had, as your learned Counsel has said, brilliant and meteoric success as a racing driver. I strongly suspect that it was your known talent as a driver which enabled you to play an important part in the perpetration of this grave crime. It may be, as you say, that you personally have never resorted to physical violence, but you nevertheless stand convicted of participating with others in armed robbery and for that you must be sentenced. You have told me that you went to Leatherslade Farm knowing you were doing wrong, that you became involved, but not in the robbery, and then ran away. I do not find it possible to differentiate your case from that of most of the other accused. You will accordingly go to prison for concurrent terms of 25 years on the first count and 30 years on the second count.

GORDON GOODY

Douglas Gordon Goody, you have been convicted on the first and second counts of this indictment. You have a bad record, notably with a conviction for grave violence at the early age of 18, and you qualify for preventive detention. Yet, in some respects, you present to this Court one of the saddest problems by which it is confronted in the trial. You have manifest gifts of personality and intelligence which might have carried you far had they been directed to honesty. I have not seen you in Court for the best part of three months without noticing signs that you are a man capable of inspiring the admiration of your fellow accused. In the Army you earned a very good character assessment and it is easy to imagine you becoming, in an entirely honourable role, a leader of your comrades, but you have become a dangerous menace to society.

The Crown have said that they do not consider this criminal enterprise was the product of any criminal master-mind. I do not know that I necessarily agree with the Crown in this respect. I strongly suspect that you played a major role, both in the conspiracy and in the actual robbery. Suspicion, however, is not good enough for me any more than it would be for a jury. It would be, therefore, quite wrong for me to cause my suspicions to lead to imposing upon you any heavier sentence than upon other accused and I shall not do so. You will go to prison for concurrent terms of 25 years on the first count and 30 years on the second.

BRIAN FIELD

Brian Arthur Field, you have been convicted upon count one and count twelve of conspiracy to rob the mail and conspiracy to obstruct the course of justice. Of the righteousness of both verdicts I personally entertain no doubt whatsoever. You had earned an excellent reputation beginning with little original advantages. By a combination of native ability of no mean kind and hard work you had attained a responsible position of a solicitor's managing clerk. Your strength of personality and superior intelligence enabled you, I strongly suspect, to attain a position of dominance in relation to your employer, John Wheater. I entertain no serious doubt that you are in some measure responsible for the disastrous position in which that wretched man now finds himself, but it is for your own misdeeds and for them alone, that you now have to be sentenced. They are serious enough in all conscience. You are one of the very few convicted persons in this trial of whom it can be said with any degree of certainty what it was that you were able to contribute to the furtherance of criminal ends. Whether it was in your mind or that of Leonard Field or that of some other entirely different person that there originated the idea of acquiring possession of Leatherslade Farm by subterfuge by saying it was wanted for purely honest purposes, I have no satisfactory means of knowing. Whether it was simply a remarkable coincidence that two out of the four bags found in Dorking Woods containing over £100,000 were your property or whether the fact is an indication of your further complicity in the main conspiracy again I have no means of knowing, though naturally I loyally give effect to your vindication by the jury on both the robbery and the receiving charges.

But that you played an essential role in the major conspiracy is clear. Out of that there naturally flowed the later conspiracy to obstruct justice. I have borne in mind your antecedents, as spoken by the police, the contents of the probation officer's report and all those matters urged upon me by your learned Counsel. You express regret for the position in which you now find yourself and that is understandable. The concurrent sentences of the Court upon you are that on the first count you will go to prison for 25 years and on the twelfth count you will go to prison for 5 years.

LEONARD FIELD

Leonard Dennis Field, you have been convicted on the first and twelfth counts in this indictment. Although you have but one previous conviction, which I ignore, you are a dangerous man. Not only have you perjured yourself repeatedly in this trial to save your own skin but on your own showing at one stage you perjured yourself in an endeavour to ruin the accused, Brian Field. I sentence you not for perjury, but I sentence you solely for conspiracy. How and when you entered the major conspiracy I do not know. Whether you joined it at the instigation of another again I do not know, but an overt act committed by you in pursuance of that conspiracy is established beyond doubt and very important it was.

I cannot agree with your learned Counsel that your part in acquiring possession of Leatherslade Farm may properly be described as a small contribution to the criminal enterprise. On the contrary, it was a vital contribution. Once having joined the major conspiracy, the lesser conspiracy to obstruct justice was a natural outcome. I bear in mind your antecedent history and all those matters urged upon me by your learned Counsel. Having done so I can see no valid grounds for differentiating your case from Brian Field. You will accordingly be sentenced to concurrent terms of 25 years on the first count and 5 years on the twelfth count.

JOHN WHEATER

John Denby Wheater, your case is in many respects the saddest and most difficult of all. You are 42 years old, a married man with heavy family responsibilities and of excellent character up until the present crime. You too served your country gallantly in the war and faithfully in peace. There is no evidence that you have contributed to your present disastrous position by profligate living of any kind. Indeed your standards appear to have been distinctly lower than those of your managing clerk. Yet you, as a solicitor of the Supreme Court, stand convicted under count 12 of conspiring with Leonard Field and your managing clerk to obstruct the course of justice. The jury have acquitted you on the first count and I naturally treat you as having had no knowledge until after the mail train robbery of the criminal purpose for which you had been instructed to secure possession of Leatherslade Farm. Your conviction on the twelfth count establishes, as I interpret the verdict, that at some time after the robbery that criminal purpose became clear to you, as indeed it must have done, and you could then have given the police vital information by identifying Leonard Field as your professional client. A decent citizen would have volunteered to do that very thing whatever his strictly legal obligations must be. Instead, you professed inability to do so. That profession the jury have found was false and I regret to have to say that I have no doubt the verdict of the jury in that regard was right. At that time not a single one of the accused had been identified and, indeed, it was not until some days later that Mrs Rixon picked out Leonard Field. But for that no thanks are due to you. Instead of assisting justice you were obstructing it and that at a time when speed was obviously of vital concern to the forces of

> law and order. Furthermore, your deliberately obstructive actions clearly sprang from the conspiracy between you and the two Fields. It is in respect of that conspiracy that you must now be sentenced.
>
> Why you participated in it I do not know and you have not told me. You learned Counsel has been able merely to hazard a guess. Whether or not all the facts, if known, would speak in your favour or to your prejudice I have no means of telling and must not speculate, but I am disposed to accept the view that you allowed yourself to be overborne in some manner by your more masterful and able managing clerk. I cannot accept the submission that the fact that the maximum punishment for being an accessory after the fact to felony, with which you were originally charged, is 2 years' imprisonment, offers a sure guide to the proper sentence for this criminal conspiracy. Such conduct on the part of any citizen is gravely blameworthy. The criminality of it is gravitated when practiced by an officer of the Supreme Court and that fact must weigh heavily against you. On the other hand, I realise that the consequences of your conviction are disastrous both professionally and personally. Bearing in mind all relevant considerations I have come to the conclusion that you must go to prison for 3 years and you will be sentenced accordingly.[27]

Shocked reactions to these heavy sentences were not only evident in the public gallery but equally among the national and international press representatives who expressed their views the following day.

The *Daily Mail* editorial was a prime example:

> People everywhere are puzzled by one glaring contrast. It is this – an evil doer convicted of conspiracy and robbery as in the Train Case can be sentenced to thirty years which, with normal remission, means serving twenty years in prison. But an evil doer convicted of murder and jailed for life is unlikely to serve more than fifteen years. Does this mean that stealing banknotes is regarded as being more wicked than murdering somebody? What is the real purpose of punishment in both cases? To mete out retribution? To deter others? To reform the criminal?[28]

For once, the Labour-supporting *Daily Herald* (which, five months later would be renamed *The Sun*),[29] found itself in full agreement with the right-wing *Daily Mail*:

> Those of the gang sentenced would have got lighter sentences for non-capital murder,[30] still lighter for blackmail, infinitely lighter for breaking [a] baby's legs.

> Our legal system tends to take a sterner view of crimes against property than crimes against people.[31]

The *Daily Herald* also compared the sentences with another headline story on the same day. The Ferranti Company had been exposed for making an unfair profit of more than £4 million from a government missile contract. The irony was given full vent by the paper's cartoonist Belsky, who showed a father telling his son after reading the newspaper, 'Well, that shows crime doesn't pay – Government missiles – that's what you want to go in for.'[32]

The *Daily Telegraph* took a different view of the sentences and focused on the deterrent issue:

> Another interpretation is that killers are thought less susceptible to deterrence than thieves – a view maintained by many experts of crime. Certainly the learned judge made it clear that his severity was aimed at striking fear into the heart of the criminal world by making the penalty match the exorbitance of the offence.[33]

The liberal-leaning *Guardian*'s editorial declared that: '... the sentences are out of proportion with everything except the value of the property involved'.[34]

Probably the most telling comments were made by DCI Frank Williams, when interviewed by a BBC reporter following the sentencing:

> BBC Reporter: What do you think would have happened if Leatherslade Farm had been, as they put it, 'cleaned up' – do you think you'd have actually caught anybody?
>
> DCI Frank Williams: The job would have been very, very much more difficult of course because you know by the trial we depended to a very, very great extent on what clues were left at the farm. The mistake they made of course was not getting away straight away and by staying at the farm leaving the clues they did, which led to the eventual arrests.[35]

13

AN ACT OF WARFARE

While there were two months to go before the appeal hearings were scheduled at the High Court, DCS Butler continued his relentless search for the elusive Harry Smith. Finally:

At 6pm [on] Tuesday 5 May 1964 in consequence of a telephone call received at this office, I went with Detective Chief Inspector Williams to New Church Road, Camberwell SE5, and there saw Henry Thomas Smith in the company of Daniel Regan who left forthwith in a motor car.

I told him we were police officers and added, 'Are you Henry Thomas Smith who at [one] time lived at 262 Fieldgate Mansions, Stepney?' He replied, 'Yes that's right'. I said, 'We are engaged on enquiries into the robbery of the mail train at Cheddington, Bucks in August last year and want to ask you some questions about your whereabouts at that time'. He replied, 'Yes all right but I can tell you straight away I am making no statement'.

He was taken to Southwark police station. On arrival I said to him, 'My information is that you lived at 262 Fieldgate Mansions, Stepney until the 14 August 1963 and then disappeared'. Smith made no reply so I added, 'Do you recall a police officer answering the telephone that day in your flat and asking you to come home?' Smith replied, 'No I don't'. I said, 'Do you say you did not ring later on after first promising to come to the flat and telling the officer you had an idea why he wanted to see you?' Smith replied, 'I rang but nothing like that was said'. I said to him, 'What do you say took place?' He replied, 'I've had advice and told to make no statement even if you charge me with something'.

I said, 'Perhaps at least you will tell us why you did not go to live with your wife and child at the address at Barking Road that was bought on your behalf'. He replied, 'No I'm saying nothing except I am innocent of any robbery'.

> He was asked whether he had any objection to his finger and palm prints being taken by police. He replied, 'No, have as many as you want'. Palm prints were taken by Detective Chief Inspector Williams. He [Henry Smith] was later detained at Cannon Row police station where he gave his name as John Smith of no fixed address. His palm prints were compared with those left at Leatherslade Farm but no identification was made. On Wednesday the 6 May 1964 Smith was taken to Aylesbury police station and detained whilst arrangements were made for witnesses to attend an Identification Parade.
>
> On Thursday the 7 May 1964 Smith was placed with a number of other men on an Identification Parade. Ten witnesses who either saw or had dealings with the strangers in the Oakley or Brill districts of Buckinghamshire at the material time were introduced to the Parade but none made an identification. Smith was accordingly released on his personal undertaking to present himself at New Scotland Yard in fourteen days' time. Smith carried out his undertaking but no further evidence being available he was allowed to leave.'[1]

Smith's address at 496 Barking Road, Plaistow was also re-searched:

> A pair of boots, some shoes and sandals which were not present at the earlier search were seized. It was thought possible that markings and blemishes on the soles might correspond with impressions found in the soft earth at Leatherslade Farm. An examination carried out at the Forensic Laboratory dashed this hope. The position we reached at this juncture was that there was not the slightest doubt in our minds of police that Smith (whose name had been given to me only a few days after the commission of the offence) was one of the robbers actually at the scene and taking a very active part in the commission of the offence. Because of our failure to trace him earlier, he has received advice from one or more solicitors regarding his demeanour when interrogated by police. We have been defeated on the question of physical identification, whilst any palm and finger impressions he may have left at the Farm were erased before the arrival [of] the officers from the Fingerprint Department.[2]

At the same time as the Barking Road address was being searched on 6 May, DS Slipper and DS Suter travelled to Gosport in Hampshire where they searched two properties that had recently been purchased by Smith's friend Daniel Regan. At 32 Palmerston Way, in the wardrobe in Regan's bedroom, Slipper found two sheets of paper giving details of addresses and figures appertaining to the purchase of property. According to the schedule, Regan, with his associates:

> … bought thirty-two houses (including a row of eleven), a drinking club and a hotel in the Portsmouth and Gosport districts. In addition, there is the house in Barking Road in which Smith has been living and which has now been sumptuously furnished.[3]

DCS Butler informed Commander Hatherill that, 'It can, however, be said with virtual certainty that the cash expended on all the property is the proceeds of Smith's share of the proceeds of the Train Robbery.'[4]

While little hope was held out, the appeals on behalf of all those convicted at the Buckinghamshire Assize trial in April had been lodged and commenced on Monday 6 July 1964. They were held at the Court of Criminal Appeal in Central London before Justice Widgery, Justice Fenton Atkinson and Justice Lawton. Every prisoner, apart from Charles Wilson, who did not wish to attend, was brought under close police escort to the courts.

When deliberating the appeals, the judges held that though none of the robbers were identified at the scene of the crime, the fingerprint evidence against the six was sufficient for the trial jury to infer they were plotters who also took part in the raid.

Mr Justice Atkinson said, 'Last year's £2,500,000 raid was warfare against society and an act of organised banditry touching new depths of lawlessness. In our judgement, severe deterrent sentences are necessary to protect the community against these men for a long time.'[5]

Leave to appeal to the House of Lords was refused to the six. The next appeal against conviction and sentence was that of Gordon Goody. Having reviewed his case, the Court of Criminal Appeal criticised prosecution counsel Niall MacDermot QC for the 'irrelevant' questions he asked Goody at the trial concerning the 1962 London Airport robbery. Mr Justice Lawton said:

> No questions should have been asked about this matter. Still less should Mr MacDermot have asked questions which had the effects of suggesting, even if he did not intend to do so, that Goody had been lucky to be acquitted.[6]

However, Lawton went on to conclude that: 'Even if the Court was satisfied there was such gross impropriety by Mr MacDermot, as to be likely to interfere with the trial, the conviction would not have been set aside.'[7]

Both of Goody's appeals were therefore dismissed and leave for him to appeal to the House of Lords was also refused.

Brian Field's was the next appeal to be heard. He had originally been sentenced to twenty-five years' imprisonment and five years' imprisonment to run concurrently for conspiracy to rob and conspiracy to obstruct the course of justice. His conviction and sentence in relation to the conspiracy to rob charge was quashed.

Giving judgement, Mr Justice Fenton Atkinson said the trial jury at the Assize Court had acquitted Field of receiving stolen money, even though two bags belonging to him were found full of banknotes in Dorking. Once dissociated from possession of any stolen money, the remaining facts against him were therefore insufficient to enable the jury to infer he was guilty of conspiring to rob the mail train.

The appeal of Leonard Field, whom Mr Justice Fenton Atkinson described as 'a ready liar at the trial', reached the same conclusion as 'No facts had been established that he knew of the intention to stop and rob the train.'

John Wheater, who was sentenced to three years' imprisonment for conspiracy to obstruct the course of justice, appealed against his conviction and sentence. The appeals against both were dismissed.

The final appeals were those of William Boal and Roger Cordrey. Boal was originally sentenced to twenty-four years' imprisonment. Arthur James QC for the Crown admitted to the court that the prosecution was now 'unhappy' about Boal's case. Scientific evidence at the trial, he said, had turned out to be inconclusive. This in itself was a major revelation, for surely if the scientific evidence against Boal was not conclusive, how could the same evidence put forward by Dr Holden against Goody at the earlier trial not also be so?

Arthur James QC further went on to say, 'Looking back on it now, I should have invited the jury not to convict Boal of being one of the actual robbers. If Boal had pleaded not guilty to armed robbery but, like Cordrey, guilty to receiving £151,000, the prosecution would have accepted the pleas.'[8]

Mr Justice Widgery agreed that 'Boal's conviction of armed robbery might result in a miscarriage of justice' and so quashed the conviction. The court then substituted a fourteen-year sentence of imprisonment for conspiracy to rob for three charges of receiving. Mr Justice Widgery commented that, 'a significant difference in sentence is justified for those who were not the inner-circle of plotters'. Boal was to die of a brain tumour in prison on 25 June 1970 a broken man.[9]

Roger Cordrey, who had pleaded guilty at the Buckinghamshire Assize Court to conspiracy to rob and three charges of receiving, and had been sentenced to twenty years' imprisonment had his sentence reduced to one of fourteen years, the same sentence as Boal, a man who had no involvement at all in the crime and nothing like the same degree of involvement as others who were handed down sentences of no more than three years for receiving.

On Monday 20 July 1964 the Court of Criminal Appeal dismissed the appeals of Brian Field, Leonard Field and John Wheater against their sentences for conspiracy to obstruct the course of justice. Mr Justice Lawton said that the five-year sentences on Brian Field and Leonard Field, and a three-year sentence on Wheater, were not wrong in law.

By the time the appeal process had come to an end, Charlie Wilson was already in the later stages of his escape preparations. Just over two weeks after the appeal, he made headlines all over the world with a daring escape that further fuelled the public's fascination for the train robbers.

It was just after 3 a.m. on 12 August that Wilson was freed from the maximum security Winson Green Prison in Birmingham by three men who had broken into the jail. In one of two Metropolitan Police files on his escape is a report by Flying Squad officers summarising the facts relating to the jailbreak, written on 12 and 13 August.[10]

The three men who rescued Wilson were believed to have stolen a ladder from a nearby builders' yard to break into the grounds of a psychiatric hospital situated next to the prison. They then used a rope-ladder to climb the 20ft prison wall and proceeded to knock out William Nicholls, one of two patrolling prison officers, and tie him up. They next opened the outside door to C Block and unlocked a steel grille door, before making for Landing No 2 where they silently opened Wilson's cell door before retracing their steps out of the prison.

Winson Green authorities were unable to account for how the master key had been obtained, and a copy made. Only one member of the prison staff held the keys to open cells at night. The police seem to have been of the view that a prison officer or official had more than likely been induced by bribery to provide a copy of the master key well in advance of the escape.

Detectives also unsuccessfully tested the prison keys for any traces of soap. They also interviewed the governor, all of the 120 prison officers, the civilian staff working at the prison and a number of the 180 inmates and former inmates. Peter Marshall of Hyde Road, Ladywood, who had previously served three sentences at Winson Green and was known as an expert locksmith, was among those interviewed. He expressed the view that a copy of the master key could not have been made by wax impression, because 'if any part of the key was even a thousandth of an inch out it would not work,' he said in a statement. This was a view that Dr Ian Holden at Scotland Yard also concurred with.

Mrs Rose Gredden, who lived close to the prison, also made a witness statement in which she said she had noticed three men talking on the prison side of the canal towpath at around 2.35 a.m. shortly after she had been awakened by her baby daughter. 'They were respectably dressed. Two were rather tall,' she recalled. 'Some prison officers must have seen them. Their social club is only a few yards from where the men were standing and I heard officers leaving the club around that time.'

At 3.20 a.m., William Nicholls, the guard who had been bound and gagged, came to and immediately reported the incident to the night orderly officer, although it was a further thirty minutes before the police received a call logged at 3.50 a.m. Ten minutes later they arrived at the main gate, but were unable to enter until a senior prison officer appeared with the keys.

When the prison governor Rundle Harris was woken and told of Wilson's escape, he immediately phoned the Home Office duty officer, who in turn sent a telegram to Home Secretary Henry Brooke, who at the time was on an official trip to the Channel Islands. Brooke cancelled the rest of his engagements and immediately flew back to London.

A special watch was put on all airports and sea ports, including Dublin, Cork and Shannon airports in the Republic of Ireland, where the police thought Wilson might initially head for. Notices to Interpol, requesting the circulation of Wilson's description and photograph, were also sent out.

However, DCS Butler also thought that Wilson might visit the house near Boscastle, so he 'arranged for the local police to search the house but there was no trace of Wilson'.[11]

Wilson was, however, heading for London not Ireland. There, he stayed in a safe house for six months, eventually making arrangements to leave the country and start a new life abroad with his family. In December 1964 he obtained a passport in the name of Ronald Alloway and, in March 1965, disguised as a teacher on a backpacking holiday, took a cross-channel ferry to France.

DCS Butler continued to believe, however, that Wilson was still in Britain:

> On 9 June 1965 Chief Supt Butler informed me that he had good reason to suppose that Tracey, aged 7 years, and Cheryl, aged 9 years, two of Wilson's 3 children, were attending school at Ilford and living with Wilson's sister and her husband, Charles Edward Woollard at 29 Laurel Close, Hainault, Essex. At Chief Supt Butler's request, a Home Office Warrant was obtained to intercept the telephone Hainault 3478 at the address and for a check of correspondence delivered to the address since it was considered that Wilson may well be communicating with his sister.[12]

Interception continued for a month until it became apparent that no one else was living there other than Mr and Mrs Woollard and their young son.

No communication of any kind from Wilson was either heard or seen. A year later, in May 1966 (by which time Wilson had settled down in Canada), Butler was still 'of the opinion that Wilson may now be living in or near London'.[13]

The police apparently had suspicions as to who might have been behind Wilson's escape. The identity of the man they investigated, who was 'suspected of harbouring and assisting' Wilson to escape, remains in a file that at the time of writing is closed until 2043.[14]

While prison security had apparently been tightened following Wilson's jailbreak, further embarrassment for the Home Office, and for the new Labour Home Secretary Sir Frank Soskice, was not long in coming:

> On the 8 July 1965 Ronald Biggs, together with Eric Flowers, CRO 2046/50, Robert Anderson, CRO 41542/55 and Patrick Doyle, CRO 36738/57 escaped over the north wall of Wandsworth Prison into a waiting pantechnicon and two private cars. Biggs and Flowers are still at large but Anderson and Doyle have been returned to prison. The following have been prosecuted to conviction for assisting the escapes:
>
> Paul Seabourne, CRO 37440/44
> Henry Holsgrove, CRO 36780/54
> George Ronald Leslie, CRO 5563/55
> George Albert Gibbs, CRO 20253/61
> Ronald Brown, CRO 36394/55
> Terrence Mintagh, CRO 70184/62[15]

Biggs and Flowers were initially hidden in a series of safe houses in London and Sussex, before being given new passports and taken out of the country by boat from London to Antwerp. Biggs's new identity was that of writer Terence Furminger. On arrival in Belgium, he and Flowers were sheltered for some weeks before having plastic surgery at a clinic in Paris. They flew out to Australia at the end of December 1965.[16]

According to IB officer W.J. Edwards:

> Following Biggs' escape Chief Supt Butler arranged for a further call at the house near Boscastle by the local police. Biggs was not there but Miss Sleep, who was then alone, produced two biscuit tins containing £9,349 in £1 notes which she said her dog had unearthed in the garden besides the garage. She appeared to be distressed because her dog had recently died. The £1 notes and the biscuit tins clearly bore signs of having been buried for some time.

> Chief Supt Butler visited Miss Sleep in September, 1965, and in the presence of her solicitor she admitted that she knew that Daly and Black had buried £100,000 in the garden; that Black subsequently took half of it and that Goodwin bricked into a wall in the kitchen the remaining £50,000. She said that following the failure of the hot water system in the house the landlord told her he would install a new oil fired system and she knew this would involve structural alterations in the kitchen so decided to remove the money from the wall. She admitted that she took a few pounds herself, alleged that she burnt the £5 notes because she thought they could be traced and said she buried the remainder in the garden. Chief Supt Butler is of the opinion that Miss Sleep was living alone, became distressed after the death of her dog and was on the point of reporting the facts concerning the money when the local Police visited her.
>
> The £9,349 is held by the Police and the facts have been reported to the Director of Public Prosecutions suggesting Daly be prosecuted for receiving. The DPP has decided not to prosecute at this stage but the case will doubtless be reopened should any new evidence come to light. This may well materialise when Edwards or Reynolds are arrested.[17]

W.J. Edwards's reports also indicate that DSC Butler felt, 'There is good reason for thinking that Biggs and Flowers, who escaped from prison at the same time, may still be together and in South Africa.'[18]

According to DI Frank Williams, Butler:

> … became so obsessed that as time went on he even spent his holidays on the beaches touring the South of France, parading up and down with binoculars and photographs, scanning the sunbathing crowds through the glasses in the hope of spotting one of the missing robbers (he particularly favoured the view that they were on the Riviera). He spent considerable time talking to English visitors at these resorts, showing them the photographs and asking if they had seen any of the robbers.[19]

In October 1965 information was received by Chief Supt Butler that a man named Chiandano Vittorio had been living in a caravan in a camp at Antibes and that Ann Killoran and Mabel Hume were living in adjacent caravans. It was considered that Vittorio may well be Reynolds but inquiries revealed that this was not the case.

On 24 May 1966, W.J. Edwards of the IB reported that, 'Chief Supt Butler has good reason for thinking that Reynolds has been living in the South of France but that he may now have returned to this country.'[20]

Of course, Reynolds was neither in the South of France nor in England, having flown to Mexico the previous year.

While Biggs, Reynolds and Wilson remained on the run,[21] Jimmy White was finally arrested on 21 April 1966[22] and Buster Edwards eventually gave himself up to DI Frank Williams on 19 September 1966 in a deal brokered between Williams and Freddie Foreman.[23]

Their arrests were by no means the beginning of the end, so far as the train robbery story was concerned. In many ways, they were more the end of the beginning.

14

THE END OF THE BEGINNING

The saga of the Great Train Robbery has continued unabated for the past five decades. Speculation centred on many of the unanswered aspects of the robbery has been hotly debated by a host of authors and TV documentaries.

One of the principal sources of conjecture has been the identity of the 'Irishman' or the 'Ulsterman' who allegedly provided the inside information that enabled the robbery to be committed.

There have been a number of views over the years. DCS Butler was always sceptical about the 'insider' theory. He believed his view was substantiated when, after Jimmy White's arrest, he was closely questioned about the robbery and how it had been organised. Without betraying any names or identities, White spoke in some detail about the preparations, which appear in his arrest file. Butler placed particular emphasis on the following quote:

> I asked what kind of money could be expected and I was told that after the August Bank Holiday we could expect about £2,000,000 to be on the train, but in any event there would be someone in Glasgow to count the bags when the coach was being loaded and no move would be made unless there was a known large amount in the coach. Later on one of the men left the farm to go to a telephone. He returned with the news that the Scottish Night Mail Train was well and truly loaded and the spy in Glasgow had reported that lots of high value bags had been put aboard.[1]

Butler's view was that the 'spy in Glasgow' was not necessarily anyone working for the Post Office, and that the information supplied by this individual was all that was needed to launch the operation to hold up the train.

Bearing in mind that it was supposedly Brian Field who had contact with the insider, the police and IB had hoped that Brian Field or John Wheater, who they saw as the weakest links, might eventually reveal further details in prison. However, once Brian Field's sentence had been downgraded on appeal, he no longer saw any benefit in the possibility of talking and instead concentrated on his early release. Wheater, however, was a different kettle of fish. In 1966 he divulged that:

> I did get the impression that there were some other people involved who were not brought to trial and have not been named by the Police. And one thing I learned pointed back to well before the raid – to a link between the gang and somebody in Post Office security. This somebody made contact through an intermediary with one of the men who stood trial, and it was this man – one of my fellows in the dock – who gave me the information when I was discussing with him how he became involved. The intermediary – a relation, I think, of the Post Office security man – put up the proposition that large sums of money were being moved by train at various times, and that it was there for the taking so to speak. This made my fellow prisoner a lynch pin in the whole thing. I was never able to discover who the intermediary was. I was told that after the robbery money was passed to the intermediary for himself and for the Post Office man. Each was said to have received one full share of the total sum stolen and that would be between £140,000 and £150,000.[2]

Percy Hoskins, the crime editor of the *Daily Express*, also later recalled that a certain senior Scotland Yard officer had called at his Park Lane apartment and over a drink divulged off-the-record that a senior Royal Mail officer was strongly suspected of being the man mentioned in Hoskins's 20 April 1964 story speculating about the 'inside man'. According to the information given to Hoskins:

> The man had joined Royal Mail in Belfast twenty or so years before, had worked his way up through the ranks and eventually moved to England after the war where he settled into a quiet middle class suburb in south London.[3]

Hoskins's informant had added that the man now held a key post in Royal Mail security, and had written down his name and address on the strict understanding that the brief background information he had given Hoskins would only ever be used in a story if the man in question were to be arrested.

Hoskins knew that he had no legal grounds for a story of any kind, but his curiosity, if nothing else, had to be satisfied.

One Wednesday a few weeks after his conversation with the Scotland Yard officer, Hoskins took the train to Beckenham Junction and walked a short distance to the 'pleasant tree lined road of spacious semi-detached houses' where the man lived with his wife and mother. It was the middle of the day and Hoskins (rightly) sensed that the man would be at work. When he knocked at the smart bay-windowed house, the wife opened the front door and Hoskins spoke to her for a few minutes on a pretext.

This man certainly fitted the bill in every sense, but was he really the man who had, on several occasions, supplied top-grade information to a gang of criminals, albeit through an intermediary? He was apparently a popular and outwardly honest man who was spoken of most highly by his superiors and colleagues.

One mystery surrounding Brian Field was eventually solved by Tommy Butler. While the appeal hearings were in progress he had received information suggesting that:

> ... the persons who deposited the bags and the cash at the spot were Brian Field and his father. We were informed that this action had been taken because (a) Wheater's (and therefore Field's) part in the affair was under active investigation, and (b) because Karen Field insisted upon its removal from her house, where Brian Field had taken it. Therefore, at the Appeal Court, shortly after the conclusion of that part of the proceedings involving Brian Field, I saw Field senior and inferred in general terms that he might have something to impart to police concerning the money found in the woods. He declined to discuss the matter, but was patently fearful.[4]

Six months later, Butler received further information to the effect that a visit to Brian Field's father, Reginald Field, in the near future would probably lead to a full disclosure of what had happened. Butler therefore visited Reginald Field's home at 141 Constance Road in Whitton, Middlesex on 9 February 1965 with DS Nevill. Apparently, after some hesitation, Field made a full written statement:

> I Reginald Arthur Field wish to make a statement. I want someone to write down what I say. I have been told that I need not say anything unless I wish to do so and that whatever I say may be given in evidence.

I am the father of Brian Arthur Field who is at present serving sentence. I can't be certain of the exact date but one day in August 1963 I came home from work sometime about 6.30 pm and went into my garage. There are two doors but I do not use a padlock on them. I keep the doors shut with a bolt. I don't know exactly when it was but on the weekend before the Bank Holiday Monday my car was struck by another vehicle whilst I was stationary in the kerb. It was somewhere the other side of Guildford. There was a lot of damage to the car and I could not drive it away. It was towed to a local garage the name of which escapes me. The matter was reported to the police because my wife had to be taken to hospital as she had slight concussion. My car was a Hillman index No MP 4393. Because of this fact when I came home on the night I have mentioned there was no car in my garage. The garage is normally kept in a very tidy condition because I like to put my hands on anything I want.

I went into the garage to get a piece of wood I had left there. The garage lies to the back of the house and there is a driveway to the street. On opening the door of the garage I saw on the floor at the back of the garage one case and three bags. There was one holdall, an embossed leather case, a brief case and a round leathery sort of hat box. I had not been into the garage for several days so I don't how long they had been there. I naturally went and looked into them and found that they contained money. The money was done up in separate bundles tied with brown paper bands. I immediately realized that this must be money to do with the train robbery which was reported in the papers at that time. I had no idea how it came to be in my garage. I decided that the best thing to do was to get rid of it as soon as possible. As I had no car I had to give the matter a lot of thought because there was too much to carry. Eventually I thought of Gordon Neal who lives in Blandford Avenue and who had grown up with my son. I told him that I had found some money in my garage which I felt sure had come from the train robbery and asked if I could borrow his car to go and get rid of it. Gordon volunteered to drive the car for me. I put the money in the car and we drove out to Dorking where I threw the money out of the car and we continued our journey and came home. I feel sure that I dumped the money at about 11 pm on the night before it was found at a place I know to be Leaf Hill, Dorking. I got out of the car and threw the money into the woods. I want to get this off my chest as it has been playing on my mind for a long time and it has been making me ill. Now I have told you about it I wish to God I had done so before. I feel as though I can have a good night's sleep now it is over and done with.

I have read the above statement and I have been told that I can correct alter or add anything I wish. This statement true. I have made it of my own free will.

(signed) R A Field[5]

Butler and Nevill then sought out Gordon Neal who corroborated everything Reginald Field had said and made a statement as such. Butler's conclusions, in light of the new disclosures, are outlined in a report to Commander Hatherill:

> The amount found leads one to strongly suspect that it is not the total share awarded to Brian Field for his participation in the offence. It therefore follows that someone diverted a portion of it prior to dumping that found in the wood. Although there is no evidence to prove it, there are firm grounds for believing that Brian Field accompanied his father and Neal to Dorking. His presence would have probably been insisted on by both.[6]

When Brian Field was released from prison in 1967 he changed his name and identity and promptly disappeared without trace. A decade later he died in a motorway accident. The truth about the Ulsterman and Field's other secrets died with him.[7]

So far as the legacy of the robbery and the sentences handed down to those involved was concerned, it undoubtedly contributed to an upsurge in armed robbery during the following decade. The net result is probably best summed up by South London gangland boss Eddie Richardson:

> If they could be given thirty years for when they weren't carrying guns, what was the point in not being armed? Guns reduced the risk of being caught, and if you did get caught, they couldn't give you longer than thirty years. There was nothing to lose.[8]

Appendix 1

JACK MILLS

Sir, The sad death of Mr Mills, driver of the diesel in the Mail Train case, frees me from a promise I made to him some five years ago, of which the convicted men are fully aware. It also allows me to comment on the identity of the man who injured him.

When I interviewed Mr Mills on, I think, the actual diesel used in the raid, I asked him whether it was true, as the robbers maintain, that his worst injuries resulted from a fall and not from the blow to the head. To this he replied with some hesitation, 'if I tell you something, will you promise not to write it in your paper? They hit my scalp and it bled a lot but when I stumbled, I caught my head *here*' – and he indicated the curved steel dashboard which runs under the driver's window. 'They say this was the bad injury.'

I said: 'Why did you not tell the court this and why did you not repeat what I believe you said early on to a reporter, that they treated you "like a gentleman", which at least suggests that they had not meant so much violence? It would not have made any difference to their *guilt* but it might well have made a difference to their *sentence*. Why did you not tell the court the whole story?'

He became very agitated and said: 'Oh, please do not ever repeat this as I have been warned that my pension would be affected if this came out.' Well, I did not betray his confidence during his lifetime, though the robbers have often asked me to, since it corroborates the fact that they had not intended serious violence – something which could not be said in court because of their plea; and I did not, in view of my husband's involvement in their defence, think it proper to ask by whom the threat about his pension had been made.

Nor can I say what was the medical view, other than what was given in evidence, of when his leukaemia developed. I did, however, offer him, through the then Public Relations Officer to Midland Region, a consultation with a leading neurologist and sufficient time in the National Hospital to ensure that everything possible had been done. This he refused, to my lasting regret. He was a brave and pleasant man and everyone is sad about his fate, including Parkhurst. But who struck the fatal blow? All those in the 'know' in the underworld (and certainly the convicted men themselves) maintain that it was a man who was never on trial but who slipped through the net. This they have never said openly during Mills' lifetime, lest, if the man were charged, he might be recognised by the driver, who heard him speak. This, if true (and there is reason to think it is), is surely the supreme irony of the thirty-year sentences.

I am, Sir, yours sincerely
PETA FORDHAM
4 Paper Buildings, The Temple, EC4[1]

'Leukaemia with complications due to bronchial pneumonia was the cause of Jack Mills' death. I am aware that Mr Mills sustained a head injury during the course of the train robbery in 1963. In my opinion, there is nothing to connect this incident with the cause of death.'[2]

Appendix 2

THE VEHICLES

The three vehicles found abandoned at Leatherslade Farm were as follows:

A new Land Rover bearing false index plates BMG 757A. It was light blue in colour but over-painted khaki. The vehicle was later identified as having been stolen from Oxenden Street, London, WC1 between 7.30 pm – 11 pm, 21st July 1963. The vehicle when stolen was fitted with a radio set. The radio set was still in position, attached to the dashboard of the vehicle when it was recovered.

An ex-War Department Land Rover bearing index plates BMG 757A. This vehicle passed through the auction of ex-War Department Vehicles at Ruddington, Nottinghamshire, on 2nd July 1963, and was sold to a London motor dealer, trading in the name of Cross Country Vehicles. The Vehicle had been re-sprayed a deep bronze green [by] the purchaser. Cross Country Vehicles re-sell their vehicles to the public through the medium of advertisements in the Exchange and Mart. On 26 July, Cross Country Vehicles received a telephone call about the vehicle and as a result two men called at Cross Country Vehicles. One of them who gave the name Bentley agreed to purchase the Land Rover for £195. The vehicle was registered and allocated the number BMG 757A. On 1 August 1963, Bentley telephoned Cross Country Vehicles, was given the number, and called to collect the vehicle with the registration number plate on either 3 or 4 August 1963. He signed the duplicate receipt for the vehicle 'F Wood pp C Bentley'. Bentley was later identified as James E White CRO 26113/55.

An Austin Goods Platform Truck bearing false index plates BPA 260. This vehicle when found was dark green in colour with the front and cabin crudely over-painted yellow. It was traced as having passed through the auction of ex-War Department vehicles on 24th April 1963, and was purchased by D A

Mullard & Company Limited, Government Surplus Contractors of Edgware. They re-sprayed inside and out olive green. This vehicle was purchased from D A Mullard & Company Limited by a man giving the name of F Blake, 272, Kenton Lane, Middlesex (false), for £300. On 30 July 1963 Blake collected the vehicle, saying he had registered it. He had no index plate with him and chalked a registration number on the original blanks. This number could not be remembered. A man similar to Blake and referred to as 'Jimmy' by a second man was directed to Mullards by H & A Motors of Edgware. 'Jimmy' later returned to H & A Motors and said that he had bought a lorry at Mullards. 'Jimmy' has been identified as James E White, CRO 26113/55.

The false number BPA 260 referred to a Ford car. This vehicle was broken up by a scrap dealer in Gloucester two or three years ago. The Road Fund Licence displayed on the lorry relates to a vehicle VJD 35. The licence was stolen from this vehicle at Warner Place, London, E2 between 7.30 pm, 29 July 1963, and 2pm 30 July 1963 and was reported to police at Bethnal Green on 30 July 1963.[3]

Appendix 3

THE COURT

Judge: Mr Justice Edmund Davies

Counsel:

Mr Arthur James QC, Mr Niall MacDermot QC, Mr Howard Sabin and Mr Desmond Fennell appeared for the prosecution.

Mr William Sime QC and Mr Edward Eyre appeared for the accused William Gerald Boal.

Mr John Mathew and Mr John Speed appeared for the accused Charles Frederick Wilson.

Mr Wilfred Fordham and Mr Cyril Salmon appeared for the accused Ronald Arthur Biggs

Mr Joseph Grieves QC and the Hon. Patrick Pakenham appeared for the accused Thomas William Wisbey.

Mr Frederick Ashe Lincoln QC and Mr Joseph Gamgee appeared for the accused Robert Alfred Welch.

Mr R. Kilner Brown QC and Mr Gavin Freeman appeared for the accused James Hussey.

Mr Walter Raeburn QC, Mr Wilfred Fordham and Mr John Speed appeared for the accused John Thomas Daly.

Mr William Howard and Mr John Speed appeared for the accused Roy John James.

Mr Sebag Shaw QC, Mr Wilfred Fordham and Mr Cyril Salmon appeared for the accused Douglas Gordon Goody.

Mr Lewis Hawser QC, Mr Ivor Richards and Mr George Hazledine appeared for the accused Brian Arthur Field.

Mr Michael Argyle QC and Mr Edwin Jowitt appeared for the accused Leonard Dennis Field.
Mr Graham Swanwick QC and Mr Felix Waley appeared for the accused John Denby Wheater.

Appendix 4

FORENSIC EVIDENCE ON GORDON GOODY'S SHOES

Statement by Dr Ian Holden
I am a Doctor of Philosophy in the Faculty of Science, a Bachelor of Science, a Fellow of the Royal Institute of Chemistry, and a Principal Scientific Officer at the Metropolitan Police Laboratory.

On Thursday 29 August 1963 I received at New Scotland Yard, from Detective Constable Milner, Buckinghamshire Constabulary, Aylesbury, items from Leatherslade Farm. On 19 September 1963 at Buckinghamshire Headquarters, Aylesbury, in company with Detective Constable Milner, I examined the large new Land Rover. I removed a sample of yellow paint found smeared on the pedals of this vehicle. I also took a sample of the Khaki top coat of paint from this Land Rover.

On 28 September 1963 in company with Detective Chief Superintendent CO, C8 and PC Cullen, Buckinghamshire Constabulary, I went to Leatherslade Farm and examined the large open garage and took samples of the yellow paints on the floor of the garage.

I examined the exhibits I had received together with the various samples I had taken myself. The rubber soles of the shoes had raised lines across the soles to form a pattern of squares. This pattern had been worn away from the main tread area of the soles. There was khaki paint on the shoes of Goody which had gone on in the wet condition. It was mainly on the right shoe under the instep and along the outer edge of the rubber sole. There was a small spot of khaki paint on the top of the right shoe and on an area on the inner aspect of the edge of the sole near the toe of the left shoe. The paint appeared to have been sufficiently wet to run down the sides of the soles. Some of the khaki paint under the instep of the right shoe was free from contamination and was found to be identical in colour and chemical composition with the khaki top coat of paint from the large Land Rover taken by Detective Constable Milner and by myself.

There was an area of yellow paint under the instep of the right shoe of Goody and some small circular areas of yellow paint under the toe of the left shoe where they were partially protected by the remain of the raised lines of the sole pattern. This yellow paint on the shoes had gone on in the wet condition and would be consistent with the wearer of the shoes treading on an area splashed with this yellow paint.

This paint under the instep of Goody's shoes was mixed with fine mineral material. This mixture had the same colour and chemical composition as the paint and fine mineral mixture from the pedals of the Land Rover and the paint and fine mineral material from the large area on the floor of the garage at Leatherslade Farm.

The uncontaminated paint separated from this mixture on the floor of the garage, the paint splashed on the floor at the rear of the garage, the paint from the squashed tin and the yellow paints from the large lorry were identical in colour and chemical composition.[4]

At the trial, alternative forensic evidence was placed before the court:

The Defence for Goody called before the Court Mr Cecil Hancorn Robbins BSc FRIC, a director of Hehner & Cox Ltd, Fenchurch Street, City of London, who are consulting and analytical chemists.

He was called to negative the evidence given by Dr Holden that the paint on Goody's shoes was identical with yellow paint contaminated with mineral found on the floor of the garage at Leatherslade Farm and khaki paint found on the Land Rover at Leatherslade Farm. Mr Robbins tried to do this by disputing the interpretations by Dr Holden of spectra of paints which he and Mr Robbins had prepared from samples taken from exhibits. Mr Robbins summarised his findings regarding the khaki point in this way:

(1) In two spectra of paint prepared from samples taken from the Land Rover, one by Dr Holden and one by himself, there were lines of chromium in strong intensity.

(2) a spectrum of rubber without paint prepared from a sample taken from the shoes, there were lines of chromium of less intensity and,

(3) a spectrum of soil without paint prepared from a sample taken from the shoes, there were lines of equal intensity as those in (2),

(4) a spectrum of paint prepared from a sample taken from the shoes, there were lines of less intensity than (2) and (3).

He argued that the chromium lines in (4) were the result of contamination from the surface of the shoe when the sample of point was scraped off and that chromium was not a constituent of that paint. He said, therefore, the paint on the Land Rover and that on the shoes were different paints.

Mr Robbins summarised his findings regarding the yellow paint by saying that having examined the spectra, prepared by Dr Holden, he could not pledge himself to a distinction between the point taken from the lorry and the paint taken from the shoes. They had the same composition.

The Defence then called to the box Mr Douglas Nicholas who is employed at the Fulmer Research Institute at Stoke Poges in Buckinghamshire. He is an Investigator in charge of the Department of Spectroscopy. His qualifications are by experience and not by academic diploma. Mr Nicholas agreed with the readings of Mr Robbins of the spectra relating to the khaki paint and said that it seemed likely that there were difference in the compositions of the khaki paint taken from the Land Rover and the Khaki paint taken from the shoes. He said he was not an expert on paints and could not say whether it could be accounted for by the fact that the samples may have come from different parts of the same pot of paint. He agreed it would depend on whether the paint was a homogeneous mixture. He concluded by saying that if they had been the same paint he would have expected the spectra to have been identical.[5]

Appendix 5

METROPOLITAN POLICE STRUCTURE 1963

The Metropolitan police consisted of four departments each headed by an assistant commissioner:
A Department – Administration
B Department – Traffic
C Department – CID
D Department – Recruitment and Personnel

C Department, the department referred to throughout this book, was in turn subdivided into divisions:
C1 – Murder Squad
C2 – Crime Correspondence
C3 – Fingerprints
C4 – Criminal Records Office
C5 – CID Policy
C6 – Company Fraud Squad
C7 – Laboratory
C8 – Flying Squad
C9 – Provincial Crime Branch
C10 – Stolen Car Squad
C11 – Criminal Intelligence

Appendix 6

ROY JAMES'S MOTOR RACING RECORD

16.3.63	Oulton Park	Spun off
23.3.63	Goodwood	Spun off
15.3.63	Brands Hatch	Spun off
28.4.63	Snetterton	1st Prize
5.5.63	Snetterton	2nd Prize
19.5.63	Brands Hatch	1st Prize
3.6.63	Snetterton	1st Prize
8.6.63	Aintree	1st Prize
22.6.63	Goodwood	1st Prize
23.6.63	Cadwell Park	1st Prize
13.7.63	Oulton Park	1st prize
14.7.63	Snetterton	2nd Prize
27.7.63	Phoenix Park Ireland	3rd Prize
5.8.63	Aintree	Circuit lap record
18.8.63	Cadwell Park	1st Prize
22.863	Goodwood	Practice[6]

ABBREVIATIONS USED IN SOURCE NOTES

AN	BTC/BRB papers at TNA
ASSI	Courts of Assize files at TNA
BL	British Library
BPMA	British Postal Museum & Archive
BRB	British Railways Board
BT	Board of Trade
BTC	British Transport Commission
BTCP	British Transport Commission Police
CAB	Cabinet
CFS	Company Fraud Squad (Section C6 of CID Department C)
CID	Criminal Investigation Department
CPS	Crown Prosecution Service
CRO	Criminal Record Office (Section C4 of CID Department C)
DDG	Deputy Director General
DE	*Daily Express*
DPP	Director of Public Prosecutions
DPS	Director of Postal Services
FOI	Freedom of Information
FO	Foreign Office
GPO	General Post Office
HMB	Home Mails Branch
HO	Home Office
HVP	High Value Packet

IB	Post Office Investigation Branch (known as POID after 1967)
J	Ministry of Justice
LO	Law Officers
LPR	London Postal Region
NLW	National Library of Wales
MEPO	Metropolitan Police
NLW	National Library of Wales
OMB	Overseas Mails Branch
PACE	Police and Criminal Evidence Act
PHG	Postman Higher Grade
PO	Post Office
POID	Post Office Investigation Department
PMB	Postal Mechanisation Branch
PMB (S)	Postal Mechanisation Branch – Security
PMG	Postmaster General
PSD	Postal Services Department
RDC	Rural District Council
RM	Royal Mail
SRA	Solicitors Regulatory Authority
TNA	The National Archive, Kew
TPO	Travelling Post Office
TUC	Trades Union Congress

SOURCE NOTES

Introduction

1. Sources for the early history of the IB and its predecessors: POST 23/13–66; Missing Letter Branch case papers, 1839–1859; POST 30/1492 Confidential Enquiry Branch (GPO): Revision, 1907; Historical summaries of Branch workings and grades employed, 1793–1907; POST 74 Solicitor's Department; POST 74/199–203 Prosecutions in England and Scotland, 1800–1896; POST 74/204–344; Prosecution Briefs in England, Ireland and Wales, 1774–1934; POST 122/13084 Investigation Branch Annual Reports 1957/58–1966/67.
2. *Ibid.*
3. *Ibid.*

1 The 2.25 to Brighton

1. POST 120/95 (originally closed until 2001; opened 2002).
2. POST 120/90 (originally closed until 1985; opened 1986).
3. *Ibid.*
4. POST 120/93 (originally closed until 1985; opened 1986).
5. *Daily Express*, 27/1/62, p. 7.
6. POST 120/95 (originally closed until 2002; opened 2002).
7. POST 68/849.
8. POST 120/102 (originally closed until 1996; opened 1997).
9. *The Times*, 9/7/62, p. 6.
10. *The Times*, 31/8/62, p. 8.
11. *Daily Express*, 31/8/62, p. 1.
12. POST 120/129 (originally closed until 2014; opened 2011).

13. *Ibid.*
14. *Daily Express*, 21/2/63, p. 1.
15. POST 120/95 (originally closed until 2001; opened 2002).
16. Among those questioned but released without charge during this three-year period included Roger Cordrey and Robert Welch, who would later be charged and convicted in connection with the Great Train Robbery of 8 August 1963.

2 The Hold-Up

1. The Class 40 diesel locomotive used that night was D326 (later renumbered 40126). It was withdrawn from service in February 1984 and scrapped two months later. When the 1967 film *Robbery* was made, starring Stanley Baker, Class 40 locomotive D318 was used by the film company. The 1988 film *Buster*, starring Phil Collins, used Class 40 locomotive D306. The technical information about the train, its coaches and layout are to be found in POST 120/110 (originally closed until 1993; opened 1994).
2. The basic narrative of this chapter is drawn from the regular investigation reports written by DCS Gerald McArthur (original reference 202/63/943), which were originally closed until 2045. They were opened on 25/6/10 as a result of a Freedom of Information application made in connection with research for this book (TNA, DPP 2/3717/1). A significant number of sections in these reports were redacted under Section 40 (2) of the FOI Exemptions regulations (and at the time of writing remain redacted until 2045). However, full and unredacted zerox versions of some of the McArthur reports that were originally copied by Scotland Yard to the Post Office Investigation Branch are to be found at the British Postal Archive; see POST 120/96, 120/97, 120/98, 120/99. While some of these have deteriorated over the past fifty years due to light exposure, they remain the only unedited copies available to researchers.
3. POST 120/96 (originally closed until 1993; opened 1994).
4. DPP 2/3718, part 3 of 6 (originally closed until 2045, but opened under FOI request 25/6/10).
5. *Ibid.*
6. Although McArthur was, in theory, a Scotland Yard adviser to the Chief Constable of Buckinghamshire, Brigadier John Cheney, he was effectively in charge of the police investigation in Buckinghamshire.
7. POST 120/96 (originally closed until 1993; opened 1994).
8. DPP 2/3718, part 1 of 6 (originally closed until 2045, but opened under FOI request 25/6/10).

9. POST 120/96 (originally closed until 1993; opened 1994).
10. DPP 2/3718, part 1 of 6 (originally closed until 2045, but opened under FOI request 25/6/10).
11. POST 120/96 (originally closed until 1993; opened 1994).
12. *Ibid.*
13. *Ibid.*
14. HO 287/1496 (originally closed until 1995; opened 1996).
15. BTPC/Euston A.001718.

3 The 30-Minute Club

1. DPP 2/3718, part 2 of 6 (originally closed until 2045, but opened under FOI request 25/6/10).
2. HO 287/1496 (originally closed until 1995; opened 1996).
3. POST 120/96 (originally closed until 1993; opened 1994).
4. Osmond's estimate was to prove prophetic; at this early stage many were estimating the loss in the hundreds of thousands.
5. HO 287/1496 (originally closed until 1995; opened 1996).
6. *Ibid.*
7. *Daily Express*, 9/8/63, p. 1.
8. POST 120/134 (originally closed until 1993; opened 1994).
9. BBC TV News, 9/8/63.
10. POST 122/15954 (originally closed until 2014; opened December 2011).
11. *Ibid.*
12. DPP 2/3718, part 2 of 6 (originally closed until 2045, but opened under FOI request 25/6/10).
13. After Jack Mills's death on 4 February 1970, *The Times* published a letter on 21 February 1970 by Peta Fordham, the wife of Wilfred Fordham QC (who had defended Ronald Biggs, John Daly and Gordon Goody at the 1964 trial), which reinforces this conclusion (see Appendix 1 for the full text of this letter).
14. DPP 2/3717/1 (originally closed until 2045, but opened under FOI request 25/6/10) and POST 120/97; the identity of Welch's two associates is not revealed in McArthur's report.
15. Makowski was born in Poland in 1926 and came to Britain during the war, where he soon became involved in black-market criminality. He was first arrested and convicted in 1951 (CRO file 50130/51). He died in London 26/4/93.
16. POST 120/146 (originally closed until 2039, opened November 2011).
17. HO 287/1496 (originally closed until 1995; opened 1996).

18. *Ibid.*
19. *Ibid.*
20. *Ibid.*
21. DPP 2/3717/1 (redacted version opened 25/6/10) and unredacted version POST 120/96 (originally closed until 1993; opened 1994).
22. *Daily Express*, 9/8/63, p. 2.
23. The *Sunday People*, 11/8/63, p. 1.
24. DPP 2/3588 (still closed until 2045 at the time of writing). The police believed that the following individuals were among those who took part in the robbery: Bruce Reynolds, Ronald Edwards, Gordon Goody, John Daly, Michael Ball, Charles Wilson, Joseph Hartfield, Terence Hogan, Roy James and James White. See also *Daily Express*, 28/11/62, p. 3.
25. *Daily Mail*, 9/8/63, p. 3.
26. *Daily Telegraph*, 10/8/63, p. 1.
27. *Ibid.*
28. *Sunday Telegraph*, 19/4/64, p. 4.
29. HO 287/1496 (originally closed until 1995; opened 1996).

4 Robbers' Roost

1. DPP 2/3718, 1 of 6, part 2 (originally closed until 2045, redacted version opened 25/6/10).
2. DPP 2/3717 (originally closed until 2045, redacted version opened 25/6/10).
3. *Ibid.*
4. HO 287/1496 (originally closed until 1995; opened 1996).
5. DPP 2/3718, part 3 of 6 (originally closed until 2045, redacted version opened 25/6/10). For further details of the three vehicles found at Leatherslade Farm, see Appendix 2.
6. *Ibid.*
7. DPP 2/3717 (originally closed until 2045, redacted version opened 25/6/10). The majority view today is that Mrs Nappin was mistaken about a motorbike heading the convoy, although the rest of her statement conforms to what is now known and established fact about the convoy of vehicles.
8. *Ibid.*
9. POST 120/102 (originally closed until 1996; opened 1997). Investigators were of the view that the driver of the Jaguar was James White, who had shaved off his moustache shortly before the robbery.

10. POST 120/103 (originally closed 1997; opened 1998). This was viewed as a very accurate description of Henry Isaacs, a long-time associate of James White, who investigators believed played a key role before and after the robbery in a behind-the-scenes capacity.
11. DPP 2/3718, part 2 of 6 (originally closed until 2045, redacted version opened 25/6/10).
12. DPP 2/3718, part 3 of 6 (originally closed until 2045, redacted version opened 25/6/10). This incident took place on the afternoon of Monday 29 July 1963. While Mrs Brooks stated that she was not sure if she could recognise the man again, the police assumption was that the man who collected the keys was Brian Field.
13. DPP 2/3717, part 2 of 6 (originally closed until 2045, redacted version opened 25/6/10). The man Wyatt saw and spoke to for several minutes was Bruce Reynolds. From the physical description given, police were of the view that it best matched 'Bruce Richard Reynolds, CRO 41212/48'. Reynolds himself confirmed that he had, in fact, been the man who spoke to Wyatt and related the incident in his book *Crossing the Lines: An Autobiography of a Thief* (Virgin Books, 2003), p. 192.
14. The man sitting in the deckchair was a former train driver recruited by the robbers to move the train for the half-mile journey between Sears Crossing and Bridego Bridge.
15. The police were sceptical about Wyatt's description of the man, who was considerably older than any of those involved or suspected of involvement in the robbery. Nor did it remotely match anyone on the police list of suspects. Wyatt's recollection was, however, a very accurate description of the man who was to evade arrest and prosecution for his involvement in the robbery, and whose role is covered later in this book.
16. DPP 2/3717, part 2 of 6 (originally closed until 2045, redacted version opened 25/6/10); MEPO 10571 (still closed at time of writing); DPP 2/3911 (closed until 2045).
17. 'Mr Richards' was in fact an alias used on this occasion by Bruce Reynolds (see Reynolds; p181 ff).
18. DPP 2/3717/1 (originally closed until 2045; redacted version opened 25/6/10) and POST 120/ 96–97 (originally closed until 1993; opened 1994).
19. Leonard Field (no relation to Brian Field) was the brother of Henry Alexander Field, a client of the firm James, Wheater & Co. Alexander Field had been convicted of horse doping and was serving a prison sentence at the time.

20. DPP 2/3717/1 (originally closed until 2045; redacted version opened 25/6/10) and POST 120/96–97 (originally closed until 1993; opened 1994).
21. Rachman's property empire was located in West London and consisted of over 100 residential properties and several nightclubs. He tended to purchase old mansion blocks and convert them into multi-occupation dwellings, a good number of which were used for prostitution. When the Profumo scandal hit the headlines in 1963 it emerged that both Christine Keeler and Mandy Rice-Davies had been his mistresses. 1 Bryanston Mews West, London W1, where Keeler and Rice-Davies lived, was owned by Rachman.
22. Of the initial three partners, only Hocking had a criminal record (CRO 18147/55); POST 120/96 (originally closed until 1993; opened 1994).
23. DPP 2/3718, part 2 of 6 (originally closed until 2045; redacted version opened 25/6/10).
24. *Ibid.*
25. DPP 2/3718, part 2 of 6 (originally closed until 2045; redacted version opened 25/6/10).
26. DPP 2/3717 (originally closed until 2045; redacted version opened 25/6/10).
27. DPP 2/3718/1 (originally closed until 2045, redacted version opened 25/6/10).
28. DPP 2/3718, part 3 of 6 (originally closed until 2045; redacted version opened 25/6/10). The five fragmentary fingerprints that DS Ray speculated upon but were not of a sufficient standard to put before a court, more than likely belonged to Field's father, Reginald Arthur Field, who was thought to have been minding the money for his son (the discovery of the cases and bags near Dorking is documented in MEPO 2/10571, which remains closed at the time of writing).
29. POST 120/131 (originally closed until 1994; opened 1995).
30. DPP 2/3717, Report 4 (originally closed until 2045; redacted version opened 25/6/10).
31. *Ibid.*

5 The Poppy

1. For Roger Cordrey it was a double irony, for he was one of the few robbers at Leatherslade Farm who had kept his gloves on for the full duration of the three days he spent at the farm. Indeed, when the exhaustive fingerprint search was completed by the police, no trace of any print belonging to

Cordrey was found at the farm. Had it not been for his chance encounter with Emily Clarke he would most likely have evaded detection and arrest; DPP 2/3723, part 2 of 3 (originally closed until 2045; redacted version opened 25/6/10).

2. HO 287/1496 (originally closed until 1995; opened 1996).
3. DPP 2/3718, part 2 of 6 (originally closed until 2045; redacted version opened 25/6/10).
4. Before his arrest, Cordrey had given the Pilgrims £860 in £5 notes and Rene Boal £330 in £5 and £1 notes from his share of the stolen money.
5. HO 287/1496 (originally closed until 1995; opened 1996).
6. DPP 2/3717, Report 11(originally closed until 2045; redacted version opened on 25/6/10); DPP 2/3718, 1 of 6, part 2 (originally closed until 2045; redacted version opened 25/6/10); Inspector Roberts's report appears on p. 258 of this file – the whole of the following page, 259, remains closed until 2045. McArthur's report in DPP 2/3717/1 (originally closed until 2045; redacted version opened 25/6/10) is also redacted in respect to Charles Lilley, although an unredacted copy is to be found in POST 120/96 (closed until 1993; opened 1994).
7. POST 120/95 (originally closed until 2001; opened 2002). Without a definitive fingerprint report, a theoretical compilation list was the best that could be done at this stage of the investigation.
8. Henry George Pitts, of East Lane, Walworth, London SE, (CRO File 30286/51) – sentenced to an eight-year jail term in 1958, Pitts died of tuberculosis, aged 51, at Parkhurst Prison, Isle of Wight on 10 November 1962.
9. Michael David Kehoe, a car hirer of Barry Road, East Dulwich, London SE, (CRO File 20937/54) – eliminated as a suspect. A known associate of Anthony Thomas Lucraft (see note 16, Chapter 3), whose name had been mentioned by another informant in connection with other mail offences.
10. Terence Michael Sansom, a car dealer of Leighton Gardens, Kensal Rise, London NW (CRO File 34126/52) – eliminated as a suspect. Was found not guilty of the non-capital murder of James Hawney, a guard, after a £9,400 bus payroll hold-up in Wimbledon on 26 January 1961.
11. George Sansom (CRO File 10076/60), brother of Terence Michael Sansom – eliminated as a suspect.
12. Frederick Robinson, a car dealer of Holland Road, Willesden, London NW (CRO File 24078/39) – a string of robbery convictions stretching back to 1939. In January 1962 he was sentenced to eighteen months' imprisonment for receiving money from a wages robbery at Lots Road Power Station, Chelsea on 17 August 1961 – eliminated as a suspect.

13. John Charles Cramer of Camgate Mansions, Camberwell Road, London SE (CRO File 21846/47) – eliminated as a suspect.
14. Hayden Francis Smith (CRO File 15918/58) – younger brother of Henry Thomas Smith – eliminated as a suspect.
15. William David Ambrose, a car salesman of Stepney, London – eliminated as a suspect.
16. Kenneth Shakeshaft, a club owner of Essendine Mansions, Maida Vale, London W (CRO File 15847/42) – eliminated as a suspect.
17. POST 120/96 (originally closed until 1993; opened 1994).
18. Michael (Mick) Regan was an associate of South London bookmaker and publican Frederick Foreman. See *Freddie Foreman: The Godfather of British Crime* (John Blake, 2008), chapter 7 *ff* for references to Regan.
19. DPP 2/3919, part 2 (originally closed until 2045; redacted version opened 25/6/10).
20. POST 120/96 (originally closed until 1993; opened 1994) and DPP 2/3717, Report 16 (originally closed until 2045; redacted version opened 25/6/10).
21. The prospective buyer was Bruce Reynolds (see 'Reynolds, p. 200 *ff*).
22. DPP 2/3718/1 and DPP 2/3718, 1 of 6, part 2 (originally closed until 2045; redacted version opened 25/6/10).
23. DPP 2/3713, Report 16 (originally closed until 2045; redacted version opened 25/6/10).
24. DPP 2/3719, part 2 (originally closed until 2045; redacted version opened 25/6/10).
25. *Ibid.*
26. Terence Hogan (CRO File 38593/45) was a close friend of Bruce Reynolds over many years (see Reynolds p. 47*ff*). Both Reynolds and Piers Paul Read use the alias 'Harry Booth' when referring to Hogan in their respective books. See also 'Crime paid for my privileged childhood' by Karen Hogan (*Daily Mail*, 15 May 2011).
27. DPP 2/3717, Report 16 (originally closed until 2045; redacted version opened 25/6/10).
28. DPP 2/3718, 1 of 6, part 2 (originally closed until 2045; redacted version opened 25/6/10).
29. George Stanley was in fact born George Albert Sturley in Stepney, London on 11 July 1911 (Volume 1C, p. 645, Register of Births, Stepney Registration District, County of London). His role in these events will be explored later in this book.
30. Mac's antique shop in Portobello Road, London W11 was owned by her

husband. Both Bruce Reynolds and his brother-in-law John Daly claimed to be antique dealers operating from this address.

31. DPP 2/3718, 1 of 6, part 2 (originally closed until 2045; redacted version opened 25/6/10).
32. DPP 2/3723, 2 of 3 (originally closed until 2045; redacted version opened 25/6/10).
33. DPP 2/3723, 1 of 3 (originally closed until 2045, redacted version opened 25/6/10).
34. DPP 2/3717, Report 2 (originally closed until 2045; redacted version opened 25/6/10.
35. DPP 2/3718/1 (originally closed until 2045; redacted version opened 25/6/10).
36. Ibid; DSgt Nigel Reid admitted under cross-examination by Mr J.C. Mathew, Wilson's counsel, that the officer did not have a search warrant. He justified this by stating that Wilson 'had no objection to the search'.
37. *Ibid.*; Reid, however, perjured himself at the trial by stating under cross-examination by Mr Mathew that, 'up to the time we arrived at Scotland Yard there was no decision to arrest Wilson otherwise he would have been cautioned'. Wilson's fingerprints were the first to be identified and this in itself was the basis for publicly naming Wilson, Reynolds and White on 22 August. It is equally clear from DPP files that all three men were arrested on the strength of the recovered prints and not on an ad-hoc decision made as the result of searching his home. This is also confirmed by Commander George Hatherill. See George Hatherill, *A Detective's Story* (Andre Deutsch, 1971), p. 202.
38. *Ibid.*
39. *Ibid.*; Butler's report essentially confirms that Wilson was arrested on his instructions, which were issued before the Flying Squad officers left Scotland Yard. By Butler's own admission, Wilson was not cautioned until the end of the interview.
40. Wilson was dubbed 'the silent man' on account of his reputation for saying little or nothing when under arrest. This was certainly borne out in the two robberies with which Wilson was charged prior to the train robbery, i.e. the London Airport robbery (November 1962) and the National Provincial Bank robbery in Clapham, London (August 1962) (DPP 2/3588, closed until 2045 at the time of writing). He was discharged on both counts. Lord Justice Edmund Davies commented on Wilson at the train robbery trial that, 'No one has said less than you throughout this long trial. Indeed, I doubt you have spoken half a dozen words.'

41. The Police and Criminal Evidence Act 1984 (PACE) was specifically introduced to tackle police abuses, especially the practice of verballing, i.e. officers saying that a suspect had made some kind of admission when in fact no such conversation took place. PACE introduced a number of Codes of Practice: Code C governs the detention, treatment and questioning of persons by police officers. The code provides at C11.7 (a) that an accurate record must be made of each interview; in practice this means that interviews are now recorded.
42. Goody had been acquitted of the London Airport robbery by jury tampering (to ensure a failure to agree at the first trial) and by bribing a police officer to switch a key piece of evidence at the retrial (DPP 2/3588; closed until 2045 at the time of writing).
43. DPP 2/3717, Exhibits (originally closed until 2045; redacted version opened 25/6/10).
44. DPP 2/3718, 2 of 6 (originally closed until 2045; redacted version opened 25/6/10).

6 An Inside Job

1. POST 120/95 (originally closed until 2001; opened 2002).
2. *Ibid.*
3. The name of Ronald Biggs is noticeably absent from this list. The view later taken by the police was that the informant's contact with the gang, direct or indirect, must have ceased before Biggs joined the gang. This was also the view taken by Biggs himself (see Biggs, *Ronnie Biggs: His Own Story*, p. 81, and Reynolds, *Crossing the Line*, p. 201).
4. POST 120/95 (originally closed until 2001, opened 2002).
5. While this list is to be found in POST 120/445 (originally closed until 2017, opened 2003), three of the thirty-five names are omitted for reasons that can only be speculative at this point in time.
6. POST 120/95 (originally closed until 2001, opened 2002).
7. POST 120/445 (originally closed until 2017, opened 2003).
8. POST 120/129 (originally closed until 2014, opened 2011).
9. POST 120/95 (originally closed until 2001, opened 2002).
10. From the very beginning of the investigation, Butler was sceptical if not completely opposed to the idea of an 'insider' within the Post Office. In this, he was at odds with the IB, many of his Flying Squad colleagues as well as his immediate superior Commander Hatherill.
11. POST 120/129 (originally closed until 2014, opened 2011).
12. POST 120/128 (originally closed until 2014, opened 2011).

13. *Ibid.*
14. *Ibid.*
15. POST 120/146 (originally closed until 2017, opened 2011).
16. POST 120/447 (originally closed until 2017, opened 2011).
17. *Ibid.*
18. POST 120/129 (originally closed until 2014, opened 2011).
19. *Ibid.*

7 Through the Looking Glass

1. POST 120/146 (opened in 2011; some material still closed until 2017).
2. *Ibid.*
3. *Ibid.*
4. *Ibid.*
5. POST 120/146 (opened in 2011; some material still closed until 2017) – Millbank's mother, Louisa Millbank, resided at 127 Arlington Road, London N1.
6. POST 120/146 (opened 2011; some material still closed until 2017).
7. Millbank and McGuinness were subsequently found not guilty in relation to the two charges; Millbank was released and McGuinness sent to Glasgow under the terms of the arrest warrant (CRO File 2019/39). See also *The Times*, 17 September 1955, p. 4 and *The Times*, 21 September 1955, p. 4.
8. See Reynolds's accounts of 22 August 1963 and in his book *Crossing the Line*, p. 204 *ff.*
9. POST 120/146 (opened in 2011; some material still closed until 2017).
10. *Ibid.*
11. POST 120/95 (closed until 2001; opened 2002).
12. DPP 2/3717, Report 5 (originally closed until 2045; redacted version opened 25/6/10). See Chapter 4, note 11.
13. POST 120/131 (originally closed until 1994; opened 1995).
14. The shop at No 14 was 'Vanity Fayre' which held the lease for a five-year period, 1961–66.
15. POST 120/130 (originally opened in 2011; some material remains closed until 2014).
16. POST 120/449 (officially opened 2003; some material still closed until 2017).
17. *Ibid.*
18. POST 120/130 (officially opened in 2011; some material still closed until 2014).
19. POST 120/133 (officially opened 2011; some material still closed until 2014).

20. POST 120/130 (officially opened 2011; some material still closed until 2014).
21. *Ibid.*
22. *Ibid.*
23. *Ibid.*
24. Lola Willard was in fact the mother of Peter Collinson, who six years later directed the widely acclaimed film *The Italian Job*, starring Michael Caine. Collinson's widow, Hazel, spoke at length to the author about Lola Willard. Willard was 'a glamorous woman in her early 40s who worked in nightclubs in London's West End such as the Pigalle Club. She had never been a prostitute', said Collinson, 'although she certainly had a host of male friends and acquaintances who supported her financially and were no doubt observed by Mr Billington coming and going from the house'.
25. Identified by tailers Gray and Fowler as Albert Millbank; POST 120/133 (officially opened in 2011; some material still closed until 2014).
26. POST 120/448 (officially opened in 2003, although the reports on 99 Pollards Hill South were only opened in November 2011; some material remains closed until 2017).
27. DPP 2/3717, Report 10 (originally closed until 2045; redacted version opened 25/6/10).
28. *Ibid.*
29. *Ibid.*
30. *Ibid.*
31. POST 122/15954 (officially opened in 2011).
32. *Ibid.*
33. George Hatherill, *A Detective's Story* (Andre Deutsch, 1971), p. 210.
34. *Ibid.*

8 Blind Man's Bluff

1. Atkins is referred to as 'Ivy' by Bruce Reynolds in his book *Crossing the Line* (p. 130 *ff*) and as 'Rose' by Ronald Biggs in his book *Ronnie Biggs: His Own Story* (p. 41 *ff*). According to the Electoral Register, Biggs lived with Atkins at 138 Malmstone Avenue, Merstham, during 1957–58.
2. DPP 2/3718, 1 of 6, part 2 (originally closed until 2045; redacted version opened 25/6/10).
3. *Ibid.*
4. *Daily Mirror*, 12 August 1963, p. 1.
5. Alf is referred to by Piers Paul Read as 'Old Stan' in his book *The Train Robbers* (W.H. Allen, 1978). Ronald Biggs refers to him as 'Old Peter' in *Ronnie Biggs: His Own Story*, as does Bruce Reynolds in *Crossing the Line*.

6. POST 120/95 (originally closed until 2001; opened 2002). While 'Old Alf' was never definitively identified, the principal police suspect was one Alfred Stevens, who ultimately was neither arrested nor charged.
7. MEPO 2/10571 (still closed at time of writing); DPP 2/3718 2 of 6 (originally closed until 2045; redacted version opened 25/6/10).
8. DPP 2/3717, Report 3 (originally closed until 2045; redacted version released 25/6/10).
9. DPP 2/3718, 1 of 2, part 2 (originally closed until 2045; redacted version released 25/6/10).
10. POST 120/130 (opened 2011).
11. The address in the statement was misspelt: it was in fact 1 Redcross Way. The betting shop was owned by three partners: Frederick Foreman, William Gorbell and Thomas Wisbey (Frederick Foreman alludes to this and other business interests in his book *Freddie Foreman: The Godfather of British Crime* (John Blake, 2008), p. 151 *ff*.
12. DPP 2/3718, 1 of 6, part 2 (originally closed until 2045; redacted version opened 25/6/10).
13. *Ibid.*
14. DPP 2/3717, Report 5 (originally closed until 2045; redacted version released 25/6/10). According to DCI Frank Williams, he had told Copeland that he stood to lose his licence if it turned out that he had given a false alibi. See Frank Williams, *No Fixed Address: Life On The Run for the Great Train Robbers* (W H Allen, 1973), p. 41 ff.
15. DPP 2/3717, Report 4 (originally closed until 2045; redacted version released 25/6/10)
16. *Ibid.*
17. *Ibid.*
18. The Antecedent History of Brian Field, J82–245 (opened 1994).
19. *Ibid.*
20. *The Times*, 6 August 1958, p. 5.
21. DPP 2/2861 (opened 1991).
22. Solicitors Regulatory Authority; Wheater was admitted to the Roll of Solicitors of England & Wales in March 1949 and had formerly practised in partnership with Richard Lomer at 48 Beaufont Gardens, Brompton Road, Chelsea SW3 between 1956 and 1959. In 1959 he began practising as a sole solicitor under the name 'TW James & Wheater' at 3 New Quebec Street, London W1.
23. Brian Hocking, Property Agent, Flat D, 4 Leinster Square, Bayswater, London W2 (CRO File 18147/55).

24. DPP 2/3718, 2 of 6 (originally closed until 2045; redacted version released 25/6/10).
25. BT 31/765560; 765622; 765633; 765634.
26. ASSI 13/658 (opened 1993), & DPP 2/3735 (originally closed until 2045; redacted version opened 22/9/10).
27. BT 31/734607; In *Freddie Foreman, The Godfather of British Crime* (John Blake, 2008), p. 154 *ff,* Frederick Foreman describes how and why he set up the company under the aegis of his associate Derek Ruddell (also referred to in the book as 'Ding Dong'). The company was dissolved on 11 August 1966.
28. MEPO 2/10571 (still closed at time of writing).
29. DPP 2/3718, 1 of 6, part 2 (originally closed until 2045; redacted version opened 25/6/10).
30. DPP 2/3718/1, part 2 (originally closed until 2045; redacted version opened 25/6/10).
31. POST 120/95 (originally closed until 2001; opened 2002).
32. MEPO 2/10575 (still closed at time of writing).
33. By common consent today, Boal had no involvement in the robbery and was unknown to all those who participated in it with the exception of Cordrey (see Reynolds, *Crossing the Line*, pp. 203, 221 and 287).

9 And Then There Were Six

1. DPP 2/3718, 1 of 6, part 2 (originally closed until 2045; redacted version opened 25/6/10)
2. *Ibid.*
3. *Ibid*; Dr Ian Holden was the Scotland Yard forensic expert who had testified at the 1962 Regina v Goody trial at the Old Bailey, where Goody was charged in connection with the London Airport robbery at BOAC's Comet House. After being found not guilty, Goody had left the dock elated and spoken briefly with the prosecution counsel, pointing out that, 'your expert isn't much good is he? He never even noticed this.' Goody then proceeded to show the counsel an artificial link in the piece of chain that Holden had examined in his laboratory and testified about earlier in the trial. This oversight by Holden was a great embarrassment to him personally and indeed to the prosecution case (see Piers Paul Read, *The Train Robbers*, p. 33; DPP 2/3588 (still closed until 2045 at the time of writing)).
4. DPP 2/3718, 1 of 6, part 2 (originally closed until 2045; redacted version opened 25/6/10).
5. HO 287/1496, POST 120/96 (originally closed until 1993; opened 1994).

6. DPP 2/3718, 1 of 6, part 2 (originally closed until 2045; redacted version opened 25/6/10). Goody's defence counsel viewed this deposition as a further example of a fabricated case. Goody had apparently not said, 'Yes, Mr Butler they are mine' but given a non-committal answer, not knowing for sure that they were his.
7. DPP 2/3719, part 2 (originally closed until 2045; redacted version opened 25/6/10).
8. Frank Williams, *No Fixed Address*, p. 111.
9. CRO File No 18605/1929 and Michael Black (real name was Ronald Clarke), CRO File No 12922/49, were former housebreakers. Bruce Reynolds refers to Black as Michael Hackett in *Crossing the Line*, p. 210, and Piers Paul Read refers to him as Godfrey Green in *The Train Robbers*, p. 139.
10. DPP 2 3719, 1 of 3 (originally closed until 2045; redacted version opened 25/6/10).
11. *Ibid.*
12. POST 120/97 (closed until 1993; opened 1994).
13. *Ibid.*
14. *Ibid.*
15. MEPO 2/10571, MEPO 2/10575 (both MEPO files still closed at time of writing).
16. *Ibid.*
17. If over £200,000 was being held at Beaford, this would indicate a quantity of money well in access of one person's share of the robbery proceeds, and the possibility that two gang members who were on full shares might be at the house. According to Piers Paul Read, one of the robbers who evaded arrest and prosecution was among those who were staying at Beaford (Piers Paul Read, *The Train Robbers*, p. 138.
18. POST 120/95 (closed until 2001; opened 2002).
19. Lincoln & Lincoln were Bob Welch's solicitors.
20. POST 120/448 (opened 2003; some material still closed until 2017).
21. This would be the equivalent today of buying drinks with a £50 note.
22. MEPO 2/10571 & 2/10575 (both still closed at time of writing); POST 120/131 (closed until 1994; opened 1995).
23. POST 120/448 (opened 2003; some material still closed until 2017).
24. *Ibid.*
25. Frank Williams, *No Fixed Address*, p. 43. MEPO 2/10571 (still closed at time of writing). Much later it was finally decided that Beaford Farm should be raided and DS Steve Moore, a team of Flying Squad officers and Devon police officers undertook the search. This was after the five individuals

had left. No money or items of interest were found.

26. POST 120/448 (opened 2003; some material still closed until 2017).
27. *Ibid.*
28. *Ibid.*
29. According to Welch he was to go abroad after a farewell meeting with his brother (Piers Paul Read, *The Train Robbers*, p. 138 ff).
30. MEPO 2/10571 & MEPO 2/10575 (both files still closed at time of writing).
31. DPP 2/3718, 1 of 6, part 2 (originally closed until 2045; redacted version opened 25/6/10). According to Flying Squad enquiries, the red Cortina Reg No 796 FXC Welch was driving had been hired by Charles Lilley from Fry's Hire Ltd of 43 Glenhouse Road, Eltham, London SE9.
32. POST 120/95 (closed until 2001; opened 2002).
33. ASSI 13/643 (opened 1995); DPP 2/3718, 1 of 6, part 2 (of pages 142–150 covering the Flying Horse Hotel incident, pp. 143–150 remain closed until 2045).
34. The file contained this newspaper clipping – 'The Cup Final looks like being a flop for ticket touts. Last night the price for a pair of 63*s* tickets dropped to £20 against £75 for a pair of 50*s* tickets paid for last season's Spurs v Burnley final.' (*Daily Express*, 25 May 1963, p. 1). When the case came to court, Judge Edmund Davies ruled that the jury should ignore the entire issue of the Flying Horse Hotel (J 82–245).
35. Consideration was given to charging Lilley in connection with the robbery, possibly on a charge of 'receiving proceeds of the mail train robbery'. However, Lilley's DPP file records 'no action taken'. DPP 2/4006 (still closed until 2045); MEPO 2/10571 (still closed at time of writing).
36. James Kensit, CRO File 3850/34; born 1915, alias George Downey. Nicknamed 'Jimmy the Dip', a known associate of a host of names including Reginald and Ronald Kray, Charles and Edward Richardson and William Howard (a key player in the 1952 Eastcastle Street TPO robbery). Kensit was also the father of actress Patricia (Patsy) Kensit (born 1968) who has starred in *Absolute Beginners*, *Lethal Weapon 2*, *Emmerdale* and *Holby City* and was married to Rock stars Jim Kerr and Liam Gallagher.
37. DPP 2/3718, 1 of 6, part 2 (originally closed until 2045; redacted version opened 25/6/10).
38. MEPO 2/10575 (still closed at time of writing).
39. DPP 2/3718, 3 of 6 (originally closed until 2045; redacted version opened 25/6/10).
40. *Ibid.*

41. POST 120/104 (originally closed until 1996; opened 1997); MEPO 2/10575 (still closed until 2045 at the time of writing).
42. *Ibid.*
43. MEPO 2/10571 (still closed at time of writing).
44. *Ibid.*
45. MEPO 2/10571 (still closed at time of writing); *Daily Express*, 25 January 1964, p. 1.
46. *The People*, 1 March 1964, p. 1.
47. See note 41 above.
48. POST 120/97 (closed until 1993; opened 1994).
49. Ibid.; when Daly's case came to court, Wilfred Fordham QC successfully argued that references in DI Frank Williams's statement to the gun licence in the name of Michael Black found during the search of 65a Eaton Square should not be produced to the jury. He contended that there was no evidence that a gun had been used in the commission of the robbery or that the other documents had been used by Daly illegally.
50. *Ibid.*
51. *Ibid.*
52. DPP 2/3719, 1 of 3 (originally closed until 2045; redacted version opened 25/6/10). The 'colonel' was an alias used by Bill Goodwin (Colonel Summers).
53. *Ibid.*
54. POST 120/97 (closed until 1993; opened 1994).
55. MEPO 2/10571 (still closed at time of writing).
56. *Ibid.*
57. DPP 2/3717, Report 15 (originally closed until 2045; redacted version opened 25/6/10). Those suspected 'of assisting Roy John James to evade arrest' were George Frederick Wright, Kenneth Thomas Simmons, Peter Alan Kelliem and Maureen Jean Willers (DPP 2/3858; still closed until 2045 at time of writing).
58. See note 54 above.

10 Operation Primrose

1. DPP 2/3717, Report 15 (originally closed until 2045; redacted version opened 25/5/10). Only the first paragraph of the report on the Great Dover Street incident, reproduced here, is publicly available. From the end of this paragraph onwards, the entire page that follows has been redacted and remains closed until 2045.
2. Frank Williams, *No Fixed Address*, p. 76 ff.
3. According to a former Flying Squad officer, who was a close colleague

of Frank Williams and who accompanied him later that evening on the Roy James arrest, this was not in fact what happened, but what was retrospectively entered into the police report. According to the officer, who spoke privately to the author in July 2010, Williams himself made the 'anonymous' call to place it on record having already arranged the time and location of the drop with his contact. Frederick Foreman also alludes to this incident and his own involvement in his book *The Godfather of British Crime* (John Blake, 2008), p. 130 *ff.*

4. *No Fixed Address*, Frank Williams, W.H. Allen, p. 76 *ff.*
5. Malcolm Fewtrell, *The Train Robbers* (Arthur Barker Ltd, 1964).
6. George Hatherill, *A Detective's Story*.
7. According to Williams, it was not until 1970 that he discovered Butler had not, after all, kept Millen and Hatherill informed of his activities nor passed on his reports regarding those robbers still at liberty. See Williams, *No Fixed Address*, p. 74.
8. *The Godfather of British Crime*, Freddie Foreman (John Blake Publishing, 2008, p. 131 *ff*).
9. See Foreman, *The Godfather of British Crime*, p. 130 *ff*; Williams, *No Fixed Address*, p. 78 *ff.*
10. POST 122/15959 (opened 2011).
11. *Ibid.*
12. A possible Weybridge–Woking TPO robbery planned around February 1963 was eventually aborted (see Chapter 1; Chapter 1, notes 15 and 16).
13. *Ibid.*
14. POST 120/95 (originally closed until 2001; opened 2002); DPP 2/3718, 2 of 6 (originally closed until 2045; redacted version opened 25/6/10).
15. POST 122/15959 (opened 2011).
16. *Ibid.*
17. *Ibid.*
18. The name chosen for the operation, ie 'Primrose', seems from police files to be derived from the activities of a group of suspects whose common denominator was 69 Belsize Park Gardens, London NW3, where the phone number was 'Primrose 0218' (see Chapter 7).
19. POST 122/15959 (opened 2011).
20. *Ibid.*
21. *Ibid.*
22. *Daily Express* (20 April 1964, p. 4). It seems likely that DCI Peter Vibart was Hoskins's source for the story.
23. POST 122/15959 (opened 2011).

11 Fish on a Hook

1. County Quarter Sessions were presided over by two or more Justices of the Peace, one of whom would act as chairman, and sat with a jury. Quarter Sessions in county boroughs were usually presided over by one Recorder Judge.
2. Courts of Assize were presided over by judges of the King's/Queen's Bench Division of the High Court of Justice, who travelled across the seven judicial circuits of England and Wales, summoning juries at the Assize towns within each circuit.
3. ASSI 13/643 (opened in 1996).
4. Commons at a 1957 by-election in the Warwick and Leamington constituency, caused by the resignation of Prime Minister Sir Anthony Eden after the Suez debacle. The Constituency Association were seeking another rising star to succeed Eden, and Hobson quickly gained promotion to ministerial rank in Harold Macmillan's government. Sir John was re-elected at three General Elections and tipped for greater things when the Conservatives lost office in October 1964, but was to die an early death at the age of 55 in 1967.
5. Letter dated 23 April 1964, from Sir John Hobson, Attorney General, Royal Courts of Justice, to The Hon. Mr Justice Edmund Davies (National Library of Wales; Lord Edmund-Davies Papers, files 10/1–10/13, opened following his death in 1992). It is apparent from the letter that Edmund Davies had written to Hobson immediately after the trial ended commending the work of the prosecution team, who seem to have been personally chosen by Hobson.
6. *Ibid*; A noteworthy example are two letters from King's College Faculty of Law, dated 2 May 1964 and 4 July 1964.
7. While the police and the DPP held what they regarded as incontestable evidence against Reynolds (DPP 2/3717, Report 16; originally closed until 2045, redacted version opened 25/6/10) they were understandably unwilling to produce it before Reynolds had been arrested, charged and put before a court. The main consequence of not compromising such evidence was to withdraw the charges against Manson, who the DPP clearly believed was guilty of the charges against her.
8. HO 287/1496.
9. Brian Field had asked, when arrested on 15 September 1963, 'Will this case go to the Old Bailey or Bucks Assize Court?' (DPP 2/3718 6 of 6, originally closed until 2045, redacted version opened 25/6/10). He knew full well that a country jury would be more likely to convict and that conversely, a London jury would be easier to influence.

10. HO 287/1496.
11. ASSI 13/643 (opened 1996).
12. HO 287/1496.
13. *Ibid.*
14. *Ibid.*
15. *Ibid.*
16. *Ibid.*
17. ASSI 13/643 (opened 1996).
18. J 82/420–441 (opened 1994).
19. HO 287/1496 reveals that the banks were extremely remiss in that of all the banknotes totalling £2,631,684, only £1,579 of the notes had their serial numbers recorded by the respective bank branches before transit to the TPO pick-up point.
20. HO 287/1496.
21. J 82/420–441 (opened 1994).
22. *Daily Mirror*, 15 February 1964, p. 1.

12 Case for the Defence

1. POST 120/95 (closed until 2001; opened 2002).
2. POST 120/95 (closed until 2001; opened 2002), MEPO 2/10571 (still closed at time of writing) and MEPO 2/2/10575 (still closed at time of writing).
3. See note 2; Black died on 9 March 1964. Two months later, William Goodwin too died suddenly of a heart attack while staying at Endelstowe.
4. HO 287/1496.
5. *Ibid.*
6. DPP 2/3719, part 2 (originally closed until 2045; redacted version opened 25/6/10).
7. J 82/420–441 (opened 1994).
8. Brian Field married Brenda Spencer on 1 March 1958 (Entry 117, Register of Marriages, Registration District of Middlesex South), and they were divorced three years later. Field married Karin Klemich on 20 January 1962 at St Marylebone Register Office (Entry 155, Register of Marriages, Registration District of St Marylebone).
9. HO 287/1496.
10. *Ibid.*
11. J 82/420–441 (opened 1994).
12. *Ibid.*
13. *Ibid.*

14. *Ibid.*
15. *Ibid.*
16. *Ibid.*
17. HO 287/1496.
18. J 82/420–441 (opened 1994).
19. DPP 2/3718, 1 of 6, part 2 (originally closed until 2045; redacted version opened 25/6/10).
20. *Ibid.*
21. DPP 2/3718, 3 of 6 (originally closed until 2045; redacted version opened 25/6/10).
22. The Rixon family moved to the Post Office Stores at Dunsden near Reading, where Bernard Rixon became the sub-postmaster.
23. DPP 2/3718/1 (originally closed until 2045; redacted version opened 25/6/10).
24. DPP 2/3717, Report 3 (originally closed until 2045; redacted version opened 25/6/10). Two pages of McArthur's report on Biggs and the fingerprint evidence regarding him have been redacted under FOI exemption (s) 40 (2) and therefore remain closed until 2045.
25. *Ibid.*
26. HO 287/1496.
27. J 82/440 (opened 1994).
28. *The Daily Mail*, 17 April 1964.
29. In 1960 the TUC sold *The Daily Herald*, which was losing readers and advertising revenue, to the pro-Labour Mirror Group Newspapers. On 15 September 1964 MGN changed the name on the paper to *The Sun* and relaunched it as 'a radical, independent newspaper'. It was not until 1969 that Rupert Murdoch purchased the still ailing *Sun* from MGN.
30. Since the 1957 Homicide Act, there had been two types of murder on the statute book – capital murder punished by the death penalty and non-capital murder punished by a life sentence in jail. The death penalty was suspended in November 1964 for a period of five years before final abolition in 1969.
31. *The Daily Herald*, 17 April 1964.
32. *Ibid.*
33. *The Daily Telegraph*, 17 April 1964.
34. *The Guardian*, 17 April 1964.
35. *BBC Nine O'Clock News*, 16 April 1964.

13 An Act of Warfare

1. MEPO 2/10571 (still closed at time of writing).
2. *Ibid.*
3. *Ibid.*
4. *Ibid*; when Harry Smith died in 2008, his death certificate recorded his occupation as a Property Consultant (retired); Record of Deaths, London Borough of Redbridge, Entry No 232, 16 October 2008.
5. HO 287/1496 (opened 1995).
6. *Ibid.*
7. *Ibid.*
8. *Ibid.*
9. *Ibid.*
10. MEPO 2/10581, MEPO 2/11298 (closed until 2045 at time of writing).
11. POST 120/95 (originally closed until 2001; opened 2002).
12. *Ibid.*
13. *Ibid.*
14. MEPO 2/11298 (closed until 2045 at time of writing).
15. POST 120/95 (originally closed until 2001; opened 2002).
16. LO 2/244, MEPO 26/282. See Frederick Foreman, *The Godfather of British Crime*, p. 127 *ff*; Ronald Biggs, *Ronnie Biggs: His Own Story*, p. 108 *ff*. In his book Biggs refers to Alfred Gerrard and Frederick Foreman as 'Raymond Macclesfield' and 'Kenny Lisle'.
17. POST 120/95 (originally closed until 2001; opened 2002).
18. *Ibid.*
19. Frank Williams, *No Fixed Address*, p. 21.
20. POST 120/95 (originally closed until 2001; opened 2002).
21. All three were later to be returned to prison; Biggs gave himself up on 7 May 2001, Reynolds was arrested on 8 November 1968 and Wilson on 25 January 1968.
22. POST 120/102, POST 120/103 (originally closed until 1996 & 1997; opened 1997 and 1998 respectively).
23. POST 120/104 (originally closed until 1996; opened 1997). Frederick Foreman, *The Godfather of British Crime*, p. 131 *ff*; Frank Williams, *No Fixed Address*, p. 144 *ff*.

14 The End of the Beginning

1. POST 120/102 (originally closed until 1996; opened 1997).
2. POST 120/95 (originally closed until 2001, opened 2002); DPP 2/3735

(originally closed until 2045; redacted version opened 22/9/10).

3. Percy Hoskins Papers.
4. MEPO 2/10571 (still closed at time of writing).
5. *Ibid.*
6. *Ibid.*
7. Brian Field changed his name by Deed Poll to Brian Mark Carlton. He died on 28 April 1979 (Register of Deaths 1979, Registration District of Hounslow, Entry No 232).
8. Eddie Richardson, *The Last Word* (Headline, 2006), p. 108.

Appendices

1. *The Times*, 21/2/70.
2. Statement of the West Cheshire coroner in ruling that there was no reason to hold an inquest into the death of Jack Mills, who died on 4 February 1970 at Barony Hospital, Nantwich, Cheshire (Ellis, Ellis & Bolton solicitors, Crewe).
3. HO 287/1496 (originally closed until 1995; opened 1996).
4. DPP 2/3718, 2 of 6 (originally closed until 2045; redacted version 25/6/10).
5. DPP 2/3717, Report 17 (originally closed until 2045; redacted version 25/6/10).
6. ASSI 13/658 (opened 1994).

BIBLIOGRAPHY

Biggs, Ronnie, *Keep on Running* (Bloomsbury, 1995)
Biggs, Ronnie, *Odd Man Out* (M Press, 2011)
Biggs, Ronnie, *His Own Story* (Sphere, 1981)
Clarkson, Wensley, *Killing Charlie* (Mainstream Publishing, 2006)
Coates, Tim, *The Great British Train Robbery* (SP, 2003)
Delano, Anthony, *Slip-Up* (Coronet, 1986)
Fewtrell, Malcolm, *The Train Robbers* (Arthur Barker, 1964)
Fordham, Peta, *The Robbers' Tale* (Hodder & Stoughton, 1965)
Foreman, Freddie, *The Godfather of British Crime* (John Blake, 2008)
Gosling, John & Craig, Dennis *The Inside Story of the Great Train Robbery* (W.H. Allen, 1964)
Guttridge, Peter, *The Great Train Robbery* (Crime Archive/National Archive, 2008)
Hatherill, George, *A Detective's Story* (Andre Deutsch, 1971)
Hoskins, Percy, *Two Men Were Acquitted* (Secker & Warburg, 1984)
Mackenzie, Colin, *The Most Wanted Man* (Hart-Davis, MacGibbon, 1975)
Read, Piers Paul, *The Train Robbers* (W.H. Allen, 1978)
Reynolds, Bruce, *Crossing the Line* (Virgin Books, 2003)
Richards, Ross, *The Great Train Robbery* (Consul Books, 1964)
Richardson, Charlie, *My Manor* (Pan Books, 1992)
Richardson, Eddie, *The Last Word* (Headline, 2006)
Sandbrook, Domnic, *Never Had It So Good; 1956–63* (Little, Brown, 2005)
Sandbrook, Dominic, *White Heat; 1964–70* (Little, Brown, 2006)
Shirley, John & Short, Martin *The Fall of Scotland Yard* (Penguin Books, 1977)
Slipper, Jack, *Slipper of the Yard* (Sidgwick & Jackson, 1981)
Wheen, Francis, *The Sixties* (Century, 1982)
Williams, Frank, *No Fixed Address* (W.H. Allen, 1973)

INDEX